**Praise for the Novels
of Katie MacAlister**

The Art of Stealing Time
A TIME THIEF NOVEL

"I highly recommend this book for the humor, the romance, and the wild ride it takes us on."
—Cocktails and Books

"[MacAlister is] still a brilliant writer, funny, fast, silly, and completely irreverent.... Her sassy wit and crazy characters will still entertain her fans."
—Bitten by Books

"Great.... If you enjoy a delightful combination of humor and character-driven stories, MacAlister's latest is a must-have." —*RT Book Reviews*

"A laugh-out-loud mix of modern and medieval times, full of nonstop action and unforgettable characters ... very entertaining and endearing!" —Harlequin Junkie

Time Thief
A TIME THIEF NOVEL

"If you enjoy a good murder mystery mixed with familial betrayal, the otherworld, and a romance, then this is the book for you." —Dark Faerie Tales

"Silly, sassy, and salacious—Katie MacAlister ... gets up to her usual tricks in this comical paranormal romance." —The Urban Book Thief

continued ...

D0050131

It's All Greek to Me

"This author delivers again with yet another steamy, sexy read with humorous situations, dialogue, and characters. The plot is fast-paced and fun, typical of MacAlister's novels. The characters are impossible not to like. The hiccups in their relationship only serve to make the reader root harder for them. The events range from amusing to steamy to serious. The reader can't be bored with MacAlister's novel."   —*Fresh Fiction*

"A fun and sexy read."   —*The Season*

"A wonderful lighthearted romantic romp as a kick-butt American Amazon and a hunky Greek find love. Filled with humor; fans will laugh with the zaniness of Harry meets Yacky."   —*Midwest Book Review*

"Katie MacAlister sizzles with this upbeat and funny summer romance. . . . MacAlister's dialogue is fast-paced and entertaining. . . . Her characters are interesting and her heroes are always attractive/intriguing . . . a good fun, fast summer read."   —*Books with Benefits*

"Fabulous banter between the main characters. . . . Katie MacAlister's got a breezy, fun writing style that keeps me reading."   —*Book Binge*

Sparks Fly
A NOVEL OF THE LIGHT DRAGONS

"Once again I was drawn into the wondrous world of this author's dragons and hated leaving once their story was told. I loved this visit and cannot wait for the next book to see just what new adventures lie in wait for these dragons."   —*Love Romances & More*

"Fast-paced . . . an entertaining read and a fine addition to MacAlister's dragon series."—*Bookshelf Bombshells*

"Balanced by a well-organized plot and MacAlister's trademark humor." —*Publishers Weekly*

The Unbearable Lightness of Dragons
A NOVEL OF THE LIGHT DRAGONS

"Laugh-out-loud moments . . . a welcome addition." —*Publishers Weekly*

"[Katie MacAlister is] a gifted humorous paranormal author." —*RT Book Reviews*

"MacAlister continues with her witty and fun style." —Bookshelf Bombshells

A Tale of Two Vampires
A DARK ONES NOVEL

"A roller coaster of giggles, chortles, and even some guffaws. In other words, it is a lighthearted and fun read." —The Reading Cafe

Much Ado About Vampires
A DARK ONES NOVEL

"A humorous take on the dark and demonic." —*USA Today*

"Once again this author has done a wonderful job. I was sucked into the world of Dark Ones right from the start and was taken on a fantastic ride. This book is full of witty dialogue and great romance, making it one that should not be missed." —Fresh Fiction

"An extremely appealing hero. If you enjoy a fast-paced paranormal romance laced with witty prose and dialogue, you might like to give *Much Ado About Vampires* a try." —azcentral.com

"I cannot get enough of the warmth of Ms. MacAlister's books. They're the paranormal romance equivalent of soul food." —Errant Dreams Reviews

A MIDSUMMER NIGHT'S ROMP

Katie MacAlister

A SIGNET SELECT BOOK

SIGNET SELECT
Published by the Penguin Group
Penguin Group (USA) LLC, 375 Hudson Street,
New York, New York 10014

USA | Canada | UK | Ireland | Australia | New Zealand | India | South Africa | China
penguin.com
A Penguin Random House Company

First published by Signet Select, an imprint of New American Library,
a division of Penguin Group (USA) LLC

First Printing, May 2015

ISBN 978-0-451-47138-3

Printed in the United States of America
10 9 8 7 6 5 4 3 2 1

Many, many thanks to my adorable and extremely patient agent, Michelle Grajkowski, who despite my never naming a character Honey Grajkowski still keeps me sane when the world around me goes nutso-cuckoo. Not only is she a fabulous agent, charming as all get-out, and cute as a button, she makes a heck of a male pirate. Yarr, my dumpling!

A MIDSUMMER
NIGHT'S ROMP

Chapter 1

"I get that Gunner is an amateur archaeologist. But why is an archaeology reality TV show coming to the castle?"

Gunner Ainslie made a face at his sister-in-law. "'Amateur' is a bit rough, Alice. I took a degree in archaeology, after all."

She looked even more confused. "Then why are you a photographer now instead of an archaeologist?"

"Because he didn't want to be a burden to the estate like all my other siblings," his brother Elliott, the current Baron Ainslie, answered, giving his wife a squeeze. "Or so he said. Frankly, I think it was a cover so he could take pictures of unclothed women."

"My job, as you very well know, is about as far from taking pictures of nude women as you can get," Gunner said with dignity, ignoring the way that Alice, sitting on the arm of Elliott's chair, leaned over to whisper something into his ear. Gunner kept speaking. "Old decaying buildings aren't particularly sexy, but they can be lucrative in the right developer's hands, and yes, dear sister-in-law, Elliott is absolutely correct that I wanted a job that would allow me to support myself. Archaeology, while fascinating, isn't a profession known for money. In fact, it's damned hard to even make a living from it, let alone thrive."

"I got that," Alice said, reluctantly pulling her attention away from Elliott and back to Gunner. Since the two had been married for only a few months, Gunner was prepared to give them a little leeway as far as displays of affection went. "But why did you call in your archaeology buddies in the first place? Yes, the tower in this castle you call home fell down, but there's nothing there that screams archaeology, is there?"

"We wouldn't know if there was," Elliott answered. "Not until the rubble is cleared away, that is."

"Crop marks are the answer to your question, Alice." Gunner gave her a smile that immediately had Elliott pulling her down onto his lap. Gunner grinned inwardly, never failing to find amusement in how jealous his brother had become. "During the summer, here in England, it's possible to see areas where archaeology exists, because the crops grow differently when stone walls or ditches are beneath the topsoil. The drought this summer made it clear that the remains of some large structures were beneath the surface of the estate's pastures, so I called a friend who works for the county archaeology office, and he passed on the news to the Claud-Marie Archaeology people."

"Speaking of which, who are these Claud-Marie people? You said they're some kind of archaeology company, but you also just said no one makes money in the old-buried-stuff business. How does this company survive if that's the case? They don't work with a university, do they?"

"No, they're privately funded by a number of companies. Adam—my friend who now works for the county—volunteers now and again for the CMA, and told them about our crop lines. We were actually already on their list of potential sites to visit in the future when the television studio contacted them."

"And the TV show joined forces with them . . . why?" Alice asked, her brow wrinkling in puzzlement.

Gunner shrugged. "That, I don't know, beyond the fact that they want to make a monthlong TV show about an archaeology dig."

"And they offered us money for it," Elliott said quickly. "Lots of money. Which, as you know, my dear wife, despite my lofty title and thriving career as a novelist, we desperately need before our castle falls further down around our heads."

"I like lots of money," Alice said approvingly. "Even if it means digging up the pastures a bit. The tourists who come to visit the castle might like it, too. Do you think we should have some new brochures printed up that describe what's going on?"

"That would be a bit premature, since we don't know what, if anything, will be found at the dig site," Gunner pointed out.

"Yes, but a TV show will be filming while the dig is going on. People love to watch that sort of thing. Maybe we should have some new merchandise for the gift shop made up with archaeology stuff on it. Hm."

Alice, who had taken wonderfully to the business side of Ainslie Castle's tourist programs, was clearly getting caught up in considering a whole new range of products, and scooted off Elliott's lap to take a position behind his laptop. Before long, she was busily typing up some notes to herself.

Gunner smiled, grateful his new sister-in-law had taken up the challenge of her husband's impoverished family. Given how many of them there were—the late baron and his wife had had two children of their own and adopted nine others—helping the family over the hump of insolvency was no small feat. But it was Alice's greater intention—the one to see them all happily married—that gave Gunner pause.

"Are you sure you're going to be able to cope with the TV crew while we're gone?" Elliott asked Gunner. "With the family making its yearly exodus to their various holiday destinations, there will be no one here but you to deal with any problems."

"It'll be fine. I'll be back from Portugal before they start, and Cressy will be here by then."

"Oh, that's right—your daughter is coming for the summer." Alice looked up from the laptop. "I'm excited to meet her. She's seventeen, right?"

"Yes."

"So she'll probably be boy-mad, and indulging in *all* the drama," Alice said, nodding.

"Actually, she's not. Cressy is a bit . . ." He paused, trying to find the words to explain his daughter's particular joie de vivre. "She's a bit enthusiastic about things. No drama in the sense of door slamming and pouts, just lots of running around, and everything is either *super awesome* or *dead grotty*. There's no in-between with Cressy. Her mother claims she's immature, but I prefer to think of her as unsophisticated and excitable."

"Well, she sounds adorable, nonetheless, although I have to say that you're the last person I'd have expected would have a seventeen-year-old daughter. You're so . . ." Alice stopped, suddenly looking guilty.

"Dashing?" Gunner supplied. "Debonair?"

"A bit of a dawg, actually."

Elliott gave a short bark of laughter. "Truer words were never spoken, my dear."

"On the contrary," Gunner protested. "I would say just the opposite. I am not a dawg, assuming you mean that in the sense of a man who prowls his way through women."

"Oh?" Elliott's brow rose. "Let us examine the last few women with whom you associated yourself romantically. You were with them how long?"

Alice raised her eyebrows. "I don't know about the others, because I've been here less than six months, but the last one—wasn't her name Charity?—she lasted a whole three days. And Anna Louise, that American lady—you remember her, Elliott; she's the one who was here for one of the Ainslie Castle Experience weekends— she hung in there for a whole ten days before Gunner gave her the heave-ho."

"She had to leave," Gunner said with a frown at both of them. "I didn't tell her to go; she had travel plans elsewhere."

"Uh-huh. And if she hadn't, would you have asked her to stay on longer?"

Gunner made a sharp gesture with his hand. "That's neither here nor there."

"He wouldn't have," Elliott told his wife.

"Totally a dawg. But in a nice way," Alice added.

Gunner sighed. "Just because I'm not a fan of long-term relationships doesn't mean I'm misogynistic. I like women. Women like me. We like each other in a mutually satisfying way, and when that satisfaction ceases to be mutual, we part. Amicably."

"I will give you that," Elliott said, considering his brother. "None of your exes is vindictive or bitter. You do seem to have a knack for picking women who are just as transitory relationship-wise as you are."

"There's nothing wrong with embracing a lack of responsibility," Gunner said, getting to his feet and gathering up his camera. "Not everyone can be the worrywart you are, El. Are you clear on the situation with the dig now, Alice? If so, I've got to get ready for my trip to Spain and Portugal."

"As clear as I'll ever be." Alice's attention was clearly focused back on the laptop. "I'm just going to add a little something to the castle's Web site about the TV show filming here."

"Since you two will be off to the States on Elliott's book tour and delayed honeymoon before I return home, I'll give you a bon voyage now." Gunner embraced Alice, and patted Elliott on the back. "Have fun, and stay safe."

"Likewise," Elliott said, turning a smile on his wife. "Don't call unless something dire happens. I fully intend to give Alice the honeymoon she deserves."

"I'm sure nothing more exciting will happen beyond finding some Roman ruins beneath the pasture," Gunner predicted, an excellent example of why he would never be called psychic in any understanding of the word.

Chapter 2

"I think my best memory of you is when we were in college and you were telling me a funny anecdote that ended with the punch line 'I said, I have gas!' and right at the moment you were telling that part, the office door opened and out walked Professor Levi—you remember him?—*and* the dean of students, *and* the head of Romance languages."

"Oh, lord. Yes, I remember both Dr. Levi and that day," I said into the phone.

"And you were so mortified—" Laughter choked off Sandy's voice.

"You don't have to continue. We both know what happened."

"Lorina, you were so mortified that when you scurried away, you pooted with every step."

The phone tucked under my chin, I rested my head on my hands, not with remembered shame of that day some twelve years in the past but because Sandy was laughing so hard she was snorting. It had been months since she'd laughed, and I just wanted it to go on and on. Why did it have to happen now, when she was calling me just before boarding her flight? "We had a lot of laughs together that summer, my intestinal woes aside."

"We sure did. You were the best roommate I ever had."

"Silly woman. You haven't had any roomies other than me. In fact, if you add up the four years we were together in college, and then the eight years we've shared an apartment after that, I think we're going to have our twelfth anniversary in October."

"Good lord, so we are." There was a thoughtful pause. "That's longer than a lot of marriages!"

"I told you that we should have been gay. We'd have been an awesome lesbian couple, and we could have had kids by now," I said, a bittersweet nostalgia tinting my voice. "Although you'd probably have been the wife in the relationship, since I'm built like a brick oven."

"Oh, you are not. You're statuesque and tall and everything that petite people like me are not. I envy your ability to walk into a room and make people take notice."

"It's not so much take notice as it is stare and wonder who the Amazon is. No, no, don't go on trying to make me feel better—I'm resigned to the fact that I'm almost six feet tall, and chunky. That's beside the point, which is that we'd have made an awesome lesbian couple."

"Yes, darn us and our pesky love of men." She was laughing again, which made my spirits rise. "Although it doesn't seem to have done either of us any good. I ended up with a man who ruined my life, and you—" She stopped abruptly.

"I had exactly one relationship in that time, and it was with a man who was just as abusive as my father was," I finished for her, feeling the pull of dark memories, but not allowing them to drag me under. After years of therapy, I'd finally made my peace with the fact that some men thought it was their right to tear women's egos to shreds, but it didn't mean I had to be a victim.

I was most definitely *not* a victim any longer.

"Oh, sweetie, I didn't mean that."

"No, but it's true. My romantic life has sucked. Men are just so ... shallow. Into themselves. Looking for someone to be arm candy, or a quick roll in bed, and not anything more. Wow, I sound bitter, don't I?"

"No, you sound like someone who simply hasn't found Mr. Right yet."

"And fast starting to believe that such a man doesn't exist for me. I'm thirty-four, for heaven's sake. I'm running out of time to meet a man who doesn't have to resort to Viagra to perform."

"Now, that is a gross exaggeration, and you know it. There are lots of men out there in their thirties, or even forties, who are awesome lovers. There's bound to be one who's perfect for you. You just haven't found him yet, but you will. I know you will."

"That's because you're a romantic, while I'm a realist," I pointed out.

"You would be just as romantic as I am if it hadn't been driven out of you by that therapist you went to," she answered, her voice filled with scorn.

"Dr. Anderson made me a strong, confident woman," I said quickly.

"By stripping away all ideas that men can be just as nurturing and emotionally giving as women, yes. But really, Lorina, do you want to live the rest of your life alone because your dad was an asshole, and your ex was cut out of the same material? Not all men are like them. There are plenty of men out there who cherish women."

"I know that, silly. I know that there are perfectly nice men around—it's just that I don't seem to attract them. Hey, how did we get onto the subject of my pathetic excuse for a love life? We're supposed to be celebrating you."

Sandy laughed. "Nice change of subject."

"I thought it was." My throat tightened up. "Are you sure you're going to be all right? What if the nuns aren't as good with HIV as you think they are?"

"They've had a higher success rate than Western doctors. I showed you the medical-review paper about them, and their treatments are beyond what I could get here."

"Yeah, but it just seems foolish to trust yourself to a religious group rather than reputable doctors with cutting-edge drugs that could nip the disease in the bud."

"A religious group that has had tremendous success with their antiretrovirus drugs that are allowing thousands of people with HIV to live perfectly normal, healthy lives. No, there's no cure for it, but at least with the treatments I get with the nuns, I will *have* a life. And that's certainly worth pursuing, don't you think? I don't want to go through my life wondering if I could have done more." She paused, and said softly, "Lorina?"

I rubbed my ear. The phone had been pressed into it so hard that I was sure it was leaving a mark. "Right here, babe."

"Don't cry. You know this is for the best."

"No, I don't, but I respect the fact that you think withdrawing from the world is what's best for you. I just wish you could do it closer to home, where I could occasionally see you."

"The order doesn't work that way. When they say cloistered with no contact with the outside world, they mean it."

"But . . . you'll need doctors and medicines." It was the same objection that I had made for the last two days, and I knew even as I spoke the words what her response would be.

"I'll have doctors and medicines. Just not the same kind we have here."

"Your doctor said there were all sorts of drugs available for you to take that could let you be just fine—"

"And I will resort to them if I have to, but from everyone I've talked to who has HIV, this treatment is the best way to get a handle on it so it doesn't progress any further. Even my doctor agrees that it won't hurt me in the least, and will likely help me just as much as, if not more than, conventional drugs. Oh, Lorina, I know you don't agree with me about going away, but it really is the best answer. I'll be happy there—I really will. And after two months, I'll be able to correspond with you."

Unreasonably, I lashed out with anger that had built up for the last few months, ever since we found out that the scumbag had given Sandy HIV. "I don't know what sort of a religious order won't let their initiates talk to people for two freaking months! That's just wrong!"

"It's not wrong for them, and I can understand that they want us to focus on healing without outside distractions." Another pause. "Lorina."

"What?" I snapped, alternately wanting to slam down the phone and burst into tears.

"Be happy. And hopeful. I am."

"It's not right," I said, slumping back in my chair, the anger draining out of me and leaving me as limp as a three-day-dead cod. "We should be going after him for what he did."

"Vengeance is mine? No, sweetie, I can't. But I have written to him telling him what's happened."

"And how did he take it?"

She was silent for a few seconds, then admitted, "He said . . . he said some pretty harsh things, as a matter of fact. Threatening me if I said anything about it to any-one, and . . . well, he was quite abusive about it. I'll admit it was ugly, but you know, Lorina, people strike out like that when they're hurting, especially if they know they're guilty of harming someone else."

"Oh, come on! Paul doesn't give a damn for anyone but Paul, and you know it."

"I do not know that. He is basically a decent man—he's just had some bad breaks, and chosen to go down a path that isn't, perhaps, the wisest."

"I have no problem with him making his own hell—my objection is the way he's dragged you into it as well."

"We all have to take responsibility for our actions, myself included," she said softly. "I am at peace with my decisions, and have to trust that Paul will rectify his ways and seek help."

I said nothing, knowing that it was of no use. We'd had *that* argument all too often in the past. "So this is it, then? I lose the best friend and roomie a girl ever had without a backward look?"

"That's not fair," Sandy chided. "Lorina—"

"It's OK," I lied, making an effort to send her off with a smile, not that she could see it. "I'm just being hor-monal and cranky and sorry for myself because I'll have to spend my free time interviewing a new roommate, and you know I'd rather hack off my arm with a grapefruit knife than do that."

"Then take off and go do something fun. You deserve a break after looking after me for the last five months. There's a dig in Egypt that I know needs volunteers."

"Sandy Fache," I said sternly. "The very last thing I would ever think of doing is going to an archaeological dig."

"Why not? You were jealous every time I went off to one, or at least you claimed to be."

"I would think the answer would be obvious," I said with more than a little acid.

"Because of Paul? Pfft." She dismissed that objection. "He's just one man, and there are a lot of digs you could volunteer for this summer. I heard from Mom that there's even going to be one at Alice's castle."

"Who, now?"

"Alice, my foster sister. You met her once or twice when she came to see me at college."

"I vaguely remember her. Didn't she leave right after that?"

"Yeah, not long after. She's about half a year younger than me, and when she hit eighteen, the foster system kicked her out into the world. We've kept in touch over the years, although mostly just via Christmas cards. Anyway, she married a baron a couple of months ago."

"Like a land baron? A tycoon?"

"No, silly." Sandy's chuckle was warm and just hearing it made me feel better. Maybe she really *was* making the right choice, and would be able to thrive in such an isolated environment. "A real baron. You know, nobility and Jane Austen and all that."

"Wow. I had no idea they still existed."

"Well, they do, and she's a real bona fide baroness, and I read on her Facebook page that the castle her husband owns is part of some reality TV series that's going to be filmed there for a month. And that means that Alice will be on TV doing her lady-of-the-manor thing. If I wasn't in this situation, I'd be over there so fast that your head would spin."

"Where does she live?" I asked idly, not that I was really considering Sandy's suggestion to pursue a volunteer dig there just because I kind of knew this Alice person.

"Some little town in England. You should check her Facebook page—she just announced the TV show when

I checked, but that was about a month ago. There might be more info now about who's running the dig, and how you can volunteer."

"Eh."

"Don't be that way—this is the perfect opportunity for you to do something fun, and get out of the apartment, since you don't have any summer classes to teach. I'm sure if you asked my mom, she'd drop Alice a line and ask her to take you in, assuming you wanted to stay with a real baroness."

"I wouldn't dream of inflicting myself on someone I've barely even met," I protested.

"Bah. Alice was always nice, and I'm sure you'd like her. Oh, dear, that's my flight. Sweetie—"

Panic gripped me hard, squeezing my guts together. "Sandy . . . there's so much to say. . . ."

"I know, but just hold on to it for two months. It seems like forever now, but it'll pass quickly."

"If you have any doubts about this place, any doubt at any time, all you have to do is call me and I'll make sure you get out of Nepal."

"I know you will, silly girl. I've always been able to rely on you to have your head screwed on right, and your feet on the ground."

I gave a shaky laugh. "In other words, plodding and boring."

"Hardly that. You were just the rock to my butterfly. Whoops, must go. Love you bunches, girl."

"Love you, too. Be happy and healthy."

"Ditto. Later, alligator."

I won't say I didn't get a bit misty-eyed at the silly farewell that she had used ever since I'd met her, but I did sit clutching the phone for a long time after she hung up.

Once I roused myself, I got online and did a little investigating of Sandy's foster sister.

Exciting news for fans of Ainslie Castle! read an announcement on Alice's Facebook page. *The castle and grounds will be featured on an archaeology reality show called* Dig Britain!

"Never heard of it," I muttered to myself.

The dig will be broadcast each day for a month, and is sure to have lots of exciting finds. Elliott is hoping for a Roman bathhouse, while Lady Ainslie is sure there must be the ruins of a convent or two lurking around the grounds.

"Elliott must be the baron. But then who is Lady Ainslie?" I switched browser tabs to the castle's Web site, and read the description of the Ainslie family. "Ah. The baron's mom. Huh. I cannot imagine having to call your mother-in-law 'Lady Ainslie.' I wonder if Alice has to curtsy when she sees her." I clicked to read more.

Which will it be? Be sure to tune in to the Now! channel starting September first, and see what turns up under the earth of Ainslie.

"Worms and potato bugs," I predicted, more than a little jaded. It was true that I'd been jealous of Sandy and her yearly summer trips to exotic places to participate in archaeological digs, but after her experience with Paul, I'd be damned if I ever stepped foot on one, myself.

For a complete schedule, click here. And if you'd like to volunteer as a digger, sifter, or find-washer, follow this link to the managing dig company.

I glanced down at the link, and reeled backward just as if a mule had kicked me in the gut. I stared at it for a good eight minutes, my mind whirling and my stomach lurching around my insides, until I finally clicked on the text.

Wide-eyed, I stared at the resulting Web site.

Claud-Marie Archaeology, read the name at the top of the page. *Paul Thompson, director.*

"Paul," I whispered to myself, the name bringing with it a red swell of fury. Had Sandy known who was managing the dig? No, that didn't make sense—she would want me to steer clear of any dig of which Paul was a member. And now Sandy's foster sister was right there where Paul was. It seemed almost like a sign, as if fate was daring me not to take notice.

I dug through my memories to shake out those regarding Alice. I remembered her as being bubbly and nice, surprisingly cheerful despite the fact that she was in the foster system. She'd also been the possessor of a wicked sense of humor.

"I have to stop Paul from ruining anyone else's life," I said out loud to my tank of zebra fish. They flitted back and forth without a care as to what I was saying, but it made me feel better just having something to talk to. "The question is, how do I do that? Dr. Anderson's insistence that I can do anything I want aside, I'm not a superhero. I'm a low-paid, mild-mannered community college French teacher who has a very bad feeling about what might be happening at"—I checked the computer—"Ainslie Castle. The sad truth is I can't save Sandy and I can't stop a villain from being a villain."

Or can you? a voice asked in my head. I frowned, my mind surging down a new path of speculation. What if I had proof of how Paul had infected Sandy? Inescapable, solid proof that he couldn't deny? Proof that would hold up in court, if needed.

An idea started to grow in my brain, one that, after a few online searches, blossomed into a full-fledged plan.

"It may be heinous, and it may be incredibly illegal, but that doesn't matter," I told my fish, steadfastly ignoring my conscience declaring otherwise. "Sandy's faith that Paul isn't the bastard I know him to be just isn't going to cut it. Let's see, I could apply to be a digger, but I have no experience, and there's bound to be a lot of people applying for those positions, what with the TV show going on at the same time. I need something unique, something that no one else could offer them. . . ."

I mulled over the possibilities, which ranged from being a translator of all things French to what amounted to a gofer, but in the end, I decided to play on people's pretty reliable desire for publicity.

I opened an e-mail and filled in the address of the network producer. "A TV show is going to want all the publicity they can get. I'll pitch the idea of a behind-the-scenes book about the dig and show to them, and pray they like it. Otherwise, fishies, I'm going to have to fake a hell of a background in archaeology, and that won't end well. As it is, I'm going to have to do an awful lot of fudging, but at least I can pretend to use a camera. Right? Right."

The fish didn't look convinced, but I hadn't survived too many years of my father telling me I was a worthless waste of space to let my fish dis my ideas. "Dammit, I'm a strong woman now. I don't need your approval. Besides, I have a higher calling here—I have to make sure that no other innocent women's lives are destroyed by a man who doesn't care that he has a potentially deadly infection. He might not listen to Sandy, but he'll have to pay attention to me when I get indisputable proof of his illness. Beware, Paul Thompson, for your doom is nigh, and her name is Lorina!"

Chapter 3

"Well, Lorina, it looks like we've officially started." Daria Hollingberry, one of the archaeologists whom I'd just met, nodded at the cluster of people standing around a soundman bearing a large microphone swathed in a furry cover. In the center of the group was a woman who'd been introduced as Sue Birdwhistle, the director of the *Dig Britain!* reality show.

"We have?" I glanced at my watch. "Hell's bells, I haven't even unpacked. Well, anything but this." I nodded at the camera I was holding, one of the two I had borrowed from a friend, after having promised him I would guard them with my life. "Did they move up the schedule? No one told me, if they did. I had to take a train from London, and it took a lot longer than I imagined."

"No, no, they didn't move the schedule—we don't start actually digging until this afternoon. I meant we've officially started because Sue's just done her first mono-

logue to the camera." Daria gestured a small triangular
trowel toward the small clutch of people. Then, with a
smile, she used it to tap lightly against my camera in a
faux toast. "Here's to a successful dig."

"Ah, gotcha." I smiled wanly, my confusion fading.
"So, do you work for the Claud-Marie company, or are
you one of the independent diggers?"

I had an idea of how a dig site actually worked after
having listened to Sandy's tales of the summers she
spent grubbing around in the sands of the Middle East
and eastern Europe as a volunteer, and wanted to iden-
tify anyone who might be able to help me in my quest.
Volunteers probably weren't going to help my cause
much, but an employee . . . that was another matter.

"Yes, I work for CMA. It's quite exciting, really. Last
year we excavated in Tunisia, which was a blast, although
my husband complained about my leaving him home
with our twin ten-year-olds while I gallivanted around in
the sun, and had steamy affairs with various and sundry
handsome sheikhs."

I didn't quite know how to take that, so I simply said,
"Did your husband come with you this time?"

"Not him! He runs a testing facility—you know, the
people who process blood tests and urine samples, and
that sort of thing. He'd die if he had to spend his day in
what he calls unsanitary dirt." She giggled. "I've made
him sound like a jealous clean freak, but he's not. He's
actually quite understanding, although he does like to
pretend that I'm surrounded by countless diggers who
lust after me, which couldn't be further from the truth.
Just look around—by tonight we'll be knee-high in dirt
and mud, and the only thing we'll lust after is a hot bath.
Are you going to be here for long? Oh, dear, that
sounded rude. What I meant to ask is how long you expect it will take to get your book done."

"Oh, you know," I said, trying to look sage. "These things are hard to pin down. It could take a few days, or a few weeks."

"I've never met a photojournalist before," she said with obvious interest. "It must be thrilling for you to be able to take a few pictures and then voilà! You have a book."

"It's a bit more complicated than that," I said with what I hoped looked like learned professionalism. I tried to dredge up every morsel of information I had ever seen about journalists and photography. "There's fact-checking and things, naturally. And the photos have to be processed. That takes a lot of time."

She nodded, and I breathed a sigh of relief that she obviously had no clue I was bluffing like crazy. "I'm sure there's a lot of work involved. I take it you're a fan of Roman history? Or are you just covering the dig because . . . well, because?"

"I'm interested, but afraid I know squat about it." I'd already decided that it would be dangerous to try to pass myself off as someone interested in history around a group of people who fairly dripped expertise on the subject. "And a friend's friend is married to the owner, so she was happy to let me putter around taking pictures."

"You're a friend of the baroness?" Daria looked impressed.

"I've met her a couple of times, but that was years ago. She's a friend of my roommate's, actually."

"What made you choose us for your book if you're not overly keen on Roman history?"

Guilt dug deep in my gut. "Well, I've always wanted to come to England, and when I read about the dig and the TV program that would be filming it, I suddenly had an idea for a behind-the-scenes book. I know those have been popular for other reality shows, and thought that maybe people would like one about an archaeology dig."

She blinked at me, but said nothing.

My palms started to sweat. "Have you seen the producer's other reality shows? They all had books done about them, and they were really popular, so he—Roger d'Aspry—was totally on board when I suggested doing a book for this project. It may be a bit unorthodox to record the filming of an archaeological dig, but Roger thinks it will do well."

To my relief, she smiled. "Well, I think it's impressive that you're going to publish a book about us—about the dig. I'll be sure to make everyone in my family buy a copy."

The guilt in my gut dug deeper. How many more lies would I have to dish out before I could go home with the proof I needed? "That would be awesome."

"What's the name of the book?"

"Er . . . I haven't picked one yet."

"How long will it be? Will it be one of those coffee table books, or something smaller?"

I was in hell, liar's hell. This was what came to people who wantonly told untruths, my conscience told me with smug satisfaction. I squirmed slightly, trying to think of something to end the conversation. "I'm afraid I can't talk about it yet."

"Top secret, eh?" Daria said, nodding knowingly. "I heard authors are like that."

I tried to summon up a confident smile, but failed. "More like inspiration hasn't yet struck."

"Let's just hope that we have a productive month to justify a book about us." Daria watched as Sue argued with Roger d'Aspry, noted producer of various British reality TV shows. "There they go, at it again. You've met both of them, yes?"

"I met Sue when I got here, although I actually met Roger two days ago in London. I was a bit of a fangirl,

I'm afraid. I loved the show he produced with an American woman who played a duchess during a monthlong Victorian reenactment."

Daria squinted in thought. "Oh, I think I remember that. There was some controversy around it, wasn't there? Sabotage or something?"

"I don't know anything about that. I just thought it was cool, and of course, it was interesting that the lead couple hooked up in real life. I mean, that's kind of a fairy tale, isn't it?"

"Absolutely."

As I watched Sue and Roger, my thoughts turned to just how wonderful it would be to meet a man I could trust, one who wouldn't use his power against me, one who would be there beside me, supportive and loving and sexy as sin. "There's nothing like that in my future, for sure," I said on a sigh.

"Nothing like what? Arguments with a bossy producer? Don't fool yourself—I worked with Roger on the *Anglopalooza* show he did two years ago—we tried to locate an Anglo-Saxon castle, but it was a miserable failure—and I can tell you in all honesty that he's the pushiest man in TV."

"Pushy, how?" I asked, looking worriedly at the red-haired, balding man who was still arguing with the pretty blonde Sue. "When I met him, he was quite nice. Although that might be in part because I was telling him how much I liked the Victorian show he did."

"For one, he worries more about getting what he calls 'good TV' than us doing proper archaeology. And he's a stickler for everyone keeping to the schedule, no matter how much we tell him that we have to go where the archaeology is. But worst of all is that he loves having everyone doing reenactments of anything even remotely related to the subject at hand."

"What sort of reenactments?" I tried to look like I was interested from a purely journalistic viewpoint, but the truth was that I had a secret love for such things, and couldn't wait to watch them in progress.

"Everything from spending twenty-four hours as a medieval nun or monk to making pottery, weapons, clothing, food . . . you name it, Roger will have us doing it. You better watch out, because when he's in the throes of one of his big ideas, he ropes in everyone he can find. And I do mean everyone. In *Anglopalooza*, he had not only the whole crew but also all the bystanders dressed up as Saxons reenacting what a siege was like."

"That can't be too bad," I said, considering the subject. "You guys are looking for Roman remains, aren't you? It wouldn't be horrible to dress up like Romans. I mean, they had nice hair arrangements, and lovely jewelry, and their dresses weren't bad, either. Flattering to those of us who are more substantial than others."

"Just you wait," Daria warned, nodding toward the group, which at that moment broke up and scattered. "And pray you don't end up being picked to play the part of the servant."

"Ew." I remembered a television show I watched a few weeks back in preparation for the trip. "It would be just my luck that I'd be the servant who has to mop up the vomitorium."

"Pfft," Daria said, making a dismissive gesture. "Vomitoria were passageways into large places, not rooms where people went to barf up their feast so they could go indulge in more. That's nothing but a fallacy."

"I'm happy to hear it," I said, relieved despite the fact that I hadn't been called on to do anything more than stroll around and take pictures. "Let's just hope Roger knows that, too."

"That is extremely unlikely. He'd love nothing more

than to have people vomiting everywhere. He doesn't really care much for accuracy so long as it's dramatic."

I let my gaze wander over to where the big television studio trucks had parked alongside an old barn. The members of the dig team had set up a tent camp in an unused pasture well out of sight of Ainslie Castle, per an agreement with Alice and her baron husband. Roger had told me they were worried that tourism would drop if archaeologists were cluttering up the place. Apparently, the castle was partially supported by the tourists who visited it a couple of days a week, so it was important to keep them happy.

In addition to the two dozen or so tents that had been set up as the dig and TV crews' home away from home for the next month, five RVs had been parked along the fringes, where the producer, the director, and the other VIPs would live. One RV had been converted into a miniature processing studio, complete with satellite uplink, editing computers, and a huge whiteboard where the producer mapped out each day's shooting schedule. Although Alice had offered me accommodations at the castle, I didn't want to take advantage of our tenuous acquaintance, and instead had taken up Roger's offer to stay in one of the staff tents. But it was one of the RVs that held my attention.

I decided the time was right to do a little probing. "I'm surprised that Paul would allow things to be presented that weren't true. He's such a stickler for accuracy."

"Paul Thompson?" Daria gave me an odd look. "Do you know him?"

"A little," I said, adopting a coy expression that I hoped would lead to further confidences.

She continued, but not along the lines I had hoped for. "Have you ever seen him dig? Most of his finds come from the spoil pile."

"Um ... that's what?"

"Sorry, technical lingo. Spoil pile is the dirt and debris that is excavated. We go through it to check for small items like bits of pottery or glass or even bone that's missed while we dig."

"Ah, gotcha."

"Anyway, a more incompetent choice for head of the company than Paul I can't imagine. Yes, I'm biased—I was up for the job, and the board gave it to him, instead— but seriously, if you want to photograph proper archaeology, stay away from Paul."

I pursed my lips. Daria's comment about the spoil pile was an insult, pure and simple—it implied that Paul wasn't paying enough attention to what he was digging. "It's never easy when someone else gets a job instead of you, but surely the board must have felt he was qualified for it."

"There's qualified, and then there's qualified," Daria said opaquely, nodding over toward the line of trailers. "He may swank around and think he's a god of the archaeological world, but the truth is that it's us diggers who really know what's going on. Take Dennis Smythe-Lowe, for instance. He's had his hands in the dirt since he was a kid, and worked for CMA almost as long as I have, and yet the powers that be passed us both by when they hired Paul to head up the company. It's politics, nothing but politics."

Now, that was interesting. There was obviously no love lost between Daria and Paul. . . . I tucked that fact away, and looked interested. "Is Dennis the man who looks like Indiana Jones had a love child with a hippie?"

Daria laughed. "That's him. He's the salt of the earth, and a damned good archaeologist. Just don't get him going about the Stone Age, or he'll spend all day teaching you how to map flints."

"Map? Like draw?"

"No, in this case it means to chip away at a flint until you have a pointed end that can be used as a tool or weapon."

"Gotcha." I dredged up a morsel of information I'd seen during my planning phase for this trip. "One thing I'm confused about—you called yourself a digger, but I thought diggers were the grad students and unpaid volunteers who did the grunt work, not the proper archaeologists."

"Well, it's a bit of both, really," she said with a bob of her head. "The term digger does generally refer to the nonprofessionals, but sometimes we archaeologists also refer to ourselves as diggers."

"As a way of being one of the common folk?" I asked lightly.

"That and because it's what we all do," she said, her eyes back on the group of TV folk.

I watched them with her for a moment before commenting, "I've seen a TV show about some people who salt sites in order to fool people. You don't think that Roger . . . ?"

"No, I can't accuse Roger of doing that." Daria gave a little shrug. "Not that I think he wouldn't if it had occurred to him, but luckily, his mind doesn't usually run to deviousness like that. Hey, isn't that the baron's brother? I heard he broke his leg falling off a cliff in Turkey. If that's him, then I shall certainly volunteer to push his wheelchair around the dig site. Mmrowr."

"I thought you were married," I said with a smile before turning to look where she had nodded.

"Married, but not dead. Damn, but he's a fine, fine sight."

The producer, Roger d'Aspry, stood with a man who sat on a bright blue motorized scooter. I couldn't see much of the man until I moved to the side a couple of steps, and then it took me a moment to be able to speak. "Wow."

"Glad I'm not the only one to have that reaction. I wonder if he needs help bathing."

With an effort, I managed to drag my eyes from the man on the scooter to look askance at Daria.

She giggled, and nudged me with her elbow. "Don't tell me you wouldn't offer to help him bathe if he asked you."

Unbidden, my eyes returned to the man who was at that moment swinging a leg in a bright pink cast with Velcro straps around it so he could get to his feet. He towered over Roger, which meant he must have been well over six feet, with impressively broad shoulders, the tops of which were brushed by straight dark brown hair. His skin was the color of milky coffee, and although he was in profile to me, I could see he had a softly squared chin. All that, combined with a natural grace evident despite his having to clunk around in a walking cast, meant he really was worth looking at.

But I was not in the market for a romantic entanglement, I reminded myself. I had a job to do, an important job, and nothing could distract me from that.

"I don't know that I'd offer to give him a bath," I said slowly, trying hard to pretend that I wasn't, at that moment, thinking a number of lascivious thoughts, "but I certainly wouldn't kick him out of bed for eating crackers."

It was Daria's turn to stare at me.

"Sorry. Idiom. Might be too American to be known here."

She made a face. "Hardly. Our version is 'I wouldn't kick him out of bed for farting.' Yours is nicer."

"What's he doing here?" I asked, unable to quell my

curiosity. "Just making sure no one harms the castle grounds?"

"Far from it—he has a degree in archaeology, although evidently he didn't pursue it. He's here to lend a hand, so far as he can, or so I gather from what Sue said about him. Frankly, I don't care why he's interested in helping. I'm just happy he is."

There was a note of sly cunning in her voice that I chose to ignore, telling myself that what Daria did in private was her own business.

Besides, this man was way out of my league, and that was good as far as I was concerned. Men who looked like him not only had giant egos; they also had to beat women away with a stick. Big, gawky women like me probably didn't even enter his sphere of notice, not that I'd want to be noticed by a handsome egomaniac. "I suppose I should go see to unpacking the rest of my stuff. I dashed out before I finished because I was so excited. Oh, speaking of excited—I was told that I should be at a staff meeting this afternoon. Do you know exactly when it is?"

"After lunch." Daria hadn't taken her eyes off Roger and the baron's brother, who were slowly meandering toward the line of RVs. "I think I'll just go over to Roger and say hello, and remind him that I've worked with him before."

"Subtle," I called after her, smiling at her thumbs-up gesture in response.

Chapter 4

The smile stayed with me until I reached the tent that had been assigned to me. The archaeology folk's temporary housing consisted of standard camping fare—orange and white domelike tents with little screened windows, and a large matching screened opening with an inner flap for privacy—while the film team were arrayed in fancy RVs bearing the name of the network.

I was in the middle of unpacking the borrowed photography equipment, trying hard to remember which lens went with which camera, when noises of an altercation seeped through from my next-door neighbor.

I peeked out the door to eye the tent next to me. It bulged and rocked in an alarming manner. Unlike my tent, though, this one resembled an orange and white hippopotamus with its butt in the air, and its front end wallowing in the water. Worse were the noises coming from it.

"Gran, no, that's not helping! You're pulling my hair."
That was a very young-sounding American woman's
voice.

"Well then, what about this?" answered a much more
dignified, definitely British older woman's voice.

A side of the tent bulged outward.

"Ack! No! Balls, now the other end is going!"

There was a metallic snap, and gently, as if it were a
giant orange and white butterfly alighting on a flower,
the far end of the tent wafted to the ground, leaving beneath it two squirming forms.

I stood outside the now collapsed tent, hesitating before asking, "Hello? Hi! I'm Lorina, your neighbor to the
south. I can't help but notice that your tent appears to
have deflated. Is everything all right in there?"

The squirming stopped for a few seconds.

"Oh, hi, Lorina. I'm Cressy. Cressida, really, but everyone calls me Cressy. And we're fine, Gran and me, that is.
Gran and I? Whichever, we're fine, but the tent is totes
sucktastic."

"Perhaps the lady might unzip the door to allow us
out?" came a gentle voice.

"I'd be happy to, Mrs. . . . er . . . Cressy's gran, but I'm
afraid I don't see a zipper." I pulled up a long length of
flaccid tent hunting for it. "Are you sure it was closed?"

"Gran's name is Salma Raintree, and yes, we're sure.
We were trying it out to see how much light would be let
in with the door closed. But then I tripped, and fell into
the side of it, and broke one of the thingies that goes
around making the curved part, and then Gran tried to
help me put it back together, and my hair got caught
when we snapped the rod together, and then I got a charley horse in my leg, and I couldn't get it straight, and
Gran said I should walk the charley horse off, but my
hair was still stuck to the rod, so I couldn't, and then I

had to wee, so Gran said we should just take the rod out of the little pocket it sits in, and then it just all went horribly wrong."

"You don't have to explain any more," I interrupted, laughing despite the note of desperation in Cressida's voice. I dug around in more of the tenting, searching for the collapsed entrance. "I can see that it just went downhill from there. Are you still attached to the tent rib?"

"Not anymore," came Cressy's sad reply.

It took five minutes, but at last I extricated both Cressy and Salma from the remains of their temporary prison. Cressy emerged red-faced from the exertion, her T-shirt rumpled, and her shorts creased and grubby. She was an inch or so taller than me, which had to put her at six feet, with butt-length straight brown hair pulled back in a messy ponytail. Despite her experience with the tent, she grinned at me, quite cheerful as she stuck out a hand. "Hi, again."

"Hello," I said, shaking her hand, then glancing down at my hand in dismay.

"Oh, sorry, I should have warned you that my hands are sticky." She held up a pair of hands that were grubby in the extreme. "Had a candy bar in my pocket, and I forgot about it, and it melted all over. It ran down my outer leg, but I licked it up. You wouldn't happen to know where the bathroom is, would you?"

I refrained from commenting about the dubious act of licking chocolate off one's own leg, and confined myself to pointing at the barn, where I'd been told that the production company had set up not only a row of portable toilets but makeshift showers for the use of the dig crew.

"It really wasn't her fault," Salma said, brushing herself off to stand beside me, watching as Cressy galloped off in that way that only long-legged, six-foot-tall teenage girls can. "Cressida meant well, but she's at that awkward stage where her mind doesn't quite realize where her limbs are."

"I went through that phase," I said with a bit of a grimace. "I was forever falling down stairs, or tripping over my own big feet. Luckily, it stopped by the time I went off to college."

"Cressida is only seventeen, so I suspect she has a few more years before mind and body are one." Salma frowned at the tent. "I don't trust this contraption."

We both eyed the remains. Salma was what I thought of as a Miss Marple sort of Englishwoman—early sixties with a beautiful complexion, perfectly styled white hair, and gentle blue eyes surrounded by a mass of tiny lines that bespoke character. She wasn't the least bit rumpled despite the tent experience.

"The tent does look like it's a goner," I said. "But maybe it can be repaired?"

She sighed. "I have an uncomfortable feeling that it can."

I couldn't help but give her a doubtful look. "Perhaps there's somewhere else you can stay if life in the tent would be too hard—"

"Oh, no, no," she interrupted gently. "I wouldn't dream of discommoding anyone. Really, I'm just happy to spend the time with Cressida, since my daughter seldom allows her to visit this country."

"And is Cressy a fan of archaeology?" I asked, amazed at a grandmother who would tolerate roughing it for a month just to be near her grandchild.

"Not really, no. Her father is, though. She's here to see him, and I'm here to keep an eye on Cressy, and enjoy her company. And there is the fact that my husband was a historian, so I have a fondness for all things historical."

"That really is dedication to want to stay in a tent for

a month," I said with a nod toward the blob of fallen fabric.

She sighed. "Yes, I will admit that I hadn't anticipated this accident. I cannot help but worry about the structural stability of the mechanism now that it's been . . ."

"Mauled?" I asked.

"Compromised," she corrected with another of those Miss Marple smiles, the one that made me think of having tea with shortbread cookies.

I reminded myself that her problem wasn't mine to fix, and that I had more than enough on my plate without worrying about whether the tent was going to give way onto the nice old lady.

Which is why it surprised me to hear myself offer, "If you like, we can swap tents. I did a lot of camping when I was a child, so I'm used to tents being a bit temperamental. There's no reason you shouldn't have a stable structure."

"That's very sweet of you, but I couldn't think of putting you to such trouble."

"What trouble?" Cressy asked, galloping up to us with another of her blinding grins. "You're talking about me, aren't you? I'm such a trial."

I couldn't help but giggle a little at the sorrowful way she said the last sentence. "I doubt if that's true at all. I offered to let your grandmother and you have use of my tent, since it appears to be hale and hearty. I'm sure I could beat your tent into submission, or as much as would be needed for me to stay in it for a week or so while I document the dig."

"You're a journalist?" Cressida asked, scrunching up her nose as she looked over at my tent. Her scrunch faded as a pensive look swept over her face. "That's really nice of you, but my dad would kill me if he thought

I broke a tent and then dumped it on someone else. He's always telling me that I have to own my problems. Oh, I know!"

Her expression changed in a flash to one of jubilant triumph. "Gran can have your tent, because she's old and my dad said she looks like she'd break into a million pieces if a big wind blew."

"Cressida," Salma objected.

Cressy patted her grandmother on the arm. "He meant that nicely."

"I'm sure he did, but regardless—"

"You wouldn't really mind if Gran had your tent, would you? I'll move your stuff to our tent, and her stuff to yours, so no one will have to lift a finger. That way I won't worry about Gran, and yet I'll still have to suffer with our tent, so no one can say I'm taking advantage of you, right?"

I hesitated for a few seconds, trying to think of a polite way to tell her that I'd prefer being on my own—it was very difficult being the instrument of justice if one had a seventeen-year-old stumbling over one's plots and connivings.

But at that moment, I looked at Cressy, and caught the hint of uncertainty in her eyes, a painful awareness that I all too well remembered from my own awkward teenage years. She was trying to put a brave face on it, but it was evident that if I refused, she'd take it as a personal comment about rooming with her, rather than my own desire to be alone.

"That sounds like a lovely idea, as long as you don't mind sharing the tent with an old fuddy-duddy like me."

"Cool!" she said, giving me a grin. "You're not old at all, and if you fuddy-duddy, I'll simply go bother Gran in her tent, and Gunner won't be able to say boo about it, right?"

"Gunner?" I asked, confused.

"He's my dad," she said, tossing a cheerful smile over her shoulder before she dived into the collapsed tent and began hauling out their luggage. "He was a mistake like me."

"Cressida," Salma objected, giving me a little shake of the head. "Just because you have taken advantage of Miss . . . ?"

"Liddell. But do please call me Lorina."

"Such a pretty name. Just because you have taken advantage of Lorina's generous nature does not mean you must blight her with irrelevant details of your life."

"She's a journalist, Gran. She lives for those sorts of things. Don't you, Lorina?"

"Absolutely," I said, ignoring the twinge of guilt at the fact that this innocent young woman had taken my lie to heart. "I love talking to people about their lives. But I'm also going to be very busy—"

"See?" Cressy threw herself under the wad of deflated tent, and emerged with two suitcases. "It'll be just fine, Gran. Lorina's cool, and I promise to not bother her, and Gunner can't say I wasn't being nice, and everyone is happy!"

There are just some people that it's very hard to get through to, and Cressy was clearly one of their crowd. So in the end I helped her transfer Salma's belongings to my tent, and mine to the grass between the tents while we struggled to resurrect that structure. After an hour of swearing, sweating, and seeking assistance from two passing diggers, we finally got the tent resurrected, fortified by a judicious use of duct tape.

"Good as new," Cressy announced when I stood back with our two helpers to admire our handiwork. "Dibs the bed in the back. I know you'll probably want the one nearest the door so you can go potty in the middle of the night."

"Cressida!" Salma said on a horrified gasp.

"What?" Cressy paused at the door, shooting her grandma a puzzled look. "I don't see why you're wearing that 'Oh my god, I can't believe what Cressida has said now' face when I didn't say anything wrong."

"You implied that Lorina has a bladder that can't make it through the night, and that, my dear, is insulting."

"It also happens to be true," I intervened with a smile at Cressy, who sighed in relief, and plunged into the tent to arrange her air mattress and belongings.

Salma looked vaguely distressed. "Regardless, Cressida should learn when things should be spoken, and when they should be confined only to thought."

I tossed in my suitcase and shoved the bag with the extra camera equipment next to my air mattress, which Cressy was thoughtfully inflating for me. "Don't worry about it. I'm not in the least bit offended. . . . Oh, hello."

The woman who leaned her head into the tent was one of the diggers. I wasn't quite sure of her name, but thought it was Florence. "I've been asked to tell you that Roger would like you to go to his caravan. He said something about wanting to discuss a project with you."

"Project? What project?" I sat back on my heels. "Oh no! It's the Roman reenactments, isn't it? Look, I'm as willing to help out as the next person, but I have a gag reflex, and if I see people barfing, I'm going to barf, too, Florence."

"Fidencia," she corrected, and gave me a scornful look. "I'm afraid I don't know why Roger wants you for a project when there are so many more qualified people, but he asked me to bring you to him. If you are ill, I suggest you visit the doctor."

"I'm not sick. I just meant . . . oh, never mind." I sighed and got to my feet, doubling over to exit through the doorway, and hurrying out to follow Fidencia. "Just shove my things out of the way if they bother you, Cressy. I'll be back later to finish unpacking."

I found Fidencia a few tents down the line, speaking rapidly into a walkie-talkie.

"—don't know what happened to the potable water, but it's not my problem, and I resent you treating me like I'm a lowly production assistant. I have better things to do with my time than to run around worrying about water for Roger."

"Roger," came a staticky reply.

"That's what I just said!" She slapped one hand on her leg in an irritated manner.

"Sorry, I got caught up in tent drama," I apologized softly.

"I know you did. I was saying 'Roger' in acknowledgment," said the person on the other end of the radio.

"Oh. Well, that's just confusing. Stop it," Fidencia said before punching a button on the radio and attaching it to her belt. "Evidently I am to play nursemaid amongst other indignities. Are you ready? This way."

"Are you sure Roger's not going to ask me to be a servant?" I trotted after her, worrying unduly about anything that would get in the way of my plan. "Not that I'm *not* a team player or anything, but honestly, I don't think I'd be good vomit-scraping servant material. If I have to be a Roman, couldn't I wear a long gown and pretend to play a lyre? I used to know how to play a guitar, so I could mime playing pretty well."

Fidencia evidently had other thoughts on her mind as we hurried out of the tent village and toward the line of RVs. "What? What are you saying?" she snapped. "I don't have time for this!"

"Sorry. I'm just grousing to myself."

A static burst from a walkie-talkie had Fidencia pausing, listening intently for a few seconds, then responding, "Oh, for the love of . . . no, I do not know why someone is trying to move the portable toilets. I'm an archaeologist, not a lackey! Ask Roger what's going on."

More static, this time with a testy note to it.

"Look, just because I agreed to be a liaison between Roger's people and the CMA doesn't mean I am everyone's bitch. Roger's not paying me enough to run around and fix everything!"

"That's exactly what you *are* being paid for," the disembodied voice said out of the radio. "And if you don't want the job, we can find someone else—"

"You push me any harder, and you're going to have to! I'll see to this, but it's the last straw, do you hear me? I have digging to do this afternoon!" Fidencia viciously turned off the radio with a little snarl. "A waste of a perfectly good education . . . I can't stay to babysit you," she said, giving me a shove toward the line of RVs. "Evidently I must now go deal with some sort of issue catering has with the grills. I swear to god, no amount of money is worth this aggravation."

"Sorry. I'll find my way to him just fine. You go deal with catering."

She stormed off, muttering rude things under her breath. With a growing sense of worry, I hustled my way to the RVs, which were lined up nose to tail. I whipped around the farthest one, intent on things I would say to Roger if he insisted I do some playacting for the camera, but the sight of a man on a scooter about to mow me down drove all thoughts from my head.

"Ack!" I yelled, and tried to leap to the left, but the man jerked the handlebars at the same time, with the result that he drove right over the top of my foot.

Chapter 5

"Bloody, buggery hell!" I shouted, clutching my poor abused foot, and hopping in pain.

Tears pricked in my eyes, which is probably one reason for what happened next. The aforementioned propensity for escapades is another, and lastly, the scooter driver's decision to circle around was the final nail in the coffin of my supposed grace and elegance. In midhop, my ankle twisted, and when I landed, I listed to the side, about to fall hard on the ground, except the man on the scooter was in the way, which meant I ended up draped across his lap, and clutching his shoulders to keep from sliding off.

"Hullo," he said, and wrapped both arms around me to hoist me up so I was sitting across him. "I can't apologize enough for running over you. You just seemed to come out of nowhere, but that's no excuse. How bad is your foot? Is it broken? I hope not, because I can tell you from firsthand knowledge that a broken foot is the very devil. Can you wiggle your toes?"

It was the brother of the owner, the very man with the long hair, chiseled jaw, and sexy profile who had Daria drooling. I gazed up into his pale blue eyes, absently noting that they were ringed in black, which made them quite noticeable. And attractive. Oh, who was I fooling? He was downright gorgeous, and his driving skills notwithstanding, I almost enjoyed sitting so intimately across his lap, with his arms around me, and those stunning eyes peering concernedly at me.

"Foot," I said, unable to get my brain working. "Hurt."

His forehead wrinkled. "I knew it. I did hurt you. I'll take you up to the house and we'll call a doctor. Just stay where you are—assuming you don't mind sitting on my lap, that is."

"Foot," I said stupidly, but as the scooter jerked forward, my wits suddenly returned and I realized that I was being transported toward the castle. "Oh, man alive. No, you don't need to take me to a doctor—I'm fine, really. Your tires are pretty big, and although my foot does hurt, I don't think anything is broken. See? I can wiggle my toes."

He stopped and we both looked at my foot.

"You have a boot on. I can't see your toes."

"No, but you can take it from me they're wiggling." I winced as I did, in fact, move my toes around. "The steel toe saved them, although the top of my foot is a bit tender. But nothing's broken."

"Steel-toed boots . . . you must be an archaeologist," he said with a quirky half smile.

"Not really, no." It was on the tip of my tongue to tell him that my old roommate had been an amateur digger, but I stopped myself in time, appalled at the fact that a few seconds of sitting on his lap and I was ready to blab everything. "But I do know that boots are *de rigueur* for dig sites."

"They are indeed. I'm glad to hear your foot wasn't injured." He stared at me for a second, and it crossed my mind that I should get off him. But one of his arms was still wrapped around me, holding me firmly to his torso. "I do apologize, but as I said, you just came around that corner unexpectedly, and there was nothing I could do. I'm Gunner, by the way. Gunner Ainslie. And you are . . . ?"

"Lorina Liddell. Wait, Gunner as in the father of Cressy?"

His eyes seemed to light up. "You've met my little girl?"

"She's hardly little," I said before realizing that he might be insulted by such honesty. "That is, she's a smidgen taller than me, and I'm a behemoth."

"You are not a behemoth. Far from it."

"I am. I'm just shy of six feet, and I won't tell you my weight because it would probably make you run screaming from me."

"Women and their body issues," he said, shaking his head. "I've never understood why women feel that men find bony bodies desirable."

"Television," I said sourly. "Movies. Magazines. Every other form of media."

"Yes, well, they're wrong," he said, waving away such paltry things. "I happen to like women with some substance to them. Cressy takes after her mother in that respect, and I have no doubt the day will come when I will be carrying a shotgun around just to keep the boys off her. If she ever expresses an interest in them, that is. Her grandmother assures me that it's only a matter of time before she ceases being horse-mad and turns to romance."

"Ah, the horse stage," I said, remembering my own youth. "I kind of hope she doesn't change too much. She's quite charming, actually."

"She is that. Don't know where she gets it from—certainly not her mother, and I'm just an old crusty photographer who does better with inanimate objects than people."

I stared at him in horror, my stomach contracting with a sudden spurt of concern. For a minute, I thought I might hyperventilate. "You're a photographer?"

"There's a more technical title relating to building sites and forensics, but I like to think of myself as being a photographer at heart. I'm also a minister in an Internet religion if you want to get married."

My eyes widened to the point where I wouldn't have been surprised if they bugged out. "Did you just ask me to marry you?"

"No, I offered to—oh, I see what you're asking." His smile, which had been pleasantly lopsided, turned into an outright full-fledged grin. "Although the Ainslie men tend to wed after a short acquaintance, I think that even my brother, who married a perfectly charming American—you're a Yank, too, aren't you?—even Elliott would have something to say if I offered myself to you after having known you for only five minutes."

"Oh, good, I didn't think . . . but it just seemed like . . ." I remembered that he was the enemy, a man who could potentially destroy the cover I'd built for myself, and returned to feeling sick to my stomach. "Well, thank god you're not into me."

"That is a *very* risqué thing to say when you are sitting on my lap."

"I'm sorry." I sighed, and pushed myself off his lap, flexing my foot before putting my weight on it. "Things always come out of my mouth wrong. See? Like that. Also risqué, although wholly unintentional, I assure you."

He laughed. "I like what comes out of your mouth. Oh, lord, now I'm doing it."

"Sadly, it appears I'm contagious. It's nice to meet you, Mr. Ainslie—"

"Gunner, please."

"It's nice to meet you, Gunner, but if you'll excuse me, the producer of the TV show has requested my presence, and he's probably wondering where I am."

I hurried off at a fast limp before he could respond, desperate to get away from him before I blabbed something untoward at him. The knowledge that I was a fake and a liar burned a hole in my gut. "Just my luck there's a bona fide photographer waiting out there to expose me," I muttered to myself. "And a handsome-as-sin one, to boot. Like I don't have enough issues with him without enjoying sitting on his lap the way I did."

And that in itself was an oddity. With most men, my initial response was a level of wariness and caution, but there I was sitting on Gunner's lap and enjoying it greatly without the least little concern as to what sort of a man he was, or how he might react to me.

And long, hard experience had taught me how foolish it was to trust a man.

Which made it all that much more curious that my unconventional meeting with Gunner didn't immediately push me into assessing the situation, and my position therein.

That and similar dark thoughts were dismissed when I arrived at my destination. "Oh, hello. I understand you wanted to see me?"

Roger was in the process of emerging from his RV when I hobbled up.

He looked appalled at the sight of me, causing me to wonder if I had fallen into dog poop or something equally repulsive without being aware of it. "Good lord! Are you injured?"

"Not really. Just a little minor accident, nothing serious. Oh, is that why you're looking so horrified?" I gave him a relieved smile. "I thought my deodorant had failed. I'm fine, really."

"Accident? What sort of accident? Christ above, I'll have the health and safety people down upon us before the shooting has even begun!"

"No, no," I said soothingly, "it wasn't really an accident. Just my clumsiness."

He looked doubtfully at me. "You didn't hurt yourself on any of our equipment, did you? Because if you did, the production would still be liable—"

"Actually, the lord of the manor's brother ran me down with his mobility scooter, but I'm not really hurt. Just a little bruised on the top of my foot. My boots are pretty sturdy."

"Oh, it was Gunner's fault," he said, visibly relaxing. "Then it's the estate's responsibility. That's excellent. Now, I have a little project in mind, and as you are one to appreciate quality television such as the shows that I have produced in years past, I thought you might be interested in participating."

"What sort of project?" I asked warily, trying to form an excuse for avoiding anything but the most minimal involvement.

"Ah, well, this is where my brilliance lies, in thinking up truly spectacular opportunities. And one of them is you."

"It is?" My voice squeaked a little with surprise. "I don't think anyone has ever thought I was any sort of opportunity, let alone a spectacular one. This wouldn't have anything to do with Roman slaves, would it?"

"No, no, although . . . hmm. I'll think on that. Might have possibilities. But this is truly a wonderful opportunity for you to really get to know the dig process, and should provide us both with some wonderful coverage—you for your book, and us for the viewers."

"I'm a little confused—"

"Everyman," Roger interrupted, beaming with pride. "You'll be our everyman."

"I will?"

"Yes, yes, don't you see? You're the only one here who doesn't have any archaeology experience—all the volunteers have some sort of training, either from a university or with an amateur archaeology club. But you have none! Sue believes that the viewers will be lost with all the technical talk if we don't present them with someone who is just as ignorant as they are."

I wondered if I should be insulted or not, and decided to go with not.

"She had an idea, and I think it's really an excellent one, of picking a person to stand in for the audience, someone to whom the experts can explain things, so that it's all understandable and fun and exciting for even the dullest of persons."

"OK, now I'm going to be insulted," I couldn't help but say.

"Don't be," he said, waving away my objection. "It isn't meant to insult. It's meant to praise your accessibility. You're perfect for the job—you're well-spoken without being snooty, are personable and have a nice presence that will translate well on-screen, and you aren't too pretty, so you won't give Sue a run for the spotlight. Viewers will relate to the fact that you have little experience with archaeology. Plus you'll look good with Gunner."

"I beg your pardon?" I wasn't sure I heard him correctly. "Look good with him in what way?"

"Didn't I tell you? I'd forget my own head if it wasn't stapled on. Since the others are busy getting the dig started, I've asked him to show you the ropes." He waved a hand around vaguely. "Turns out he's got some kind of relevant degree, and knows all about the Romans and Celts and whoever else lived here, but because of his leg, he can't dig much."

Oh, dear lord, that was all I needed. "No!" I said somewhat wildly.

Roger looked askance. "No?"

"Er . . ." Mindful that I was there by the good graces of his production company, I tried to summon a friendly smile. "That is, no, I'm not personable, and I look terrible on film. That's . . . uh . . . that's why I became a photographer, so I could take pictures and not have to have them taken of me." He just stared at me. I felt like an idiot babbling away, but I couldn't seem to stop. "I appreciate the fact that you thought of me, I really appreciate it, but I'm sure there's got to be someone else who would be much better suited to the role."

A little frown appeared between his eyebrows. "I am quite well-known for my productions, you know."

"Of course you are," I said hurriedly, wanting to smooth over his obviously hurt feelings. "I've told you how much I liked your other shows, and it's clear you're a master at the job of . . . er . . . producing."

"Yes," he said coolly. "I am. And part of that mastery is knowing who is right for what role. Is there a reason you don't wish to be filmed? Some secret reason? Perhaps an illegal one?"

I gawked at him for a second, my gut spinning around like a hamster's wheel. "No! I just . . . I'm not comfortable. . . . I'm not here illegally or anything, if that's what you're thinking—"

"Then there is no reason why you can't spend an hour or two a day with the film crew, allowing us to film short segments that will make the project clear to the viewing audience." His words were clipped and had sharp edges. "I'm sure that since we have been so accommodating as to allow you unfettered access to the filming schedule, not to mention arranging for you to stay, at no little expense, with the crew itself, that you will be agreeable to helping us out where you can."

My heart turned to lead and dropped to my feet. My stomach compacted into a little black hole of misery. My spirits took one look at the next week or so of trying to pretend I was a photographer while spending time with a real one, and evaporated to nothing.

I tried one last protest, but my heart—leaden and in my feet—wasn't in it. "I'd be happy to just chitchat with the people digging if that would help out. . . ."

"You will be personable and interesting, and the audience will love you." It wasn't a prediction; it was an order, one that was spoken in an unyielding tone.

I was beaten, and I knew it. "I see. Well, if you feel that way—"

"I do. Gunner has all the qualifications to bring you up to speed on the dig, and will start this evening. I'm sure you'll have no trouble making yourself available to him for that."

"Er . . ." I had planned to "accidentally" run into Paul that evening.

"We'll film you while he teaches you the ways of the dirt—nice turn of phrase, that; I'll have to give it to Sue for the narration—which will show the audience just what it is the archaeologists do, and why they do it."

"Well, I suppose—"

"Of course, you are encouraged to ask questions that

our audience might ask, and I have no doubt that you'll also want to participate in some of the reenactments that we have scheduled."

"If I have time," I said weakly. "Books take a lot of work, you know."

"Must remember to add slaves to that list. I think we'll try for your first piece to the camera this afternoon when we officially open the dig. Just some basic information, nothing too complicated." He beamed at me just like he'd done me the biggest favor in the world.

I closed my eyes for a moment, trying desperately to find a way out of this scenario, but failing miserably. "I guess I could do that. But I do have a lot of work to do on my own, what with all the pictures to take, and the . . . er . . ." I struggled for something that sounded journalistic. "All of the interviews to be conducted."

"That's why this opportunity is so perfect for you!" He whapped me gently on the arm. "Gunner can help you out! Any extra time you spend away from your work to be with him will be more than offset by the information he'll be able to give you. It'll be wonderful for you, because not only does he know his potatoes, archaeologically speaking, but he's also the brother of a baron. Your readers will eat that up with a spoon and ask for seconds."

"Yes, of course it will be wonderful for the book." My smile was wan at best.

"Smart girl," he said, clapping a hand on my shoulder in a way that had me wincing. He pulled out a walkie-talkie, and shoved it at me. "I knew I could count on you to be a team player. We'll let you have one of these so we can alert you when we want to do a piece for the camera. Channel four is Gunner's channel. Two is dig personnel. Three is production team—don't use that channel except in emergencies. And of course, I am on channel one. Now, I must go see what the geophys people are up to."

"Geo . . . what?"

"Geophys. Stands for geophysics. They're the folks who use the machines to look into the earth and find our Roman remains. It looks like they're out doing their shtick already, and they know full well we need to film them for the intro. . . ."

He hurried off, leaving me staring glumly at a walkie-talkie. What the hell had I just gotten myself into?

Chapter 6

"Hello, my lovely one. Any luck selling my brother the baron to Hollywood?"

The smiling face of Alice, Gunner's new sister-in-law, broke into a laugh before making a little moue. "I wish. Hollywood doesn't seem to be interested in his fabulous spy books, which is just stupid beyond words, given that they are such fabulous best sellers. Plus Elliott's books are much better than a lot of what makes it into movies these days. How's your foot? You're staying off it, aren't you?"

"Yes, Mum," he said, making a face of his own at her.

She laughed again, the picture of her on the videoconferencing software glitching for a moment before it settled down. "Sorry, Gunner, I didn't mean to mother you, but as your mom is in Africa, I figured it was up to me as second lady in command to make sure you're OK."

"You're the first lady in command in my book," he

said gallantly, never above a little light flirtation with Alice.

The screen suddenly jerked, and Alice disappeared to be replaced by Elliott, his look so pointed that it was quite clear even from halfway across the world. "Still trying to seduce my wife, Gunner?"

"Only when you're not around," he said smoothly. "Besides, I have to have something to look forward to. It's been so quiet around here with you two gallivanting all over the States. Book tour going all right?"

Elliott shrugged. "I suppose so, although I'm not best suited to this life. I'd much rather be home. Is everything there all right? You're not having any trouble keeping the tourists away from the tower?"

"No, it's suitably fenced off. No one but the dig crew will have access to it, and they have all sorts of insurance, so if a falling brick hits one of them on the head, it won't be our fault."

Elliott made a face, and absently rubbed his shoulder where he'd broken a bone by being hit by one of the bricks falling from the decrepit tower himself a few months before. "I'd rather we not have any more accidents. How is the archaeology going?"

"All right so far." Gunner gave his brother a rundown of the details of the show, adding, "They've asked me to be a presenter, and do an on-air thing with some neophyte. They'll film me explaining how the dig process works, that sort of thing."

"You? I thought you were just going to dig when the cast comes off your leg."

Gunner shrugged one shoulder. "The producer seems to think that a nonprofessional will reach the viewing audience better than an academic."

"Better you than me," Elliott said with a sour look that made Gunner smile.

"That's because you're an introvert. Extroverts like me enjoy such things, not to mention having a zillion brothers and sisters around us."

"It only seems like a zillion when you're all together," Alice said in the background, pushing Elliott a little to the side. "It must be nice to have the castle to yourself while they're all out doing vacations and whatnot."

"To be honest, it's a bit lonely," Gunner admitted. He'd been battling a sense of loss with his siblings scattered hither and yon on various trips and visits to other family members, or off at assorted universities.

He even missed his mother, who had taken the two youngest boys on her annual trek to Kenya to check up on the charities she endowed there.

"It's damned quiet here," Gunner said apropos of those thoughts. "Just the tourists twice a week, and the dig crew, and they're all housed down by the old barn and stables."

"Alice and I will be home in a week; I'm sure you'll survive just fine until then what with all your nascent TV stardom."

"I don't think there's much stardom to be had with an archaeology show, but the money they're paying the family to use the grounds will make it all worth it."

"Truer words were never spoken," Elliott agreed. "And stop fussing. You'll have the cast off soon, though, and then you can go back to work."

"My boss has me booked to go to Venice in October—until then, I'll be kicking around here."

"Lucky bastard," Elliott said with affection. "How many people find themselves taken to glamorous places like Venice to do their jobs?"

Gunner grinned. "Glamour doesn't enter into it; it's damned hard work climbing all over those abandoned factories documenting them, as you well know."

"Yes, but it doesn't make me any less envious of a job where all you have to do is snap a few photos."

"'Architectural forensic photographer' is the official title, thank you very much. Anyway, did you and Alice get any time away from your book tour to enjoy your belated honeymoon?"

The talk turned purely familial as the two men spent another ten minutes hashing over various estate issues that Gunner had been handling while his brother Dixon, who normally handled such things, was off taking a much-needed vacation. Or at least he was handling things until Elliott returned from his three-week American book tour. Once the video call ended, Gunner hobbled around the residential section of the castle, his fiberglass walking boot echoing loudly down the wood-paneled hallways, making him very aware of his isolation.

He settled down in the small, dark library, propping his leg up on an ottoman. He picked up a book, but it wasn't the words on the page that he saw. His mind went to the soft feel of the woman he'd run down as she sat on his legs, one of her breasts pressed enticingly against his chest, the warm curve of her hip nicely solid under his arm. He'd been honest when he told her that he favored curves, not understanding why so many women felt it necessary to starve themselves into thinness that seemed to him to be borderline creepy. He'd seen enough survivors of famine, pestilence, and war in his life to keep him from seeking skeletal qualities in a female companion.

"Lorina," he said aloud, savoring her name on his lips. She was a substantial woman, close to six feet tall, which was another point in her favor. At six feet three, he didn't like women who were so small that they gave him a crick in his neck when he kissed them. And he very much liked kissing women—he also liked holding them, and touching their breasts, and stroking his hands up their long, long legs. . . .

He had to stop himself from mentally stripping Lorina, guessing she would not be one of the women who easily tumbled into his bed. Long experience had taught him to quickly assess who was after him for his supposed wealth and relationship to the Ainslie family, and although he wasn't above indulging himself when so offered, of late he had begun to feel there was something important missing in his fleeting relationships.

"Damn Elliott," he said aloud as an orange cat wandered into the room, looked around, and leaped onto his legs, kneading his thigh briefly before curling up on his lap. Absently, he stroked the cat while glaring out of the small paneled window. "He had to go and get married, Captain, and live happily ever after with a charming woman who makes him laugh, and stay in bed half the day until he emerges with a besotted look plastered all over his face, and now it's made me feel like things are lacking in my own life. They aren't, though. You see that, don't you? I'm not the marrying type. Elliott is. I'm a free spirit. I like women, and they like me, and we both understand that although we can enjoy each other for some time, it's not going to be permanent. I come and go like the wind, without any responsibilities. Elliott's the one with those, and he can have them. I'm as free as a bird."

His words sounded odd, hollow almost, as if he was trying to convince himself or the cat, Captain Wedderburn. He felt vaguely uncomfortable at the thought that maybe there was more to life than flitting around doing whatever he liked without any strings attached to anyone but his mother, his siblings, and his child. "Although even my time with Cressy is limited to visits every other year, and weekly video chats. No, Captain, I'm as free as they come."

That's the way I like it, he thought to himself, and pushed away the idea that perhaps lack of responsibility wasn't as attractive as it had been in the past.

"Lorina," he repeated, thinking again of her warmth. "She's a Yank, I think. Or Canadian. I should find out, don't you think? It's only proper to treat visitors to our fair isle with politeness and interest. She's smart, too. The producer said she's a journalist, and that takes a certain amount of brains. I like brains in a woman." In fact, he liked much of what he saw in Lorina, from the freckles all over her face and arms, right down to the shapely ass that was visible when she had pushed herself off his lap. And her legs—dear god, her legs! "The one odd thing about her is that she doesn't act like any journalist I've ever met. Curious, eh?"

He slammed shut the book, making the cat look up in surprise. "Sorry, Captain, you're going to have to move. I think it only right to go check on how things are going with the television crew. Yes, I was just there an hour ago, but they may need something, and with Dixon off in the Bahamas, it's right that I'm there to help out as much as I can. No, don't say it. I know I just discounted Lorina because she's most likely not the type interested in a harmless fling, but I've changed my mind. A man can do that without untoward comments from his family, can't he? Besides, I could be all wrong about Lorina. It's best not to guess about people when you don't know them well, and I sense a bit of a mystery about her. You know how I love mysteries."

The cat shot Gunner a dirty look when he rose and thumped his way out of the room, down the stairs, and through the kitchen to the small anteroom where his rented scooter was parked. It was a Tuesday, one of the two days a week that Ainslie Castle was open to the public, and it had been his habit the last few weeks to be on hand to greet the groups. It took the edge off his loneliness to chat with the tourists, but today, with the arrival of the TV crew, he had better things to do.

And a delicious woman to ogle.

"It wouldn't hurt to apologize to her again. Perhaps I can figure why she doesn't appear like any other journalists I've met. It could be because she's American," he mused as the scooter bumped its way past the outbuildings, and around the section of the castle that the family called the tower but was actually a crumbled heap of brick, slate tiles, broken glass, and broken mortar. He double-checked that the temporary fencing was secure, and continued on toward the stables, waving and smiling at the few tourists who recognized him. "Maybe I should talk to that Roger fellow and tell him that I want him to pair me up with Lorina rather than whoever he was going to assign. That way I can not only enjoy her, and her legs, and freckles, and all the other parts of her that I'd have to be blind not to admire, but in the process figure out what it is about her that's striking me as a bit different."

He was mentally forming a request for just that when he arrived at the production company's row of caravans. No one was present. He pointed his scooter toward the barn that had been set up for the dig team's use, and was rewarded with the sound of voices.

"—you know, we anticipate this show to be the big hit of summer. More than a hundred archaeology clubs will be participating with their own digs in conjunction with this show, and along with the chats and interviews that we'll be presenting online, we should have record-high viewer numbers. But it all rests on you, our brilliant team of archaeologists. You've all been handpicked to take part in this project, and I know you will throw all your energy into ensuring that we have top-notch work done."

There was a smattering of applause. Gunner stopped

his scooter at one of the big double doors, open to show the interior of the barn. The side with a drain had been hastily partitioned into temporary showers, while the other side was set up with several long tables and chairs. Around those, about forty people were arranged in varying degrees of comfort. Standing on a chair was the blond woman who Gunner remembered was the director. She turned to Roger, and said, "That's it from me. I believe Roger has a few words to add?"

"Just a couple," Roger answered in a loud voice, the top of his head shiny with sweat. He surveyed them all with a brilliant smile. "I know you're all champing at the bit to get working, but I want to remind everyone that this is a team effort, and that only by pulling together will we reach the pinnacle. So get out there and dig like the wind, but also remember that there will be millions of viewers who will be watching your every move with fascinated eyes, and it's up to you to show them just how exciting history can be!"

There was a bit more applause.

"And now let's have a quick rundown of the schedule for the next two days. Len, can you bring the whiteboard? Ah, excellent. Now, I shall take you through here point by point to make sure we are all on the same boat. So to speak. The geophysics team will commence scanning the garden to the south of the fallen tower promptly at noon. The film crew will be filming them, and Sue will be recording appropriate explanations of how the geophys business works. At four, Paul and Sue and I will put our heads together and decide on where to put the first trenches, and by five the minidiggers will be moved into place and the trenches opened. That's when you lot come into play. We'll usually have a dinner break at seven, but due to the late start today, we plan on digging until nine. Now, let's go through the shots we expect to take. . . ."

"That man sure does like to hear himself talk," a voice said behind Gunner.

He turned with a smile, wondering for what seemed like the thousandth time how his genes had produced such a miracle as Cressy.

"Gran says he's some important dude, though, so I have to be nice to ... holy Gorgonzola and beans!"

"Holy Gorgonzola?" he repeated, wondering if it was some new Internet-speak that he had missed.

"He's gorgeous," she said, then slapped her hand over her face and turned bright red. "Ohmigosh, I didn't just say that, did I? Out loud? So you could hear it?"

A little smile curled his lips. "You did, you know. Who is the object of your lust, if you don't mind my asking?"

She slid her fingers apart and spoke through them. "I'm not lusting, and I don't think I'm supposed to tell you. Gran says you'll go all medieval if I have a boyfriend, not that I want one, because they are just so much work, you know? They always expect you to do the things they want to do, and be interested in their friends, and never want to do things you want. It's so unfair! But he really is gorgeous."

Gunner turned to look into the barn, scanning over the male faces. The one that seemed to have caught Cressy's attention belonged to a lad who looked just a few years older than her, but who already had both arms covered in tattoos. Mentally, he sighed. He had a feeling he would be investing in more than one shotgun. "You can look but don't touch."

Cressy rolled her eyes at him. "Jeez, Gunner, I'm not going to walk over to him and touch him all over, you know. I just like looking at him. And his tats. Those are really fabulous. Oh, look, there's Lorina."

He turned back to the barn, finally picking out the head of Lorina in the semidarkness. She was sitting next to a dark-haired man whom he remembered as being the lead archaeologist. "So it is."

"You know her?" Cressy gave him an odd look.

"I met her earlier, yes."

"Oh. Did she ... um ... did she say anything about me?"

An odd note in her voice had him considering his child. "She said she thought you were charming. Why, what have you done to her?"

"Done to her? Me?" Her voice rose into a guilty squeak, which she quickly fixed by clearing her throat. "I don't know why everyone assumes I *do* things to people when I meet them."

Gunner waited, pursing his lips a little.

"Fine," Cressy admitted with obvious exasperation. "I may have collapsed our tent on Gran and me, and Lorina had to rescue us because my hair was caught and Gran couldn't figure out how to uncatch me, and then Gran was upset by the tent falling down and breaking, and Lorina said we could have her tent, but I said no because I knew you wouldn't want me dumping a broken tent on someone, so in the end, Gran took Lorina's tent, and she is in my tent with me. The broken one, although we got it fixed up with some duct tape, and I'd like to point out that none of that is *doing things* to Lorina. She offered to swap tents. I didn't even hint at it."

"Hmm," he said, wanting to laugh, but knowing that it would only hurt Cressy's feelings. He hadn't seen much of his daughter in the seven years he'd known about her existence, since her mother kept her in Canada most of the time, but what he did know hinted at a delicate ego that could be wounded easily. "So long as Lorina offered and you didn't put her in a position where she felt obligated to do so, then I agree that you did the right thing. And as a reward, I have decided to let you have those riding lessons you've been asking for."

With a squeal of delight, she hurled herself onto his lap, giving him a big hug that made him feel like the best father in the world. "Oh, thank you, Gunner! I just knew you'd let me take them. I mean, England is known for their show jumpers, so it would be a total waste to spend a whole summer here and not be able to do a little training. When can I start?"

"Tomorrow, if it's possible," he said, wincing when she kicked her foot against his cast in her enthusiasm.

"Oh, sorry." She leaped off him, so excited that she seemed to vibrate as she continued to chatter about the proposed lessons, her arms waving about as she talked. She was at that age where she was all arms and legs, but he had a feeling that in a few more years, she'd be a stunner . . . and with that thought, he made a mental note to purchase an entire armory's worth of shotguns.

"I'm so glad Mom sent me here this year instead of making me go to my stepgrandma's house. She's in Alberta, and there's nothing there but wheat! It's so bleh, but England is fabulous, and I have the bestest dad in the world, not at all the dickwad who isn't good enough for me, like Mom says. You're totally cool, and even Gran says that Mom is totes ballistic when it comes to you, and you know Gran—she's never wrong." She laughed a loud, burbling laugh that made Gunner want to laugh with her. "I shouldn't have said what Mom calls you, should I? Gran would say it's not polite, but I'd rather know what people say about me than pretend everyone loves me. Besides, there's dickwad, and then there's dickwad. My friend Cankles said it about her brother, but he's actually kinda nice. Cankles is my English friend, not one of my friends back home in BC. Her real name is Catrin, but everyone calls her Cankles. I met her last month when I moved in with Gran. I'll need a riding helmet, but I can wear my jeans and ankle boots. You don't mind getting me a new helmet, do you?"

"Not if it means keeping your brain from being scrambled," he said quickly, enjoying her stream of consciousness. It gave him much insight into her personality, quirky as it was. "Just keep in mind that if I hear you're annoying Lorina, the lessons will be off."

Her eyes widened until he thought they might pop out. "I'm not going to annoy her! I *like* her!"

"See that you remember that." He glanced back at the barn full of diggers. They were still going at it, which annoyed him. He wanted to talk to Lorina again.

"Gran's having a lie-down, as she calls it, but it's really a nap. She gets worn-out fast. When's the baroness coming back to Ainslie? Gran says I have to watch my manners around her, although I think that's silly because it's not like I'm a baboon! I *know* how to be polite."

"Which baroness?" he asked, absently watching Lorina as she took a few notes during the talk by the production heads. His eyes narrowed when she leaned over to make a comment in the ear of the man next to her.

"The one who's your mom, not the new one, although I suppose she's nice, too."

He turned at the note of worry in his daughter's voice, giving her a little one-armed hug. "Alice is lovely, and she told me herself that she is thrilled to meet her niece, and can't wait to get back home so she can do just that. And likewise my mother is anxious to see you again. You may not remember it, but you did meet her about five or six years ago."

Cressida scrunched up her nose in thought. "I kind of remember it, but not really well. None of my other friends have a grandmother who is a baroness, which makes Cankles crazy, because she's got the hots for Prince Harry, and she thinks you're like royalty or something because you have a castle and Uncle Elliott has a title and stuff."

Roger d'Aspry continued to drone on in his self-important manner. Now the man next to Lorina was whispering something to her that had her stifling a laugh. Gunner frowned at that.

"Who's that?" Cressy asked suddenly.

"Who is who?"

"That man who's necking with Lorina."

"They aren't necking," Gunner said quickly, a bit surprised by the spurt of anger that followed the words. He reminded himself that although Lorina was pleasing on the eyes, and had a sense of humor he enjoyed, he had never been a possessive man, and he'd be damned if he started down that path now. "They're just speaking to each other quietly."

"Huh. Looks like necking to me."

He turned a suspicious eye on her. "And what would you know about that, mademoiselle? You just got done telling me you weren't interested in having a boyfriend."

She giggled, and punched him in the arm. "I'm not, but that doesn't mean I don't recognize necking when I see it. Did I hurt your foot when I sat on you?"

He adjusted once again to her quicksilver conversational offerings. "No."

"When will you be able to walk around again?"

"Most likely next week."

"Cankles said she thought it was stupid of you to break your foot in the first place."

"It was stupid—I could tell the balcony was rusted, but I thought I could get a couple of shots without anything happening. I was wrong, a fact I'd like you to remember when I ask you to stay away from the part of the castle that's out of bounds to everyone."

She made a face. "I already said I was sorry for climb-

ing over the fence, and swore I wouldn't do it again. I
don't like the non-necking guy next to Lorina. He's"—
her nose scrunched again—"smarmy. Is that a word?
Cankles said that her sister's boyfriend was smarmy, and
I think it means kind of blechy, so if it does, then yeah,
he's smarmy."

"Smarmy is a very good word for people like that,"
Gunner agreed, ignoring the fact that when he had met
the man earlier, he had no such impression. "You are a
good judge of people. You get that from me."

She shrugged. "I don't know about that. Mom says I
think with my heart instead of my head, but that's just
silly, because hearts can't think, can they? Why don't you
have any horses here? I'm not complaining, but you have
a big stable, but no horses. I just thought if you had a
horse here, I could ride it instead of taking lessons, and
that would save money."

"No one has time to take care of a horse, although we
do have one elderly Shetland pony who is so old he
creaks when he walks, and a three-legged donkey who
keeps him company out in one of the pastures."

"Rats."

"Those we do have. In the stable, and possibly this
barn, although I couldn't swear to that."

Cressida considered him with eyes that were almost
identical to her mother's. "You're funny, Gunner. Cankles is jealous because I have a dad who has a black
mom and a white dad, and when I tell her that you're
funny, she's going to go mental. I can't wait."

"And you are an odd child who I think takes more
after me than I'm comfortable with." He gave her another smile. "I'll take you into town later to get the riding helmet, all right?"

"Awesome!" she cheered, and before he could blink,
she loped off. Gunner wondered if he'd ever been that

free and easy, decided he hadn't, and turned his attention back to the people inside the barn. Thankfully, Roger had reached the end of his discussion, and now another man was standing and briefly reviewing which teams would work on what projects.

After a moment's concerted thought, he finally dredged up a name for the man next to Lorina.

"Paul Thompson," he said softly to himself, his eyes narrowing on the fellow. But even as he recognized the fact that he was unusually hostile toward someone who had done him no wrong, he admitted that it annoyed him that someone else might have his eye on Lorina for a late summer fling.

Dammit, he saw her first. Therefore, the unwritten rules of a gentleman dictated that he should be allowed to proceed unhindered by competition. Only if Lorina chose to spurn his attentions should Thompson make a move. Perhaps he should point out the rules to the man, since it was obvious he was too obtuse (or ill-bred) to understand them on his own.

The crowd broke after one last round of mild applause. Gunner moved his scooter to the side, passing out pleasant greetings and smiles as the television and archaeology crews streamed past him. His smile grew a little when Lorina strolled past, but he reminded himself that he had never had to chase after a woman. Women always seemed to come his way without much effort.

"Oh," Lorina said, stopping a few feet away, and looking hesitantly toward him.

He smiled his very best smile.

She pursed her lips a little. "I suppose we should probably chat."

"If you like, certainly."

"Do you have your equipment with you?"

He gave her a roguish grin despite his best intentions. "I find it best to carry it with me at all times."

"Oh, good. Well, I suppose you can give me a rundown on how to use it." She glanced at her watch. "I have so much to do today. Can we make it tomorrow morning?"

He knew that she had to be speaking of something other than what he first thought she meant. He knew that, and yet he was unable to keep his roguish grin from turning into an outright leer. "I'd be delighted to show you how to use my equipment, although I should mention that I'm less flexible than normal due to the cast. In addition, I will warn you that despite your belief earlier that I was asking you to marry me, I'm not actually in the market for a permanent attachment. That doesn't mean we can't enjoy our time together—far from it. Nothing spices up a summer more than a little dalliance, don't you think?"

She gawked at him, outright gawked with open mouth and wide eyes. "Did you just proposition me into, for lack of a polite term, hooking up with you?"

"I believe we could find much mutual pleasure in each other's company, yes," he said with a startling lack of his usual finesse.

She shook her head. "Man, I just—no one has ever just come right out—not so blatant as that—no, Gunner, I am not interested in casual sex, with you or with anyone else." She took a deep breath, and continued on before he could respond. "And can I just say that you really have some kind of balls coming on to someone who you just met. The fact that you think you can just stroll up and dominate me in that way . . . no sir! It's not going to fly with me! I don't do dalliances, as you call them. I happen to prefer a meaningful relationship with a man who values me, and doesn't have to make himself feel better by showing he's stronger, or more dominant, or any of those things men feel they have to prove. You really have *some nerve* assuming that I'd fall victim to your pretty face, and nice chest, and all the rest of you."

"Are you finished?" Gunner asked politely when she paused for breath.

"Not even close!" she said with a dignified sniff. "Who do you think you are that you can hit on me like that without even so much as a by-your-leave?"

"I apologize if my attempt to flirt offended—"

"Flirt? Offended! Oh, you are so beyond offended!"

"For the record, I don't feel the need to dominate women. I much prefer them lively and engaging rather than cowed and submissive."

"Oh, tell me another," she said with irately flared nostrils. "All men say that when they're trying to get into a woman's pants. But after the bloom is off the rose, then the domineering comes out, and the 'How dare you question me? I'm a man!' attitudes fly all over the place, and the next thing you know, you're a doormat married to a monster."

He said nothing for a moment, waiting to see what she'd say next. When she did nothing but look vaguely appalled at her outburst, he said slowly, "That is very specific, but really isn't applicable to me."

"I'm sorry," she stammered, her cheeks pinkening. "I got off on a rant and couldn't seem to stop. Just ignore me."

"Now, that I will not do, although I will be happy to forget your rant if you'd like."

"I'd appreciate that. It must be the jet lag wearing me down, although I've been in England for four days."

"I'm sure that must be it," he said graciously. "Does it make you uncomfortable to be complimented?"

"Me?" She opened her eyes wide. "No, not at all. But I don't like being hit on."

"So I gathered. Would you mind if I told you that the reason I was flirting is because I like that you say things without thinking about whether or not they will be acceptable? It's a form of honesty that I particularly enjoy."

She flinched at that, and he would have continued, but at that moment a shadow fell across them, and suddenly the man Thompson was there touching her on the arm and murmuring, "Lori, I need to speak to you as soon as you're free."

Gunner caught the expression of annoyance flicker across Lorina's face, but it was gone so quickly that he doubted a less astute man would have seen it.

"Is there something wrong?" she asked.

A strong desire to punch Thompson rose within Gunner. He reminded himself yet again that he wasn't a jealous man. His inner self didn't seem to care—his fingers were fisted to keep from reaching out and jerking Thompson's hand from her arm.

"Nothing wrong, no. I just wanted to go over a few aspects of the dig with you, in case you were confused. I know it must be overwhelming for someone new to archaeology." Paul's gaze slid over to Gunner, acknowledging him with a little nod of the head and a murmured, "Ainslie."

Gunner nodded back, gritting his teeth against the sharp words that he feared would slip out.

She smiled, making him feel as if he'd been kicked in the gut. "That would be lovely, Paul, but I'm going to be busy taking pictures of the dig gearing up before the light goes. Roger told me when I met him in London that people like behind-the-scenes shots like that, so I promised I'd get first-day pictures."

"Tomorrow is soon enough," Paul said with a dismissive wave of his hand, although just what he was dismissing, Gunner didn't know.

"I'm sure I'll be able to give you a few minutes then," Lorina agreed.

"Not too many," he heard himself saying.

Both of them looked at him in surprise.

"Oh?" Lorina's forehead wrinkled.

"Yes. Don't you remember? I offered to show you around the castle." That was a blatant lie, which Lorina clearly recognized, but thankfully, she didn't dispute him; she simply shot him a curious look before turning back to Thompson when he murmured something about not keeping her long.

The man gave her a smile that Gunner felt showed entirely too many teeth. (What sort of man bared his gums when he smiled? It was unsightly at best, and grotesque at worst.) Then he moved off to join Roger and the director, Sue.

Lorina watched him go, absently rubbing her arm. Gunner was pleased by the action, and even more pleased when he heard her say under her breath, "I *hate* that."

"Hate what? Casual acquaintances who manhandle you while bare yards of glistening gums blight your vision? I couldn't agree more. It's annoying as hell."

She turned back to him with a puzzled expression. "What *are* you talking about?"

"You said you hated Thompson."

"I didn't realize I said that aloud. 'Hate' is a word I don't often use for people, although Paul . . . he's . . . oh, never mind. It's too complicated to explain."

Before she could leave him, he caught her hand, gently rubbing his thumb over the backs of her knuckles. "I like complicated. If not Thompson, then what do you hate?"

She gave him a weak smile and slowly pulled her hand from his. "Being called Lori. I just really dislike it when people do that. Why did you lie to him?"

"You seemed to need rescuing, and I would have offered to show you around the castle sooner or later. We might as well make it sooner, assuming you're interested in it."

To his surprise, she bristled. "What makes you think I need rescuing? I don't need any man to rescue me. I'm a strong person on my own, and can take care of myself. Your opinion is your own, and not at all pertinent to me."

He was silent a moment, wondering what had brought on a second outburst. Hell, now he wondered about the first one as well. Was she just defensive as a rule, or had something he said stirred her up? Out of the blue, he was reminded of his brother Rupert, who was adopted when he was seven from a father who had regularly beat him. For a few years until he'd settled down, Rupert had been prone to the same sorts of outbursts.

"I can see you are a strong woman," Gunner said slowly, speaking to her just as he used to speak to Rupert when he was in one of his wild, defiant moods. "I assure you that I had no intention of implying that you need my help in getting rid of Thompson. If I've offended you, I apologize."

The antagonism in her posture melted away, leaving her with a wary look. "Sorry, I did it again, didn't I? I didn't mean to snap your head off. I just . . . men being domineering like that is one of my pet peeves."

A memory of just how fearful Rupert had been of their father for a few years gave Gunner a sudden insight into Lorina, but what surprised him was not the fact that she'd obviously been on the receiving end of some sort of abuse, but that he was instantly swamped with a need to protect her from any further such trials. He hadn't felt that way since Rupert had grown up.

"I promise not to dominate you unless you ask me to," he said with a little wink in order to lighten the moment.

She just stared at him.

He sighed. "I was hoping you'd take that as a compliment as to how much I admire you."

"You don't know me," she pointed out, the wariness growing in her eyes.

Dammit, he was just making things worse with her. So much for humor. "I apologize again, this time for trying to flirt."

"Oh." She looked a bit contrite now, and made a little gesture of conciliation. "I'm being rude, aren't I? Sorry about that. Although I have to ask, do you always flirt with women you've just met?"

"Not always. There are occasionally some women who I can't resist, though."

She rolled her eyes. "Oh, right, and I'm one? No, I wasn't fishing for a compliment, so you needn't tell me how much you like six-foot-tall women built like linebackers. I'm simply saying that it's unlikely that you'd fall victim to my charms, such as they are, at first glance. Not unless you're a serial love-'em-and-leave-'em sort of guy."

"Hardly that. I might not be seeking a permanent addition to my life, but that doesn't mean I'm a devotee of one-night stands. I simply prefer women who seize the moment without worrying about what the future will hold. And as a matter of fact, I do admire six-foot-tall women of stature. I always have."

She was silent a moment. "I suppose your moral code isn't really a concern of mine. To answer your comment earlier, I would like to see the inside of a real castle. But don't think you're going to try any of your moves on me, all right? Because I can take care of myself, and yes, that means what you think."

He spread his hands in a gesture of acquiescence. "I've yet to have to force a woman. It shall be as you desire."

She glanced over his shoulder to where the castle stood. "Well ... if you really don't mind taking me, I'd like to have a tour, but I'm afraid I won't be free until tomorrow. Would that be OK?"

"Do you know," he said conversationally, "it's almost beyond my ability to keep from making a joke about my willingness to take you, but given your attitude on such things, I shall refrain."

To his delight, she giggled, smothering it with a hand. "My mouth again."

"Yes. I like it."

"Seriously?" She thinned her lips at him. "Can't you say anything that isn't filled with innuendos?"

"I don't know," he said, thinking about it. "I've never tried. Tomorrow would be fine for a tour, by the way."

"Sounds good. I'll see you in the morning, then."

"I'm an early riser, no pun intended," he called after her as she hurried off, and wondered why it was she had wanted to meet him in the first place. He was no stranger to women seeking out his company, but Lorina hadn't given him that vibe—on the contrary, he had a strong suspicion she was almost afraid of him. He watched her go, noting that she had a more graceful version of his daughter's lope, one that showed off her ass and her long legs to their best advantage.

He didn't want her afraid of him. Quite the opposite: he felt an odd need to prove to her that he wasn't like the men who had obviously treated her so badly. Not like that Thompson, he thought, narrowing his eyes. He knew the type well—all self-aggrandizement and conceit. Not at all the sort of man Lorina should be with. No, what she needed was a man who would take care of her while giving her the freedom to be who and what she wanted. Thompson was sure to be the sort of man who put women into categories, and insisted they conform to type.

The trick was to get her to see him as someone who wasn't a threat. With Rupert, he had simply made sure that he was always there, always supportive no matter how much Rupert had acted up. Gunner had survived numerous bouts of violence from his troubled brother, both physical and verbal, but he'd always responded with calm acceptance.

The challenge was to do the same with Lorina. She clearly wasn't interested in him as a sexual partner, but that didn't stop him from wanting to comfort her the way he had Rupert at his worst.

"There's nothing I love so much as a challenge, unless it's the mystery of womanhood," he said aloud, and with a waggle of his eyebrows at one of the barn cats, he turned the scooter around and went to find Roger d'Aspry. What better way to prove to Lorina that he wasn't a typical man than to ensure she spent several hours a day with him? Roger d'Aspry would simply have to designate her to be his sidekick in the video explanations of the dig.

He'd be the perfect gentleman, and return Lorina's suspicion with kindness until she, like Rupert of years past, finally realized that he was a man to be trusted.

A little kernel of warmth deep inside him glowed happily at the thought.

Chapter 7

The second day started with a complaint from my tent-mate.

"I thought there was going to be more to do here. Gunner says he can't take me into town to get my riding helmet and sign me up for jumping lessons until later this afternoon. Gran is still taking a nap. And there's not even any cool stuff to watch being dug up. It's all just dirt so far."

"You can help field walk at two," I told my roommate as she lay sprawled on her air mattress in our tent. I'd heard all about how wonderful her father was for agreeing to let her have riding lessons, and how her mother was dead wrong about him, and what an oddly named friend thought of her having a baron for an uncle, and to be honest, after all that, I was a bit worn-out.

"Field walk?" She lifted her head and gave me a quizzical look. "I heard them talking about that yesterday. What is it?"

I held up a photocopied daily schedule. "Evidently it's where people walk around on the pasture that they're going to dig in, and look for stuff on the surface. I got shots of them doing it yesterday afternoon when they were out on the small pasture. Today they are going to tackle the big field."

"Looking for what, cow poop?" Cressy's nose wrinkled.

"I gather that little bits of artifacts and coins and things like that work themselves to the top over time, and before people dig, they comb the ground for that stuff lest it get lost in the digging process."

"Oh." She rolled over onto her stomach, saying into the pillow, "Sounds boring."

"Why on earth did you come to an archaeological dig if you aren't interested in it?" I couldn't help but ask.

"Gunner likes it," she said, waving a hand in the air. "And Mom said I could come here for the summer, so I said it would be fun, but now that I'm here, it doesn't look that great. It's nice being in England, though. Also, I thought Uncle Elliott would have at least a couple of horses."

"And now the truth comes out—you're here solely for the horse action," I said with a smile.

She giggled. "Have you ever heard of a castle that didn't have horses?"

"No, but I'm not conversant with castles. Regardless, I'm sorry there are no horses here, but it was nice of your father to let you have lessons."

"Gunner's cool," Cressy said with another wave of her hand, which I'm sure she intended to be languid, but there was nothing even remotely languid about her. She fairly teemed with energy. Even now she'd had enough of lying down and leaped to her feet, smacking her head on one of the aluminum tent struts. "He's much nicer than my stepdad, Steve. All Steve wants to do is ski and snowboard, and things like that. He's afraid of horses." The last came out in a bit of a sneer. "I'm pretty sure Gunner's not afraid of horses."

"I'm sure he's not. Do you mind my asking why, if your dad lives in the castle, you decided to stay in a tent? I'm fairly certain that your grandmother would be more comfortable with a real bed than on an air mattress."

"I told you earlier," she said, spinning around until she located a hair scrunchie. "Gunner said we could stay there, but Gran knew I like camping, so we agreed to be out here with the archaeologists. Gran says they're interesting, and we can be independent."

"Why do you call him Gunner?" I couldn't help but ask.

She shrugged, and yanked aside the tent flap, making the whole structure wobble for a minute. "Oh, hi, Gran. I didn't know you were up. I'm going to see if I can find the old pony and three-legged donkey Gunner told me about yesterday. Then I'll do the field thing to find Roman junk that's lying around on the ground. Laters!"

I emerged from the tent to find Salma seated gracefully on a camping chair, unscrewing the lid on a thermos. "She calls Gunner by his Christian name because my daughter didn't bother to tell him that he had a child until Cressida was almost ten. Which is a shame for many reasons, not the least of which is he took to being a father extremely well."

I hesitated, wanting to know more, but reminding myself that just because I had to work with Gunner on Roger's project didn't mean I had to feel empathy for him. On the contrary, the more I could keep him at arm's length, the better. I knew I wouldn't be able to hide the fact that I wasn't a photojournalist from him for long, but I had a faint hope that I'd be able to avoid all technical conversations with him. Despite that, I couldn't help but ask, "Why didn't your daughter want him to know about Cressy? She is delightful, if a bit energetic."

"She is charming, and wonderful, and I thank god daily for bringing her into my life," Salma said simply. Then she added a bit more pragmatically, "My daughter is an only child, and unfortunately, my late husband and I spoiled her horribly. We didn't realize our mistake until she was in her teens, but by then the die had been cast. She decided that Gunner wasn't worthy of knowing about Cressida until she met her current husband. That was when she changed her mind. I think the fact that her husband likes to travel had something to do with it—at the time, I was caring for my husband as he was dying of cancer, and couldn't take care of Cressida. There was no one else with whom she could be left, so Clarice suddenly contacted Gunner, told him he had a daughter, and left Cressida with him for six weeks. That was about seven years ago."

"I have to say, I have kind of a hard time reconciling the image of the drop-dead gorgeous Gunner, a man who felt it was perfectly fine to flirt immediately after meeting me, with Gunner the responsible dad."

Salma poured herself another cup of tea. "He does have a bit of a history with women—that's true. And perhaps it was disapproval of his lifestyle that kept Clarice from telling him about Cressida. I do not know her reasons why she kept them apart; I simply am grateful that they have found each other at last. Despite what you may think, Gunner is truly an excellent father. He loves Cressida very deeply, and would, I believe, move heaven and earth for her."

"I'm glad to hear it," I said, keeping my lips zipped about the fact that Gunner evidently hadn't changed his ways too much if he managed to proposition me pretty much within minutes of our meeting.

"He would love to have Cressida on a more permanent basis, but her mother retains custody of her until next year. After that, we will see. I hope Cressida chooses to live here, either with me or with her father."

"I can't imagine what girl wouldn't want to live in a real castle," I said with a nod at the building in the distance. "Although to be honest, I can't imagine anyone preferring to stay in a tent rather than luxury. Still, she seems to have a bunch of energy, so I'm sure she appreciates having the entire castle grounds to explore."

"Indeed. I used to worry about her, since her unique sense of enthusiasm is frequently taken for immaturity, but this summer, I began to see the potential that life holds for her. She'll find her feet, just as I'm sure you will."

"Me?" I froze in the act of setting up a second camp chair, suddenly worried that Salma knew the truth about my plan. "What makes you think I need to find myself?"

She watched me silently for a few seconds before answering. "There's a sense of excitement about you, an aura of hidden agitation that leads me to believe that you're undertaking a grave quest. One, I suspect, that you are unsure of completing. Or is it that you're simply unclear why you're doing it?"

I dropped my gaze from hers, damning my inability to hide my emotions. How could she know so much about me after such a short acquaintance? And if she was that prescient, how on earth was I going to live next door to her without her ferreting out every last secret?

I threw down a red herring tinged with just enough truth to hopefully distract her. "Well, hell. You've sussed the truth about me—I'm not really the experienced journalist that everyone thinks I am. They wouldn't let me shoot everything for my book if they knew the truth, that I'm just a wannabe." I slid a glance up through my eyelashes at her, trying to ooze sincerity from every pore. "I can only hope you won't let others know my secret."

"Why would you care if people knew that you weren't an experienced journalist? Books are written all the time by people with similar lack of credentials."

"It's not so much the lack of credentials. . . ." I bit my lip, hating like the dickens that I was lying to this nice old lady, but I had to keep Sandy at the forefront of my mind. "It's just that I'm afraid I'll be asked to explain something and I simply won't be able to make my brain work. I've never done well under stress, and if people are suspicious of me, if they think I don't know what I'm doing, well . . . then I won't. And I won't be able to explain myself. And Roger will kick me off the dig site. I really don't want that." My words trailed off in a manner that reeked of pathos, but evidently, there was enough truth to sway her.

"Indeed, that would be a shame, if for no other reason than Cressida likes you, and will look forward to seeing your book."

Guilt zapped me like a red-hot poker, but I summoned a smile. "Thanks, Salma. I appreciate your support. I should get going. Er . . . will you be all right on your own? Can I get you anything?"

Salma gave me a calm, gentle smile. "My dear, I have been on my own since my dearest Gerald died seven years ago. I assure you that I will be just fine alone for a few hours. I have brought several books to read."

"You're not one of the volunteers? I assumed you were."

"I won't be doing any of the digging, no. I have offered to help clean the finds, though. I think it will be very rewarding to take a dirty piece of pottery and clean it up so one can admire it."

"Very rewarding," I agreed, feeling a sense of relief

that she wasn't going to be participating in the hard work. "And wise to stay out of the hot sun while doing manual labor. Not that you couldn't if you wanted to . . . oh dear. I put my foot in my mouth again."

She gave a little laugh. "Not at all, although I do appreciate your concern. Cressida and Gunner take very good care of me, you know."

"I'm sure they do. I'll see you later, then."

She waved me off, and I toddled away to go meet with Paul, my mind torn between chastising myself for misleading such a nice lady and thoughts about what I needed to do next.

It hadn't taken much to maneuver myself into sitting next to him during a crew meeting the day before, and a few innocent questions about archaeology that were guaranteed to pump his ego had done the trick—he had gone from polite to mildly flirtatious in just half an hour. I rubbed my ear, thinking of how he'd whispered answers to my leading questions, his breath hot and unpleasant.

"So everyone is allowed to do this field walking?" I had asked him midway through the meeting, and he'd leaned into me to answer.

"If they know what to look for, yes. Do you know what to look for, Lori?"

"Depends what you're talking about," I had answered lightly, making myself sick with a false show of archness.

"I will be happy to tutor you later, my dear. In *all* things that interest you," he had breathed into my ear, leaving me even now with a massive desire to bathe my head in antiseptic.

"You're doing this for a good cause," I told myself, and, accordingly, slapped a smile on my face when I stopped outside the last RV in the row. Given the heat that was starting to ramp up, I couldn't help but be grateful for the shade that the expandable awning cast down over a small card table and a couple of chairs. The latter were occupied by Paul and Fidencia, both of whom were poring over several sheets of paper bearing black-and-white blotches.

It wasn't what they were doing that had me raising my eyebrows, but how closely Paul was lurking over the young woman's shoulder. I had a momentary pang of sympathy for her—the poor girl probably had no idea what she was letting herself in for—but the idea of what he could do reinforced my resolution to end his tomcat ways once and for all.

"Ah, there you are." Paul smiled and hastily moved away from the woman. "Fidencia and I were just going over some of the magnetic imaging results."

"I can see that. Hi, Fidencia. Nice to see you again."

"Yes." Her tone was as terse as her manner toward me. She flipped back her long, glossy black hair. "Roger told us we must answer any questions you have about what it is we're doing, so you can document it properly. I suppose I can do that, so long as you don't need me to hold your hand again."

"I never asked you to hold my hand—" I bit off the rest of my protest, not wanting to get into a petty argument for no reason.

"Girls, girls, there's no need to get your respective knickers in a twist," Paul said blithely, helping Fidencia up from the chair. "Don't worry your head about Lorina, my dear. I'll be sure to take care of her. I know how busy you are being a liaison, and helping Roger in so many ways."

The look Fidencia slid him said she knew exactly what he was doing, but he bustled her off with a smooth manner that must have been honed over the years. "And now, why don't you take these results to Roger, and point out where I think we should put the first trench of the day.

Your trench, if you like. You've worked so hard to make things happen, I want today's first trench to be yours."

Fidencia cast me a doubtful glance, but duly trotted off, the papers clutched to her ample chest. Paul waited until she was out of earshot before turning to me. "Lori, my sweet. I'm so delighted that you are going to be here for the next few weeks. It will be a particular joy to fully investigate our . . . acquaintance."

I tipped my head to the side the better to consider him, hoping for a coquettish air. I had planned on saying something noncommittal, but instead what came out was, "You are aware of the fact that I could not only see you almost drooling down that poor girl's front, but could also hear you murmuring in her ear, yes?"

He had the balls to look surprised and, more obnoxiously, pleased. "Me? Murmur? My dear, how you wound me! How can any woman compete with the vision of loveliness that is you?"

I bit back a reply about believing him when pigs flew, realizing that he thought I was jealous. Me! I'd have disabused him of that idea except that might just be the tack I needed to worm myself into his graces. Instead, I simpered and murmured something about being grateful for any help he could give me.

"I can do more than just answer questions," he said with an oily smile. "Angelica, our resident photographer, has decided to extend her maternity leave by two months, and her replacement cannot stay the additional time. A position of dig photographer is available for two months beginning in October, and if you'd like it, I would be delighted to recommend you to the board."

"Me?" I asked, surprised. Was the man really so deranged that he'd offer a job to someone he just met? "But . . . we just met. You don't know me at all. And you haven't seen any of my stuff. Er . . . photos."

"I watched you photograph the field walk yesterday, and you seemed quite competent. I have every confidence that you are fully qualified, since Roger only hires the best people."

My lips tightened involuntarily. Man alive, I was horrible at deception. Even now, I had the worst desire to correct the false impression that Paul had about my so-called employment.

"It's for that reason that I don't need to see your portfolio, and as for the other . . . I pride myself on my ability to assess people quickly, and it's quite clear to me that you are intelligent, perceptive, and imaginative. In other words, just the person for the job. In addition, I anticipate that working side by side for two months, as we surely would be, your career would grow in a way that would bring satisfaction to all parties. In short, you would be a great addition to the team."

"That's . . ." I paused, unsure of what I wanted to say. I had to keep on his sweet side, but at the same time, I didn't want to hold up the hiring of someone who was truly qualified for the job. "That's very nice of you, Paul. But if you don't mind, I'd like to think about it, if for no other reason than I had plans for the next couple of months."

"Naturally, you may think about the offer, although don't take too long making up your mind." He gave me a smile that showed all of his blindingly white teeth. "There are other candidates who would kill for such a chance as soon as they hear about the opening, and the board will be asking me for my recommendations within the week."

He waxed rhapsodic for a few minutes, painting a gloriously Technicolor image of life with the two of us working together. But my thoughts were of a more mundane nature, mostly focused on how long it would take me to get the proof I needed before I could get the hell out of Dodge.

Paul continued his self-aggrandizing speech for a few more minutes before I made a show of exclaiming at my watch, and tossed a quick apology over my shoulder as I ran off. "Sorry, Roger asked me to make myself agreeable to Gunner Ainslie."

"My dear, you couldn't be anything but agreeable, although I fear your attentions are wasted on him. Dare I hope you'll be able to spare me a little time later tonight? Say, after dinner? Journalists always have a million questions, and I'd be delighted to let you have the benefit of my expertise."

I wanted to let the double entendre go without comment, but I had to keep him thinking I was madly interested in him, so I batted my eyelashes, and murmured something about that being just what I'd like most. I escaped at a fast trot.

It occurred to me as I passed Tabby and Matthew, who constituted one of the three film crews, that I had no idea where to find Gunner Ainslie. Not that I was anxious to see him, I told the knowing little voice in my head that noted how eager I appeared.

"OK," I told myself as I walked up and down the paths running through the gardens, "so he's not as bad as you first thought. Despite his handsome face, and obvious tomcat ways, he appears to be a loving, supportive father." I took a deep breath, acknowledging that part of me envied Cressy her father, while another part wanted to know Gunner more, despite the fact that he could expose the truth about my lack of photographic experience.

"Stupid conflicting emotions," I growled to myself when I slowed, frowning in thought. Gunner couldn't walk much with a broken leg, which limited him to one of the graveled paths. But after a half hour of searching with no sign of him, I returned to the tent area in defeat.

"Will you be participating in today's field walking?" Daria asked as she passed by. "Or taking photos again? You might want to try doing some of the field walking yourself, you know. It might not be wildly interesting, but it's an important part of the archaeological dig process."

"I'll try to do both, assuming I get done with Gunner soon enough. You haven't seen him, have you?"

One of her eyebrows rose as she pursed her lips. "You're looking for Mr. Sex-on-a-Stick?"

"Not for the reason that your jaded look is implying," I said quickly. Too quickly.

She burst into laughter, her expression returning to normal. "More fool you, say I. No, I haven't seen him, but Roger did say I should get you a standard kit, so Gunner can explain things to you on camera. One moment, I have one. . . . No, that's the first-aid kit. Ah, here we go. This is the sample that Sue was planning on demonstrating to the camera, but it'll be much better having Mr. Sexy explain the tools to you. Just remember not to peek inside it ahead of time — we wouldn't want you knowing what everything is."

"Because nothing is so flattering as looking like a complete idiot in front of millions of people," I said drily as I took a beat-up leather satchel roughly the size and shape of a shoe box. It reminded me of nothing so much as an old doctor's bag.

"Are you kidding? I'd be happy to look like the village idiot if it meant I had Gunner whispering sweet nothings in my ear." Daria sighed dreamily.

"Sweet nothings? Why sweet nothings? Is it some sort of thing to titillate viewers? Because I don't want him whispering sweet nothings to me. I don't want him whispering anything to me, no matter how much the audience would get their jollies from seeing his face, and his chest, and probably those really nice hands touching my hair, or my shoulder, or even, god help us all, my neck." I shivered in delicious awareness, ignoring the fact that I had repeatedly told myself that I wasn't interested in him. "Not even if Roger threatened to rescind permission to be here would I allow that."

I realized that Daria was staring at me openmouthed.

"What?" I asked, confused.

She blinked a couple of times before shaking her head. "Nothing. Just remember to look ignorant when Gunner explains to you what the tools are used for. When he's done touching your hair and neck, that is. Oh, and the last time I saw him, he was heading to the castle."

I shivered again, and rubbed the goose bumps on my arms. I couldn't help thinking how much nicer it would be if my plan called for me to seduce Gunner instead of Paul. "Thanks."

She looked like she wanted to say more, but kept silent while I took the bag and headed off toward the castle lawn. Perhaps Gunner was outside having tea or something British like that. With visions of *Downton Abbey* firmly in my head, I skirted a couple of disused outbuildings, and tromped my way back to the castle.

I really did not want to see him. If he saw through my lies, he'd probably blab to everyone that I wasn't a real photographer, and then where would I be? No, I did not want to see him, not at all. The less I was around him, the happier I'd be.

Which did nothing to explain why I broke into a run on the way to the castle.

Chapter 8

"I cannot imagine living with this," I said aloud as I picked my way through what was obviously a small kitchen garden. I emerged into a larger formal garden, one side dominated by lovely shades of blues and purples, the other a blaze of red and orange. Verbena and sweet William tumbled out of stone vases, while snapdragons, lupine, and irises swayed gently in the breeze. The scent of roses and sweet rocket was heavy on the air, leaving me with the desire for a chaise lounge, a tall glass of lemonade, and a country house mystery novel.

Unfortunately, what I got was a number of tourists listlessly wandering around the garden with me, pausing occasionally to smell a flower, or take a picture. I smiled when I encountered a group, and tried not to look smug over the fact that I was staying on the grounds that they had just paid to see. Then I noticed a small hole that had been dug at the end of a bed of asters.

I looked at the hole.

I looked across the garden to the side of the castle that was facing me.

I thought about being filmed while Gunner explained things to me, thought about looking like an idiot on the camera, and started scooping dirt out of the hole, careful to dump it on the mound of soil that had already been excavated. The sun beat down mercilessly as I dug down, wishing I had a small shovel to help me, but not wishing to go in search of a gardener's shed.

Sweat was trickling down my back by the time I heard a familiar electric hum.

I looked up, flushed with heat but at the same time almost chilled, and wiped a hand across my sweaty forehead, saying quickly, "Oh, hello. I didn't make this trench—it was here when I walked by, but I thought so long as it was here, I might try my hand at a little archaeology. But I didn't put it here to begin with. The trench, that is. I wouldn't do anything to hurt your nice garden."

He raised an eyebrow. "You are not hurting the garden, and I'd be happy to have you excavate whenever and wherever you like, but that's not a trench. It's likely a hole dug by our gardener to plant more of the azaleas that my sister-in-law loves."

"Sorry. I should have known better than to mess up your nice garden." I started to scoop the dirt back into the hole. "I should have thought to ask permission—"

"The problem, my dear Lorina, is not the fact that you want to dig, but how you are going about it."

"Really?" I looked down at the messy hole that had been gouged into the dirt. "I'm not sure that I understand what I'm doing wrong. Archaeologists dig, don't they?"

"Yes, but in a very specific manner." He gestured toward the hole, plucking a triangular-shaped tool out of the leather satchel. "A properly dug trench is not at all the same thing as a hole dug for a rosebush. Yes, a hole is a hole, but your methodology is at fault. For one thing, your trowel is a garden tool, not an archaeological one. We use bricklayers' trowels. See the difference?"

I eyed the trowel he held out. "Ah. Yes, it's pointier."

"And another thing, we don't just dig at random. A trench has vertical sides that are perfectly straight, not chopped in at whatever angle we feel like. That way you can see the stratification."

"You're doing that on purpose," I accused.

"Doing what? Educating you? I believe that's what I'm supposed to do."

"No, not that. You're using big words at me in an attempt to intimidate me with your knowledge. Well, it won't work. I'm not confused by stratification. I know all about it. I'm an educated woman, one who has no problem asking questions and finding answers. I'm all over stratification."

He cocked his head to the side, the laugh lines around his eyes deepening.

"Fine," I said with an annoyed sigh. "I can see you're dying to explain it to poor little me. We might as well practice for today's stint in front of the camera. Tell me, Gunner, just what is stratification in the archaeological world?"

"Layers of context."

I felt my nostrils flare of their own accord, and with no ceremony took the trowel and pointed it at his chest. "If I stabbed you with this, no one would know."

He laughed, took the trowel from me, and proceeded to dump the bag of other items out onto the lawn.

"These are trench reports. They're a pain in the ass to fill out, but a vital part of digging," he said, laying a handful of papers on the ground. "Now, let's see. . . . Mind if I borrow your foot?"

"Huh?"

Little frissons of fire seemed to tingle along the top of my foot when he lifted it and gently placed it on top of the paper. I was desperately grateful that I had on a pair of sandals rather than the boots most people wore when digging. His fingers seemed to linger for a second on my ankle before he scooted over next to me, and crossed his unbroken foot over mine.

"Is my leg too heavy for you?" he asked politely.

The leg of his jeans had slid up slightly, allowing the flesh of his calf to rest on my bare foot. I'd never thought of a foot as having an erogenous zone before, but holy moly, was I aware of that skin-to-skin contact. "Hrm? Oh, no, it's fine."

"Good. Finally . . ." He glanced around, his eyes narrowing a little as he took my hand and tugged me forward enough so that it could lie on top of his leg. He kept his hand on mine, his fingers not exactly curling around my hand, but as with my foot, I was very much aware of the weight and warmth of it. "Here begins the lesson of context. Imagine your foot is a piece of archaeology. Say, a potsherd. When you dig, you uncover layers that represent different times. So my hand on top is the most recent time—the present, if you will."

He wiggled his fingers against mine, and I swear my breath caught in my throat. "My hand is context one. If I remove it, the second layer—your hand—is revealed. That's context two."

I regretted the loss of his hand the instant he took it off mine, and then chastised myself for being so silly as to get turned on by a little hand-and-foot touching. "Context two. Gotcha."

"Because your hand—context two—is beneath my hand, your hand is going to be older than mine. Likewise—"

He twisted his foot back and forth.

I sternly ordered myself to stop wanting to rub my leg against his, and focused. "Your foot is context three, and it's older than both our hands."

"Correct. And this?" He removed his leg, and lifted my foot off the ground about a foot, his thumb gently stroking the pulse point on the inside of my ankle.

"Context four. Below it would be the oldest stuff."

"Exactly."

"How do you know that there's nothing underneath the paper that isn't older than it?"

"That's a very good question. Until we remove a layer, we don't know what's beneath it."

I frowned down at the paper, my mind struggling to keep its thoughts on archaeology and not on the fact that Gunner was stroking my ankle in a very distracting manner. "So you just keep digging until . . . what? There's nothing more to see?"

"In a manner of speaking. We call the undisturbed layer 'the natural.' It means that beneath that point, we won't find anything else, so there's no reason to keep digging. But you have to understand that archaeology is a destructive process, which is why we take such pains to record every context before we remove it to dig deeper. Oh, I suppose I should explain that, shouldn't I?"

"Context? You just did. You should probably give me my foot back, though."

"I suppose I should, although it's a very pretty foot," he said with a smile that I seemed to feel down to the tips of the foot he set down. "You'll notice I didn't comment on your legs."

"I'm wearing pants," I pointed out. "You can't see my legs."

"There are few secrets to be hidden by skinny jeans," he said with a hint of a roguish glint in his eyes. "Now, we were up to recording information, weren't we? Archaeologists use forms to record all the details about each context. And then make drawings of anything of interest, and also photograph the entire thing. Roger said you were a journalist and a photographer, so you should be familiar with documenting and photographing. What publications have you worked for?"

The lovely warm thoughts that the lascivious side of my brain had been enjoying for the last few minutes froze solid, a sudden spurt of fear leaving me speechless for a few seconds. "Uh . . ."

"I have to admit," he said with a smile that I'm sure was friendly to everyone but those of us with hideously guilty consciences, "that you don't strike me at all like the journalists I know, but I will admit that they are an odd lot who tend to hang around war zones and countries with internal conflict, swilling whiskey and trading stories of how they were almost shot or blown to pieces. I gather you're not that sort of journalist?"

"Well . . ." I coughed a couple of times in order to give myself some time to think.

Gunner continued on, apparently unaware of my dumbstruck state. "What sort of camera do you prefer? I use a Nikon, myself."

"Er . . ." I tried desperately to remember what the name was on the camera back in my tent. I think it started with an *N*.

"What subject matters do you prefer? I tend to do a lot of urban with my job, but I will admit to taking the opportunity to doing as much landscape as I can fit in around jobs. Or are you a portrait person?"

"Well . . ."

"I seldom do portraits," he mused, flipping over the sheet of paper he still held. "I just don't seem to have the patience for people."

My breath whooshed out all of a sudden. "Portraits!

That's what I love most. Can't get enough of them, as a matter of fact."

"Really?" He tipped his head on the side again, an act that I realized was more of a habit than not, and one I found oddly appealing. "What sort of lens do you use? High f-stop, or low?"

I blinked a couple of times, crossed my fingers in silent prayer that I picked the right choice, and said, "Oh, high. Like way high."

"F/4? F/5?" he inquired.

"Between those," I said, waving a vague hand. "About the archaeology stuff . . ."

"F/4.8? I imagine you must use a fish-eye lens with that."

"Of course," I said, desperately aware that I could be walking into a verbal trap, but unable to find any other way around the subject. "Doesn't everyone?"

"I myself prefer a 300mm f/2.8 lens with a close-up filter. It gives such nice soft lines and edges."

"I try to stick with my eyeball lens," I said with a little shrug.

"Fish-eye."

"That, too. So. These dig reports. They look like a lot of trouble for some broken pottery. It sounds sacrilegious to say, but they look downright boring."

"They can be," he said with a little grimace, making me sigh with relief. At least I had distracted him from the horrible conversation about photography. "It's one reason why I went into photography instead of staying with archaeology. Recording everything is a necessary evil, however. Without it, you lose all context. Imagine if someone handed you a Roman coin. All that tells you is that it's a Roman coin. But what if you found that same coin while excavating a spring, and it was accompanied by various other coins of differing eras? That would tell you much more about how the spring was used, by whom, and for how long. There's a lot more data to be extrapolated if you have the context around the finds."

"I feel like I'm sitting in an archaeology class," I couldn't help saying, and dumped the dirt back into the hole. "And now I'm ashamed of my hole. Oh hell. I didn't just say that!"

"You did, but it was so bad, I'm not even going to touch it. . . . Lord, now I'm doing it."

I couldn't help but laugh when he grinned. "It's so nice to know I'm not alone in having the mind of a ten-year-old boy. Lesson learned, Professor. I won't try digging on my own again."

"There's no reason to feel that way—you're welcome to dig wherever you like, so far as I'm concerned. But do it properly, so we can record anything you find. And my apologies on lecturing you. I didn't intend to do that. In the future, I'll try to keep the pontificating down to a bare minimum."

"I don't mind if you go into full professor mode." I put the tools back in the bag, suddenly feeling shy. I wished again that Paul weren't around, because I had greatly enjoyed the few minutes Gunner had spent teaching me about archaeology. He was so patient, and seemed as interested in explaining things as I was in hearing what he had to say. I had a strong suspicion that, subjects like photography aside, I'd very much like to get to know him better. In all meanings of the phrase. But, of course, I couldn't. He was dangerous, not just because he could expose me, but because he was proving to be much too distracting on a personal level.

I'm not looking for a man, I sternly told the part of me that very much wanted to continue spending time with Gunner. *I don't need a man to have a happy life. I am complete on my own. Just because he's sexy as sin, and*

*smells nice, and dear god, his hands make me want to
swoon and rub myself all over him, doesn't mean anything other than I might want to investigate getting a new
battery-operated boyfriend.*

The part of me that Dr. Anderson said provided an
inner balance to life responded with what I imagined
was a raised eyebrow. *Didn't you learn anything in all
that therapy? There's no reason you can't enjoy a perfectly
healthy, happy relationship with a man. Being strong
doesn't mean you can't trust a man . . . or love him.*

Love, I scoffed. *I have ample proof of what happens
when you fall in love with the wrong sort of a man.*

Who's to say that Gunner is the wrong sort? my inner
balance asked, and I'll be damned if I could answer her.

"Are you feeling ill?" Gunner pulled out a water bottle and handed it to me. "You're as white as a sheet and
making the oddest faces. . . . If you need to be sick—"

"No, no," I said hurriedly, taking the bottle and sipping at it. "I'm not sick to my stomach, although I do feel
chilled, which is weird considering I'm sweating like
crazy."

"Could be a touch of heatstroke. Keep sipping that
water. I wouldn't want you falling over during one of our
filming sessions because you've had too much sun."

Something occurred to me then. "How on earth are
you going to be able to dig?" I waved a hand toward the
pink walking boot. "Are you going to even be able to get
into a trench without hurting yourself?"

He grimaced and rose clumsily, grasping the handle-
bar of the scooter before shifting his weight onto his broken leg. "That remains to be seen. I'm hoping that a
campstool will suffice until I get the beastly thing off in
a week."

"What did you do?" I asked as we headed off the
lawn. "Is it your leg or foot that's broken?"

"My ankle. I was on the balcony of a factory in Portugal when it gave way underneath me. It was only a one-story fall, but I landed wrong and shattered my ankle. There are three plates and five pins in this beauty," he said, indicating his cast.

"Ouch."

He shot me a curious look. "You're not going to comment on the wisdom of being on the balcony to begin with?"

"Why should I? You're the one who's suffering from the results of your experience. I'm sure you wouldn't do it again, not without having a death wish. Why did you agree to do the spots for the TV show people?"

"Nice change of subject, there."

"Thank you. It's a skill I've honed over the years."

"To answer your question, as you pointed out just now, I can't do a lot of digging, which is what I'd prefer to be doing. Since I have knowledge about archaeology, but I'm not a professional, Sue thought viewers would relate more to me as an average person rather than one of the academic types like Thompson. Now it's your turn: what made you pick this dig to be the subject of your book?"

The panic that had gripped me earlier returned in full force. "Oh. Uh ... well ..."

"Who's your publisher?" His face expressed nothing but polite interest, but I could have gladly shoved him off his scooter and run away. "My brother Elliott is an author, you know. Perhaps he's familiar with your publisher."

Hell. I was in hell. Somehow, in the last half hour, I'd gone from ankle-stroking heaven straight into a hell of my own making. Desperately, I called to mind the cover story I'd concocted. "Um. I was thinking of self-publishing, actually. A lot of people do that. My aunt did it with a family history. And when my roommate—she was Alice's foster sister. I don't know if I mentioned that. Anyway, my roommate recommended that I spend my summer here, and the idea of the book just kind of came to me."

It was the lamest-sounding explanation I'd ever heard, let alone dreamed up, but Gunner didn't seem to notice. "I think the idea of a behind-the-scenes book is intriguing."

I swallowed back a lump of tension, frantic to change the subject. "How did you get involved in archaeology to begin with?"

He waved a hand around. "I was adopted by a couple who lived in a five-hundred-year-old castle. When you're raised with things this old, you either love history or hate it. Luckily, I found it all fascinating, and wanted to know more about the people who lived and died here."

"It must be wonderful. I don't blame you for being interested."

"Not as interested as I am in certain other subjects," he said in a tone that had my palms clammy. I swear, if he started talking photography again, I'd make some excuse and run off.

"Oh? Such as?"

"Such as women who have an uncanny ability to change the subject."

I paused, unsure of what to say. Was he teasing or criticizing me? Damn my damaged psyche that forced me to stop and determine what was going on. "I . . . I'm sorry. . . ."

"Don't apologize." He stopped next to me and gave me that tipped-head look that seemed to make my stomach turn upside down. "I meant that in a complimentary way, you know."

"But you don't appreciate my changing the subject

away from photography?" I decided to brazen it out. As I'd found out from life with my father, and later my sole boyfriend, confrontation was often the test of whether a man was going to lash out. I braced myself, just in case. "To be honest, I feel that there's more to life than what you can see behind a camera. I just don't get off talking about cameras and lenses and filters when there's life to be lived right in front of me."

"Very true. And you put me in my place nicely. I won't bother you anymore with photographic talk."

Relief swamped me when he didn't defend his position, but the relief was tinged with something uncomfortable— guilt. I felt like the world's biggest heel at that moment, and couldn't help but say, "I didn't mean to offend you, Gunner. I sound like the worst sort of reverse snob by not wanting to talk shop at all, but really, there's so much going on around here that I'd much rather talk about."

"I agree, and I am not offended. Or I won't be if you would tell me what you're doing later."

"Later? There's field walking going on right now that I should be out photographing."

"No, later tonight."

A slight noise behind us made the skin on my arms prickle. I turned my head slowly, and found myself staring down the lens of a film camera mounted on the shoulder of Tabby. Behind her stood Matt, with his fuzzy-covered boom microphone.

I turned away quickly, remembering Roger's lecture of the day before about how everyone should pretend the cameras weren't there unless asked to explain some archaeological point to the audience. I cleared my throat, was horribly aware of just how awful that sound was, and turned back to Gunner.

"I . . . uh . . . what did you ask?"

"What you are doing later tonight?" he prompted,

laughter now visible in his eyes. I couldn't tell if he was laughing at or with me, but both made me feel cross and annoyed, and with that, came a startling revelation.

I was comfortable around Gunner.

Not just in a physical way, like his touching my leg, and my increasingly detailed mental fantasies regarding his naked person, but it was *him*, all of him, that I was comfortable with.

I poked that thought around a few times, just to see if it set off any of the warning bells that always went off around men I was interested in—and subsequently left alone for just that reason.

Nope. There was nothing there but an awareness of him as a man, an enticing and interesting man, and the fact that I felt perfectly able to be annoyed by him without the fear of showing that emotion.

Mindful of the camera, I leaned forward until my mouth brushed against his ear. It was a strangely intimate move made all that much more meaningful by the fact that I was deliberately breathing in the citrusy smell of his aftershave. "Are you asking me out?" I finally managed to ask him.

"Yes," he whispered back.

"I told you earlier that I'm not going to have sex with you."

"I didn't ask you to engage in sex. You said that you wanted to see the castle, so I thought later tonight would be a good time to show you around."

"So . . . no sex." I felt it was important to make sure he understood that I would not be one of the bazillion women who fell victim to his chest.

And arms.

And lord above, his mouth. Why had I never noticed

his mouth before? It made me feel tingly and flustered and a level of hot that had nothing to do with the sun.

"Are you asking for sex, or telling me you don't want it?" Gunner asked, a little frown between his eyebrows.

"If I told you that you annoyed me, how would that make you feel?" I asked without thinking.

He looked thoughtful. "I would feel contrite. Have I annoyed you with something I've said? Do you not wish to engage in a little lighthearted sexual banter? I assumed you did because you tend to mention things that lead me to believe you'd be open to that, not to mention the way you are staring at my mouth, which of course makes me want to look at your mouth. You have a very nice mouth. I like it. It is pleasantly shaped, and looks as soft as a cloud. Would you bite my finger if I rubbed my thumb across your lower lip?"

"Possibly." I tilted my chin up a smidgen just to let him know I wasn't mentally swooning at the thought of kissing him. "Contrite, hm? I'm glad to hear that."

"Should I apologize for what I've said?"

"No. I just wanted to know how you'd feel if I said you had annoyed me."

"At the risk of truly annoying you, I'll point out that you didn't answer my question."

I frowned. "Which question?"

"Were you telling me you didn't want to have sex, or implying you did want to?"

"Oh for mercy's sake!" I was simultaneously amused and irritated, and reveled in the fact that Gunner didn't trigger any self-preservation worries. "How many times do I have to tell you? I do not want to have sex!"

Tabby and Matt smiled at me.

"Very well, but don't expect me to believe you're interested in that lecher Thompson."

A little niggle of worry returned. "And what if I am? That's really no business of yours."

"No, it's not, except I saw the look on your face when he touched your arm earlier. It was not the look of a woman who is desirous of further touches. In fact, I'd say you appeared to be rather sickened by the whole experience."

Once again, I mentally damned the fact that every thought I had apparently showed on my face. "You're wrong. I wasn't sickened."

"You also don't lie very well."

"Stop it!" I snapped, punching him in the arm.

I held my breath for a moment, but released it when he simply said, "Stop what? Making sense?"

"No. Stop flirting with me."

"Why? Does it make you uncomfortable? Are you gay? Bisexual? Into something that would shock me to find out?" he asked with growing interest. "Are you one of those fifty-shades-of-bondage people? I haven't been into that in the past, but I might be willing to try with you. Although I would want to be the one to do the bondaging, while you would have to be the bondagee."

I cast another glance over to Tabby and Matt, flashed a smile that denied how I really felt, and turned back to glare at Gunner. "No, I'm not into anything weird, and that includes threesomes and girl-on-girl action, which I assume was going to be the next thing you asked."

"Ah, Lorina, Lorina," he said, shaking his head in mock disappointment. "How well you know me after such a short acquaintance."

"That's just the point, you obtusely irritating man!" I slapped my hands on my thighs before remembering the camera. In a lower volume, I added, "I don't know you at all, and it just seems all shades of foolhardy to flirt with someone with no purpose."

"No purpose? There's *always* a purpose to flirting."

"Not when one of the flirters is interested in someone else," I said with so much self-righteousness, it almost choked me.

"I thought we went over that."

"We did, but you seem to refuse to believe that I'd much rather spend my flirting time with Paul than indulge in something with you that has absolutely no meaning to it."

"Oh, sweetheart," he said with a deep rumble of laughter that somehow set up a thrumming response inside me. "I can assure you there's every reason to flirt whenever and wherever possible. It's scientifically proven to lower blood pressure, ease stress, and provide a great lucidity of mind."

I looked hard at him.

He smiled a slow, lingering smile at me.

"You're just talking to hear the sound of your own voice now, aren't you?" I couldn't help but ask.

He laughed a genuinely amused laugh. "I like you, Lorina Liddell. You aren't at all swayed by the fact that my brother is a baron, are you?"

"I'm American," I said with a little lift of my chin. "Plus, he's married to my roommate's foster sister, so, no, I'm not overly impressed with your family's noble history. That sort of thing doesn't mean a whole lot to us. Besides, I value people for what they make of their lives more than for what's handed to them, or how handsome their face is, or the fact that they have a nice chest and really nice thighs, and a butt that is probably in the category of droolworthy, not that I would know because I'm not the sort of person who objectifies men that way."

"I and the rest of male humanity thank you for such consideration." He leaned forward, pulling me down so that my head was level with his. His breath ruffled my hair, and that same scent of citrus soap and aftershave wafted around me with little fingers of current. "I'll tell you a secret, shall I? I much prefer someone who makes their own way in life, too. It's one reason why I don't work for my brother, as most of our siblings do."

"Stop it," I repeated after the moment or two required to recover from the wave of pleasure his closeness had sent coursing through my body.

His nose bumped mine as he turned his head slightly. If I tipped my chin up any higher, my lips would brush against his. "Do you really dislike my talking to you?"

"No," I said on a breath, fisting my hands and pressing them into my sides as I pulled back. "That's just the problem."

"Good," was all he said before his lips met mine.

The heat and sensation of his mouth seared me to my core. I was shocked, frankly shocked by such a bold move. He was kissing me! Right there in the middle of a garden, with Matt and Tabby's camera watching. It was a heedless, irresponsible move, and I was shocked. More than that, I was appalled that even though I knew I should be giving him short shrift for such behavior, I kissed him back.

Life focused to a tiny little moment filled with Gunner, and I was about to totally lose myself in that moment when he stopped kissing me.

A group of tourists had wandered into the garden and, upon seeing us, immediately began tittering.

"That," I told Gunner, refusing to admit that I was shaking from the intensity of the kiss, "is never going to happen again."

His answering smile was slow and seductive.

Merciful heavens, I was *so* over my head with him. And yet . . . damn, it was good to finally meet a man who didn't trigger all my inner warning systems. And one who loved his daughter. And who had a sense of humor, and pretty eyes, and a chin that made my mouth water, and . . . I shook my head to stop categorizing everything about Gunner that I liked. I turned my back and headed for the field where we would be walking, deliberately setting a pace that I knew his scooter would be hard-pressed to maintain.

"You can run from me, but you can't hide," he called after me, adding, "Don't think you can get rid of me this easily, Lorina. You're going to have to be by my side to-day, and every other day of the dig, and I'm not going to be happy until I get to the bottom of your supposed at-traction to that wolf in man's clothing. Dammit, I prom-ised Cressy I'd take her to her riding lesson in a few minutes."

I hurried off, my emotions in turmoil. I wanted des-perately to continue interacting with Gunner, the first man I'd felt safe with since . . . well, ever, to be honest. But at the same time, he posed a massive threat to blow-ing my cover. "Just because he's sexy and nice, and evi-dently I'm as sexually frustrated as they come, doesn't mean I'm going to throw over my plan," I said aloud as I marched back to the tent camp. "Look, but do not touch—that's going to be my new motto. Until I've dealt with Paul, I'll simply practice some self-control where Gunner is concerned. I mean, how hard can that be? I'll focus on what's important: the plan with Paul. It'll be a piece of cake to keep Gunner at arm's length."

Dr. Anderson would not have been very pleased with how persistently I ignored the obvious, but she wasn't here, and I was.

I forged onward.

Chapter 9

"Gunner, you must be thrilled to have been the one to discover such fabulous artifacts as the medieval jug rim and bit of a storage vessel. What are your feelings upon seeing tangible proof of Ainslie Castle's past?"

Gunner looked up from where he sat on a small, three-legged metal stool. The director, Sue, was standing behind him, with cameraman and sound person in tow, the same two who had been in the garden with Lorina and him. He gave them a nod of recognition before he held up to the camera a dirty bit of broken pottery that had the archaeologists extremely excited. "Well, it's nothing I'd donate to the British Museum, but the archaeologists seem to think it's a good start. Actually, though, it was Lorina who uncovered it."

"Only because you told me to," Lorina murmured, ducking her head so that she was out of frame.

Sue ignored her. "As a member of the noble Ainslie family, you must be thrilled to know that so many hidden treasures lie buried in your ancestral home. How do you think finds like these will affect your life?"

"Not a great deal, I'd say," he said, gesturing with the potsherd to Lorina, who was now on her knees scraping with a trowel. "I was just explaining to Lorina that this is the rim of a common drinking jug, and although it's fascinating, it doesn't say a whole lot about the history of the castle itself."

"And does it open up new avenues for you?" Sue asked, waving the cameraman, Tabby, forward. "You're obviously a natural at archaeology—do you have any plans to switch careers?"

Gunner gave Sue a long look before answering. Although he was used to being the center of attention due to his family and, to some extent, his appearance, he had an aversion to being used, and there was something about the way that Sue ignored Lorina that set his teeth on edge.

"It is definitely a life-altering moment," he said gravely, smiling to himself when he heard Lorina snicker. "But I'm happy to leave the archaeology to the experts."

Sue gestured toward the film team, and they obligingly stopped filming. "Excellent job with the commentary, Gunner," she said with a glint in her eyes that was all too obvious to him. "I know most photographers prefer to be on the other side of the lens, but you're a natural at this. I can't wait until we can get some action shots of you. I just know the viewers will be thrilled to see that."

"Thank you. I'm not sure how much actual digging I'll be able to do once the boot is off, but Lorina takes instruction very well, and has been extremely useful by digging in my place."

"Ah. Yes. Lorina. I understand that your first pieces to the camera were filmed. How are you getting on with your familiarization?"

"Just fine." Lorina kept her head down, scraping carefully and with much attention around what Gunner hadn't the heart to tell her was just a rock.

"Unfortunately, it's not going as good as I would like," Gunner said in seriousness. "I tried flirting with Lorina, but she seems to want none of it. I can only hope that an invitation to a late supper at the castle will help matters along."

Lorina gawked at him over her shoulder.

Sue frowned, and shook her head, saying gently, "No, no, I meant familiarization with the archaeological process." She allowed her gaze to drift over to Lorina, busily at work excavating her rock. "Not ... er ... the diggers. Actually, I was going to suggest that you stop by my caravan later, so we can go over some presentation ideas I had for you. Naturally, if you'd like to eat, I can have a meal prepared—"

"Thanks, but I already have plans for the evening," Gunner replied.

"Not with me, you don't," Lorina said sotto voce.

Gunner ignored her. He gave Sue one of his most benign smiles. "But I do appreciate the invitation, and look forward to hearing your presentation ideas later. Shall we say tomorrow? After lunch?"

Sue agreed, albeit hesitantly, and obviously would have stayed to continue her not very subtle assault on him if her radio had not at that moment squawked, and she went running off trailing explanations behind her.

Gunner watched her amble off, then considered the woman working so diligently in front of him. The number of mysteries was beginning to mount. First it was her pretended interest in Thompson, then a belief that she wasn't a journalist, and finally awareness that she had only a scant working knowledge of photography. Crowning all those unknowns was the suspicion that at some point in her life, she'd suffered from some form of abuse, and it was that, he decided, that made him feel like Lorina needed him. She needed a protector just as Rupert had.

Lorina snorted again and gave a particularly vicious stab into the dirt, distracting him from his introspection.

"Thank god they're gone," Lorina said softly, releasing her breath as if she'd been holding it the entire time they were being filmed. Her shoulders slumped in relief.

Gunner was a bit taken aback by such a reaction to what he thought of as a perfectly nice film team. "Don't care for Tabby and Matt, I take it?"

"On the contrary, I think they're both quite nice. Did you know that Tabby has been twice widowed? Her first partner died of ovarian cancer, and the second was killed while she was doing some humanitarian work in Bosnia. Imagine losing two loves of your life and still having the strength to go on. I don't think I could do that."

"And yet you're happy to see the back of her," Gunner pointed out.

"Not her—it's her camera I'm glad to see out of sight." Lorina slid him a look out of the corner of her eye, giving her a mischievous quality that pleased Gunner.

"Now, that is guaranteed to make me want to know more." Carefully, he edged himself off the campstool and onto the grass at the edge of the trench, sitting with his bad leg stretched out before him. He'd been confined to using the screens to sift through the dirt dug out of the trench, one eye on the dirt as it drifted through the screen to the ground, the other on her. "I don't know what I've done to give you the impression that I'm so lofty I wouldn't understand something that embarrasses you—indeed, given the reason for my accident, I would have thought the opposite would be likely—but I assure you that if there is something about being filmed that bothers you, I will do my utmost to address the problem."

He sounded pompous even to his own ears, but there was little he could do about it once the words left his lips except offer her a friendly, supportive, "perfectly happy to hear your inner secrets and fears" sort of smile.

Lorina was silent for a few minutes, bent over some stones as she scraped the dirt around them. "I bet you're eating all this up with a spoon," she finally said.

"Dirt?" He curled his lip. "I can't say that I have that habit."

"No, the attention from Sue. I bet you love women fawning all over you." She straightened up and gave him a long, cool look. "If you're expecting that from me, I'm afraid you're going to be disappointed."

"Because you're so desperately interested in Thompson?" He knew full well she wasn't, but hadn't yet figured out why she pretended she was.

"This has nothing to do with Paul, and everything to do with you."

"Indeed. This wouldn't be about the flirting reference earlier, would it?" he asked, somewhat confused. "Are you angry because we shared a perfectly delightful kiss?"

"No. Yes. Not really, but possibly just a little bit. It's mostly about you looking like you do, and not being worried about doing things on camera, and everyone going gaga over you because you're handsome and you have a nice accent, and a chest that would make a nun perspire."

"Doing what sort of things on camera?" It took him a few seconds to work through her sentence, but he settled on the one thing that she seemed to be truly distressed about. "You don't suffer from stage fright, do you? I don't see how being filmed while I talk to you about archaeology would make you feel like you were onstage, but I suppose—"

"No, you idiot." She made an abrupt gesture, *tsk*ed at herself, and apologized. "I'm sorry, I didn't mean to call you an idiot. It's just that ... that ...."

"That I'm being an idiot?" he suggested, something inside him warming at the flash of laughter that was gone from her eyes before he could comment on it.

"Possibly." She bent over the rock again for a few minutes before adding, "Why do you keep trying to flirt with me? You know I'm interested in someone else."

"I know you *pretend* to be interested in someone else."

She looked up sharply, then glanced around just as if she was afraid of them being overheard. How very curious. He looked around, too, pleased on the one hand to note that no one was near enough to hear them, but still wondering why she worried about it.

"Look, I realize it's a blow to your ego to find someone who isn't susceptible to your charm—"

"On the contrary, there are quite a few women who are immune to me," Gunner admitted. "Far too many for my sense of self-worth, but at least those women are—" He was about to say "honest," but decided that would be too insulting. "They are quite clear about their disinterest."

"I'm being as clear as I know how!" Lorina protested. "That kiss wasn't my fault!"

He thought of pursuing the subject, but it was obvious she was almost as distressed by this conversation as she was by discussing photography. Yet another aspect of the mystery, he mused to himself as he sifted the spill.

"You didn't say what you were doing later tonight, and whether or not the idea of dinner in an authentic, historic castle could sway you into dining with me despite your preference for another man."

She started to say something, stopped, and then gave herself a little shake of the head. "Paul asked me to stop by and see him later."

"Does that appointment preclude you having dinner with me?" He felt a little pressure was allowable. If she really was disinterested in him, he'd back off, but her body language was at such odds with what she said that he couldn't help but ask. "Dinner won't be a fancy affair— I'm shifting for myself while my family is away doing various exciting things without me, but I'm told I make a tolerable spaghetti. I can have it ready whenever suits you."

She glanced at him from under her eyelashes, a gesture that oddly delighted him. And aroused him. He shifted, suddenly and painfully aware of his penis.

"I suppose . . . Paul didn't say anything about dinner . . . and I do love spaghetti . . . but . . ."

He waited, having learned from his experience with Rupert the value of patience.

"I suppose that would be all right." Her lips tightened momentarily. "But I should warn you that I've had a couple of self-defense classes, so if you're one of those men who don't understand that no means no, then you will be doing a whole heck of a lot more than limping around on a broken ankle. I am not a victim, and won't ever allow a man to make me one."

He sensed an unspoken hurt again, but said nothing about that. It took Rupert years before he would speak about what he had suffered before he'd been adopted.

Instead, Gunner said, "You must have quite the opinion of me if you think I'd attempt to ravish you in front of my daughter and her grandmother."

"What?" Lorina's mouth sagged open for a moment while she blinked rapidly. "Oh, you mean Cressy and Salma will be there?"

"Yes, Cressy will be at dinner tonight. And every other night while she's here. I don't get to see her very often, and I don't intend to waste any of the time she's here. I enjoy Salma's company almost as much as I do Cressy's, so if you don't care to dine with them—"

"Oh, lord, no! I like them both very much."

To his secret delight, she turned pink with embarrassment, her words tumbling over one another as she tried to explain. "I thought you were going to try some moves on me, what with the proposition, and kissing in front of the camera."

"That was a delightful kiss."

She slumped down, ducking her head in that shy way she had that he found almost as charming as the through-the-lashes look. "Great, now I sound like I'm an egomaniac who thinks all men are trying to get into her pants. Can we just forget about the conversation of the last five minutes and go back to you explaining how I can tell the difference between a plain old boring rock and a piece of ceramic?"

He laughed, and leaned down to take her hand in his, intending on giving it a friendly squeeze, but instead, he dusted off her knuckles, and pressed his lips to her fingers. "There. That was a bona fide kiss, so you can stop worrying about whether or not I find you attractive."

Immediately, she bristled, pulling her hand back. "I am not worried about anything so ridiculous. You really can't go for a minute without flirting, can you? Sheesh." She bent over her precious rock, scraping around it with far too much vigor for a trench. "I bet that gets old really fast."

"You must not have experience flirting if you imagine that to be the case. And no, that's not pottery. It's a bit of rock. See the edge on it? Pottery would have a sharper edge. Ah, it looks like Roger is calling an end to the evening's digging."

As if on cue, Roger strode by them, waving a hand toward the stable and saying, "We're closing up for the night. Put away your tools, and get something to eat."

"Rats." Lorina looked disappointed. "I was just getting into it, too. Oh well. Gunner, would you mind if I did a little more digging tomorrow? Finding that bit of a beer mug was really exciting, and I'd like to have another go at digging up something else."

He grinned at her, pleased that she'd taken to his favorite hobby so quickly. "It's addicting, isn't it? I don't mind at all if you help dig tomorrow; actually, the opposite is more appropriate, since I'm limited to what I can do with this cast on, and it's nice to have my trench produce something. Although I'd hate to interfere with your schedule."

She damned near dropped the trowel she was holding, her head swiveling around, eyes wide with surprise mingled with something else. Was it fear? Confusion? Distress? "Schedule? What schedule? What do you know about my schedule?"

"Now, *that* is a very suspicious thing to say," he said gently, offering her a hand to help her out of the one-foot-deep trench.

She stared at his hand as if it were made up of pus-filled worms.

"Suspicious? Me?" Her voice rose to a near squeak. She tossed her tools into her satchel, and clambered out of the trench without assistance, adding, "You're quite,

quite insane if you think I'm suspicious or I have a schedule of nefarious acts plotted out. I'm not at all a schedule sort of person. Or suspicious. I'm just plain old me, just boring Lorina Liddell, with no thought on my mind at all. No sir. I'm going to go wash up. Innocently, I might add."

Without waiting for him to respond, she marched off, her shoulders twitching.

Gunner looked after her, silently whistling to himself. Why on earth had she got her knickers in a twist over the use of the word "schedule"? And what were the nefarious acts that she so vehemently denied? "She's not at all the sort of person who'd do something underhanded," he said slowly, hobbling over the few yards to his scooter. He sat watching her for a few minutes more before shaking his head.

The mystery surrounding her appeared to be growing with every passing minute. He made his way slowly back to the castle, thinking long and hard about just what it was she was hiding . . . and why he was possessed with the growing feeling that what she truly needed was him.

Chapter 10

"Oh, hi, Lorina. Did you have fun digging with Gunner? Gran and I just got back from town, where I had my first jumping lesson, and it was awesome! I got to ride a real jumper, not a horse they give to beginners, because I told Madame Leigh that I had done some jumping back home in BC, and she said that if I continue to do as good as I did today, she'll assign a specific horse to me, and let me train with the people who are working for regionals. I'm so excited! Gran picked me up because I can't drive in England, even though I have a driver's license. Isn't that stupid? I mean, I know they drive on the other side of the road here, but how hard can that be to do? You just drive ... you know ... on the other side! Are you ready for dinner? Gran says you're having spaghetti with Gunner and us. He makes awesomely good spaghetti. How come you're lying down?"

I rolled over from where I had been lying facedown

on my air mattress. Cressy, brimming with horse-induced happiness, fairly bounced around the tent, oozing youthful energy. I wanted to swat her away, but decided that was unfair.

"I wasn't feeling too well, and thought I'd have a little rest. Um. About dinner . . ."

"Yeah, I was kinda sleepy after my riding lesson. Did you and Gunner dig up anything cool like a skeleton or gold coins?"

"We found the rim to a beer mug."

"Huh. No coins? I like coins. Coins are pretty. What are you going to wear tonight? Oh, that sounds like I'm asking if you are going to dress up, and I don't mean that you should, because it's just us and Gunner, and he doesn't care if we show up in shorts and a tee. But I thought if you were going to dress up, then I would get my skirt from where Gran is keeping it from being too wrinkled."

"Actually, I was thinking of not doing dinner." If I hadn't felt sick earlier, I did now, with the memory of Gunner making comments that indicated he was close to revealing my secret. That and the fact that I seemed to have absolutely no resistance to him. It was one thing to see him at the dig site, where everyone's attention was focused on archaeology, but quite another when we were in an intimate family setting. That was just asking for him to reopen the subject of Paul, or photography, or even that steamy kiss we shared.

"You're not going?" Cressy's happy face quickly crumpled. "Why not? Are you heatstroky? Gunner said you were earlier. You should drink a lot of water really slowly. I got heatstroke a couple of weeks ago, and that's what Gran had me do. I felt a butt-ton better afterwards. Want me to get you some ice?"

"No, thank you, I'm hydrated now. It's just . . ." I waved a hand, fighting back the words that wanted to come out. *I'm guilty. A liar. Deception personified, and your dad is close to figuring that out.* "I'm just feeling a bit puny tonight, and thought I'd skip dinner. Would you mind telling your father that, and ask if maybe we could do dinner another time?"

"OK." She gave me a thoughtful look; then her sunny smile broke through. "I'm going to make mac and cheese tomorrow night for dinner. It's the only thing I know how to make, but I do it really nice, with bacon and sautéed onions, and sometimes, if I feel daring, paprika. You can come to that, all right?"

"That sounds divine. Hopefully, I'll feel better tomorrow," I lied. I wanted to crawl into a hole. What the hell was I doing? Not only was I deceiving everyone, but now I was making an innocent girl do my dirty work?

"For shame, Lorina," I said to myself as soon as Cressy bustled off to have dinner with her father and grandmother. "You couldn't even tell the man to his face? That's pretty pathetic, girl. Oh, god." I slumped over my knees, my forehead in my hands, rocking with misery. "I just wish this was over so I didn't have to be such a jerk anymore."

Another ten minutes or so were spent in self-pity before I managed to get a grip on myself.

"Just get it done," I said sternly while slipping on a sleeveless gauze dress. "It's only going to be worse the longer you take about it. So get it done, and then see how you feel about Gunner."

Not the least bit buoyed by the pep talk, I gathered up a small vial of pills that I'd smuggled into England, along with a syringe, latex gloves, and a packet of sterile wipes, arranging them all into the small backpack that was serving as my purse. With a peek out of the tent to make sure that Cressy and Salma had really gone to the castle, I hurried out, and headed to where bright whitish blue lights indicated the RVs.

Near the dig site, a couple of large metal barbecues had been set up. Several long tables and white plastic chairs had been arranged in small clusters, most of which were now filled with the crew and archaeology people sitting bathed in the light of the setting sun. Voices laughing and talking happily drifted across the field, and the scent of the sun-warmed earth mingled with that of grilling meat. Normally, the latter would have me salivating, but I hadn't been lying to Cressida when I told her I didn't have much of a stomach for food.

Lying to perfectly nice people did that to me.

Roger and Paul were a short distance away, the former holding a wineglass filled with inky wine. I headed straight for them, trying to look as if there were nowhere else I'd rather be.

"—think it went very well for the first day, the disaster with the waterline notwithstanding. Gunner assures me that the baron won't take action since we weren't alerted as to the presence of the pipe in that field." Roger paused to give me a friendly nod.

Paul leered in my direction.

"That said," Roger continued, "I'd like to see more actual trenches opened up tomorrow. I realize we had limited time today what with the disappointing field walk and opening of the second pasture, but I'd like to see more results tomorrow."

Paul frowned at Roger. "The field walk was anything but disappointing. We recovered several medieval bits of pottery, a handful of pipe stems, and a couple of chips of what surely are Samian ware. So all in all, I'm quite pleased with the results of today's work, and have no doubt my team will continue to produce excellent results." He turned to me. "Good evening, Lori. You look charming in that dress. Dare I hope you are wearing it to please me?"

Roger and I both stared at him in surprise, but at least I managed to change my expression from slight shock to one that I hope passed for coy interest. "Of course, Paul. Don't I do everything with you in mind?"

He smirked to himself. Roger, with a murmur about getting some dinner, went off to collect a plate of barbecued meat.

"At last. I thought the old windbag would never take himself off. Now, my dear—" Paul took me by the arm and steered me in the opposite direction. "I take it you haven't had supper yet? Excellent. I prefer to have my meals in a place where I can think, not be drowned out by a lot of chat from the diggers. They're nice people, you understand, salt of the earth, but once they get talking . . . erm . . ."

We stopped at Paul's RV. Outside of it sat a small table covered in a real linen tablecloth, complete with two chairs, and a champagne bucket to the side. On one of the chairs Fidencia lounged, her arms crossed, and her toe tapping in an annoyed manner. She was wearing a short flame red dress with plunging neckline, a copious amount of makeup that was totally unnecessary since she was a very pretty woman to begin with, and an expression that turned to anger when her eyes lit on me.

"What is she doing here?" she demanded to know.

"Fidencia, my dear one. Did you perhaps confuse your evenings?" Paul's fingers tightened on my arm when I tried to pull away. "You were to dine with me tomorrow, not tonight."

"Like hell I was!" she snapped, jerking to her feet, and throwing down the napkin that had been in her lap. "I'm not playing this game with you, Paul. Either you want me to have dinner with you, or you want her, but you can't have both of us. So make up your mind."

"My dear, I assure you that I made this appointment

with Lorina yesterday—no, no, Lorina, don't leave—we'll clear up this unfortunate misunderstanding. My dear Fidencia . . ." Paul released me, leaving me to rub my poor abused arm. I knew I'd have bruises there in the morning.

He hustled over to where Fidencia stood in a posture of tense anger, and spoke in a lowered voice that all but dripped honey. "I assure you that I have nothing but the most innocent of interests in Lorina. She is the press, as you are very aware, and it doesn't do to anger them, not when we count so much on her goodwill to promote Claud-Marie Archaeology to the world. You are an understanding woman, so you will realize that we must all make sacrifices occasionally. This is one of those times."

"*Sacrifices,*" Fidencia snorted, casting me a black look. "Oh yes, I can see just how much you're sacrificing. Well, it's your loss." She whipped around, giving me a wide berth as if I were tainted, pausing long enough to say to me, "I really hate people who abuse their power."

I watched her leave with a sick feeling in my gut that had little to do with Paul, and a lot to do with the sort of person she believed me to be. I'd be lying if I didn't admit that I came very close to calling off the whole thing right then and there, but a look at Fidencia angrily striding away quelled that thought. "There's no way on earth," I said softly to myself, "I will let him destroy another woman's life."

"Pardon?" Paul asked, turning to me.

"Nothing. Paul, if this is a bad time, I can come back—"

"No, no, just a little miscommunication." He held out a chair for me, making sure to touch both the back of my neck and my arm as he scooted my chair in. He shook Fidencia's napkin and draped it across my thighs. "You know how it is with these young girls—they would die before they admit to hero worship, but that's really all it is."

"But she works for Claud-Marie Archaeology with you, doesn't she?" I asked, confused about their relationship. "Are you two ... er ... for lack of a better word, together?"

"We have an understanding," he said with a tight little smile. "We enjoy many things together, but not exclusively, if you know what I mean."

"I think I do." The last thing I wanted to do was discuss his relationship with Fidencia, not when I was trying to get him into a romantic mood. My stomach twisted at that thought, so to distract myself, I said, "You know, I don't think I understand how a private company can make a profit on archaeology, since you have to give any treasure you find to the government. How does the CMA do it? Do you sell the other finds, the nontreasure ones?"

"No, we donate all finds to appropriate museums and universities. Most of our work is paid for by various private companies who represent entities involved in development projects, such as housing construction, or rezoning properties, or dealing with roads being widened and such. An archaeological assessment must be conducted, which is where we come in. Without our clearance, construction couldn't begin."

"Is the baron going to have something built here?" I asked, confused.

"No, in this instance, we were approached by the *Dig Britain!* people to conduct the dig while they televised it." He gave a little shrug. "It's not an ideal situation, since we are having to modify our practices in order to suit the needs of the film crews, but as they are footing the bill, the board decided it would be worthwhile."

"I can see that. I thought the digging today was very exciting, even if we did only find a beer mug rim."

"Indeed. Now, I do hope you're hungry. I had my as-

sistant pick up a few things from town. Not that the catering isn't delightful, but I prefer to pamper myself
when I'm out on a dig—we give up so many creature
comforts that it helps to keep the spirits up, you know.
Allow me to pour you a glass of wine. Ah, I forgot the
bread. I will return momentarily."

He popped into the RV before I could protest that
the last thing my stomach wanted was alcohol. I swore
and reminded myself that I might be about to do something despicable and desperate, but I had a good reason
for my actions. I stared at his wineglass, sitting there so
open and unprotected.

It was there. Right in front of me. The moment that I
had been waiting for, the culmination of my plan. All I
had to do was reach out, drop the drugs in the glass, and
my job would be done.

I sat as frozen as a block of marble, my palms sweating, and my brain shrieking that the end didn't justify the
means.

I swallowed hard when my stomach seemed to turn
over. Now that I was so close to achieving my goal, I just
wanted to leave. My innards felt cold and clammy, and
the air was suddenly too thick to breathe. My hands, un-
pleasantly damp, were shaking. I clutched them together
in my lap, and told myself to get a grip.

No! my inner voice shrieked. *What you're doing is
wrong!*

I shivered despite the heat, fighting bile as it started
to rise, panic filling me, as did piercing doubts that tore
my confidence to shreds.

Why was I doing this? Surely there was another way,
something that wouldn't involve me staining my soul!
There *had* to be another way. I just couldn't do this.

I tried to ignore the word "coward" as it echoed
around in my mind, but it was small comfort to know

that it was better to be a coward than to do what I'd planned. Just when I thought I was going to either burst into tears or start shrieking, a low humming buzz caught my attention.

I turned around to see Gunner zipping along on his scooter, heading straight for me.

The look on his face was truly chilling. He stopped, and gave me a long, level stare. "Cressy told me you were feeling queasy and couldn't come to dinner. We were worried that you were still suffering from too much sun, so I said I'd check on you in case you needed something."

"Oh, Gunner . . ." I swallowed hard, trying desperately to think of something to say. "I . . . I just . . ."

"She simply would rather dine with me than you." Paul emerged from the RV with two covered plates, and a basket of rolls. He set them all down on the table, and cocked an eyebrow at Gunner. "I'm sure no more need be said."

Gunner looked from the plates to me. His eyes, those pretty blue eyes, were as cold as polar ice. "No, nothing more need be said."

"Wait," I said, standing up. Earlier panic turned to despair in my gut at the sight of Gunner's cold expression.

"Don't bother, my dear." Paul blocked me from going after Gunner, although I hadn't the slightest idea what I would say to the man if I did follow him. "I think the facts have been made clear to him at last. He won't be pestering you any longer."

"Gunner, wait." I shook off Paul's confining hand, my mind warring a battle of desperation and self-loathing.

Gunner stopped and looked back. "Yes?"

"There's . . . I don't want you to think . . . it's just that . . ." I swore to myself, wanting more than anything to explain it all to Gunner—from Sandy's horrible betrayal, to my plan to save others, right on down to the fact that I had a hard time keeping my hands off him— but the memory of Sandy had me clamping my lips closed. That and the knowledge of what he'd think of me should I tell him the truth.

"It's just what?" Gunner asked, his voice as arctic as his eyes.

"I'm sorry," I finally managed to say. "I'm just . . . sorry."

"Indeed," was all he said before he resumed his trip back to his castle.

My stomach gurgled, warning me that swallowing all that emotion was going to have dire consequences if I didn't relax.

Paul, smirking at Gunner's back, pushed me back into the chair. "There, now. We can have a quiet dinner without any further interruptions, just you and me, and your fascination with archaeology . . . and archaeologists."

He gave me a smile that I was fairly certain he thought was seductive, and whipped the covers off the plates with a flourish. Rich, hearty scents wafted upward. I stared down at what was probably a nice coq au vin, but appeared to me to be a nauseating blob.

"Bon appétit." He lifted his untainted glass to me. It was a banner of both my failure and my triumph of sorts. "And can I add that it's been a long time since I had such a charming dinner companion?"

My throat hurt from keeping things down when they wanted to come up. I fought my stomach, almost shaking with the effort to sit in the chair.

"Now, then. I expect you have a good many questions about what it is I do. But first, a bit about my background. I went to the University of Exeter more years ago than I care to admit." He gave a light little laugh and shoveled a forkful of food into his mouth. "I was named promising

young archaeologist for three years in a row during my
college years—which no doubt was why Monsieur
Claud-Marie snatched me up as soon as I graduated."

My stomach turned over on itself a couple of times. I
focused on breathing, taking one little sip of water to see
if that would help the situation.

"I headed up a dig in Turkey my first year with CMA,
and was responsible for leading the team that uncovered
the temple at Ankara."

The water was a mistake. My innards all seemed to
lurch to the left. I turned to the side, panting slightly in
hopes that it would ease the nausea.

"You're not eating, my dear. Is something the matter?"

I opened my mouth to excuse myself, but things
started moving of their own accord, so I leaped to my
feet and dashed around the front of the RV, hoping to
make it away from the row of vehicles before my stomach unloaded itself.

"Are you all—oh." Paul stood at the front of the RV.
"Erm . . . yes. Just so. I can see you are unwell. I had no
idea. . . . You should have told me. . . . Perhaps it would
be best if we put off dinner for another night?"

I looked up from where I was on my hands and knees
retching into the still-warm earth. With the back of my
hand, I wiped a tendril of slobber from my lips, and said
simply, "Good idea."

To my relief, he didn't stay around and try to help
me—although I was willing to bet if I puked up my guts
in front of Gunner, he would have at least offered to get
me a glass of water. Paul simply wished me well, and
took off at a fast walk, heading in the direction of the
archaeology team.

It looked like Fidencia would get her fancy dinner after all, I thought with a wry twist of my lips. Assuming
she forgave Paul.

What the hell was I going to do now that I had clearly failed my one goal? Despondently, I staggered back to my tent, brushed my teeth, brushed my tongue, brushed my teeth again, and then lay down on my air mattress and wished I were dead.

"Self-pity," I told the tent rails, "is never as satisfying as you think it's going to be. Dammit. I'm not going to get any sleep until I go fix at least one thing I've screwed up."

All the way to the castle I lectured myself, pointing out that people who had intended on conducting an illegal act upon another person—no matter how well-intentioned—did not get to claim finer feelings toward those they've hurt. "Which means, you idiot, that it's only right and proper for you to apologize to Gunner for hurting his feelings, but no, you don't get to feel noble about doing it. You shouldn't have hurt him in the first place. Own your mistakes—that's what Dr. Anderson always said." I took a deep breath, marched up eight stairs, and considered the castle's wide double doors. "Awkward. How are you supposed to enter a bona fide castle? Do I knock? Is there a doorbell? Will there be a butler, and if so, do I have to tell him I want to apologize to Gunner because I was an ass?"

I faced the doors, took a deep breath, and then, before I lost courage, opened one of them and poked my head inside. "Hello?"

In front of me was a large room that pretty much fit all my ideas of what a grand hallway should be. Across the big stretch of black-and-white tile stood a fireplace large enough to roast the tent that Cressy and I inhabited. There were also several antique-looking chairs, banners, crossed swords on the walls, and murky paintings of indistinguishable scenes—pretty much everything that you'd expect to see on a movie set of a medieval castle. There were also blue rope barriers with little signs at various spots. "Clearly the tourist section of the castle. Hmm." I entered the hall and, after a quick look around for any directional signs (*This way to the master of the house's hunky brother* would have been handy, but, alas, did not appear to have been installed), began my search.

I tried to keep myself to the public rooms as much as possible, feeling for some reason that it made my presence less intrusive, but after going through four rooms with no sign of life, I branched out and headed down a hallway that had been roped off.

From there, it was simply a matter of following my nose. Little wafts of onion and garlic kept me pointed in the correct direction until I rounded a corner and found myself at the entrance to a surprisingly small kitchen. Seated at a table that had been pushed up against one wall were Gunner, Cressy, and Salma, all of whom bore identical expressions of surprise when I came to an abrupt halt.

"Oh. Here you are. Um. I'm sorry if I'm trespassing, but I wanted to explain about earlier." I summoned up a smile for all three of them. "It was nice of you to check on me, and I thought it was only right that I explain what happened."

Gunner set down a fork loaded with salad. His face, which had been wearing a happy expression, iced over. "I think the explanation of what happened is fairly clear. You preferred to have dinner with Thompson rather than us."

"No, honestly, I didn't. I don't. He's ... he's ..." I stopped, aware that once again I was about to bare my conscience, and that would never do. I might be a horrible person and a coward to boot, but I didn't have to let Gunner know all that. "Oh, it doesn't matter what Paul is. What does matter is that I asked Cressy to tell you I was not having dinner with you, when I should have had the balls to do it myself." I paused, distracted. "I really hate that expression. Why do balls signify courage? Women have just as much courage as men. Why isn't it 'I should have had the uterus to tell you'? Why are balls the standard of bravery?"

"Ovaries," Cressy said around a mouthful of garlic bread.

I waited for my stomach to lurch at the sight and smell of it, but it seemed to have settled down. In fact, I felt the faintest gurgles of hunger around the edges. "'Ovaries' is better. You should have had the ovaries to tell Gunner that you'd rather have dinner with Paul than us, although honestly I don't know why you would. Do you fancy him?"

"Cressida!" Salma said, dabbing at her lips with a napkin. "You know better than to ask such a personal question. No doubt Lorina had a perfectly sound reason for preferring dinner with Mr. Thompson, although I will admit I'm hard put to imagine what that could be."

My courage—in the form of ovaries or balls—fell in the face of Salma's gentle chastisement. I felt lower than a worm's belly at that moment, especially since Gunner was still considering me with that frozen nonexpression. "It's . . . there's . . . I have this plan, you see . . . and . . ." I stopped, aware that they were all staring at me. With a sigh, and shoulders that slumped a good two inches, I waved a wan hand. "It's a long, long story, and not one I can tell."

"So in fact you came here to explain why you chose to spurn my invitation to dinner, but have no intention of actually presenting an explanation except to say that it's a long story and not one you can tell?" Gunner's voice, which before had reminded me of warm brandy sipped by a log fire on a cold winter's night, was now sharp and flinty and clipped. He reminded me of an upper-class character on any BBC drama.

"Yes, I guess that's what I'm doing." Wearily, I rubbed a hand across my face. "I feel awful, and I want to apologize to you. To you all, but especially Cressy for using you as a messenger. I am truly sorry. I'll leave you now so you can get on with your family dinner."

If I was hoping that they would stop me as I turned and left the kitchen, demanding that I stay and have dinner with them (or at least sit and chat while they ate) amid declarations that all was forgiven, and everyone was happy with me again, then I was in for a sad, sad reality.

No one stopped me as I left the room. No one said a word. No one chased me down as I found my way out of the castle and stomped my way across the grass and dirt to the tent camp. And two and a half hours later, when Cressy stumbled over my legs, cracked her head on one of the tent struts, and fell onto her air mattress while trying to get a shoe off, even then she said nothing to me.

Good job, I told myself a short time later. Cressy had fallen asleep almost instantly, the soft, steady sound of her breathing reassuring in a fundamental way. *Good job not only blowing your entire plan to smithereens, but also alienating just about everyone you've met. Not only do Gunner, Cressy, and Salma hate your guts, but Paul no doubt thinks you're a weirdo, and Fidencia would gladly hang your scalp from her belt. Way to triumph, Lorina.*

I groaned aloud. What was I going to do now that I had failed my plan, failed Sandy and all those potential other victims out there? I had to come up with another plan pronto. I gnawed my lip as I tried to find some way to get the sample I needed from Paul without resorting to drugging him, but my brain just whirled around miserably, not at all focused on Paul, but on Gunner, and how I had damned myself in his eyes.

I shouldn't care about his eyes, pretty though they are,

I argued with myself. *I don't need his approval, and just because he's the only man I've ever been comfortable with doesn't mean there's any sort of a future with him. Far from it—one of these days he's going to discover that I'm not a photographer, and then where will I be? Elbow deep in it, that's where. No, my girl, you stay away from him, and stick to Paul like glue. If I hang around him enough, I'm sure to think up some way to get the proof I need.*

And if you don't think of something? my brain asked, going right to the source of that particular worry.

"Oh, shut up," I said aloud, and rolled over, ignoring a sleepy query from the other side of the tent.

Chapter 11

"I don't know how much more of this I can take."

Salma turned from where she was watching Cressy. "I told you that I'd be happy to drive her to her lessons."

"No, not *this*." Gunner waved a hand at where a group of four women were cantering around an arena, on command periodically veering aside to take a low hurdle. One of the four was his daughter, so happy she almost danced when they arrived at the stable. It was a happiness that was contagious, but which sadly faded when Cressy was elsewhere. "I don't mind this. This is nice. This is Cressy having fun, and telling me I'm the best dad ever, and sending selfies of the two of us standing in front of some slobbering horse or other. This I like. What I don't like has been the last five days of hell."

"Ah," Salma said, returning to watch the action in the arena. "You mean the television show."

"Yes. I thought it was going to be different. I thought I'd be able to get some time in doing actual digging. I didn't know that I'd be stuck babysitting a . . ." His lips tightened. He wouldn't say what he wanted to say about Lorina. He might not be a nobleman like his brother, but he had been raised to be a gentleman.

"A woman who knows nothing about the subject?" Salma finished.

He shot her a quick look. The tone of her voice was pure innocence, which instantly made him suspicious. "A woman who has lied to me since the first minute I saw her."

"I understood that she made it clear from the beginning that she had no archaeological experience."

"That's not what I'm referring to." He made an abrupt gesture. "She's an irritating woman, and it's annoying to have to spend so much time on camera with her explaining various aspects of the dig."

"That producer said that you two were quite the hit, though," Salma protested in her gentle fashion. "He said you had obvious chemistry on-screen, and that viewers were saying how much they loved your sections."

"Bah." He waved the idea of viewer opinion away. "We have chemistry, all right. Doing the pieces for the camera is like acid eating away at my skin."

"It would be unfair of you to expect Lorina to have any expertise in front of a camera," Salma pointed out. "She is obviously more at home on the other side of the lens."

"Bollocks," he said shortly. "She's no more a photographer than my broken ankle is. That's the first thing she lied to me about." He took a deep breath. "And it wasn't the last."

"Perhaps *that* is what is really irritating you."

Gunner swung around to face Salma. She was considering him now with a slight smile, her pale blue eyes expressing faint amusement. "You mean my ego?" He shrugged, and applauded when Cressy took a turn alone going over a series of three low jumps. "I've been turned down by women before, Salma. I don't really give a damn if Lorina prefers another man to me."

"Now who's telling an untruth?"

"Stop it," he said, not bothering to look at Salma. He didn't want to face the hurt that seemed to lace every interaction he'd had with Lorina for the last five days. The only time he had any respite was when he was chauffeuring Cressy to and from her lessons, and even then, her joy and general state of happiness was affecting him less and less.

"Very well, but before I leave the subject alone—one that you brought up—I'd like to point out that it's not wise to always believe what your eyes see."

He pursed his lips for a few seconds. "Are you referring to the fact that Lorina is spending an inordinate amount of time with Paul, a man she professes to want to be with, yet obviously can't wait to get away from?"

"That, and the fact that you appear to be a coldhearted man who hasn't the graciousness to accept an apology, and yet I know for a fact you are just the opposite."

That startled him into spinning around again to face her. "It wasn't just me she insulted that night she didn't bother to come to dinner!"

"She sent her regrets via Cressy, so we were not expecting her."

"The very fact that she dumped us—you and Cressy as well as me—in order to have dinner with that weasel in human form proves that she has no finer feelings to hurt, as you are implying I have done."

"You don't know what her feelings are, though, do you?"

"I know she can't wait to get away from me in order to hang around that bastard Thompson," he snapped, and was instantly contrite. "I'm sorry, Salma. I have no quarrel to pick with you. It's just . . ." He rubbed his head much as Lorina had done a few days before, when she had unexpectedly appeared in his kitchen. "I'm not sleeping well, and this business with the filming is wearing me out."

"Yes, I imagine a painful conscience is not a pleasant thing to bear."

"*I'm* not the one who has anything to be sorry about," he protested. "*I'm* the victim!"

"Pfft." Salma stood and clapped lightly when Cressy and her classmates paraded around the arena before riding to the stable block. "When you stop acting like an adolescent who's had his feelings hurt, and start acting like a man who is interested in a woman who quite clearly is just as interested in him, then you'll be able to sleep at night."

"Haven't you heard anything I've said?" Stiffly, Gunner got to his feet, and with the assistance of his crutches, hobbled after Salma toward his car. "Lorina can't stand being with me. The second those blasted TV spots are filmed, she's off to watch Thompson dig at his trench. That's not a woman who is so smitten that she would invade a man's house just to tell him she can't explain why she dumped him."

"Isn't it? It seems to me that it would take a great deal of courage, testicles and ovaries notwithstanding, to face a man in just such a situation. It also bespeaks a sensitivity and concern for the goodwill of the man in question. You simply have to ask yourself why she would do so if she didn't care what you thought about her."

"Ha!" he said without a shred of mirth. "That's all part of the mysterious front she puts out, no doubt to snare unwary men like myself who love a challenge. She lures us in with promises of hidden depths to reveal, and a vulnerable, damaged psyche in need of protection, not to mention the tantalizing secrets that she is no doubt keeping. Oh, it's all there, and it snared me good and proper, but I won't have it anymore—do you hear me? I refuse to be intrigued and protective and tantalized."

"Yes, I can see that you do. Cressida, my dear, you were splendid. Your seat seems to be coming along quite nicely."

Cressida, with a saddle slung over one arm, and a bridle flung over the opposite shoulder, bounced over to them. "Thanks, Gran. I didn't think I'd get the chance to do the triple combination today, but Madame Leigh said I did so well yesterday that she'd let me try one of the low ones. And it was a blast! Gunner, are you sure you wouldn't like to get a horse? I'd be happy to take care of it while I'm here this summer."

Gunner, who had been crutching slowly toward them, didn't answer for a minute. He hadn't once forgotten the mysteries that seemed to wrap around Lorina, but perhaps Salma was correct. Perhaps he should look beyond the appearance of Lorina to what she truly was.

"No," he said aloud, answering his own question.

"Balls," Cressy said in response, flinging the tack into the back of his car. "I didn't think you'd do it. Madame Leigh says there's a nice jumper for sale, too."

"Hmm?" He held the door open for Salma before limping his way around to the other side of the car. "Oh, no, no horse. Not until you're done with school; then we can talk."

"Really? Yay! That's only a year away. Mom says I have to go to the University of Alberta, but if I went to school in England, then I could live with you and could take care of a horse."

Cressy prattled away happily during the drive back to the castle. Gunner listened to her with half his attention, the rest being focused on what he'd say to Lorina the next time he saw her.

As that turned out, it was a lot sooner than he imagined.

"There you are!" He'd just put away the car when Roger loped toward him, trailing Tabby and Matt and their accompanying equipment. "We've been looking all over for you. We've had an exciting find, and Sue wants you and Lorina to explain it to the audience."

Gunner glanced at his watch. "Isn't it rather late? Couldn't we do it in the morning?"

"Never put off until tomorrow what you can do today," Roger said sagely, despite the fact he was somewhat out of breath.

Tabby grinned at Gunner. He rolled his eyes.

"All right, but I hope Sue isn't going to make this a lengthy piece. I intend to spend the evening with my daughter at the local cinema."

"I'm sure you'll be done well in time for your movie. Tabby! You and Matt go with Gunner. I have to meet with costuming about an idea I had regarding slaves...."

Gunner watched him go, slowly turning toward the field with the trenches. "I suppose Sue will be there."

"Bound to be," Tabby answered, giving him a little shove. He hobbled the few feet to where the scooter stood, and sat down heavily on it. "You know she never misses a chance to be there when you're filming. I think she fancies you."

Matt snickered.

"I hope not. She could do better than a bloke like me." The scooter bounced over the lumpy earth, jarring more than just Gunner's teeth. He didn't know whether it was seeing his brother and closest friend, Elliott, so head over heels in love with his new wife, or whether there was something in Gunner that had slowly been changing over the years. Or hell, it could just be something about Lorina that had him thinking that maybe Elliott had it right.

Maybe it was time to think about giving up the carefree days of his youth. After all, he was a man with a seventeen-year-old daughter, one who was impressionable. He had a sudden vision of a few years hence, stumbling home from yet another casual encounter only to find Cressy in the same situation. Was that the sort of message he wanted to give her? He had to be a role model now, and the thought that his Cressy, his bright, shining, happy girl, could stagger home doing the walk of shame made him grind his teeth.

He'd be damned if he let her follow in his footsteps! It behooved him to get, as the Americans said, his act together while he could still influence Cressy to the good.

It was with such noble intentions that he bounced his way across the field to an open trench. Clustered around it were Sue, the other two sound- and cameraman teams, whose names he could never remember, Paul Thompson, Lorina, and a couple of diggers who looked hot, tired, and dirty.

He didn't fail to notice that Thompson was as fresh as if he'd just stepped from a shower in an expensive hotel.

"There you are!" Sue called loudly as he pulled to a stop. "We've been looking everywhere for you, you silly man. Didn't you hear us call for you on the radio?"

"I was watching my daughter take her riding lesson, so I didn't have the radio with me," he answered, getting off the scooter and maneuvering to the other side of it so as to force Sue to drop her hold on him. Unbidden, his eyes went to Lorina, but she was on her knees next to the trench, using a small toothbrush on a bit of stone. "What's the big find?"

"It's so exciting! Let me do a short piece to introduce it," Sue said, pointing dramatically to the trench while smiling at the camera that Tabby obligingly turned on. "As our viewers remember, four days ago we uncovered the first signs of the large building buried under this field, and several outbuildings, including one that was snuggled up right next to Ainslie Castle itself. Following that was the excitement of the skeletons of seventeen poor souls that we found in the trench we'd put in the grove. The last of those skeletons was taken out earlier today, which is why we decided to take a peek at what was in this trench. About an hour ago we found some plain tesserae, and Paul Thompson told me that he had hopes that we'd uncover a painted mosaic. And now, his hope has been fulfilled. Take a look at what Paul found just a short hour ago."

"Mosaic, eh?" Despite himself, he was interested. One of the things that he'd hoped for was proof of a Roman villa on the grounds of the castle. Local history had claimed there was once a fort, but Gunner had hoped for a more personal building, one that had housed a family, not a group of soldiers bent on subduing the population by force. "That sounds unusual for a fort. Ah, yes, I see what you mean. That is outstanding, truly outstanding."

Paul moved aside to reveal an uneven surface about a yard wide, made up of small, roughly square stones that had been painted in what once must have been glorious blues, greens, and reds. The colors formed waves and swirls, clearly meant to depict an aquatic scene.

Sue signaled to Tabby, who stopped filming. "I think my introduction set up a segment for you to explain to Lorina the importance of painted tesserae over the plain ones, and then Paul can take over with the more technical talk. Tabby?"

Carefully, Gunner sat down at the edge of the trench,

swinging his legs into it before cautiously making his way over to where the mosaic was exposed. Paul and the diggers moved out of the way, standing behind the film crew. Gunner cocked an eyebrow at Lorina. She was still on her knees on the ground next to the spoil pile, frowning over the piece of stone.

"Lorina, if we could have your attention for just a few minutes, we'd all be ever so appreciative." Sue's voice was acid, but Lorina didn't seem to notice it.

She glanced up, blinked twice, and said hurriedly, "Oh, sorry. I was just ... sorry. Yes, of course." She jumped down into the trench and, without even so much as sending a look his way, squatted next to Gunner, donning the expression that he'd come to think of as her pliant face. It was devoid of expression, no doubt intended to leave the viewers to believe she was stupid and needed to have everything explained to her. It irritated Gunner, who knew full well that she had as sharp a mind as anyone there—sharper, if her deceptions were anything to go by.

"What we have here are tesserae," Gunner began, gesturing toward some of the stones that had been dislodged from the rest of the mosaic. "The Romans used thousands of tesserae to create a mosaic, which decorated their floors. They were stuck down by a type of mortar which, amazingly, still binds the tesserae together in some places. If you look at this one, you can see the pattern forms waves, which indicates that the tile has a nautical theme, and might have been used in a bathhouse. Until we uncover more of the mosaic, and the surrounding room, we won't know why the owners chose to have this pattern laid down, but one thing we can be sure of—only the wealthy had painted mosaics, which means that this structure must have been something other than a common building to house soldiers."

"How interesting," Lorina murmured. He caught her casting a covert glance at the stone she held in one hand, and wondered just what it was about it that so absorbed her.

"Recently, enormous floors of mosaics in courtyards and baths were discovered in a port near Rome." He went on for a few more minutes, ostensibly lecturing to Lorina on everything he knew about mosaics, ending with a hope that much more of the Ainslie mosaic had survived the centuries.

"That was excellent, Gunner. Very well done. So insightful, and yet, brought down to the level of the common viewer," Sue gushed, bustling over to the edge of the trench. She was about to jump down into the trench, now about a yard deep, but stopped when Paul Thompson cleared his throat meaningfully. "Oh, of course. Forgive me."

"Hmm?" Lorina looked up, clearly distracted by the stone she held.

"What is it you have?" Gunner asked, despite his intention not to give in to her obvious attempt to intrigue him.

"A stone mouse." She gave him a curious look, and handed him the stone.

"Shall we film my in-depth discussion of the mosaic now that Ainslie's general explanation is done?" Paul asked.

Sue looked disgruntled, and waved a vague hand toward the setting sun. "This late light isn't very good—"

"All the more reason to do it before any more time passes," Paul said, brushing past Gunner in a way that sent him staggering forward. "Pardon."

Gunner shot him a look, but hobbled forward to the edge of the trench and hoisted himself onto the grass, Lorina following with much more grace. Tabby and Matt moved into position and began filming Paul when he went into a lengthy explanation about other famous mosaics discovered in England, and how this related to them.

"*Mitto tibi navem prora puppique carentem,*" Gunner murmured, reading the inscription on the stone.

"Do you know Latin?" Lorina asked, moving in close and speaking in a low tone that wouldn't be picked up by the microphone.

He was distracted by her nearness for a few seconds. A floral scent that seemed to accompany her teased his nose, making him want to breathe in deeply. Wildflowers—that's what it reminded him of. The wildflowers encountered on a Greek hillside in summer. "I do, as a matter of fact. Do you?"

"No, I'm a French . . . er . . . I'm afraid not. French, yes, but not Latin. What does it mean? Is it something about the mouse?"

"No. It says 'I send you a ship lacking a stern and bow.' Which, in case you didn't know, is a riddle by Cicero."

Her frown grew as she took the stone from him. "Really? It's a riddle? What does it mean?"

"*Navem* is Latin for 'ship.' If you remove the *n* and the *m*—the fore and aft letters—then you are left with *ave*, which is a common greeting. So in effect, the stone says hello."

"How bizarre," she said, rubbing her thumb along the edges, careful not to touch the painted surface. "Why the mouse?"

He shrugged. "No clue. Perhaps it's supposed to represent whoever painted the greeting. Why are you so interested in it? It's likely just a bit of a student's lesson. It's interesting, yes, but the subject matter isn't earth-shattering. The riddle is an old one, and well-known."

She gave him another of those looks through her eyelashes, the one that did a good deal to melt the ice of his reserve toward her. "Because there are two other mouses. Mouse stones. Mice. Whatever, there are two more of them. And it's just kind of odd seeing a third one. I thought maybe it was—oh, I don't know—like a storybook or something. Did the Romans have such things?"

"Not painted on stones. They had graffiti, some of which were rude comments; others were signs and notices. But not stories, at least, not that I know of." He thought for a moment. "Where were the other two stones found? If they were part of a wall, then it would definitely be graffiti."

"One was in trench five, at the outer edge of the castle, one was in the trench at the temple in the grove where they found all the skeletons, and this one was in Daria's trench."

"So scattered all over. Interesting," Gunner said, getting to his feet. "Let's go see the stones."

Lorina waited until he was settled on the scooter before asking, "Are you really interested in the mouse stones, or are you setting me up solely in order to be snotty to me?"

He stopped the scooter and stared at her. "Snotty! I am not snotty. I have never been snotty. I don't even know how to be snotty. Snarky, yes—snarky, I know—but snotty?" He gave a loud sniff. "I do not snot."

"Oh, you know how to be snotty. Snotty is exactly how you've behaved to me during the last five days. Snotty is having your nose out of joint because a woman doesn't inflate your ego with comments about how nice your chest is, and how pretty your eyes are, and how your little bit of stubble is sexy as hell without looking like it would scratch like a hairbrush, as some men's beards do. So don't tell me you don't know snotty, because I've been on the receiving end of it for the last five days, and frankly, I'm sick and tired of it. Just get over yourself already!"

He looked down at himself. "You like my chest?"

"No, of course I don't," she said, striding ahead of him. She stopped and contradicted herself. "Just because you have all sorts of nice swoopy bits without looking like a bodybuilder, and your shoulders are broad without being obscene, and you have biceps and that little line of muscle on the back of your arms that says you work out, does not mean that I like your chest." She jerked her chin in the air in a gesture of defiance.

He smiled. He couldn't help himself—she was just so damned adorable. Yes, she had lied to him, but perhaps she had a reason for it, something along the lines of an aged parent dying if she didn't play up to Thompson, or perhaps he held the mortgage to her grandmother's house, or maybe she was doing an undercover documentary on self-centered men? She could be keeping any one of those as a secret, but he would have to be dead not to realize that she was intrigued by him and not Thompson. And with that thought, the last of his resistance fizzled away. He upped the wattage in his smile, and added, "You should have stopped at the shoulders."

She kept her nose pointed upward for the count of five, then sighed, and slumped dejectedly. "I know. It was too far, wasn't it?"

"The triceps muscle pushed it over the line," he agreed.

"My mouth," she said, shaking her head, and strolled forward toward a disused tack room that was serving as finds storage. "I just can't take it anywhere."

"There are many responses I could make to that provocative statement, but I won't make any of them. I don't suppose you feel inclined to tell me why you pretend that you're not as interested in me as I am in you?"

he asked with a casualness that he didn't in the least bit feel.

"Interested in me? You hate me after what I did!" Lorina protested, her eyes wide with surprise and concern and something that melted him entirely.

"Far from it, I assure you, although I will admit that I was sufficiently annoyed to display a little coolness toward you."

She looked like she wanted to argue, but swallowed it back. "To be honest, I deserved your snottiness."

"That is debatable, but lest we fall into a self-blaming circle, shall we release the bygones and focus on the here and now?"

"That would be nice." Her smile seemed to warm him a good ten degrees.

"Since we are at a state of congeniality, perhaps you'd tell me why you insist on chasing Thompson when he clearly *doesn't* interest you at all?"

"Oh, he interests me," she said grimly, pulling open the door to the tack room.

The air inside was thick and musty, heavy with the ghostly scent of generations of saddles that had been stored within, touched slightly by the odor of hay, mildew, and rodent droppings.

"He doesn't interest you in a romantic way. Nor a sexual way." Gunner got off the scooter to enter the room with her. One naked bulb hung crookedly from the ceiling, its light both sickly and dim, casting down obnoxious yellow rays on the stacks of trays holding plastic bags of finds. Each bag had been carefully labeled with all pertinent information, as well as an identifying number. "Not in a way that makes your pupils dilate, like they do when you're talking about my chest and biceps. Can you reach that tray to the left? I don't suppose I should attempt a stepladder with one foot in a cast."

"Stop noticing my eyes dilating; it's none of your business what they do around you, and for the record, I'm not responsible for their reaction to you. Your chest is nothing to me, nothing at all. Would you hold the ladder steady? It's a bit wobbly. Where was I? Oh, yes—my eyes lie. Ignore them. Can you take this tray? I'm not sure if the other two stones are in this one or the other one."

He took the heavy plastic tray that she handed down, careful to keep one hand on the ladder so that she wouldn't fall. He couldn't help but admire the shapely derriere that waggled directly in front of him. "Eyes never lie. Would you drop something heavy on my head if I told you that you have a very nice bum?"

She looked down from where she was easing a second rack from the top of a tall metal shelving unit that had been set up to hold all the artifacts. "No, but only because the heavy objects here are priceless. But your comment is way over the politically correct line. Men aren't supposed to comment on women's behinds unless they are in a relationship, and then only in a positive fashion. Anything else is sexual harassment."

"Do you feel sexually harassed?" he asked, releasing the ladder in order to set down the first tray. He accepted the second one she carefully slid toward him.

"Well . . . no. But that's beside the point." She hopped down from the stepladder and knelt at one of the trays.

"I don't see how. I paid you a compliment. Yes, it was for your ass, but that is as much deserving of a compliment as any other part of your body. Would you tell me I was sexually harassing you if I told you that you have lovely eyes, or nice hair, or that your scent is distracting in the extreme?"

She reared back, her eyes almost shooting sparks of ire at him. "My scent? *My scent!* I do not stink! The showers in the stable may not be very sophisticated, but I take one every day, and—"

"And now you're jumping to a conclusion," he interrupted, taking a potsherd from her hand, since she seemed about ready to crush it in her fury. "I meant that in a positive manner as well. You have a very nice scent. Unusually nice. It reminds me of a summer I spent in Greece. It's very floral and seductive, but not overpowering like a perfume."

She blinked a couple of times, then relaxed and actually gave him a shy little smile. "Oh. That's probably the botanical soap I use. A friend of mine is a Buddhist nun, and she makes soap and sells them to fund her causes. I had no idea anyone could smell it, though. I guess I'm used to it."

"I approve of your choice of soap," he said gravely, and plucked a plastic bag holding a small triangular piece of gray stone from the finds tray. "I believe this is one of the stones you are looking for. It appears to have part of a mouse in the corner."

"Oh, is that the half-a-mouse stone? Let me see."

He offered it to her.

"That's it. I looked, but I couldn't find the rest of the stone. Can you decipher the writing?"

He leaned over the stone, very aware of the warmth of the woman pressed against his arm. "It's not all here, but let me see what I can make out. *De terra nascor, sedes est semper* . . . hmm."

"Hmm?" She leaned down, blocking his view of the stone. Her hair brushed his cheek, causing him to breathe deeply of that wonderful flowery scent. "What hmm? What does it say? Does it mention who the mouse is?"

"I don't know. I can't see the rest because your head is in the way."

"Oh, sorry." She jerked back and gave him another little smile, but this one he felt down to the tips of his toenails. "Translate away."

"Well, this part says more or less, 'born of earth, my place is still . . . something . . .'" He frowned at the faded paint. Part of it had been chipped away, and the rest of the inscription had not fared as well as the previous stone. "This part says something about 'being covered with dew,' but 'am soon dry.'" He winced, and stood upright, flexing his leg as he did so.

"Are you hurting?" Lorina watched him with obvious sympathy. "You shouldn't be on your feet."

"It's fine if I stand, but crouching like that hurts. Let's take the trays outside. We can sit more comfortably, and the light is better."

"We don't need to take the trays—we can just find the other stone."

"But then we wouldn't know for certain that there weren't other puzzle pieces. I'd like to search through the finds from those trenches for myself." He hefted one of the trays and, with a cane in the other hand, thumped his way out of the tack room to the dining area, now occupied by only a few diggers who were loitering over their beers.

"Puzzle? You mean that's another riddle?" Lorina hurried after him, setting down her tray next to his. To his sorrow, she didn't scoot her chair close. "That thing about the dew and earth, you mean?"

"Yes, it's another famous riddle. I'm quoting from memory, but I believe it goes something like: 'From earth my body, strong through fire am I, though born of earth, my place is on high, and drenched with dew, I soon am dry.'"

She stared at the bit of stone, her fingers tracing the upper body of a mouse. "What on earth is that supposed to mean?"

"It's a reference to a roof tile." He sorted through the

bits of pottery and stone and occasional lumpy twists of metal that were likely either nails or hobnails. "Judging by the charring on the potsherds, and the melted metal, it's pretty clear that a fire was responsible for the destruction of this building."

"Why would someone write riddles on bits of stone like that?"

"Your guess is as good as mine." He considered the items before him. "Let's see the third mouse stone."

"Oh, it's in this tray, I think. It's bigger than the others, which is why I first noticed it, although it doesn't have a lot of writing, and most of the mouse is missing—just his head shows up at the bottom. Here it is."

She passed him a roughly oval-shaped bit of stone. This one had a line that led away from the text, which was clearly readable. "*Homo trium litterarum.* 'Man of three letters.'" He smiled, and pointed to the line. "Do you see what those are? They're the mouse's footprints."

"You're kidding." She squinted at the stone. "Holy cow, you're right. Is it another riddle?"

"Yes. The answer is *fur*."

"Mouse fur?"

He shook his head. "*Fur* is Latin for 'thief.' A man of three letters is a thief. It was mentioned in a comedy, although I don't remember which one. My school days are long since passed, and I didn't really enjoy Latin. I admit I'm glad it was forced into me now, though."

"It is handy," she agreed, carefully sliding the plastic bags with their treasures around in the tray as she searched for more mouse-inscribed stones. "And here I thought I was smart getting a degree in French."

"French is infinitely more useful than Latin, I assure you. There don't seem to be any more stones."

"Which is a shame, because they're cute. Any ideas on what they are?"

He was about to answer when a flurry of people crowded into the dining area. "I have a very far-fetched idea of what they could mean, but your boyfriend just arrived, so I'm sure you'll want to go fasten yourself to his side."

"Boyfriend?" She looked genuinely puzzled until she glanced over her shoulder. She turned back quickly and bent over the tray, but he was able to see the disdain in her eyes. "He's *not* my boyfriend."

"Gunner!" Sue, who had entered the dining area along with Thompson and Roger, hailed him and waved, adding in a voice loud enough that everyone could hear, "Do join us. We're going to have a confab about the direction the dig is going, and your insights would be most valued, especially now that we've discovered the temple with all those skeletons. Those could have been your ancestors! Well, not yours, because—" She made a vague gesture toward him. "—and it's all very exciting. We'd love to hear what you have to say about the show so far. Wouldn't we?"

Paul and Roger murmured something.

"Oh, lord," Gunner said softly.

A little giggle slipped out of Lorina. "Looks like your girlfriend wants to see you."

"I assure you such a designation would never be applicable to her."

"Mmmhmm."

He lifted his voice to answer Sue. "I'm sure you all have it well in hand, although I appreciate the compliment. I'll leave you professionals to your work."

"Smooth," Lorina said, her voice choked with laughter.

"Not really." He ignored Sue's continued waves and gestures to join them. "I do not seek her out in order to spend time with her, whereas you . . . why *are* you acting as if you're mad about Thompson?"

She looked up, her eyes filled with a wariness that

pained him to see, her hands busily sorting and resorting the pottery shards. "I wish I could tell you, Gunner. I really wish I could. But I just can't. For one thing, it would make you despise me."

He took her hands in his, gently rubbing his thumbs over them. She had short fingers, but oddly elegant hands regardless. "Why would you think that?"

"Because I despise myself." She curled her fingers around his, giving them a little squeeze before pulling back. "No, don't ask why—I just do, and I'm not going to explain it to you. Not now. Maybe later, but not until . . . not now. What's your far-fetched idea?"

Half-tempted to tell her he wasn't about to share his thoughts if she felt unable to do the same, he decided that was petty. Besides, the little stones with their riddles had interested him, especially given the idea that was growing in the back of his mind.

He held up one of the stones. "They could be nothing more than amusing graffiti, written on the wall to entertain, or as a joke."

"I suppose so, although did the Romans use stone walls?"

"Yes, but not stone like this." He ran his fingers over the slick plastic bag. Beneath it, the surface was smooth. "These stones have been finished, finely finished, which tells me they were meant for a decoration or other artistic item. And yet they don't have a shape of, say, an urn, not that stone urns were common."

"OK, so it's not an urn or bit of wall graffiti. What is it, then?"

He hesitated, his eyes on the stone as he ran over the puzzles again. "A thief, a greeting, and a roof tile. What do they have in common?"

"Is that another riddle? Because I have no idea of what the answer is."

"Neither do I. Which makes me wonder if it's not some sort of puzzle itself."

"How do you mean?"

He set the stone down, and picked up the second one. "It occurred to me that they might be, for lack of a better word, clues."

"Clues to what?" she asked, leaning over the tray so that her hair swept over his arm. His wrist tingled in response.

"I don't know. Perhaps the stones were left by someone as a joke for a friend. Or they might have simply been a way for a scribe to practice his writing. Or it might be clues to the location of . . . something."

"What sort of something?" Her eyes widened as she sucked in her breath. "Like a treasure? Do you think the stones are clues to the location of a valuable treasure hoard?"

"Treasure hoard?"

To Gunner's dismay, Sue appeared at his shoulder, accompanied by Roger. Thompson, he was relieved to note, was bending over one of the diggers, openly staring down her shirt.

"What treasure hoard?" Roger asked, excitement spiking his voice. "You found a treasure hoard and you didn't notify me? Good god, man, do you know what that sort of thing will do to our viewership? It'll go through the roof!"

"There's no treasure hoard," Gunner protested, but was quickly interrupted.

"She said 'treasure.' I distinctly heard the word 'treasure' being used." Sue gestured toward Lorina. "What treasure are you speaking about? Did you find something that you didn't report to us? You must know that anything valuable has to be reported to the government—"

"Yes, we're well aware of the finds laws. And I haven't

found anything that you lot haven't thoroughly filmed and documented."

"Then where's the treasure hoard?" Roger asked, looking disappointed.

Lorina looked at Gunner. He shrugged. "You can show them if you like, although I would like to remind you that I used the word 'far-fetched' when I mentioned that theory."

Succinctly, Lorina explained about the mouse stones, showing them in turn to Sue and Roger.

"You can't be serious," Sue said dismissively when Lorina finished her tale. "That's just utter rot. You've leaped to all sorts of conclusions without the slightest bit of evidence. No offense intended, Lorina, but that story is nothing but a tissue of wild guesses."

Lorina opened and closed her mouth a couple of times, clearly so indignant she was speechless. Gunner gave her a grin before he said, "Actually, Sue, the suggestion was mine, not Lorina's. And I admit it's highly speculative, and likely not at all grounded in reality. It was just a thought that occurred to me given the odd nature of the stones."

"I don't know," Roger said slowly over Sue's hasty backtracking of insults. He picked up two of the stones and held them side by side. "It makes perfect sense to me. And just imagine what it would do to the ratings if we found the treasure."

"There's not likely to be any treasure," Gunner felt obligated to protest. "It's all just sheer speculation—"

"But speculation that could be grounded in truth," Roger insisted.

"How so?" Gunner asked.

"Well, for one, we know now that we're excavating a villa, not a military base," Roger said, ticking the item off on his fingers. "That means a family of wealth, right?

And then there's the fire. Paul says there's definite proof that there was a big fire at some point, and the villa could have been destroyed by it."

"Yes," Gunner drawled, frowning in thought. "Although from what I've seen of the artifacts, the fire was subsequent to an attack of some sort. Recall the skeletons in the temple in the grove."

"Exactly!" Roger ticked off another item. "The skeletons with the cleave marks on their skulls. Paul said that was a sure sign that the villa had been attacked, most likely by a Boudiccan Revolt."

"I never did understand who Boudicca was," Lorina said, looking at Gunner. "I take it she didn't like the Romans?"

"Not very much, no. You might know her as Boadicea, although that's just a variation on her name. She banded together several tribes, and led them in attacks against the invading Romans around sixty AD."

"And the stuff you found with the skeletons matches that date," Lorina said, nodding her understanding.

"Roughly, yes. Give or take a year."

"You see!" Roger was on his feet, clearly running with the idea of treasure being hidden somewhere. "It all fits! If you know that Boudicca and her gang are in the area attacking Roman villas, what do you do? You hide your valuables."

"But would you take the time to paint riddles on stones telling you where those valuables are?" Lorina asked.

Gunner gave her an approving nod. He was delighted that she could see the flaws in the theory.

"You might, if you didn't want Boudicca to find it! Lord, what a stir we'll make when *we* find it." Roger rubbed his hands together. "It'll make all the news stations. Hell, it could go global, just like when they found Richard the Third's remains!"

"What we need," Sue said, clearly thrilled by the idea of a treasure trove, "is to find more of these mouse stones. Roger, we should put the entire crew on locating stones. These clues don't mean anything the way they are, so clearly there have to be more stones. We must find them to locate where the valuables were hidden."

Gunner sighed, and looked at Lorina. She curled her lips at him, obviously as amused as he was.

What had they started now?

Chapter 12

"Morning, Cres—oh. Hello, Daria." Startled, I clutched my bag of shower accessories and a damp towel to my chest. "I didn't realize you were right there."

Daria had an odd look on her face. "Did you—" She paused, looking indecisive. "Did you see him?"

"See who?"

"Paul. I was on my way out to one of the trenches, and I could have sworn I saw him coming out of your tent."

I glanced around hurriedly. "I was in the shower, so I haven't seen anyone. Although I thought Cressy was in there sleeping." I moved the door of the tent open. "Oh. I guess she's up already."

Daria gave a little laugh, and rubbed her hand over her eyes. "This is what happens when you don't have a cup of coffee before you start work—I must have been seeing things."

"Maybe it was Cressy you saw. She's as tall as Paul."

"Most likely that was it. I'd better get to work before my brain completely leaves me. Are you coming by to do photos of me cleaning some archaeology?"

"Sure. We can do that in a few minutes, if you like."

"Sounds good. See you then."

I slipped into the tent and eyed the contents. Nothing looked out of place, or otherwise disturbed. Could Paul have really been into my things? And if so, why? He'd done his best to avoid me for the last six days, ever since I'd ralphed behind his RV, so if he had been in here, it certainly wasn't from a desire to be nearer to me. Far from it—I'd had a devil of a time sticking to him, finally having to resort to telling him I wanted to do a feature on how he worked. Not that it had helped much—I was still struggling for some idea as to how I could get the proof I needed. The best I'd come up with was to organize a spontaneous blood drive on the dig site, but that idea wasn't feasible on any level. I sighed, and prayed that something would occur to me soon.

Twenty minutes later, I knelt down next to an open trench where Daria was working.

"You'd think I'd have this protocol down by now." I took a deep breath, and counted off the items. "Never step into a trench without first asking permission."

"Because you could destroy something that is in the process of being cleaned." Daria nodded, and continued scraping at a collection of stones that she assured me were part of a road that led directly under the castle.

"And you never dig out something without first spending copious amounts of time photographing and drawing it. That part I remember." I grimaced to myself. All the archaeologists were well versed in taking photos of their dig sites, but I had been called on twice by Roger to take pictures of particularly thrilling artifacts. Both times I felt I had botched the pictures horribly.

"Always, always document." Daria brushed her wrist across her head, leaving an earthy smear behind.

"And most of all, don't walk over the spoil pile, because there could be hidden treasures in it. Oh, crap."

Daria groaned. "You said the word!"

"I know, I'm sorry." I glanced around quickly. The bulk of the crew was having a prebreakfast meeting with Sue and Roger, being briefed on their new treasure-hunting assignments. "Luckily, no one heard me. Why aren't you at the meeting?"

"No one heard you now, but evidently they did last night." Daria gave me a sour look.

"I said I was sorry! Besides, it's not my fault if they eavesdropped on a conversation I was having with Gunner and took one of his comments out of context."

"You and I know that, but the end result is that half the team will be in my trench mucking everything up, while the other half goes on a mad scramble to find more of those stones." She shook her head to herself. "I decided to forgo the meeting, since Paul won't listen to anything I have to say. Honestly, Lorina, at this point I almost wish I'd stayed home. This treasure hunt is going to be a nightmare."

"Maybe if you talked to Paul—"

"Not likely. He's as thrilled as the TV people, since it means additional attention for CMA. I just wish the board could see how he's prostituting good archaeology for a bit of money. No, we're simply going to have to write off this dig. It was promising, but once the treasure bug bites people, it's all over. All they see is one object, and all else is trivial."

I stood up from where I'd been kneeling on the edge of her trench, remembered I was supposed to be documenting her work, and snapped a few pictures. "I'd apologize again if it would do any good, but since Roger and

Sue seem to have their minds made up, I won't bother. Although you'd think Paul would have the good sense to put a halt to their treasure hunt."

She gave an irritated jerk of one shoulder, and said, "You can try talking to him. Maybe he'll listen to you. You guys appear to be pretty close these last few days."

"Er . . . well . . ." I managed to not make a face.

"I didn't mean to pry. You look like you're savvy enough to know how to take care of yourself around a man like him, so I'm sure I don't have to point out the obvious." She glanced up and saw the obvious look of surprise on my face, and laughed. "Sorry. That's what comes from being the wife of a man who spends his day doing health and STD tests. I'm forever warning women to be sure to use protection when they're having dig romances."

"I . . . There's nothing like that going on," I protested. "To be honest, he's been avoiding me ever since I didn't feel well at dinner. He thought I had something contagious. Evidently he's a bit of a germophobe, which is ironic considering—" I stopped, horrified that I was once again so close to blurting out the truth.

Damn that Gunner. What was it about him that had me lowering my commonsense defenses? He didn't even have to be here and I was still in "tell everyone the truth" mode. I stiffened my resolve to stop talking.

"Considering what?" Daria asked without lifting her head.

"Considering he spends his day grubbing around in dirt." It sounded lame, but she accepted it.

"Well, if you can get Paul to see reason, more power to you. But I don't hold out much hope—I've seen this happen before, and I know how good archaeological practices can get trampled in the lust for high-publicity finds."

"I'll do what I can," I said, tucking away the camera in its little case. "Good luck preserving your road."

She snorted, and tipped her head toward the castle. "I had been hoping to ask the owner if I could extend it across his lawn to the pasture, but now Paul won't let me have any diggers go in that direction. They'll all be focused on the other end of the trench."

I waved good-bye, and hurried to the tent area, planning on leaving off the camera and its bag of accoutrements while I went in search of breakfast. Cressy had returned from taking a shower, and was pulling on her usual pair of shorts and grubby T-shirt.

"Ah, you're back. Good morning," I said, feeling horribly awkward. Although we were sharing a tent, I hadn't spoken more than a dozen words to her since that terrible night when I burst in on Gunner's dinner. My own embarrassment and the fact that I was sticking to Paul in hopes of finding some way to get a blood sample, along with Cressy's busy schedule, had guaranteed that we'd see each other only briefly.

"Hiya." She twirled her damp hair into a knot on the top of her head. "I haven't seen you in a while. If I didn't see you sleeping at night, I'd have thought you left."

"I've been busy." I remembered the camera bag and held it out toward her. "Taking pictures. Digging. Doing bits with your father in front of the camera."

"Sounds like fun. I've been at the stable every day. Did I tell you about my riding lessons?"

"Yes," I said quickly. "Are you enjoying yourself?"

"So much!" she said, hugging herself. "I get to clean the tack and wash down the horses, and Madame Leigh said that she'll let me help lead the tourists on their cross-country hacks. Won't that be awesome?"

"Totally," I agreed, and tucked away the camera. "It

sounds like you're spending your summer very productively."

"Yeah, it's great. Ugh, I'm so hungry I could eat a whale! Gran's not up yet. Are you going to get some breakfast?" She strolled with me out of the tent.

"I was, but I don't think there is any breakfast yet. It looks like the entire crew is still at their meeting." The tables clustered around the cooking trailer were empty.

"Yeah, I heard that Roger guy yacking when I went in to take a shower." She tugged at her T-shirt, and made a face. "I'm going to die if I don't get some food."

"I'm a bit famished, myself. I didn't get much dinner because your father . . ." I stopped.

"Because Gunner what?"

I didn't want to tell Cressy that a conversation with Gunner had left me frustrated and angry with myself, so angry I had left the discussion of treasure the night before lest I drag Gunner off and have my womanly way with him.

I blushed a little just thinking about that. How had I gone from wanting to avoid him to the point where I just wanted to touch him? And kiss him. And be with him, no matter how dangerous that proved to be.

"Lorina?"

"Hmm? Oh, sorry, I was distracted."

Cressy screwed up her face. "Are you still mad at Gunner? Because if you are, you really shouldn't be. He's not mad at you, even if Gran says he's acting like a dickwad. That's my word, not hers. Gran would turn cartwheels before she ever said that word. But Gunner isn't mad about you telling me to tell him you'd rather eat with Paul than us. I mean, he was at first, but then he chilled, and now he's totally copacetic."

"I'm delighted to hear that. And no, I'm not mad at

him. Far from it—" I swore to myself. Really, my mouth could not be trusted to speak around anyone. "I was having quite a pleasant conversation with Gunner last night while he translated some interesting texts for me."

"Oh, the treasure thing." She made a horrible face. "Ugh! Stomach growling! Let's go up to the castle and make Gunner feed us."

"Er . . ." I stopped, not sure if I wanted to face him again so soon. Although we'd parted amicably enough the night before, I still felt all shades of uncomfortable around him despite the fact that we did several short bits in front of the camera each day. I'd done so much lying. . . . Where was it going to end? And what would I do when he found out the truth about me? Worse, I seemed to be losing the desire to keep him at arm's length, as I'd previously decided. Weakly, I protested, "Maybe he's busy. We have to do a piece later about the possibility of treasure."

"Naw, he always fixes me breakfast. It's a bonding thing. Come on, you're hungry, aren't you?" She took my arm and tugged me forward. Reluctantly, I let my own desire to see him override my better judgment, and followed her. "I heard one of the diggers talking in the shower about a change to their schedule, and that they were going to go after some treasure that Gunner found."

"He didn't actually find a treasure; he simply translated some stones that have riddles on them that he jokingly said might be clues to a hidden treasure."

"Cool!" She charged ahead at a pace that had me almost trotting to keep up. "We can get all the details from Gunner while he makes us breakfast. He's really good at waffles. I love waffles, don't you? Especially the big fluffy kind with strawberries and clotted cream. Num!"

I hurried after her, trying to think of some excuse to give Gunner for showing up uninvited and expecting to be fed. But by the time I followed Cressy through the maze of rooms that made up the ground floor of the castle, and emerged into the small kitchen, I was breathless, clueless, and downright flabbergasted. That last bit was due to the fact that Gunner was standing at a large stove with his back to us, clad only in a pair of silk sleeping shorts.

I couldn't stop staring at the expanse of his back, noting the lovely lines of muscle in shoulders, arms, and flanks. He half turned when Cressy stomped into the room, demanding, "I hope you're making lots of something, Gunner, because we're famished."

"I was making an omelet, actually. If you'd like one, I'd be happy to—" He stopped, evidently having seen me behind Cressy. "Ah. Good morning, Lorina."

"Morning." Lord, the man had a gorgeous chest. And now that it was unclothed, I could see just how gorgeous it was. He wasn't horribly hirsute, but not naked as a plucked turkey, either. There was a lovely line of hair that led down his chest to his belly button. I made an effort to swallow, and tried to drag my eyes off all that naked flesh. "I apologize for inviting myself to breakfast, but Cressy seemed to believe that you wouldn't mind."

"Not at all." He turned back to the stove, and I willed my eyeballs back into their accustomed places. The silk shorts he wore seemed to caress his behind, a lovely, lovely behind, one that made my mouth water, my hands itch, and deep, secret parts of me tingle in a most distracting manner. "I hope you don't mind an omelet, though."

"No waffles?" Cressy rummaged around in a cupboard and pulled out a couple of plates and mugs, setting them haphazardly down on the table. "I love waffles!"

"I know you do, but you can't eat them every day. Or rather, *I* can't eat them every day." Gunner flipped the omelet out onto a plate, and thumped his way over to the refrigerator to get a bowl of eggs, then returned to the stove.

"Why not? Oh man, I need some juice bad. Juice and coffee. And maybe some fruit. Ooh, is this ham? I want some of that, too." Cressy, who had her head in the fridge, pulled out milk, orange juice, a bunch of grapes, and a packet of ham, and set them on the table before moving over to another cupboard and grabbing a package of cereal. "Juice, Lorina?"

"Coffee will be fine, thanks."

"Help yourself," Gunner said, nodding toward a coffeemaker. "Cream is in the fridge, unless Cressy has just poured it all over that bowl of cereal."

"Have you ever had cereal with cream?" Cressy asked around a mouthful of flakes. "It's awesome!"

"Oh, to have the metabolism of a seventeen-year-old," Gunner said to me with a conspiratorial smile.

I felt oddly warmed by that, and might have commented on it if my brain weren't still stuttering to itself over the fact that a nearly naked Gunner was within arm's reach. "You certainly don't look like your metabolism is falling down on the job," my mouth said wholly without my permission.

Gunner's eyebrows rose for a second before he looked down at himself, then over to me, another smile forming on his lips, this one slow and very knowing. "Your eyes are dilating again," he said in a volume that was barely audible over Cressida's humming as she crunched her way through a bowl of cereal.

"I have no doubt they are." I glanced at Cressy, and kept to myself the fact that there were a lot of other parts that were equally aware of him.

He opened his mouth to say something, but evidently

thought better of it, saying simply, "Sit down. Do you like your omelet with or without cheese?"

"With, please. Can I help you? I suspect you shouldn't be on that ankle."

"On the contrary, the cast comes off tomorrow, so I consider this practice for walking again. An omelet is entirely within my culinary purview."

"Your father," I told Cressy, sitting down with a mug of coffee, "likes to intimidate me with that plummy accent and fancy words."

Gunner laughed.

"Don't let him," Cressy said, stuffing her mouth with a handful of grapes. Thankfully, she waited until she had chewed and swallowed before adding, "We had to take a semester of psychology last year, and I can tell that he's just trying to impress you. It's because he's not the oldest son."

"Hey!" Gunner protested.

"And he's adopted."

"I am right here, you know, perfectly able to hear you."

"And probably has some weird thing where he thinks he's not as good as other people because his birth mom was African, and his dad was Serbian."

"I object to you speaking of me as if I was a mental patient. And in case you were thinking of defying me, your father, the authority figure in your life who has custody of you for the summer, let me remind you that I also hold the keys to the car that takes you to your beloved riding lessons." Gunner brought the omelet over to the table, sliding it onto a plate. He returned to the stove to continue cooking a third omelet. "Lorina, I forbid you to listen to this hell-spawn child of mine, for she knows not of what she speaks. Yes, I might have been trying to impress you, although I doubt if words like 'culinary purview' would do that, but even if that was so, I was motivated solely by the desire to have you think well of me, and not because of my heritage or the fact that I was adopted. Would anyone care for a grilled tomato?"

"Ew!" Cressy said.

Likewise, I made a face that Gunner caught.

"Americans," he said, shaking his head.

"I'm Canadian!"

"North Americans, then. If you don't mind me asking, what are your plans for today, Lorina?"

Cressy answered before I could. "I don't know what she's going to do, but I'm going to the stable to muck out, and then going to help with a class of special-needs kids who get walked around on horses. It's going to be great fun."

"I know what your plans are, hence my directing the question to Lorina." Gunner sat down with the third omelet.

I will admit to eating more than I had planned, partly because I really was hungry, but mostly as a way to divert my attention from the sight of a naked chest sitting opposite me.

"You could come with me, if you wanted, Lorina," Cressy offered around a mouthful of egg and ham. "I bet Madame Leigh wouldn't mind extra helpers, and it's for a really good cause."

"I'm sure it is, but I have work to do here," I said, averting my eyes from the play of muscle as Gunner lifted a fork to his mouth. Really, men who looked like him should be illegal. They were pure distraction, and didn't allow a person—a normal, average female person who was self-sufficient and in control of her life—to enjoy her eggs the way she should.

"Lorina?" Gunner prompted.

Unbidden, my gaze lifted, locking on him. There he was, sitting just as if he were innocent, and yet the opposite was so clearly true. A man like Gunner filled an unwary woman's head with lustful thoughts of touching him, and rubbing her breasts on his chest, and, god help us, licking all that sleek, tempting flesh.

"Lorina? Is something wrong?"

I had a mental image of what he would look like emerging from a shower, wet and warm and slippery with soapy water. My tongue seemed to grow two sizes as I imagined stroking my hands all over that delicious body.

"Earth to Lorina." A sharp blow to my shoulder abruptly recalled me from the Land of Gunner's Naked Self. Cressy poked me again on the shoulder. "You OK? You have the wildest look on your face."

"Soapy," I said, giving myself a mental shake to dissipate those erotic images. "Er ... sorry, what was the question?"

Gunner gave me an odd look, part question, and part concern. "I asked what you had planned for the day."

"Oh. Um." It took me a couple of seconds, but I managed to get my brain working again. "Well, we have the treasure piece for the camera to do this morning, and until Roger demands we do another piece, which, knowing him, will be this afternoon, I have pictures to take."

"Ah, yes. The photography." He busied himself with a piece of toast. "That's a shame. I had an idea during the night that I wanted to investigate, and I thought you might be interested in helping me pursue it."

"An idea about what?" I asked warily.

"This supposed treasure."

"I thought we were agreed that there wasn't one? And speaking of that, one of the archaeologists has already blamed me for the production company forcing all the diggers to stop their work and now search for more of those mouse stones, assuming there are any more."

"We can hardly help that—it's not our decision to make, and to be honest, once the word gets out that there may be some treasure, the glut of publicity that will descend upon our heads will appease even the sourest of diggers. Not to mention will likely increase the tourist traffic to the castle. Hmm. I may have to warn the tour guides to be prepared for an influx of visitors."

I frowned. "Yes, but publicity at what cost?"

"At the cost of valuable archaeology, of course," he said before I could answer my own rhetorical question. "Which is to be regretted, but since the decision is out of our hands, why shouldn't we make the best of the situation?"

"By cashing in on tourists?" I asked, more than a little shocked at his crass commercialism.

He shook his head. "No, that doesn't matter. Tourists will come to the castle no matter what's going on here. What I meant is that the dig means massive amounts of attention from the public, more than what would be generated by the TV show alone, so why shouldn't we use that to further the bounds of knowledge?"

I shook my head, confused. "I haven't the slightest idea what you're talking about."

"He means it'll make archaeology seem cool and exciting. Very Indiana Jones, right, Gunner?"

"Exactly so." He beamed at his daughter. "You obviously get your intelligence from my side of the family."

Cressy giggled, and rolled her eyes.

Really, I could not continue with Gunner's chest just sitting there asking to be pounced on. It was beyond human endurance. "Exposure aside—and speaking of that, would you mind terribly putting on some clothes?—what is your idea about the treasure?"

There was a distinct twinkle in his eye as he said, "Are you one of those prudish people who doesn't like to see other people's skin?"

"Not in the least. You can be stark naked if you like," I said with a dismissive sniff that hopefully disguised the fact that I was fairly drooling at the sight of all his skin at the moment.

"Ew," Cressy said, glancing over from a small TV that had been silently displaying the morning news. "Please don't, Gunner. I'd have to go to all sorts of therapy, and who knows what they'd find wrong with me? Besides, that's just icky. I don't want to see you naked."

"Thank god for small mercies," Gunner said, and, leaning back, caught a ragged sweater off a hook, and pulled it over his wonderful chest. "Better?" he asked me.

"Infinitely so," I lied, annoyed at myself for making him cover up. At the same time, I knew I wouldn't have lasted much longer without doing something I was sure to regret. "Please go on with your idea about this stupid treasure hunt."

"Well," he said, setting down his fork and leaning forward, moving the salt and pepper shakers into formation with a napkin basket and Cressy's empty glass. "Imagine this is the trench on the north side of the castle."

"Trench ten," I said, frowning as he set a pot of jam down.

"Right. And in that trench, what did we find? Cressy?"

"Beats me," Cressy answered, giving up on the TV to pop earbuds into her ears, and pulling out an MP3 player. "Unless it's jewelry or skeletons, it's beyond boring."

"I'll tell you what they found, you heathen child— they found one of those mouse stones. And that's where the courtyard of the Roman villa was."

"Big whoop."

Both Gunner and I frowned at her.

"It *is* a big deal. It means that the building they've uncovered so far really is a villa, and not a military base, as they first thought. Although . . ." I toyed with the salt-shaker. "I thought trenches two and three were the courtyard. How could the courtyard extend this far? The villa would have to have been mega-huge."

"The answer is that the courtyard that clearly runs under the north edge of the existing castle belongs to a separate villa. In other words, we have multiple villas located on a relatively small amount of land, with the temple lying between them." Gunner sat back with an air of satisfaction. "And that means that it's likely the remains of the second villa are under the castle foundation."

I tried to picture the layout in my mind. "I don't know enough about archaeology to say whether that's a reasonable conclusion or not, but since assumedly you do, I'll go along with it. There's no way that you can dig to find out whether or not that's true, though."

"We can't destroy the castle to see what's underneath it, but there may be a way around that."

"I don't see how, unless you're talking about that high-tech ground-scanning stuff. But in any case, why are you so focused on *this* villa? Two of the stones were found elsewhere."

"Don't focus on the minutiae. You have to see the big picture." He moved a few plates and cups around on the table. "Let's say that you live in the villa that's located out in the south pasture. You hear rumors of a great army sweeping toward you, and you're well aware that the nearest fort is at Tunston—that's a good thirteen miles away. The tribes that have united under Boudicca— remember, the finds we have from the villa all date to around sixty AD, which means it was the right time period for Boudicca's attempts to drive out the Romans— those tribes are destroying everything they come across."

"That would be terrifying," I said, giving a little shiver. "The people here must have felt so isolated and unprotected."

"Hence the explanation for the skeletons in the grove," Gunner said, nodding.

"Those were sad!" Cressy said, looking up from her cell phone. "All those kids in there with the women. And no men! Why weren't the men there? Where were the men? Stupid men leaving women and children alone!"

"It's likely the men were cut down defending the villas."

"OK, now I'm seriously confused," I said, trying to make sense of what Gunner was saying. "What does this attack have to do with the mouse stones, and hence the supposed treasure?"

"Let's go back to the scenario—let's say you live in the first villa."

"Gotcha. Are you going to make me a slave?"

"No, you can be the wife of the owner, if you like."

"Oooh! The one with all the clothes, and pretty jewelry, and scads of servants? I can live with being the lady of the manor."

"It's a role you're suited for." Gunner smiled at me, and I lost my thoughts for a few seconds.

Cressy looked up from her cell phone. "Can I be there, too? Only I want to be a female warrior, not a grand lady. I wouldn't mind some of the jewelry, though."

"All right," Gunner agreed, "you can be Lorina's personal guard. One who wears gold jewelry."

"Woot! I get a sword, too, right?"

"A sword and a shield. Now, the people who have escaped ahead of the advancing army tell you a tale that makes your blood run cold. Romans, all Romans—men, women, and children—are all being slaughtered by Boudicca and the Trinovantes tribe, and whoever else they gathered along the way."

"The Trinovantes sound like they sucked," Cressy said stalwartly. "I would totally defend you from them, Lorina."

"I appreciate that, although I fear that we might be outnumbered." I bit my lip and eyed Gunner. "What happened next?"

"Ideally, you women, the children, and any elderly and infirm are moved to a safe place along with your household valuables—gold and silver jewelry, and any plates that you happened to have—so that the attackers can't kill you all and walk off with your things."

"That makes sense," I said, beginning to see a light. "Get the people and the priceless stuff to safety because the house could be destroyed."

"Correct. But if the villa is caught off guard and you don't have time to get people and valuables out, then what?" He waited, obviously expecting Cressy and me to provide a reasonable answer.

"Well ..." I looked at Cressy. Her forehead was wrinkled in thought. "I guess if the attackers were marching down the Roman road to my front door, I'd run out the back with my arms stuffed full of everything I could carry."

"No, you wouldn't," Cressy said slowly. "You're the lady of the manor, aren't you? That's like the captain of a ship. You'd stay with it, and send the others away."

"Right. I like that. Less cowardly." I lifted my chin. I had enough cowardice in my real life to burden this fantasy life with it. "I'd hide the jewelry and gold plates, get the vulnerable people to a safe place, and organize the boiling-oil line to defend my home."

"Exactly. But what if you aren't sure you're going to survive the attack? What if you want to leave clues as to where you hid your valuables, so survivors can find them should you fall?"

"I'd get my brave personal guard, Cressy, to write up a

bunch of stone clues telling people who could read Latin where the valuables were, only I'd put it in riddle form because ... er ... so the Britons wouldn't get them?"

"Possibly. Remember, the riddles found so far would have been well-known to the Romans."

"Right." I turned to Cressy and waggled my fingers at her. "Write me up a few stones with some riddles telling whoever survives the attack that our stuff is hidden away safely."

Cressy pretended to write, pausing to ask, "Why am I putting a mouse on all of them?"

I looked at Gunner.

He winked at me before he answered Cressy. "Think of it as your signature. That way everyone will know that the stones are connected."

"Oh, that's good." She scribbled a mouse shape in the air, finishing with a final grand sweep of her arm. "My stones are completed! I shall scatter them hither and yon so that people will find them and dig up the jewelry we buried out behind the cesspit."

"I wouldn't think such a location would be a likely hiding spot." A little line appeared between Gunner's brows. "Sadly, with no help at hand, the attackers would likely have easily overcome the villa's defenses made up of your male family members, and any male servants and slaves, and set fire to everything."

I shivered again, and rubbed my arms. "And Cressy and me and the rest of my household?"

His eyes were grave. "Unfortunately, you were taken to the temple and sacrificed."

"And people said the Romans were brutal." Cressy scrunched up her shoulders. "Killing people who couldn't fight back is despicable."

"The Romans were just as brutal," Gunner told her. "What they did to the native Britons would give you nightmares, or at least it did me when I learned about it at school, so I won't go into it, but if you remember anything, remember that brutality isn't limited by nationality."

Cressy made a face.

For the first time since the subject had been broached, a little tingle of excitement rippled down my arms. "So those mouse stones *could* actually point to some treasure. How do we know the survivors didn't dig it up after the attack?"

"It's not likely that any Romans survived," Gunner said gently. "Think of the walls."

"Burned," I said. "And a lot of the pottery as well. The mosaic wasn't burned, though."

"No, but that was most likely to have been in a bathhouse in a pool, so it was somewhat protected."

I looked at him with a smidgen of disbelief. "You realize what you're saying, right? The idea of a real treasure is just . . . unbelievable."

"It's certainly not highly probable, but not impossible." Gunner rubbed his chin thoughtfully. "You know, my father used to curse the fact that so many plows were ruined in the fields to the south that he had to use them as pasture, instead. That makes me think that the walls of the villas ran from north to south, which is the orientation of the road that Daria found."

"So the two villas were definitely connected?" I asked.

"They could well be. Possibly siblings built near each other, for instance."

"And put a temple between them so it would give them both good luck," I said, picturing it in my mind.

"It doesn't sound like it did them much good," Cressy pointed out, and I had to agree with her.

"It would be interesting to find out if the other villa was burned, too. Or do you think—" I gasped as a sudden thought hit me.

"Hmm?" Gunner was still looking thoughtful. I smacked him on the hand with a spoon.

"If I've got a horde of advancing barbarians on my doorstep, and I'm trying to hide the good silver, where's the first place that I'd put it?"

His brows rose slightly. "That, I believe, is the point of all these ruminations—"

"No," I interrupted. "Think. If people are coming to attack me at my house, I'm going to have my trusty handmaiden—"

"Personal bodyguard," Cressy corrected me.

"—trusty bodyguard, who looks like a lovely handmaiden in order to fool people into thinking she's a wuss, take my valuables, and run quick like a bunny to my brother's villa that's just down the road."

"But why wouldn't you run there yourself so that you'd be safe?" Cressy asked.

"Because," I said, smiling at my own cleverness. "The people who lived in both villas would gather together at our house, because there's safety in numbers, and it's better to defend one house with a full contingent of men than try to split them between two. So if the valuables were hidden in the second villa, say, buried in the cellar or whatever Romans had, then even if they burned down Villa Number Two, our stash would still be safe from marauders."

"With the mouse stones telling people who come to the first villa to look at the second?" Cressida asked. "But what about the stone that was found next to the castle? That's in the second villa, isn't it?"

"Yes," I said thoughtfully, then gave a little half shrug. "Perhaps that stone was intended to tell the seeker that they'd found the right place. Or it's a final clue as to exactly where in that villa the treasure was placed."

Cressy beamed at me. "Nice going, Lorina. I'd totes fight to the death for that sort of a lady overlord."

"Thank you," I said modestly.

"And that," Gunner said with a smile of his own, one that seemed to suddenly strip all the air out of the room, "is why I think we should open up more trenches here."

"But we have no idea where to look. For all we know, the treasure, assuming there is one, could be deep under the castle, and we can't get there."

"Can't we?" The corners of his lips twitched. I had a horrible time trying to drag my eyes from his mouth. Damn, the man had nice lips. Not too full, but with nice curves that were just meant for nibbling. I was just dwelling on that thought when those lips curved, his eyes lighting.

"I'm willing to bet your brother would have a problem with you taking down his family home in order to see if anything's beneath it."

"Ah, but if I told you that at least half the cellar has a dirt floor, then would you be giving me that jaded look, or would you leap to your feet and shout with enthusiasm, 'Gunner Ainslie, you are the smartest man I know, and I would be happy to dig with you in the cellar in order to find the treasure before that bastard Thompson'? Following which you might want to kiss me, although if the look you're now giving me is accurate, I suspect that would be off the table."

I couldn't help but laugh at his statement, closing my lips on the protest that I'd take anything so wonderful out of the realm of possibilities. "It's an interesting idea, to be sure, but I repeat my objection that we wouldn't know where to dig. Wouldn't it be smarter to see if we can find all of the stones so that we could figure it out rather than relying solely on speculation?"

"My liege lady speaks wisely," Cressy told her father. "And since you're just the captain of the guard, you have to do what we say."

"Oh, it's like that, is it?" Gunner asked.

"Yup." Cressy nodded.

He thought for a moment. "I rather like the idea of being the captain. Very well, I have considered your objection, and have two of my own to mention. The first is that we have no idea how many clue stones there were, and it's unrealistic to dig up every square foot of the grounds in order to find any more."

"Damn," I said, mulling that over. "He's got a point, trusty guard."

"I hate it when he's right."

"What's the second objection?" I asked Gunner, wondering if the lady of the villa secretly fancied the captain of her guard, and if so, whether she ever had to have breakfast with him when she knew he was clad only in tiny little silk shorts and a repulsive sweater.

"Even if we had all the stones, and we could decipher the riddles properly—and honestly, I don't think that would be too difficult—then we wouldn't know what the answers pointed to. The landscape has changed quite a bit in the last two thousand years, and even if there has been a building on this location for most of that time, any pointers to a specific room, or even a tree or a rock, would be useless."

"Hell," I said at the same time Cressy said, "Balls! There goes all the excitement. Now we're back to just being slaughtered in the grove. I hope I took down at least a couple of those troglodyte dudes before they hacked us to bits and pieces."

"Trinovantes," Gunner said absently. He gave me a questioning look. "I thought if you and Cressy would like, we could make a little foray into the cellar, just to take a look at what we could find."

"Not me," Cressy said. "I get claustrophobic down there. Besides, Madame is counting on me. Ack! The time!" She leaped to her feet. "Are you taking me to the stables, or is Gran?"

"I believe your grandmother offered to take you there today, since she wanted to do some shopping in town. You know where I keep the car keys? You can take them down to her with her tea."

"Gran never has breakfast," Cressy told me, grabbing a thermos that Gunner had evidently already prepared. "She says a cup of tea is all she needs. Laters!"

"Have fun," Gunner said, calling after her, "and mind you do what the riding master says, and don't get overly enthusiastic with the children."

Cressy waved and dashed out of the room, leaving me feeling once again like I'd been passed over by some sort of a benign whirlwind.

One that left me alone with the most tempting man I'd ever met . . . who stood poised to destroy everything I'd worked for.

Chapter 13

I couldn't help but smile when Cressy whirlwinded her way out of the room, shaking my head a little. "I don't think that even in my top form I had as much energy as she does."

"She's certainly a force to behold, isn't she?" Gunner said with no little pride. "The shotgun-bearing years aside, I can't wait for her to make her mark on the world."

"I'm sure the world will never be the same." I looked away from him, irrationally sad at the sight of that wonderful flesh covered up. I began to think up a plan whereby he had to get out of the chair, and allow me to ogle his behind and legs. "Do you think it would be worthwhile to dig around randomly in the cellar? I mean, we would have no clue where we were down there in relationship to the rest of the Roman structure."

"It's as much a gamble as anything else, really. The trench next to the north wall of the castle shows there's a building in the immediate area, so it's likely under the castle." Much to my delight, he collected the empty plates and, rising, clunked his way over to the sink. "My feeling is that we won't know until we look."

"True, but it still seems very unlikely we'll find anything." I tapped a spoon against my chin, idly watching the way his butt cheeks flexed as he rinsed dishes and loaded them into a dishwasher. Good manners dictated that I should have offered to help so that he could get off his foot, but there was no way in hell I was going to miss this show. "And what will Roger say about it? He's liable to go ballistic."

"That's why I want to take a look down there first. You know how excited he gets over the sketchiest of ideas."

"I'm fine with taking a peek at the cellar, but I'd like to point out that you have your foot in a cast, Cressy doesn't want to help, and I don't know the proper way to open a trench so that I don't destroy stuff."

"I told you before that I'd be happy to teach you whatever you wanted to know." Gunner grinned as he dried his hands.

I raised my eyebrows at him, but before I could say anything in response, he said more seriously, "That's a good point, actually. I'd like the satisfaction of opening up any trenches we put in the cellars ourselves, but I'm afraid my dig work is limited. Unless we could persuade one of the diggers to covertly do a little work for us, I'm afraid we are going to be very limited in digging possibilities."

"Daria!" I said, pointing the spoon at him. He *tsk*ed, and held out a hand for it. I got to my feet and slowly walked it over to him, my mind turning over this new idea. "I bet she'd open a trench for us. She's fairly furious about Roger's plan to drop everything and focus on what she considers nonexistent treasure. She said she was thinking of going home, so I bet she'd be interested in helping us instead. As long as we made it clear that we wanted to do real archaeology, and not just find the treasure for publicity reasons."

Gunner made an odd face, tried to reach behind himself, and, with a disgusted word, pulled the sweater over his head. "This damned thing is too itchy to stand."

My entire body gave a cheer of happiness. My breasts in particular were pleased about the state of affairs. I suspected that fact was all too obvious to Gunner, because as he turned from the dishwasher to take the spoon from my outstretched hand, he suddenly froze, too.

"Oh," I said, unable to think of a single thing to say that didn't involve the words *want*, *chest*, and *lick*. "Uh . . ."

"You're dilating again," he said, but his voice was breathless and not at all its usual state of smooth.

I glanced quickly at his eyes. "So are you."

"And my nipples are—" He gestured toward his chest.

"Yes," I said, my gaze now focused on his two little brown nipples, which resided pertly in the soft bed of his chest hair. "They're really cute. Do you . . . uh . . . like people touching your nipples?"

"I'd like you to," he said, his nostrils flaring in a manner that I would have found silly in anyone else, but on him seemed as sexy as all get-out.

At that point, my brain seemed to shut down. That's all I can say in explanation for what happened, because one minute I was standing there admiring his nostrils, and the next I had both hands on his bare chest, and was letting my fingers go wild.

"Lorina," he said in a strangled voice.

"Oooh," I breathed, my fingers tingling as they stroked his chest. "I like your nipples a lot. And your muscles. And your chest hair is really soft. Do you mind if I do this?" I bent to twirl my tongue around one of his nipples.

He moaned, and gave a little shiver. "Not at all. Feel free to do that whenever the mood strikes you."

"Well, I should probably do the other one. I wouldn't want it to get an inferiority complex," I murmured into his chest as I blew my breath in a trail over to the other nipple. I gave it a friendly lick as well, seriously considering the wisdom of asking him if he'd lie down so I could frolic on his chest more easily.

"Would you mind . . ." His voice cracked. He cleared it, and tried again. His hands were at breast height, his fingers making an all-too-obvious gesture. "Would you mind if I had a go at yours?"

"My breasts would be pleased to meet your hands," I said primly, but only because my mind was, at that moment, occupied with the fact that my fingers were sliding down the slippery hair trail toward his belly button. Dear lord, I'd never been as aroused as I was at that moment, and for a second or two, I marveled that I could have such an overwhelming desire for any man, but with Gunner, it all seemed so right.

His hands were warm on my breasts, making me pause so I could arch my back and moan, his mouth close to mine, but not close enough. I de-arched a bit, and allowed my nose to bump his. At that moment, I wanted to kiss him more than anything in the world.

"You have very agreeable breasts," he murmured, his lips brushing mine as he spoke.

"I like your mouth," I answered, downright babbling at that point.

His lips teased mine. "Such compliments should be paid back in kind."

I gave up trying to will him into kissing me, and

grabbed his hair with both hands, pulling his mouth exactly where I wanted it.

He tasted sweet like the jam that he'd put on his toast, and hot and wonderfully masculine. I reveled in the way his tongue tasted on my lips, teasing the edges of them, making them part on short little gasps of sheer pleasure. And when he pulled me tightly against his body, his hands cupping my behind while his tongue did a wicked dance around mine, I just gave up thinking altogether and became one giant ball of feeling.

That lasted until I realized that I wasn't able to breathe, and slowly, reluctantly dragged my mouth from his.

I stared at him, panting.

He stared back, his breath decidedly ragged. It took a good minute before he recovered enough to speak. "That was a hell of a kiss."

"It was," I agreed, more than a little bemused. "Better than normal. You are quite good at kissing."

"I don't want to take all of the credit," he said modestly. "You put in your fair share of the work. Would it be rude of me to point out that you have a shirt on, and I don't?"

He bent over my cleavage, his thumbs rubbing gently back and forth across my nipples, making me want to do a little dance of anticipation.

My breath hitched in my throat. "That doesn't seem fair, me having a shirt when you have none."

"No, it doesn't. I'd like to take yours off of your tantalizing self."

I didn't even think about it, or the fact that I was standing in Gunner's kitchen, my hands on his chest, my tongue demanding that I taste him again, and my breasts yelling all sorts of things about needing Gunner's mouth on them. "Fine with me. Would you mind if I touched you in other places than your chest?"

His eyes crossed for a few seconds before he shook his head, and said, "You have carte blanche to touch me wherever you like."

"But you just shook your head."

He nodded. "No, I didn't. My head lies. Just keep doing what you're doing, only without your shirt. Could you move your arm this way?"

"No. I'm using it."

"Just for a few seconds, then I'll return it so you can continue to drive me insane by stroking my chest."

I obliged, then slid my hands around his sides, and down to his silk-covered behind. Cool air made me shiver as he peeled off my shirt, his hands immediately on my breasts, his mouth caressing the tops of them in a way that just about made my knees buckle. "I have a bra on," I said helpfully.

"I noticed. Might I remove that, too?"

"Gunner," I said sternly, or as sternly as a person could while she stood in a man's castle, her hands full of his ass. "You've got your hands on my boobs, and your tongue down my cleavage. At this point if I'm not yelling for the police, you can probably take it for granted that you have my consent to remove my bra."

"I like to make sure," he said, pulling his head out of my breasts for a moment. "Some women have limits."

I squeezed his cheeks. "I don't seem to be one of them. Also, too much talking, and not enough mouth on breast."

"You must be one of those women who likes to dominate men. Would you think less of me if I told you that I'm not particularly turned on by that?"

My fingers lovingly traced his thick gluteus muscles. I thought for a moment, then slid my hands inside his shorts. It seemed to me that his naked skin was even softer than the silk shorts, if such a thing were possible. "And you are one of those guys who likes to talk a lot during sexy times, aren't you? Luckily, I don't mind that. And I'm not trying to dominate you; I'm simply letting you know what I want. Strong women do that."

The grin he flashed at me was lopsided, but one hundred percent adorable. "You can let me know exactly what you want, my fair little squab. Now, about this bra of yours that is so cruelly hiding your breasts from me—"

"I can't find the car keys on your dresser, Gun—holy hair balls with big juicy spit on it!" Cressy stood in the doorway, her mouth open, her eyes huge.

I gave a little shriek and, in the best nearly half-naked-woman manner, leaped behind Gunner.

Cressy screamed at my shriek, and slapped her hands over her eyes. "Oh my god. OH MY GOD! I didn't just see you with your hands down Gunner's shorts, did I? I did! Oh my god, I'm blighted for the rest of my life despite the fact that I like you, and I wouldn't mind if you hooked up with Gunner, because he's probably really lonely and could do with a nice woman to make him stop dating all those trashy women that my mom says he dates, but clearly doesn't love, because if he did, one of them would be here right now with *her* hands down his shorts, and not you, but you are here, and you were copping a grope, not to mention the fact that he had his hands on your boobs, and holy toasted cheese, how am I ever going to get *that* image out of my brain?"

I did a horrified little dance behind Gunner, sending one arm out to snatch up my shirt from where it had fallen, hastily putting it back on and buttoning it.

Gunner, on the other hand, didn't seem to be bothered in the least. He simply moved a chair to the side so that it stood between him and Cressy. "If the keys aren't in my room, then check the sitting room. And no, I'm not going to buy you a horse to cure you of the vision of Lorina embracing me."

I pinched his butt.

"What?" he asked, looking around at me.

I made mean, but meaningful, eyes at him.

"Oh." He turned back to Cressy. "That should be the vision of me embracing Lorina."

I peered out around his shoulder. Cressy had stopped screaming and hiding her eyes, and was now glaring at her father, her hands on her hips, and her brow mutinous. "But I'm *traumatized*!"

"You are not."

"I *could* be! You could have been *naked*! Lorina could have been naked! You guys could have been *doing it*!"

"But I'm not, she's not, and we weren't, so no horse. And I'm sure I needn't point out that what I do in the *privacy* of my own home—you'll note I stress the word— is no one's business but my own. And Lorina's."

"Fine!" Cressy slapped her hands on her legs and stomped loudly out the door. "But when I'm so horrified about sex because I saw you guys hooking up in the kitchen that I can't stay married longer than six months at a time, I know who I'm going to blame!"

"If that's the sort of grammar they teach at your school, then you may have other issues to address," he called after her.

I waited until she was gone before emerging from behind Gunner, my cheeks hot with embarrassment.

"You look delightful," he told me. "Rosy-cheeked and bright-eyed, but I have a suspicion you're going to rail at me for putting you in such a position. Should I apologize now, or wait for the railing to be over and do so then?"

"I'm not going to rail. At least, not at you. What the hell was I thinking?" I grabbed up my jacket, realized that it was Gunner's discarded sweater, and dropped it, hurrying over to where my jacket lay over the back of a chair. "I'm just—seriously, Gunner, at what point did my brain flat-out stop and decide to throw what remains of my plan overboard just so I could kiss you, and lick your nipples, and stroke your chest, and smell you, and want to do all sorts of things to you with a small pastry brush and some lemon pudding?"

He looked thoughtful. "That sounds sticky. What plan?"

I stared at him in dismay. "I did it again. Or rather, my mouth did. I can't take it anywhere anymore." I thought for a moment, then pointed at him, holding the jacket tight to my chest with one hand. "It's your fault!"

"It is?"

He did the head-tilt thing that just made me want to pounce on him again.

"Oh, no!" I backed away, holding the jacket out like it was a shield. "You're not going to sway me anymore—do you hear me? My mind may be susceptible, but my . . . er . . . well, other parts of me aren't. Dammit, that was a bad analogy."

"Metaphor, I believe."

"Whatever!" I struck a dramatic pose at the door. "I refuse to be tempted by you any longer. You got that? No more touching your really fabulous butt. And your chest. And your back, not that I ever imagined a man's back could be sexy, but I'm damned if you didn't pull it off. In other words, I don't, under any circumstances, want to kiss you anymore. In fact, if I never see you again, I'll be a happy, happy woman!"

He just head-tilted a little more and said, "So I'll see you out at Daria's trench to talk to her about digging in the cellar when?"

"Half an hour!" I snarled, and, turning on my heel, marched off, swearing at my own weakness.

Chapter 14

The day did not proceed as Gunner had hoped it would. First there was a second shower of the day that was necessitated by Lorina's attentions in the kitchen. The erection he sported simply refused to go away until he doused his body in cold water, and even then it was a near thing.

The second flaw in his morning was that his continuing desire to get Lorina alone was consistently thwarted. She had attached herself to the archaeologist named Daria, and clearly was not falling in with his suggestion that they go to a quiet place where he could kiss her senseless.

In fact, when Gunner finally found her with Daria at one of the trenches in the pasture, Lorina looked anything but interested in resuming their previous actions.

"Daria agreed to help us with the cellar. She said she'd do the hard digging for you, and teach me how to start a trench without potentially harming stuff beneath the surface," Lorina explained with a pointed look that Gunner didn't have the least trouble deciphering. She obviously did not want to risk being alone with him, and strode off quickly to her tent when Daria told her to go pick up a spare shovel and her digging kit.

Daria watched her leave before turning to Gunner. "I'm not one to push myself in where I'm not wanted, but if you have your eye on Lorina, you should know that she's been spending time with Paul Thompson. The odd thing is, from what I can see, she doesn't seem to be enjoying herself with him." Daria's eyes narrowed on him. "She doesn't seem to be awfully happy to see you, either."

"No, she doesn't." Gunner wasn't one to tell tales, but he did want to find out why Lorina was pretending to be something she wasn't. "I take it you've been keeping track of her?"

"Ha!" Daria gave a harsh bark of laughter. "Not out of interest, if that's what you're worried about. I have a husband and two children running amok at home."

"Lorina is exceptionally attractive," Gunner pointed out. "You wouldn't be the first person to fall sway to her charms, I'm sure."

"Attractive?" Daria blinked a couple of times. "I suppose some men like overly curvy women like that, and with hair that's all over the place, but attractive? I don't think you could call her that."

"I think she is," Gunner said quickly, feeling defensive on Lorina's behalf. He kept to himself the thought that he'd rather have an armful of the lovely round form of Lorina than any of his previous model girlfriends.

"Beauty, eye of the beholder, et cetera," Daria said dismissively. "Regardless of what you think of her appearance, I assure you that my interest is purely one of

self-preservation. Keeping your enemies closer and all
that, you know."

"Thompson?" he guessed after eliminating Lorina as
a possible enemy. No one in his or her right mind could
consider someone as sweet as Lorina an enemy. Even
the fact that she had outright lied to him, and was deceiving everyone present, couldn't convince him that she
was enemy fodder.

"He's as capricious as the wind, and twice as unreli-
able," Daria said with a tightening of her lips. "He's also
known to fire people at the slightest whim."

"Thompson can't fire her—she's here by permission
of the TV studio."

"True, but he can put pressure on them to rescind that
permission, and since the studio wants to keep him
happy, they might listen to him. I've seen him drive other
people he didn't like from a dig site, so I know he can do
it. That's why I thought it was best to keep an eye on
things." She gave him a sidelong look. "Not that I understand her preference, mind you."

"Thank you." He made a wry face. "At least I hope
that was a compliment."

"It was." She started packing up her tools. "Besides, I
like Lorina. I just don't know why she's spending so
much time with Paul."

He was oddly relieved that others didn't understand
Lorina's preference, either, but what concerned him
most was how quickly he had fallen victim to her despite
the fact that she continued to maintain a deception. And
yet there was an obvious attraction between them that
he didn't seem able to resist. It was puzzling and frustrat-
ing and gloriously wonderful all at the same time.

"You know that Roger is going to have a fit when he
hears you are digging somewhere hard to film."

"We're just going to take a quick look to see if it's worth bringing the crew into the cellar."

She tucked away the last of her implements. "I have to admit, I am looking forward to doing a little digging, even if it does have the hint of a covert treasure hunt about it."

"Covert treasure hunt? What covert treasure hunt is this?"

Gunner slumped on his scooter for a moment before straightening up and looking over his shoulder at Roger, who stood with a look that was equal parts outraged and interested. "You have another spot to dig?"

Daria gave Gunner an apologetic look. "Sorry."

"That's all right," Gunner said, swiveling around on the seat to explain. "We would have told you the second we found anything promising, Roger."

"What's promising? Where?" Roger demanded to know.

"Gunner and Lorina think that they've found a connection between the villa here and the courtyard at the castle." Daria briefly went over the scenario that Lorina had shared.

With each word, Roger grew more and more excited, finally bursting out, "What a fabulous idea! I love it! It's brilliant! Viewers are going to go crazy with excitement watching the dig in the actual castle itself."

"It's all just speculation," Gunner felt obligated to point out. "Drawn from the admittedly tenuous evidence of the courtyard along the north side of the castle. There may be nothing in the cellar, nothing at all."

Roger brushed away such doubts. "Results would be fabulous, but even if we don't find anything, the whole idea of a treasure hunt will keep viewers glued to each episode. Now, let's see. . . . We can send one crew down to the cellars to film the digging there. That'll mean the two other film teams will have to cover both trenches in the field, but that can't be helped. Digging inside an actual castle is unprecedented! The ratings will skyrocket! Where exactly is this other courtyard, Daria?"

Gunner hobbled his way over to where Daria pulled out several printouts that showed the results of the geophysical surveys. She pointed to one. "We think it's there."

"And do we have any data on the cellars? No, of course we don't. Let me get the geophys team on it." Roger pulled out his walkie-talkie. "Terry, come in. We need your team to go to the castle to survey the cellars, stat."

A static-laden voice demanded to know what the hell Roger was talking about.

"The cellars—we need them surveyed. We're going to put in some test pits there to see if the treasure is there. There's a second villa, and it makes sense that the treasure was put there when the first one was attacked."

More staticky demands of explanations.

"No, no, it all makes sense. That's what those stones were pointing to—don't you see?"

Gunner was mildly irritated, but resigned himself to the film crew's involvement.

"I can't help it if you don't get it," Roger snapped into the radio at Terry's protestations of confusion. "The clues were a roof tile, a ship, and a thief. Clearly they meant to say that thieves were coming, so the treasure would be hidden on a roof in a ship of some sort. Probably a wind gauge or decorative bit of statuary, or something of that ilk."

"A ship statue on a roof?" Daria asked, shaking her head. "I've never heard of such a thing on a Roman villa."

"Nor I," Gunner said, smiling a little at the spate of

profanity emerging from the radio at Roger's explanation.

"Just do as I ask," Roger said, clearly losing his temper. "We'll want the full treatment. Get your team in there pronto so we can get the diggers in and find the treasure."

A staticky, but obscene, suggestion was the result of that request.

Roger looked at Gunner. "Do you think we could get the backhoe in by some means?"

"No," Gunner said acidly. "I refuse to knock down a wall for this. In fact, my brother will probably have my hide for letting you people in to dig up the cellar, but since that part isn't being used, I feel he won't mind too terribly so long as no damage is done to the castle and everything is set to rights afterward."

"Oh, we won't do any damage—that I promise you." Roger spoke briefly into the radio. "No backhoe, Terry. Now, then, Daria, where do you think we should put the first trenches?"

Daria gave a little shrug. "It's difficult to say, since I haven't been in the cellars to know their layout, but assuming that they reach to the north, I'd say against the northernmost wall first, and work our way outward from there."

Gunner thought for a few seconds. "That section of the castle is made up of a lot of corners and angles, but I bet you could open a trench across the northmost corner."

"Excellent," Roger said, and continued on excitedly about his plans for filming, and how digging would proceed, and what sort of ratings the show was sure to get.

Lorina returned with a shovel, a pair of gloves, and her dig kit. Strapped across her delectable torso was a camera case. She didn't meet Gunner's eyes, but he couldn't help but (delightedly) notice that her color rose when he shuffled over to stand next to her.

While Roger was continuing his speculation, Gunner leaned toward Lorina and said softly in her ear, "If I was responsible for creating a book that documents this project, my camera would never leave my hand."

She froze, shot a startled look his way, and hurriedly moved forward to stand with Daria. The latter was now explaining to Roger her plan for laying out trenches given what Gunner had just explained about the layout of the cellar.

Gunner forgot for a few minutes his desire to corner Lorina and not only have a few words with her about this plan she had accidentally mentioned in the heat of lust, but also more fully explore said lustful passions. "That sounds like it would work. I don't remember the layout of the cellars exactly, but it should be possible to drop pits at various points along the northern walls to see if we find any archaeology. If you can do the hard work, Daria, I'll be able to get into the trench and—"

"Ah, excellent, everyone is here."

Gunner ground his teeth at the sounds of Thompson's voice. The man himself strode confidently over to them, trailed by Tabby and Matt, and a handful of diggers.

"I understand from Terry that we have had an exciting development, and we're going to be working in the castle itself. I had wanted to do that the second we found the courtyard against the castle, but assumed we'd never get permission. I'm delighted to know that, about this, I was incorrect." Paul, without a single glance his way, began giving orders to the diggers, sending them and the film crew to the castle. "Oh, Ainslie, is that you? Excellent. You can show the diggers how to get into the cellar. Daria, you can take over my trench out in the pasture.

Roger, you may want the film teams in the cellar for maximum coverage. Lorina . . . ah. Yes. You're here, too."

Lorina straightened her shoulders, her chin rising as Thompson gave her a questioning once-over. "I am, and I'll be happy to get some shots of you digging in the cellar."

"Er . . . yes, that would be fine." Thompson looked anything but thrilled by the idea, but manfully proceeded with directing everyone to their tasks.

"Here, you can have these, since Paul's selfishly taken the best for himself," Daria told Lorina, and handed her another shovel and a small pickax. "You'll need them if you can convince he-who-shall-be-obeyed to let you dig."

"Daria, I'm so sorry—"

"Don't worry about it. Karma will out, I've always found." Daria turned and walked stiffly toward the fields.

With a last uncertain glance toward Gunner, Lorina hefted the two shovels, the pickax, and her dig kit, and started off toward the castle.

Paul, after a brief confab with Roger, clapped his hands and ordered the rest of the team to their duties. He spied Gunner and frowned. "Are you still here?"

"Obviously so," Gunner replied, calmly regaining his seat on the scooter.

"My people have gone to the castle. They'll need you to show them how to access the cellar, and I'm sure you won't wish to delay filming, so if you could just . . ." He made shooing motions.

"I wouldn't dream of doing anything so heinous as delaying the production," Gunner said, and gunning the motor of the scooter as much as possible—which really did nothing other than make the battery hum—he zoomed off, making sure to head straight for Lorina.

She didn't realize his intention until the scooter was

almost upon her, at which point Gunner reached out and simply scooped her up, pulling her, the tools, and the dig bag onto his lap.

"Ack!" she shrieked, struggling enough that one of the shovel handles smacked him sharply on the chin. "What are you doing?"

"Seeing stars right now, although that's clearing," he admitted, grabbing the shovel handles as she squirmed around to see him. "Ow. Could you move that bag? I may wish to have other children in the future, and the edge of the dig bag is coming close to ensuring that possibility doesn't exist."

Lorina's gaze turned to his crotch, which instantly hardened. Her cheeks turned dusky red as she hurriedly shifted the dig bag onto her lap. "I'm sorry. Did I hurt anything?"

"Nothing that can't be mended by some dedicated attention later," he said with a lascivious waggle of his eyebrows.

A little smile started to curl her lips, those deliciously pink lips, but sadly, it faded as she stiffened her back, and turned around to face front. "It's your own fault if you got hit with the shovel. What did you think you were doing, anyway, grabbing me like that?"

"I was thinking something along the lines of a dashing knight scooping up a fair maiden in distress and setting her atop his mighty stallion, actually. It was a very romantic picture in my head, although I admit I failed to factor in the shovels. Would you mind not flailing them about? That was my shin you just slammed one against."

"Sorry. Stop the scooter, Gunner. Two people can't ride on it."

"On the contrary, I believe we are proving that they can."

"Do you hear that noise?"

"Yes."

"That is the noise of a pissed-off scooter. One that is about to burst its gussets, or whatever scooters have. Let me off."

"No." His arm tightened around her waist, pulling her back against his chest. He breathed in the smell of her hair. It was floral-scented, just like the rest of her. "Or rather, yes, I will, but on one condition."

"I am not having sex with you!" she squawked loudly, then shuffled the dig bag so that she could slap a hand over her mouth for a few seconds. When she removed it, she glared over her shoulder at him as best she could. "Goddamn it, Gunner! You're making my mouth do this!"

He did a little more eyebrow waggling at her, and waited.

"I really object to you encouraging me to make a fool of myself." She took a deep breath, which he felt down to this toenails, and then asked, "What condition?"

His arm tightened again as the scooter lurched over a bump and they hit the gravel path that led toward the front of the house. "That you tell me what this secret plan is that you are harboring. It has something to do with Thompson—that much I know—but just why you are pretending that he fascinates you is beyond my understanding. Care to enlighten me?"

"No," she said, and tried to climb off his lap, even though they were still moving.

He held her firmly against him.

"Dammit, Gunner!" She pinched his wrist. "Stop flexing your biceps at me, and don't tell me you aren't, because I can feel it against my waist."

"Why are you pretending to be a photographer?"

She stopped squirming. It took a minute before she asked, "What makes you think I'm not one?"

"Grant me the basic intelligence to recognize a fellow professional from an amateur."

"Perhaps I don't have the level of professionalism that you have, but that doesn't mean I'm not a legitimate photographer." She stopped, swore softly under her breath, but not softly enough.

"My sweet, you may be many things—fascinating, enticing, deliciously made, and intriguing in ways I've never before encountered—but a photographer you are not."

She stayed stiff for the count of twenty, then slumped back against him. "I knew it. I just knew my mouth would give me away. What did I say? I was careful not to mention anything about those f-stop things you grilled me about the first day."

"Actually, it wasn't what you said—although the combination of f-stop and lenses that you mentioned would have been all but useless—but it's your actions that gave you away. No photographer worth her salt would let the camera stray from her side. When I'm on a job, I live and breathe through my camera."

He stopped when she turned on his lap, swinging her legs over his, careful to shift the shovels to the other side so they wouldn't hit him on the face again. "Now what? Are you going to tell Roger and Paul?"

He tempted to force her to tell him the truth about what she was up to by using the threat of disclosing her ignorance about photography to Roger, but that thought just irritated him. "I've never had to force a woman to do anything, and I'm not about to start now," he told her.

She looked a bit confused.

"Sorry. I was having an argument with myself."

"Oh. I have those all the time. It's the ones I lose that really piss me off, like this morning in the kitchen." She blushed again, but this time, it made her eyes sparkle. "You should have heard me yell at myself for giving in to the lure of your chest. And butt. And legs and back and, really, all of you. Can I say right now that I dislike intensely the fact that you're so sexy you make me forget my common sense?"

"I'd apologize, but there's not a lot I can do about my appearance."

"Oh, like hell there isn't." She now faced him squarely with a jaded expression. "I bet you love how you look, don't you? You like having women go gaga over you when you parade about in nothing but a pair of damned near indecent shorts. And really, Gunner, what sort of man stands around in nothing but a scrap of silk while a seventeen-year-old girl is in the same room?"

"A man who is the girl's father, and who made sure the sight of appropriate body parts was blocked by a chair when a certain someone aroused him to the point where it would have been noticeable to said daughter."

"Hmph. I notice you don't deny liking being so gorgeous that women like Sue follow you around just about drooling."

He gave a one-shoulder shrug. "That's like my saying that I object to you being charming. It's not something you can change any more than I can."

"Hey!" She elbowed him. "A polite man would have made sure he complimented my appearance. He wouldn't have gone straight for the personality thing, which every woman knows means he finds her physically repugnant."

He released her long enough to take her free hand and place it on his groin. "Do I feel to you like I find you repugnant?"

"Oh. Oh my. You're very . . . mercy."

He gritted his teeth against the sensation of her hand stroking his erection through the tight confines of his jeans, and got the scooter moving again. "Yes, I am very."

"Wow. I mean, not wow as in holy hell, but you're

hung like a horse. You don't feel porn-star huge or anything. You're just very . . . there."

He tried to rustle up a glare, but the feeling of her
fingers on his fly drove all other thoughts from his head.
"Are you impugning my manhood, madam?"

She giggled. "Not in the least. After all, my first word
was 'wow.' You can take that as a badge of honor."

"I accept your apology." He had to take her hand off
him before he got pushed beyond bearing. "And I will
reciprocate at a later date. You will see that as we *are* at
the library door, the scooter did indeed handle two people just fine."

"Uh-huh. Is that why there's smoke coming out of the
battery?" She got herself and her assortment of items off
his legs, and nodded toward the back of the scooter.

A little puff of pale smoke emerged, accompanied by
the smell of burning electrics.

"Balls," he swore.

"Yes, those are very nice, too, but despite what my
no-doubt-dilated pupils and tingly girl parts say—despite
that, I do not have any interest in them."

He blinked a couple of times just as if that would help
him think. "Interest in what?"

"Your balls."

"Why not? They would like to get to know you better.
And your tingly woman bits."

"The term is 'girl parts,' or, at worst, 'lady garden.'
'Woman bits' sounds like female-shaped pieces of bacon
that you'd shake onto a salad."

"Strangely specific, and yet, your whimsy in no way
makes you less endearing," he told her, getting off the
scooter. "Shall we plan to introduce my highly attractive
balls to your tingly girl parts later?"

"No. And I never said your balls were attractive. On

the contrary, it's been my experience that testicles are seldom attractive. Functional, I assume, but attractive? Not so much."

"There you are!" Sue hurried up to them, her eyes locked on Gunner. "I heard we were doing some exciting things in the castle. Well!" She stopped next to him, and looked at Lorina, then back to Gunner. "Am I interrupting an important discussion?"

"Not really," Lorina answered before Gunner could. She hefted her shovels and the dig bag. "I was telling Gunner that I think his balls aren't pretty. Feel free to feed his ego by telling him they are the best balls in the world." With that, she turned and stalked through the library French doors.

Sue's mouth formed an O as she looked at Gunner.

"She'll be back," Gunner told her, nodding toward the French doors.

"She will? But—"

Lorina reappeared in the door at that moment, her nostrils flaring in annoyance. "I don't know how to get to the cellar."

He smiled and, with a cane in one hand, grabbed the pickax that Lorina had left for him, swinging it over his shoulder and shooing her back into the castle. "Forward, my little pack mule. Take a left at the hall, go past the sign that says 'Private,' and through the second door on the right."

"Do I want to know why you two were discussing your testicles?" Sue asked, trotting after them. "Not that I'm opposed to making a judgment on them . . ."

Gunner tuned out Sue's prattle and instead gathered together the waiting diggers to follow him down into the oldest part of the castle.

He didn't stop smiling, though. Oh, it was going to be

a very long day working alongside Lorina when she simultaneously aroused him and drove him batty with her refusal to explain herself, but there was nowhere else on the planet he'd rather be.

She might claim it was by mistake, but Lorina had started to open up to him, and that was a very good sign indeed.

Chapter 15

"I can't believe you gave away our premium dig spot!" I kicked at a broken wooden crate, and stood up from where I'd been leaning against a door along with a shovel and my dig bag. "You know that if Paul finds anything, he'll grab all the glory."

Gunner stumped into one of the side passageways with a couple of oil lamps. He held them up triumphantly. "I told you that I thought there were a few of these down here. As for giving away prime cellar real estate, we wouldn't have been able to dig much before Thompson and Roger had to be told."

"Yeah, but Paul will find the treasure after *we* figured out where it was!"

"Possibly." He smiled the same self-satisfied smile he'd been giving me ever since I'd blurted out a confession that I wasn't really a photojournalist. Damn his nonthreatening, sexy self. "But it so happens that I kept a little something up my sleeve just for you."

"Really?" Unbidden, my gaze dropped to the front of his jeans.

"Well, that, too, but not here where there are so many people about. Later, perhaps, in a more convenient location, like my bedroom."

I snorted in what I hoped sounded like disinterest, but sadly, it came out more like a horse champing at the bit. "So what is it you're keeping back from the others?"

He looked like he was going to offer to swap secrets again, but, thankfully, thought better of it. Which I couldn't help but admire. It would be far too easy for a man who looked like him to use his attractiveness to force me to admit all, and the fact that he didn't simultaneously warmed my heart and made me want to admit the truth about my failed plan.

"It was a little bit of an untruth, actually. Go left up here."

I glanced in surprise at him, taking the turn he indicated. In front of me was an extremely old-looking black wooden door. Across the middle of it was a thick piece of wood held into place by a couple of brackets that were twisted with age.

Gunner reached alongside me and tried to shift the wooden bar, but it wouldn't budge.

"I was afraid of that. It's stuck." He set down the lamps, and applied his shoulder to it, jiggling it at the same time. "The wood gets warped and won't shift."

"Maybe it's locked," I suggested.

"There is no lock on this door, just the bar. Ah, there it goes." With a rough noise, he got the wooden bar to swing upward. He then spent another four minutes pulling, swearing, and prying open the wooden door, which eventually creaked open.

"It hasn't been opened in quite a while," Gunner explained, wiping his hands on his legs and bending down to light one of the lamps.

"Are you sure it's safe?" I eyed the door. It looked like a strong wind would blow it over, but evidently it was tougher than it looked.

"The door? It's just swollen over the years, but should be fine now." He held up a lamp and nodded toward the doorway. There was a whole lot of black within it. "No electricity from here on out, I'm afraid. Let me go first, just in case the stairs are bad."

"So you can break your other leg?" I blocked the narrow doorway. "You don't have to be gallant, Gunner. I'll go first and make sure there's nothing to trip you up."

He stopped me before I could go through. "I'm not being gallant, at least not for the reason you think. If something were to happen to you, legally it would be better if it happened to me."

I glared at him. "Are you implying that if I fell down your stupid stairs, I'd sue you? Or rather, your brother?"

Gunner gave a wry little smile. "Elliott *is* due back tomorrow, and he'd be hellaciously angry if I let you hurt yourself. But no, I was actually referring to insurance reasons. You're not covered by the liability insurance the film company has taken out for the crew. So if you would kindly allow me to pass, I will go down the stairs first."

"But—," I started to protest.

"Sweetness," Gunner said, pulling me forward and giving me a swift kiss, so swift that I barely had time to enjoy the taste and scent of him before he was pushing past me. "I appreciate your concern, but I've been down these stairs before, and you haven't. I would advise you to stick close, though. This light isn't going to illuminate much but a few feet around me."

My lips tingled, and I desperately wanted to kiss him

again, but as he entered the black maw of the doorway, I moved the shovel to the same hand as the dig bag and grabbed the back of his shirt, shuffling after him.

The stairs weren't wood, as I'd assumed. They were stone, very narrow, and quite uneven. "Steady," Gunner warned, pausing to lift the lamp. About six feet of stairs were illuminated; the rest of the space was swallowed up by blackness. "Speak up if I'm going too fast for you."

"You're not going too fast, but I'd like to know where we're going. I thought the dirt part of the cellar was the bottom level of the castle."

"It is. Except for the bolt-hole, which is what this is. Or part of it—the outer part was covered over during a renovation a few hundred years ago. But this was originally a tunnel that my father said emerged out by the folly."

"Folly?" I tried to remember the layout of the castle grounds. "I don't remember seeing a folly."

"That's because it's not there anymore. It was located in the south pasture."

The significance of that hit me immediately. "So there used to be a secret passageway connecting the pasture where the first villa is and the castle?"

"I find that fact significant, don't you?" he asked, his voice oddly softened in the confined space. I shivered a little despite the comfort of both Gunner and his lamp. I wasn't particularly claustrophobic, but I couldn't help but feel the weight of the castle above us.

"Why didn't you tell Roger this?"

"Because I'm not sure if there's anything down here worth his while. For one thing, there isn't room to dig, and for another, I haven't been down here since I was five or six. My father was a fairly tolerant man, but he forbade us to go into the bolt-hole, saying it was danger-ous, and that it would be easy to be trapped by a cave-in or other calamity. Evidently Elliott was down here about ten years ago, but all he said was that the passage still existed to the outer wall of the castle."

"Cave-in," I murmured, clutching his shirt all that much tighter. "I can think of other ways I'd rather perish."

We continued down another dozen steps until Gunner stopped, saying, "All right, we're at the bottom."

"Sorry," I said, releasing his shirt, and giving his back a quick brush to try to relax the wrinkles I'd put into it. "You may want to iron your shirt later."

"Actually, I was going to tell you to hold on to me, since the floor isn't level, and I have no idea if there has been any destruction since Elliott last visited."

"So long as you don't mind a wrinkly shirt." I clutched the material again, trying to peer around him as we slowly walked forward. "There aren't any rats down here, are there?"

"Why, are you afraid of rodents?"

"Not unduly so, although I could do without the mental image of being trapped by a cave-in and consumed by a horde of hungry rats."

He laughed, but it sounded muffled and unnatural, making me all that much more aware that we were deep under the castle and far away from all signs of life. "Don't worry, I won't let that happen. I have my mobile phone. Ah, here we go."

He stopped suddenly and set the lamp on the ground. "I'll be blowed. I thought Dad was making this up, but now I see that he wasn't."

"What are you blowed about?" I tried to see around him, but it was too dark.

"One second—let me light the second lamp, and then I'll show you what I hope will make up for losing the premium dig site to Thompson."

The passage was too narrow for me to see anything

around him but the brownish gray stone walls, stained black over the centuries, with various bits of roots and long-dead plant life sprouting through seams. I rubbed my nose, which was itching with the smell of earth and decay.

Gunner got the second lamp lit. He flashed a grin over his shoulder at me. "Ready to be astounded?"

I eyed him. "You're not going to drop your trousers and demand I admire your gorgeous testicles, are you?"

"Not after you disparaged their beauty." His teeth flashed again, and then he lifted both arms to raise the two lamps, and turned to the side so I could see past him. Beyond him was a whole lot of blackness . . . and dull gray shapes dotting the ground.

I gawked for a second, then dropped the shovel and bag and squeezed past him, taking one of the lamps in the process. "What is this, a wall? Or the road?"

"That, my sweet Lorina, is the corner wall of a structure. See the right angles? It's definitely a building of some form, and could possibly even be part of the second villa. When I was little, my dad used to tell Elliott and me that there was an old foundation down here. We assumed it was just a now-demolished section of the castle, but this is definitely not sixteenth century." Gunner carefully thumped past me to stand looking down at the exposed stone structure that lay crumbled and half-buried in the dirt of the bolt-hole, disappearing under one of the brick walls of the castle. "And we don't even have to dig down for it. It's just a matter of uncovering it."

"OK, that is worth giving up the prime spot for," I said complacently, mentally rubbing my hands at the thought of stealing some of Paul's thunder. Then I realized that I shouldn't be relishing that since — the temptation of Gunner aside — I couldn't forgo my attempt to bring Paul to account. Not when there were other women like Sandy out there. "We should get Daria in here, though. She's a bit hurt because Paul swanned in and took away the cellar dig from her."

He made a face, then gave a rueful grin. "I was going to protest that I'd prefer to remain with you alone, but this isn't the ideal location for seduction, so we might as well have the help she'd be able to give us."

"Look," I said when he pulled the walkie-talkie off his belt. "I realize that I fully participated in the kissing and butt-groping, and licking of nipples, and stroking of chest and arms and back, but that doesn't mean I'm remotely susceptible to seduction."

Gunner cocked an eyebrow at me.

"Dammit, how do you know I'm lying?" I demanded to know.

"I'm not sure. I just know." He turned a couple of knobs on the walkie-talkie, frowned at it, and pulled out his cell phone instead.

"No reception?" I asked a couple of minutes later.

"No. The phone says I have a connection, but it doesn't seem to want to actually connect." He sighed. "One of us will have to go fetch Daria. Would you prefer to stay here with the rats, or should I fend them off while you find her?"

I shuddered. "How about we both go?"

He shook his head and eased himself down onto the ground. "It's hard enough walking on this ground with the cast that I don't want to make extra trips. I'll wait here while you bring her."

"All right, but I'll leave you a shovel so you can whack at any rats that charge you." I shifted both the bag and the shovel so that it sat next to him. He immediately took a trowel from the former and started scraping at the exposed stone.

"Tell Daria to bring any portable lights that she can find. And possibly a camp chair if she knows of one."

"I'll go for the full 'digging in a bolt-hole' kit," I promised, and, picking up one of the lamps, carefully made my way back to the stairs.

"You might also ask the catering people if they could send us some coffee or tea in a bit. I suspect we're going to be down here for a while," Gunner called after me, his voice muffled.

"Roger will find out about this if I do," I pointed out, waving toward the archaeology.

"I'll have to tell him anyway. I just wanted to get a little digging in by ourselves. In a couple of hours, the rest of the crew will be all over it. Until then . . ." He grinned.

I saluted in acknowledgment. "Will do. Roger and Paul can just focus on finding archaeology in their part of the cellar until after lunch. I'll be back as soon as I can." I trotted down the passageway and started up the steps, carefully holding the glass lantern, mentally rehearsing what I was going to say to Daria. The door loomed at the top of the stairs. I gave it a hearty shove.

It didn't move.

"Well, of course you're stuck. That just figures." I set down the lamp and shoved at the door with both hands.

It still didn't move.

I sighed a sigh of the martyred, and threw my full weight against the door.

Nothing happened other than my shoulder protested the action.

"Great, now I have to go down and get Gunner, and he shouldn't be walking up and down stairs on his owie foot. I just hope you're happy," I told the door, giving it another shove.

I stomped back down the stairs to Gunner.

He looked up, surprised that I was back so quickly. "Change your mind?"

"No. The door is stuck. Can you work your manly magic on it so that I can get us coffee and Daria and chairs and more lights?"

He frowned, but followed me back to the door.

Ten minutes later, I started to panic. "What do you mean it's going to take more than you to get it open? You opened it less than half an hour ago! Why can't you open it now?"

"Because I was on the other side of it then, pulling the door toward me. Now I'm on the top of a narrow stair, and I can't get a running start to throw myself on it. And even if I could, I wouldn't, since I'd likely fall and break several more bones." Gunner was silent a moment, rubbing his shoulder where he'd repeatedly attempted to force the door open. "I'm afraid we're stuck here until someone notices we're gone."

I stared at him in horror. "You have got to be kidding!"

"Unfortunately, I'm not." He tried his cell phone again, shaking his head. "Still not connecting even though it shows it sees the network. Do you have a mobile phone?"

"Not one that is set up to work in England. Maybe if you get right next to the door, you can get the walkie-talkie to work?"

"I'll try." He sat on the top step and spoke into the radio, but there was no reply.

"Well, that's it," I said dramatically, taking a lamp and marching down the stairs. "We're doomed."

"Careful," he warned, following me at a slower pace. "Those steps are uneven. You could fall and hurt yourself."

"What does it matter? We're going to die down here anyway! I'd rather have a swift death due to a plummet down ancient steps than I would a slow, lingering death where I sit in the dark and wonder if I should try to eat your corpse, or use it to catch rats and eat them."

"What makes you think I am going to be the one to die first?" He limped past me back to the part of the passageway where the stone ruins jutted out of the earth. "I've got more body mass than you, so if we're going to starve to death, then logically you will be the one to go first, and I'll have to decide whether to eat your legs first or go for your arms."

I wrapped my arms around myself, and sank less than gracefully down onto a bit of stone wall. "Oh, I like that! You wouldn't even have a dilemma about whether or not you should eat me over the rats, where I'd be in all sorts of mental hell trying to justify cannibalizing you. Well, fine. If you want to be that way, then I won't even consider the rats—I'll just start in on you. Happy now?"

"Not very, no, but it's not because of your desire to eat me."

I glanced sharply at him, but there wasn't even the least little bit of a leer about him. That made me sad, and oddly irritated. "If you're going to have that attitude, then you're going to be lucky if I wait until you're dead before I start chomping on you."

He surveyed the area for a few minutes, then gave a half shrug, got down onto his butt, and with a brush and a trowel, started working at the nearest stretch of archaeology. "I wouldn't eat your legs unless you were almost dead and were paralyzed."

I gasped. "Oh my god, do you mean you'd seriously eat me while I was still alive?"

"You just said you'd do the same to me."

"I said you'd be lucky if I waited!" I threw a clod of dirt at him. "I never said I'd actually do it. My god, you're a monster—do you know that? You're just a cannibalizing monster!"

"How is it being a monster to save myself by eating you when you'd be paralyzed and near death?" he asked, brushing the dirt off his leg. (My aim sucks.) "It's not like you'd feel it. You probably wouldn't even know if I waited until you drifted into a coma."

"I am speechless with appallingness," I said, heedless of grammar, and stood up. "So speechless that I'm going to leave you to your horrible, foul thoughts, and take my very nonparalyzed legs and try to find a way out of this hellhole."

"Bolt-hole," he corrected, and, other than raising an eyebrow at me, didn't say anything more when I shuffled my way past him with one of the lamps.

Ten minutes later, I admitted defeat.

"Back so soon?" he asked, looking up.

"I had to come back." I held out the lamp. "It ran out of oil."

"Ah. Yes, that was bound to happen. Luckily, this one seems to be all right."

"Gunner," I said, and slumped down next to him. "Hold me."

He set down the tools he was still using. "Are you still angry with me?"

"No. I can't do anything about the fact that you don't have the moral compass to leave my legs alone even if I wasn't dead yet. We're trapped in here, Gunner, really trapped. There's nothing farther down the passage but a big wall of nothing."

He nodded. "That would be the cave-in that my father mentioned when Elliott and I were little. There is no more to the bolt-hole."

I scooted over so that he could put his arms around me properly, and leaned into him, breathing in the now slightly musty scent of him. "What are we going to do? I wasn't serious about eating you, you know. But I don't want to die down here."

"You won't," he said in a calm, matter-of-fact voice that did much to ease the panic that had been steadily growing inside me.

"You don't know that for certain." I swallowed back a lump of what was most likely tears waiting to be shed. "I don't see how we're going to get out of here. No one knows to even look for us here. Why aren't you doing something?"

"I am doing something. I'm holding the most desirable woman in the world."

"Yes, you are, if by that you consider that your world is limited to this passageway, but that also means I'm the *only* desirable woman in the world, so I'm not too ecstatic over the title."

He chuckled into my hair, then slid a finger beneath my chin and tipped my head upward so that his lips brushed mine when he spoke. "If I told you that at this moment, the only thing concerning me is whether or not I'm going to be able to keep my hands off you, would you think I was sex-obsessed?"

"No, but that's only because I've been trying all morning not to slide my hands under your shirt."

"Why would you stop an urge like that?" He kissed me before I could answer, his mouth warm and wonderful, and so exciting that it almost made me forget that we were more or less buried in a tomb beneath the castle.

I swear that every nerve in my body was alight at that moment. I simultaneously didn't want the kiss to end and wanted to fling Gunner to the ground, strip off his clothes, and rub myself all over him.

"Lorina?" He ran his thumb over my lip.

I quivered like a plucked bowstring. "Hmm?"

"If you want to put your hands under my shirt, you

can. I'd even take it off for you, if you like. My shirt, not your hands. Evidently I've lost the ability to grammar."

"I think that's just my mouth being infectious," I told him, and started to reach for his chest. I stopped when my brain finally recovered enough from the kiss to remind me of several things.

His eyes narrowed on me. "What are you doing? You're thinking, aren't you? I can see you are. You were about to torment my chest again, and then you thought of something, and stopped. Stop thinking. There's no reason you shouldn't touch my chest. And, for that matter, any other part of me that happens to tempt you. There's nothing to stop you, is there?"

I sat on my hands. "You know, there are times when I really wish I *could* stop thinking. But unfortunately, my brain is annoying and it picks weird moments to remind me of things, and it just reminded me of something important."

He was silent a moment. "Something to do with Thompson?"

"Yes."

"It's this secret you have, isn't it? The plan you mentioned this morning."

Me and my big mouth. "That's right."

"And that's related to why you are pretending to be a photographer?"

"Boy, you don't forget anything, do you? Elephants could take memory lessons from you. Yes, Mr. Third Degree, it's all part and parcel of that."

"Do you fancy him?"

I shuddered.

"I thought not. Then, why—no. I take that back. I don't want to know why."

Now, that surprised me. "You don't?"

"Not in the least. No, I tell a lie—I do want to know,

but at this moment, in this place, I don't care. So long as you aren't interested in Thompson in a romantic way, then I can wait for you to be comfortable with telling me."

And at that, my heart did a little flip-flop. "I don't want to sleep with him. I wouldn't do that, even if I did want to. He's . . ." I bit my lip, so tempted to tell him the truth that it almost poured out of me. Something held me back, though. The doubting side of my mind pointed out that I had known Gunner for only a few days, and had no idea how he would view my plan. If he thought I was immoral . . . I gave a mental shake of my head. I didn't want to have to address that unless I absolutely had to. "He's not exactly what he seems."

"Who among us is?" He rubbed his thumb across my lower lip again. I nipped his finger. "I'm not saying I'm not curious as hell, but if it matters this much to you, then consider the subject closed."

"Thank you," I said, my conscience yelling at me for not trusting him.

You trust him enough to snog the tongue right out of his head; how can you desire a man if you don't trust him?

It's not my secret to share! I yelled back at her. *Besides, there's nothing wrong with not wanting to look like an asshat.*

My conscience didn't answer that, but she gave me a long, knowing look that made me feel even worse.

"So, shall we have sex?"

I goggled at him for a few seconds before I realized he was teasing me. And then it struck me that he wasn't teasing at all. "I—we're in a passageway, Gunner!"

"Oddly enough, I'm aware of that." He smiled at me, and my legs quivered, as did several other, more intimate parts of me. "But you fancy me, and I sure as hell want you, and we appear to have some time to kill, so why not?"

"I didn't say I fancied you," I said, tipping my chin upward, but that was just a little pride talking. That and Dr. Anderson's insistence that I set the terms of my involvement in any relationship.

He just looked at me.

"Oh, all right, I do, but you don't have to assume I do. I am not the sort of a woman who needs a man to be happy in her life. I've got a fulfilling job, and am happy in my own skin. Well, mostly. I would like to drop a few pounds, but I refuse to let society dictate to me what I should look like."

Gunner looked a little puzzled. Before he could ask me what the hell I was ranting about, I added, "Sorry. That was just a little self-defense thing. I do like touching you and kissing you and all that, but you could have pretended to have a shred of doubt, you know. It's a bit annoying to have it assumed that I'd fall for your gorgeous self."

"I don't, as a rule, play games like that. I believe in honesty."

I flinched. "Ouch."

"Sorry. That wasn't intended to reflect upon our discussion of a few moments ago. I was referring to honesty in emotions. So, how about it?"

I shook my head. "We're trapped in a passage under a castle, with no one knowing we're down here. And you said there are rats."

He sighed heavily. "I knew that lie would come back to haunt me. There are no rats, Lorina."

"You're just saying that because you want to get busy with me," I said suspiciously.

"I want to get busier with you than you've ever busied before—that's true—but I said it because I'd hoped you'd be terrified of them, and want to cling to me."

"That's a pretty dastardly thing to do, Gunner."

"I know, but I'm beginning to feel desperate."

"Just because you say there aren't any rats doesn't mean they aren't here," I pointed out.

"Look around you. Have you seen any rats since we've been down here?"

I glanced around the passageway. "Well . . . no."

"Have you heard any sounds of rodents?"

"No," I said slowly. "But maybe they're just hiding from us."

"Hiding where?" He gestured at the stones on the floor. "There's nowhere for them to go to remain unseen, not to mention the fact that we'd see droppings if they had been here."

I rubbed my arms. "It's still a bad idea. We've only known each other less than a week, and for most of that time, you were annoyed with me. I'm not the sort who dashes into relationships, anyway. It took me six months to decide whether or not I wanted my previous boy-friend, and thankfully, it only took me a year to get away from him."

"Get away from?" His lovely blue eyes were narrowed slightly.

I shook my head. "Not ready to talk about that."

"Fair enough." His brows smoothed, and a little smile flirted with his lips, making all my internal organs melt into puddles of goo. "If I told you that my brother married his wife after knowing her for less than a week, what would you say?"

"That your sister-in-law must be one hell of a woman."

"She is that." He pulled me into a loose embrace. "Do you know what I think?"

"No, but I have a strong suspicion you're going to tell me."

"I think that you're suffering mental distress, Lorina. You've let this situation with Thompson—no, don't tense up; I'm not going to question you about it—you've let it work you into knots, and now you're worried about rats and being trapped down here, and whether or not you're falling in love with me, and that's giving you an immense amount of stress."

I shoved back on him. "I am not falling in love with you! Didn't you just hear me tell you that it takes me forever to warm up to a man, romantically speaking?"

"Ainslie men are different. My brother proved that. Regardless, you're under tremendous stress, and quite obviously suffering. That's not good. You need something to distract you from your dark and confused thoughts."

"I do?" The lure of his nearness was too much for me. It wooed me as nothing else could. I watched his mouth move as he spoke, wanting to kiss him again, wanting to touch all that gorgeous warm flesh.

"Yes, you do, and as a caring man, as a man who values you for more than just your delectable body, and enticing breasts, and truly magnificent ass, I will take it upon myself to provide that distraction so that you might be comfortable, mentally speaking."

"Oh." Unable to resist, I leaned in and gently bit his lower lip. "That is very thoughtful of you."

"Yes, yes it is," he said, and with businesslike, efficient moves, he peeled off his shirt, and spread it out on the ground.

"Noble, even," I said, my eyes huge as they drank in all that lovely chest acreage. My mouth started watering at the sight of it. "We're talking Mother Teresa sort of generosity, the kind of act that the Nobel people take note of. Are you going to take off your jeans, too?"

"Yes, it's part of the plan I just created to keep your mind from being distressed."

"I like your plan. Your plan is good. No, wait, what am I saying? We can't have sex here, Gunner." I stopped pulling his jeans off him when he carefully removed his cast. "It's wrong."

"How is it wrong? Please pull the jeans off, so I can put my cast back on. Thank you. It's a nuisance, but the doctor assures me it's necessary for another day." He strapped the cast back onto his foot, and sat watching me.

I had a horrible time trying to get my brain working in the face of his near nudity. "My god, you really are gorgeous. Hmm? Oh, it's wrong . . . uh . . . morally?"

He shook his head. "I'm not involved with anyone, and I'm assuming you aren't, either, since you mentioned a former partner."

"Still, we haven't known each other long—" I stopped. I had a hard time forming coherent thoughts in my almost overwhelming desire to lick him.

"I don't think that would make a difference in how we feel about each other, do you?"

He had a point, I had to admit. "Well . . . I suppose if I'm going to die down here, it would be better if I died happy, rather than sexually frustrated."

"You're not going to die down here." He swept his hands down my back, and around my front to cup my breasts. "I, however, may well do so if you don't let me finish what we started this morning."

My breasts were wholly on board with that idea. I let them flirt shamelessly with him for a few minutes before letting my hands do a little walking along his arms and shoulders. "I thought you were doing this to save me from mental upset?"

"Ah, yes. Good point." He cleared his throat and looked down his nose at me. "I am thinking only of your welfare, Lorina. You will allow me to kiss and otherwise fondle your breasts for your own good."

He bent his head to do just that. I moaned, and pulled away enough to run my thumbs over his naked little nipples. "I'd nominate you for Good Samaritan of the Year, but you have a raging erection, and I don't think they approve of that sort of thing at the awards ceremony."

"My erection is not raging—it's simply appreciative and attentive. And I can't help it when you kiss me like you just did." He looked somewhat offended.

"Well, now I feel like a heel pointing it out," I said, and pulled my shirt off over my head. Gunner had arranged his pants on the ground next to his shirt. "Here you are doing nothing but thinking of my own good, and I go and make you feel awkward."

"If you take your trousers off, I won't feel awkward anymore," he said, nodding at my lower half as he laid my shirt out next to his.

"Then I obviously need to do that as a sign of just how much I regret causing you even so much as a moment of unhappiness," I said grandly, and shucked my shoes, socks, and pants with panache.

He paused in the act of putting them on the ground, giving me a look that had me giggling out loud.

"Too far?" I asked.

He nodded. "I could pretend to chalk it up to the regret-causing-you-unhappiness bit, though."

"Good. I'm not sure I'm willing to face the fact that I'm so happy getting it on with you when we could be down here for the rest of our lives."

He slid my bra off, and immediately cupped my naked breasts in his hands, bending down to kiss each handful. "At most, we'll spend a day down here, just long enough for us to get a bit peckish."

"I don't know that people will know to look for us here, assuming they notice we're gone," I said more than a little breathlessly.

"Perhaps not, but my brother is due back tomorrow, and he knows I know about the bolt-hole. He'll be sure to look here once he finds out we're missing." Gunner looked up at me, his eyes a smoky blue even in the dim lamplight. "You're sure you want to do this, Lorina?"

"Oh, hell yes," I said, leaning into him and gently biting the tendon in his neck. "I've wanted it since that first moment when you ran me over and pulled me onto your lap. Oh, dammit! I didn't mean to say that. Great, now you think I'm just one of the millions of women who no doubt fall for you the second they see you."

"And that, I assume, is my cue to tell you that you are unique and there's never been a woman like you, and despite the millions of women who have fallen for me, I can see, think of, and desire only you?"

I pulled back and punched him in the stomach.

Laughing, he held my hand and pulled me down onto the makeshift bed. "Don't tell me I deserved that."

"You did," I said, giving in to my body's demands and nibbling my way along his jaw to his ear. "You're not supposed to catch me out when I'm fishing for a compliment. A polite man, a man who has the manners to live in a castle, would have said all of that and not pointed out my insecurities."

"I'm a boor and a brute, and I did deserve that punch, because it is true that I do only think of you." He rubbed his cheeks against my breasts, the slight abrasion of his beard making my whole body feel like it was made up of fire.

"Apology accepted," I said, squirming restlessly against him as I kissed him. "Although you still haven't retracted that 'millions of women' thing."

"Less than twenty," he amended, and slid a hand up my leg, bending over my ankle and giving it a little bite. "You have the most beautiful legs."

"That's because I'm on my feet all day. It builds up

the calf muscles." I gave myself up to the moment, relishing the feel of his mouth as it steamed up my flesh.

"Mmm. So sexy," he said, nibbling a path up my thigh.

"I hope that wasn't a cannibal reference. Gunner?"

"Yes, my dumpling of delight?"

"Can we skip the appetizer and go straight to the main course? Because I already feel like I'm going to explode in a thousand little pieces if you take any longer, and it's just bound to make me insane if you insist on going into the land of oral sex."

He pursed his lips and eyed my underwear. "But I was looking forward to giving you pleasure."

I lifted my hips and peeled off my undies. "Oh, trust me, this is going to be pleasurable enough. Normally I'm very thumbs-up on foreplay, but I'm feeling a bit vulnerable here. We're not really in a private place, are we? We are just out here in the middle of a passage with Roman ruins, and if anyone opened that door and came into the passage, they'd see us going at it, and then where would we be?"

"I would have to marry you," he said gallantly, and released my leg, pulling himself upward as he did so.

I snorted. "That's a pretty old-fashioned response. People don't do that anymore."

"You've never been a member of my family," he said with a twisted smile. "If my mother had her way, we'd all be married with large families by the time we hit twenty. Hell."

"I don't know that it would be hell being married to you. Not that I'm looking for a man to marry—I'm perfectly fine on my own—" I stopped, realizing that he wasn't listening. "What's wrong? You look disappointed. Did you really want the oral sex part of the event? If you did, I can go ahead with it."

He gestured toward his lap. "Do I look like I'm unhappy? I was just thinking that since this is our first encounter, we should use protection."

"Oh. You're right." I was annoyed that I was so smitten with him, I hadn't even thought of that. "And how stupid is that?" I said aloud. "Especially since it's the whole reason I'm here."

"Pardon?" he said, looking confused. "You're here just to have sex with me?"

"Of course not! I didn't even know you existed until I got here. Just ignore my mouth. It's talking again without my permission."

"But I like your mouth so very much." He got up on his knees and leaned over me, kissing me in a slow, hot manner that left my stomach quivering, and all my girl parts cheering in anticipation.

"I don't suppose you have a condom?"

"I do, as a matter of fact, and if you make so much as one comment about that, I will refuse to let you touch my chest for an entire week." He rolled me onto my side while fumbling around in the pocket of his pants, which lay beneath me.

I gasped at him, pinching him on the hip. "That's even worse than telling me you'd eat me while I was in a coma!"

He found the condom, and opened the package while I tried to adopt a position that said I was willing and enthralled without seeming needy or the sort of woman who would get down with a man in a dire situation.

He slid me a coy look. "Would you like to put it on, or should I?"

"Oooh! Let me." I took the condom from him, and sat up, biting my lip to keep from offering him help when his underwear got caught on his cast. At last he managed to wrestle it off, and lay on his side next to me, panting slightly, but trying hard to look suave.

"Now, let's see." I waggled the condom at him, unrolling it a bit. "I believe I know how this works. Why don't you lie on your back and let me see if I can't get you suited up?"

"I hope I last," he said, groaning when I trailed my hand down his belly and made a little circle around his crotch. "I'd better start thinking about famine and sexual diseases."

I froze just as I was about to kiss his belly button, glancing up at him in worry.

"Sorry," he said, waving a hand. "I wasn't implying I thought you had an STD. I'll stop talking now so you can continue."

I opened my mouth, closer than I'd ever been to just telling him the truth, but decided that it wouldn't enhance the moment. Instead, in an attempt to recapture the light mood of a minute ago, I said perkily, "Prepare yourself. I shall now apply the condom . . . using only my mouth."

At that moment, the oil lamp gave a nasty hissing sound, sputtered twice, and went out.

I heard Gunner sigh in the darkness.

I started laughing. I couldn't help myself—it was just too funny to refuse to acknowledge.

"Do you ever feel like you're doomed?" Gunner asked when I finally managed to stop. "Not doomed to die—I reiterate that we will be found sooner rather than later—but doomed on a metaphysical level, the kind where all the sins of your past return to haunt you?"

"Not really." I reached out to where I last saw his penis, found it still standing at attention and waiting for my ministrations, and leaned down to lave my tongue around the head.

Gunner sucked in approximately half the air in the passage. "Oh Christ! I really won't last if you do that."

With some fumbling, I managed to get the condom

rolled down on him, after which I crawled up his body, careful to avoid his hurt ankle. I lowered myself until I lay on top of him, his flesh warm and solid beneath me. Instantly, his hands came around and possessed themselves of my behind. "It's a bit weird doing this in pitch black, and I'm having to block the thought of rats from my mind even though you said there really aren't any, but I think if we focus, we can do this. Only, Gunner, I'm going to need a whole lot of distracting."

He chuckled, his mouth taking possession of mine, his tongue doing a wonderful little move against mine that had me feeling light-headed with passion. And when he lifted me up so that I was poised to accept him, I had a flash of insight that told me that nothing would ever again be the same.

The feel of him as he slid into me was almost overwhelming, making my muscles cramp around him in a manner that had him humming with pleasure. And when he worked up a rhythm that came close to making *me* hum, too, I let go of the last shreds of doubt, the little slivers of fear that he would turn out like my father. Gunner wasn't a man who felt he had to dominate in order to prove himself—far from it. He had been solicitous and thoughtful with me, and I realized that he must have known I would have felt threatened otherwise.

The question of how he knew that was for another time. Right now, I just wanted to glory in him, in how right he felt, and tasted, and simply *was*. Everything about him fit perfectly with me, and when he urged me to a faster pace, his fingers tightening on my hips and his breath coming short and hard, I knew that no matter how the situation with Paul ended, at least one very good thing had come from this trip.

Gunner shouted as I slipped over the edge into an orgasm that seemed to ripple outward in never-ending waves. And after I collapsed down on his chest, now heaving and damp with exertion, his ragged breath ruffling my hair, I felt a few tears prick painfully behind my eyes.

Now that I'd found Gunner, I didn't want to ruin everything. Would he understand if I told him the truth about my plan? Or would he find it so repugnant that I lost him forever?

I clutched him tight and ignored the fact that I was lying naked in the middle of a hidden passageway. If I pretended hard enough, maybe everything would work out.

Chapter 16

Gunner felt pretty damned good, even considering the cramp in his leg, the rock that had somehow wedged itself under his left hip, and the fact that he hadn't had food for almost twenty-four hours.

He narrowed his eyes in the darkness, wondering about that. With nothing else to do, and no oil left in the lamp to see by, he'd made love to Lorina two times. A man of normal stamina, usually he'd feel pretty drained after two sessions of lovemaking in a small amount of time, yet here he was not only feeling good, but also thinking more and more about waking Lorina up and allowing her to have her womanly way with him, as he'd promised her at the culmination of their previous session.

Even without her telling him what secrets she held regarding Thompson and the dig, he felt closer to her than he had any of his previous lovers. More so, because none of them had triggered in him the strange protective need that possessed him around Lorina.

Quite simply, he wanted to keep her in his life. He wanted to enjoy the warm, loving woman he had uncovered, to watch her blossom while keeping her safe from all the ills of the world.

He just wanted her, in every sense of the word, and that itself was such an alien concept, he had to stand back and look it over thoroughly.

"You're humming," Lorina's voice drifted upward to him.

Why? he asked himself. Why did he want to keep Lorina in his life? She was just a woman, like any other woman he had known.

Ah, but there he was wrong. She wasn't like anyone else—she had her own unique blend of defiance, vulnerability, and mystery that made up a heady cocktail of desire.

"Gunner?"

That didn't mean he had to think along the lines of a permanent arrangement, he argued with himself. He'd enjoyed lovers before and not yearned to wake up to them every morning, or to act the brave hero in keeping the world at bay. No, it was Lorina and Lorina alone, he decided. She was the only one who had generated such thoughts and feelings.

"Gunner, are you all right? I know you're awake."

The question was what to do about that. He considered his options, thought about what Lorina would be likely to accept, and decided there was no way for it but to make the decision for her. Oh, to be sure, she'd give him hell for it by pointing out that she was an independent woman who could think very nicely for herself, thank you. But even knowing the ire she'd display, he concluded there was no other option. If he wanted her,

wanted to keep her, then he'd simply have to change his
ways.

It was an oddly pleasing thought.

"Right, now you're making me paranoid. Are you not
answering me because you're suddenly appalled at what
we've been doing? Having second thoughts? Wishing
you were miles away from me?"

"Hmm?" He stopped making plans, and quickly ran
over her conversation. "Good morning, love. I didn't
know you were awake. I apologize if I woke you up with
humming."

"You didn't; I was awake already. I was lying here
wondering if we were going to be changed by this experience. I mean, when people eventually find us years
from now, assuming we could gain enough nutrients
from the dirt to survive, will we be pale, shrunken, giant-
eyed mole people?"

"Do you want another minute of light?" He reached
into the spot where he'd carefully set his mobile phone.

"No, we'll save its flashlight app for potty visits." He
felt her shudder. "Although what we're going to do when
the emergency tissues run out, I don't like to think. Also,
at some point, that hole I dug isn't going to remain suitable as a toilet."

"You're worrying again," he told her, and lifting her
head, he raised his hand so he could see his watch with
its lit dials.

"Yes, I am. I'm also hungry as all get-out, but I'm trying to remind myself that this is no worse than a cleans-
ing fast. How many days have we been down here?"

"Almost twenty-three hours." He was silent a moment.

Lorina uncurled herself from his side, and he knew
without even seeing her that she was eyeing him with
skepticism. "You have got to be kidding."

He held up his wrist. "You can see the time for yourself."

"I'm not talking about the time, which you very well know. I'm referring to your oath to distract me from what you call my rising panic by making love to me until I forget everything but how fabulous you are, and how I love your legs and your chest and that little spot on your neck that makes you shiver when I bite it."

He smiled into the darkness. "It's odd how we met just a week ago, and yet you know me so well."

Her hand fumbled around until it found his flesh, which she then pinched. "You can't be serious, Gunner. You're not an animal. You're not some potent stallion around a harem of mares. Normal men, men who are real and not depicted in porn movies, those sorts of actual, live men, do not have sex three times in twenty-three hours. I know you promised to keep me from being scared and worried, but even you have to admit that there is a limit to your stamina."

"You're dying to know if I have an erection, aren't you?" he asked.

"Dammit!" She sounded so irritated it made him smile again. "Stop reading my mind. Where are you?"

Her hands danced lightly across his side until she got her bearings; then she slid them down his stomach to his groin. "Holy Mary, mother of god! You are bulgy again! *Gunner!*"

"I can't help it," he protested. "There's something about you that has me sporting wood every time I think about you. I think it's your legs. And your breasts. And your ass, and your thighs, and those delicious calves of yours. I just want them all."

"Aha! I knew it! It's a return to the oral sex thing. You can't convince me that you're really brokenhearted because I wouldn't let you do that the first time."

"No, but when you insisted on pleasuring me the second time, without allowing me due repercussion, I began to suspect there's some sort of a hang-up you are too embarrassed to mention."

He felt air move above him, indicating she was waving her hand around. "I don't have sexual hang-ups! I simply wanted to go down on you, and I assumed you would enjoy that."

"I would. I did. All I ask is equal time to give you the same pleasure."

"Hrmph." She sounded disgruntled, which perversely delighted him. He'd never known a woman to think the way she did. It wasn't just the vulnerability about her that he sensed, but something within himself that reacted to her. He realized at that moment that he was wholly devoted to protecting her, to act as her champion and fight the world on her behalf.

He pulled her down, and rolled onto his side, using her thigh as a guide as he moved downward. "Would it make you uncomfortable if I indulged myself now? I won't if you really don't want me to, but it's been my experience that women who feel they won't enjoy it usually do once they allow themselves to give me free rein, so to speak."

"I think," Lorina said after a moment of thought, "that we need to have a moratorium on the mention of other people when we're about to get down and get funky. As I said, I don't have an objection, although those moist wipes that you inexplicably carry around with you—"

"I told you—it's impossible to keep your foot clean during the day when it's in a cast, even a removable one such as I have. The need arises to wipe my toes during the day lest they start to resemble those of a Hobbit."

"Regardless, as grateful as I am that you have them, they aren't as potent as a nice hot shower. Plus, you've been a-visitin' twice now, and although I cleaned up the last time I went to the toilet area, I'm not as springtime fresh as I would like."

"The same can be said for me," he murmured, kissing her inner thigh, and relishing the way she simultaneously shivered and pulled his head closer.

"Except it's easier for you to keep clean."

He paused. "I don't see how."

He felt her arm move. "It's the way we're built. Women have parts that are nicely tucked up inside, which, although preferable to the alternative—really, don't all male genitalia get in the way when you walk? I don't see how you can even sit without crushing parts of it. Anyway, lady parts are a wee bit more difficult to tend to due to their position."

"There you go again, calling my balls ugly. I can't do anything about their appearance any more than I can my face."

"I didn't call your balls ugly. I simply pointed out that having all your bits outside made it easy to clean them up. I mean, you can just dunk them in a bucket, whereas women have folds. And recesses. And many more working parts. It's not my fault that men insist on keeping their genitals outside, where they are not only visible to all and sundry, but also get in the way of things."

He squared his shoulders. "My cock and balls do not get in the way!"

"Well, not now, but I bet they do other times. Like when you want to ride a horse. Or a motorcycle. Or dandle a baby on your lap only to have him kick you right in the family jewels."

Gunner grimaced. "All right, I will allow the last one, but I assure you that I have no difficulties with my privates when riding a motorcycle. Now, shall we proceed, or is there something else you wish to discourse about?"

Lorina laughed. "I love it when you talk all lofty like that, although you really sound awfully disgruntled."

"I feel disgruntled," he said in an injured tone. "Here I am attempting to seduce you as best I can, and I'm just about to tell you that you have a lovely . . . what did you call it? Lady guardian?"

"Garden."

"Lady garden, and you throw at me the fact that you think my genitals are unsightly! I ask you, how is a man to proceed with admiring the lady garden when that happens?"

"Screw it," Lorina said, pulling him forward onto her. "Foreplay is overrated anyway. Let's skip the oral sex again, and then we can trade witticisms about crotches afterward."

He shifted his hurt leg to one side and propped himself up on his arms, humor and passion mingling within. Was there ever such a delightful woman as Lorina? "I have never met a woman who says exactly what she thinks."

"It's my lack of filter," she said sadly, and then he lost all thought when her hands took possession of him, stroking him to a hardness he hadn't thought possible. His heart sped up to match her rhythm, making the blood pound in his ears. Spots seemed to dance before his eyes, and just as he was about to sink himself in her, he realized two things.

It wasn't the sound of blood pounding that he heard, and they were no longer alone.

He looked up and saw elongated fingers of pale light licking along the bolt-hole walls, and heard the sound of footsteps.

"Christ," he swore, and, reaching underneath Lorina, pulled out his shirt, and thrust it at her at the same time he tried to pull his jeans out from underneath himself.

Unfortunately, the pants caught on the heel of the walking cast, and wouldn't budge.

"Gunner? What's wrong? Hell's bells, I can see your face! Ack!"

Lorina spoke the last word as a squawk when their darkness was suddenly illuminated by several sources of light, all of them seeming to be as bright as the sun. He shielded his eyes and blinked, trying to get his pupils to adjust after almost a day of darkness.

"Gunner? Are you all right?" a familiar voice asked.

Gunner blinked some more when a second voice said, "Crikey! He's naked, Elliott. And who's that behind him? Whoever she is, she's naked, too."

"Ah. Yes. Just so."

Slowly, Gunner's vision adjusted itself so that he could make out the people behind the lights. Sure enough, his brother Elliott was in the forefront, an ax in his hand, and behind him, smiling with delight, was Alice.

Those two rescuers, he could have dealt with. But when Cressy pushed her way through, accompanied by Tabby and Matt, he knew the situation was pretty bad.

"Gunner, we were so wor—aiiiiieeeee! You really are naked this time!" Cressy sucked in a huge amount of air, and then pointed over his shoulder. "And Lorina is naked, too! OH MY GOD, YOU GUYS WERE DOING IT!"

With an *eep*ing noise that he found oddly endearing given the situation, Lorina lunged around him and threw herself across his legs. She'd managed to get his shirt on, hiding her naked torso from view, but it was clear to all that beneath it she wore nothing. "For god's sake, Cressy, stop staring. Haven't you ever seen a naked man before?" Lorina scolded.

Gunner tapped her on the shoulder. "She's only seventeen, love."

"Oh. That's right." Lorina cleared her throat. "Never mind, Cressy. You're due a freak-out, although if you could stop panting, it would probably leave more air for the rest of us."

"I believe that Cressida and I should retire to the kitchen to make some tea," a gentle voice said from the back of the crowd, and to Gunner's dismay, Salma came forward to take Cressy's arm and drag her still-gaping self backward. "I'm sure you could do with a cup, and I know I could."

"Did you get that all on film?" Roger could be heard to ask in the background. "Dear god, the viewers are going to go insane over this footage! I can almost hear the voice-over: sex on the ruins! The Romans weren't the only ones who had deviant practices!"

"We are not deviant!" Lorina protested.

Roger ignored her. "We'll top the ratings! This'll bring all the tabloids running. It'll make *Big Brother* look like a kiddie show."

"Yes, I got it," Tabby said, giving Gunner and Lorina an apologetic look. She continued to film them as Gunner sighed.

"Good, keep at it. Sue, you're going to want to work up some new text for the next voice-over. Something about romance being in the air, and unable to resist the lusts of the ages, and how the lord of the manor's brother and an American visitor fell victim to the passions of the past, that sort of thing . . ."

Gunner met his brother's eyes. "Could I get your light, please, El? This is Lorina, by the way. Lorina, my brother Elliott, Baron Ainslie. That's Alice, his baroness, beyond him."

"Hi, Lorina!" Alice called, waving. "Good to see you again. It's been a long time, huh? I look forward to having a chat with you about Sandy. Er . . . later. When you're not so . . . occupied."

Lorina, now draped across his lap, gave a feeble smile in reply. "Nice to see you again, Alice. I'm sure you'd like some sort of an explanation about what we're doing down here—"

Gunner stopped her talking by dint of covering her mouth with his hand for a few seconds. "I don't think that's necessary."

"But they're going to want to know what we were doing—"

"No," he said firmly, the humor in the situation making his lips twitch. "I think they know exactly what we were doing." She turned beet red and started sputtering an explanation that he ended by announcing, "You may congratulate us, actually. We have decided to get married."

"We have not!" Lorina managed to say before he rolled her over so that her face was into his chest.

"Ignore her. She's a bit disconcerted by the fact that our lamp went out several hours ago."

Lorina struggled against him, but he kept her firmly clasped to his chest.

Roger gave a cheer and started babbling to Sue about the possibility of having a wedding the last week of the show in order to drive up viewers, while Alice clapped excitedly. "You can have the wedding at the dower house now that the renovations are done! Oh my god, this is so exciting! Elliott, isn't it exciting? Your mom is going to go ballistic! Good thing she's coming home in a few weeks."

"Very exciting," Elliott said, giving Gunner an unreadable look. But at least he had the presence of mind to set down the flashlight he'd been holding, and turned to shoo the clutch of people back along the passageway to the stairs. "We will get the full details in a bit, everyone. Now, I think you've filmed enough."

Roger clearly wanted to protest, but didn't wish to annoy Elliott, so with a reluctant wave of his hand, he instructed the film crew to follow him and Sue.

Gunner didn't need to catch the acid look that the latter cast him to know he was now in her bad graces, but he didn't particularly care. What he did worry about was what Lorina would say as soon as he released her.

He looked down at her. She had tried to push herself back from where he'd clasped her to his bosom, but gave up when she realized it was doing no good. Now he loosened his hold and braced himself for the barrage.

It wasn't long in coming.

"What the hell do you think you were doing? You could have smothered me with your lovely chest muscles and that soft chest hair, which I never think I'm going to like but which is really nice on you." She smacked him on the arm. "Don't you ever do that again! Not unless I ask you to, anyway. And why on earth did you tell them we're getting married? Are you insane? Did the lack of light make everything but your genitals wither away and die? You're bonkers—that's what you are. You're outright bonkers!"

"I told you that if we were discovered down here *in flagrante delicto* that I'd have to marry you, and marry you I will."

"*Have* to marry me? *Have* to? Oh, I do *not* think so," she snapped, getting to her feet. "No one *has to* marry me, especially not some oversexed, way-too-handsome-for-his-own-good brother of a lord. No sir! The man I marry is going to feel *grateful* to me, not beholden by some outdated and totally insane moral code that says men in the act of getting their jollies off have to wed their fellow jollyee."

He waited until she took a breath, and awkwardly got to his feet, shaking off his jeans as he did so, and attempting to hop his way into them. He had to sit down in the dirt to do it, which left grit in unmentionable places. "We'll talk about it later," was all he said.

"We'll talk about it when *I* say we will talk about it," Lorina yelled, then stopped, realized what she'd said, and huffily donned her own clothing, muttering all the while, "Of all the stupid things to say in front of people . . . we're going to get married, he said, just like *he* gets to decide that without me having any input whatsoever, not that I'd marry him now if he was the last man on the earth. . . . Where the hell is my left shoe? I am a strong woman, one who does not allow men to run roughshod over her, and that includes making decisions about what I do with my own life. That is *so* something my father would do! Well, I won't have it, do you hear me? You may be the only man I'm comfortable with, but that doesn't mean I'm going to let you push me around!"

Gunner took mental notes while she ranted, but wisely kept his thoughts to himself. Ten minutes later they emerged from the stairs back into the main cellar. He could hear the sounds of digging and voices coming from the northern end, but didn't stop to investigate whether anything of interest had been discovered. He escorted a still muttering Lorina up the stairs and to the kitchen, where he knew the family would be. But rather than stopping there and accepting the cups of tea that Salma held out to them, he shook his head and said, "We'll be down shortly," and gently pushed Lorina out the door and into the hall, up another flight of stairs, and finally into the small suite of rooms that had been his since his father had died, and he had inherited Elliott's former digs.

"The shower is in there," he said, pointing to the attached bathroom. "If you've got dirt in the same places I do, you'll want to get it out before facing the family."

"They're *your* family, not mine," Lorina said huffily, but immediately started removing her clothes. "I don't have to face them about anything. I'm no one to them, nothing, more than nothing. Just some chickie you got it on with in the bolt-hole. Although I do feel bad about Cressy seeing us."

"Don't," he said resignedly. "I'm sure she's going to manage to turn the event into a horse of her own."

He would have liked to join Lorina in the shower, since he could think of nothing more pleasurable at that moment than soaping her up while standing under a stream of hot water, but when he peeled off his clothes and entered the bathroom, the glare she gave him through the shower door warned that his presence was not going to be welcome. He sighed and, wrapping a towel around his waist, left his rooms.

Lorina was out of the shower when he returned. He held out a handful of clothing. "These belong to one of my sisters. She's about your size, and I thought you might like some clean things to change into. At least until I can have your own things brought here."

"And why, pray tell, would you have my things brought to your room? Do you think that just because we slept together means I'm moving in?"

"No, I think you're moving in because that's how married people live."

Lorina took a deep breath, then two more before finally managing to get words out. "I see you are confused about several points. First of all, we aren't married. Second, and this is the most important, so I suppose it should really be the first point, I am not some mousy little woman who wants and needs a man to make decisions for her. Third, and this is almost as important as the new first point, so I suppose it should be second—hell, now I'm confusing myself—third, no man tells me what to do. I make my own decisions about what I do with my life."

"I think that your third point and the first one are basically the same," he explained gently, wanting to wrap his arms around her. More than that, he wanted to take the hurt from her, the same hurt that showed in her eyes ... in between the flashes of ire, that is. "And I apologize."

She had opened her mouth to dispute what he said, but paused, a little frown pulling her brows together. "You ... you do?"

"Yes. What I said was thoughtless and high-handed. You have every right to be annoyed with me, although in my defense, I'd like to say that I said what I did with your best interests uppermost in my mind."

She crossed her arms. "And how exactly does announcing our upcoming nuptials without even bothering to ask me represent my best interest?"

"You need me," he said simply, deciding honesty was definitely the best policy with her.

"Me?" She looked aghast. "I don't need anyone!"

"Of course you do. We all need people—I need my family, and Cressy, and now you. And you need me because ... well, because."

"Because why?"

He considered her stance—it reminded him of a deer about to bolt. Carefully, mindful of her feelings, he answered, "You said earlier I was the only man you were comfortable with. I assume that means some men in your life have not been as considerate of you as they ought to have been. I will never be inconsiderate of you."

One of her eyebrows rose in a mute statement.

He made a little conciliatory gesture. "Other than announcing our engagement without first asking you, that is."

She shook her head. "You really do take the cake—do you know that?"

"Possibly, but you have to admit that a marriage between us would solve a lot of problems."

"Oh, really?" She stood before him with a towel tucked around her torso, unfortunately hiding those lovely breasts from his view. "Such as?"

"It's generally viewed as the right thing to be done when one is discovered in such a situation," he said, trying to think of valid reasons why she should marry him. He knew why he wanted her, but finding reasons for her to accept him was more difficult.

"If you're in a Georgette Heyer novel, possibly. But I have news for you—no one does that sort of thing these days."

"It would allow you to stay in England longer than a normal tourist."

"What makes you think I want to stay here?"

He didn't answer that. Searching his mind, he offered, "We wouldn't have to sneak around in order to make love. It wouldn't shock Cressy to know we were sleeping together if we were married. And it would make Salma happy. She's long wanted to see me happily settled."

Lorina hesitated. "Much as I like Salma, I'm not prepared to get married just to please her."

"You have to admit that we get on well together. Very well together," he said with a little smile. "Think of how well things would go if we weren't on a dirt floor, hmm?"

She gave a ladylike snort. "There is more to life than mind-blowingly wonderful sex."

"And," he said, presenting his coup de grâce, "if we were married, I could teach you how to be a proper photographer, so you wouldn't have to go around pretending anymore."

The color faded out of her cheeks, and her gaze

dropped. Instantly, he felt consumed with guilt and, without thinking, took her in his arms, kissing her hair. "I'm sorry, love. I shouldn't have said that. I really am an oaf, aren't I?"

"No," she said, her voice muffled as she snuggled her head into his neck. Her arms were tight around his waist. "It's not you, Gunner. It's me. I'm the one who is an oaf. And more. I've lied to you and Cressy and Salma and Roger, and, oh, everyone. And if you knew the truth about me, you'd never in a million years even joke about getting married. I'm not who you think I am. I have ... dark secrets."

"You are a warm, loving woman," he told her, wondering if she was going to trust him enough to tell him those secrets. "I'm sure you had a good reason for lying to us all."

"I do," she said, making a suspiciously wet sniffling sound. He pulled back and tipped her head up. Her lashes were damp. "Oh, god, Gunner, you're going to make me tell you, and then you're going to hate me, and you'll tell everyone about me and then they will hate me, too, and I just don't think I could take that!"

He brushed away a tear that had welled over her lower lashes. "I think it's safe to say that there's little you could do to make me hate you, and even if you did harbor some secret so heinous that it made me think twice about you—not that I think anything could—then I can promise you I won't tell anyone else about it."

She swallowed hard and slid her hands up his chest, her fingers sending little tingles of electricity along his flesh. "I'll tell you, but if you hate me because of it, I'll never forgive you."

He kissed her, and led her over to the bed, where he pulled her down onto his lap. "Fair enough. No, to the right, those are my balls. Thank you. Comfortable? All right, begin."

Lorina leaned into him, tracing random patterns on his left pectoral. "It all started with my friend Sandy. She's Alice's foster sister, or one of them. I gather Alice lived with a few foster families."

"She did. She's remarkably well-adjusted despite it, although I think she gave Elliott a few bad moments before she settled down."

"Well, anyway, she lived with Sandy's family for several years, and since they were nearly the same age, they hung out together. Then Sandy went to college, and Alice turned eighteen and left the foster system, but they stayed in contact. Sandy and I met when we were roommates our freshman year. When we left college, we got an apartment together. She went into child welfare work, and I got a job teaching French to community college students. During summers, Sandy took time off to pursue her lifelong passion by volunteering at archaeological digs all over the world."

"Ah," Gunner said. "I wondered when we'd get to Thompson. I take it she met him at one of the digs?"

Lorina nodded. "And fell for him hook, line, and sinker. Came back from a dig and told me she was in love, and couldn't wait to quit her job so she could join him, and live happily ever after, et cetera."

"Let me guess—Thompson had no serious intentions toward her?"

"Not only that, but he left her an unwanted present."

"Oh dear. A baby?"

"No, thank heavens." Lorina's jaw tightened. "Although I don't know why I say that—Sandy would have been better off with a baby than HIV."

"Ouch," Gunner said, starting to have an idea of where her tale was going.

"Worse than ouch—it's not the death knell that it was ten years ago, but it's still ruined her life and any hope she had of having a normal family. She's gone to live with some nursing nuns in Nepal who have a good rate of patient recovery, so we're hoping they can get her healthy again, and able to live a life without infection."

"I'm so sorry," he said, holding her tight. "If there's anything I can do—"

She kissed his jaw. "Thank you. She's out of contact from her family and me for two months, so perhaps there will be good news at that time. Until then . . ." She stopped.

"Until then, we have to make Thompson pay."

"No. Well, yes, it would be nice if he was held responsible for her situation, financially speaking, but so far, he's refused to believe anything that Sandy told him. He claimed she was simply being a spurned lover and making up lies about him to scare off other women, and that he'd sue her if she spread rumors about him. She tried to give him her doctor's statement, but he said that her illicit past had nothing to do with him, other than making him grateful he used condoms with her."

"If he wore a condom, then how—"

"They aren't infallible," she said with a knowing look. "And Sandy distinctly remembers one time when he forgot. She told him that even if what he said was true, then he should have himself checked, but he refused, saying he was fine and had no symptoms, et cetera. He simply refuses to listen to her. But, Gunner, he has to be stopped. I don't want another woman to go through what Sandy's had to go through."

"And that's why you've been playing up to him?" Gunner tried to work out a way that made sense, but failed. "I'm not quite sure I see—"

"I was trying to get him into a position where he was alone with me, so I could slip him a roofie and take a sample of his blood." Lorina ducked her head, peering up at him through her lashes. "I know, it's wrong. It's heinous. It's barbaric and immoral, and illegal to boot, but I couldn't think of anything else to do."

"Hmm. I agree that he needs to face the fact that he is infected and could be infecting others. In addition, he must alert any other lovers whom he has infected."

"And not be allowed to harm anyone else," Lorina added.

"Agreed. What can I do to help you?"

She stared at him for a few seconds, then said, "You want to help me?"

"I do."

"Why?"

He didn't need to consider his answer before giving it. "Because it's important to you."

"I . . . I . . . Gunner, that's the nicest thing anyone has ever said to me."

His heart seemed to give a little squeeze at that idea. "I suggest we confront him together. Yes, I know you've already chatted with him, but if we present a united front, perhaps we can get further."

She took a deep, shaking breath. "That sounds wonderful. And thank you for caring so much about Sandy that you'd be willing to do this."

He let her think his altruism was for her friend.

"So you don't think I'm a horrible person?" The look in her eyes was so stark, it left him seriously thinking about marching out of the castle and putting his fist in Thompson's face just because he upset Lorina.

"I do not think you are a horrible person. I think you're rather wonderful, to be honest. There's not many women I know who would put themselves to both the trouble and expense to fly to the other side of the world just to avenge a friend, not to mention save the lives of women she's not even met. My youngest sister might.

Alice probably would, but she'd do it on a whim without any preplanning, and then she'd get herself in a predicament that would be both funny and alarming."

To his joy, Lorina smiled at that. "I don't know Alice well, but I do think when I get to know her better, I'm going to like her a lot."

"You will. She's a delight, although not nearly so charming as you."

"Silly man. You have to say that due to your weird, antiquated idea of chivalry that kicked in when people saw us in the passageway." Her smile faded, and she looked worried again. "You're not going to tell your family about me, are you?"

"That you have breasts that make my mouth water, and an ass that's almost divine, and legs that make me hard just thinking about them wrapped around my waist? No, I won't tell them those things. I will tell them that you're fabulous in all other regards, but I won't mention a thing about the way your muscles tighten around me until I think I might just die of happiness."

"Silly man," she repeated, and got off his lap, collecting the clothes and returning to the bathroom. "We're not getting married."

"I think we are," he called after her, and idly wondered if he should be concerned why something that had started as a joke was now becoming vitally important to him.

Chapter 17

"We got one!"

It wasn't so much the volume of the shout that had me looking up from where I was sitting on my air mattress tying the laces of my boots, but the excitement rife in the words. I couldn't tell who had shouted the statement, but I thought it was one of the grad student diggers.

"Really? Where?"

That sounded a lot like Daria.

"Castle cellar. Paul's cleaning it now so we can read it. Of course he's claiming that it was all him finding it, but Simon said it was in a trench on the northeast, not the one Paul was on. Exciting stuff, huh?"

"Very."

I poked my head out of my tent and had my guess confirmed. "Another mouse stone?" I asked Daria, who stood with an especially sour look on her face, watching the retreating back of the digger.

"So I gather. I wouldn't know, since Paul won't let me near the cellar trenches." She shifted the look to me before giving me a twisted smile. "Welcome back, by the way. I heard through the grapevine that you and the hunky Gunner were trapped together overnight."

"It was a lot less fun than you're imagining," I told her, gathering up my camera bag and emerging from the tent. "No toilet, no food, no water, and after a couple of hours, no light."

"Mmhmm. But evidently you found a way to keep yourselves busy."

"OK, that is a knowing look if I ever saw one," I said, pointing to her face. We both turned and started toward the pasture where Daria's trench was. "And it's totally unnecessary. I'm too traumatized by the way everyone burst in on us to put up with that. What's been going on while we were incommunicado?"

She gave a short burst of laughter. "That's one way of putting it, eh? Well, let's see. . . . There was a search for you and Gunner when you didn't show up for supper."

"It's nice to know that the second I disappear, people think I'm having sexy fun time."

"Well, you were," Daria pointed out.

"I know I was, but everyone else doesn't have to think that way about me!" I pulled my dignity together. "At least people noticed we were missing."

"This morning the baron and his wife came back, and when he found out that no one had seen you or Gunner since yesterday, he started a proper search in the castle."

My cheeks warmed at the thought of what they had found, but I pushed it away. "Thank heavens for the baron."

"Yes, well, thanks to him *and* Gunner's daughter. The baron grilled her about what you talked about yesterday morning, and she said that Gunner had been talking about how his dad had taken them down to the cellar, and then the baron said, 'I wonder if he went to look in the bolt-hole,' and then I gather they tried the door, but it wouldn't open, so he got an ax and hacked it down." She made a moue. "I have to say, I wish I'd been there to see that. Roger said he filmed the whole thing, and it was going to get a lot of press."

"Oh, joy." I thought of all those viewers watching Gunner and me. "Like that's not going to give me nightmares for years."

"I don't see why it should—Tabby said she didn't get any shots of you, and kept the camera slightly off-kilter on Gunner so nothing untoward showed. Other than that, nothing much has happened, except this morning, before all of the excitement of finding you, Roger called a meeting and said that he wanted all the digging to be focused inside the castle. Paul tried to object, but Sue and Roger overruled him. As Paul said, we might be the archaeologists, but they hold the purse strings. All of which means today is my last day of doing proper archaeology." She kicked at a tuft of grass. "This whole treasure hunt thing is beyond ridiculous, and it isn't what I signed up for when I agreed to work for the CMA."

"I don't blame you for being upset, but look at it this way—if we do find something treasurelike, then it'll bring tons of attention to the dig, and that has to be good for archaeology, right?"

"Eh." She made a noncommittal gesture. "I'd rather just be allowed to do what I'm best at."

"I'll get some shots of you this afternoon," I promised, waving her off when she headed for the trench where two diggers were sitting and waiting, with nary a film camera in sight.

She waved back, and I hurried off to the castle, feeling a twinge of guilt at joining in the treasure fever, but excited at the thought of another mouse stone. I wondered what Gunner would think of it, then wondered where he was and what he was doing, and whether he was thinking about me. A sharp little spike of jealousy stabbed me at the thought that he was with some other woman, but then I realized just how stupid that was.

"I am not going to be one of those women," I told myself as I entered the castle through the French doors that Gunner had taken me through the day before. "I am not so insecure in myself, nor doubtful of his character, to attribute to him that sort of heinous—oh, hello."

Sue emerged from a side hall, pausing when she spotted me.

"I understand that Paul found another mouse stone," I said.

"Yes, he did."

She was as curt as she normally was with me, but I gave that no mind, smiling smugly to myself that she might have wanted Gunner, but I got him.

That thought startled me the second it cohered in my brain. Was he really mine? Did I really want him? The joke about marriage aside, he had said that I needed him, and what was better, he needed me. Was he right? Did I need him? Dr. Anderson had quite a few things to say about women who needed men, but she also said I had to trust my judgment.

The trouble was, I didn't seem to know what to think about Gunner. The fact that he seemed to know I had been abused was disconcerting, but I wasn't ready to face that just yet. No, more than anything, it was the word *need* that gave pause to thoughts of life with Gunner.

Oh, the sex was fabulous, more fabulous than I knew it could be, but was that enough to base a relationship on? Did I even *want* to have a relationship with him? That brought me back to that "need" statement. And where did that leave me?

"Confused," I muttered to myself as we emerged into the section of the house where the kitchen was located. I turned down an unlit hallway that I knew led to the cellar door.

Sue hurried after me, and we both descended the stairs to the cellar. I tossed the broken door that hung crookedly over the bolt-hole a black look when we passed it, but my attention was focused on the sounds of people and the sight of flickering lights that stretched out from the depths of the cellar. "Has Gunner already translated the stone? What does it say? I have to admit, I'm really starting to get excited about the whole treasure thing, and I didn't believe in it when we began."

"I have no idea." We arrived at the three storerooms that were currently hosting trenches. Sue murmured something about being too busy to speak with me, and escaped into the first room.

I looked around in surprise. Roger had somehow managed to get some bright lights strung along the upper walls, which gave the gloomy cellar a strangely stark look. I almost felt sorry to have the lights on, since they stripped away all the mystery inherent in the cellar ambiance.

I peered into the rooms until I found one with a large cluster of people. "Hello. Can I see the stone?"

Everyone turned to look at me, including Tabby and her camera. I'm sure my cheeks turned bright pink when I noticed several of the people smirking, but I was determined to pretend nothing unusual had recently happened to me down in these very cellars. I sauntered up to everyone with what I hoped was calm self-possession.

"Nice to *see* you again," Paul said with an impossible-to-miss inflection. It made my blush crank up a notch higher. "Yes, the stone is here. I've just been cleaning it, and have done a translation."

"Where's Gunner?" I asked, glancing around.

"Can't go an hour without him?" Paul asked with a wink at the camera. "I understand Ainslie's gone off to have his foot attended to."

"Oh no, has he hurt himself?" A little pang of worry had me wondering if I shouldn't go find him, and then I realized I didn't even have his cell number to call him. I started toward the door. "Maybe I should find him—"

"No, nothing like that," Roger said, bustling forward and shooing me over to a folding table that had been set up in a corner of the storeroom. "I understand he's having his cast off. Here's the latest clue in the hunt for the treasure. It's not a lot to look at, but Paul assures me that it has another riddle on it. Or part of one."

I looked down at the roughly rectangular piece of stone. Half of one of the sides had been chipped away, making it look like some fantastical beast had nibbled off the edge. In the lower right corner was a faded outline of a familiar mouse, partially obscured with a black stain. Above it, pale gray letters were visible, a section of the plaster surface having been flaked off, but it looked to me like the bulk of the letters were present.

"That's definitely one of the mouse stones," I agreed. "What does it say?"

Paul held the stone up and angled it to catch the light. "It's difficult to read since it's so faded, and apparently part of it has been rubbed off. I do see something about an extremity, and little weight. And I think that line there says 'making a good impression by day.' Hmm."

Roger peered over his shoulder. "An extremity? Like an arm or a leg? That would indicate a statue. We haven't uncovered any statues, have we?"

"No," Paul said, setting down the stone.

I wished Gunner were here so he could see it, and sidled over to take a gander at it myself.

"No statues, and the word extremity here could mean the extreme tip of something, so it might not mean arms or legs. It could be the top of a mountain peak, or highest point in a tower, or something like that."

"I see, I see. Hmm. But it *could* be a statue." Roger stroked his chin for a few seconds, then exclaimed, "A statue that is pointing to where the treasure is hidden! Or! What if it's a painting of a person pointing? I've seen that sort of thing before. Those Elizabethans, they loved to do that sort of thing. What if it started with the Romans?"

I looked at him in amazement. "Wow, you *really* run with an idea when you get one, don't you? Sorry, that sounded rude. What I meant was—"

"I have vision, yes," Roger said, thankfully not taking offense at what my mouth had spoken without my brain's permission. "That's why I've gotten as far as I have. Now, then, people, let's look lively, shall we? There's a statue or painting pointing to treasure to be found, and it won't show itself! Tabby, you and Matt and Sam and Vic come with me. We'll go to trench fifteen to film them lifting the skull from the skeleton. Viewers always like skulls. And then there's that suspicious shape in trench sixteen that could well be a chest of some sort. I wonder if there's a wall niche as well. Didn't Romans leave little statues of their gods in wall niches? One of them could be pointing...."

All five of them drifted out of the room, leaving behind Paul, Fidencia, and me.

"The man's an idiot," Fidencia said with an unattractive sneer.

"Yes, but one whose company is funding the dig, so it behooves us to keep such comments behind our respective teeth, hmm?"

Fidencia rounded on him. "Oh, I like that! You weren't being quite so circumspect when you ran out of condoms and wanted to go ahead despite my saying no, it was condoms or nothing. And speaking of our little rendezvous, I'm getting some sort of a rash that I didn't have before you seduced me."

Paul cleared his throat loudly to interrupt her. My heart fell at her words, though. Even though she wasn't my favorite person in the world, I didn't want to see her cursed with an STD.

He nodded toward me. "I think that talk is better left for another time, don't you?"

Fidencia evidently didn't care about having an audience. She glowered at him as she said, "I have an itch, Paul!"

"As have we all, my dear, but we don't act on them in public, at least, not unless we take precautions first."

I rolled my eyes. Paul gestured toward the far end of the room, where the white stones of an uncovered Roman wall gleamed against the nearly black soil that made up the floor. "Shall we get back to seeing where that wall leads?"

"All right, but if you've given me crabs or something, you're going to be hearing more about it," Fidencia said, stalking off.

Paul smiled widely at me. "Such a volatile girl. And how are you doing after your little embarrassment of this morning? Judging by what I saw, you have clearly gotten over whatever bug blighted you a few days ago, so if you'd like to get together this evening, I'm sure I can answer those questions you said you had."

It was too good of an opportunity to miss. "Crabs," I said to him.

He looked mildly discomfited. "As I said, she's very volatile, and she doesn't like the idea that I have many interests in life . . . both in subjects and people."

"And if you've given her something worse than pubic lice?" I asked, my heart beating wildly. I'd dreamed of the moment when I could confront him with what he'd done to Sandy, but somehow, it wasn't nearly as wonderful as I'd hoped it would be. It was actually a little scary. I desperately wanted Gunner there to help me confront Paul.

Good heavens—did this mean that I really *did* need Gunner? I shook that thought away, not able to deal with it at that moment.

Paul frowned, his voice going a few degrees colder. "Such as?"

"Try full-fledged HIV on for size," I snapped. "Have you told Fidencia how many lives you've ruined because you had unprotected sex? Have you told her how HIV can ravage your body? How it can leave you helpless or worse? How it can destroy the lives of sweet, innocent women who make the mistake of falling in love with you only to find out you're a heartless monster? Have you told her all that, Paul?"

"Who *are* you?" Paul asked, his face black with anger. His hands were clenched into fists, causing me to take a couple of involuntary steps backward.

I lifted my chin. "My name is Lorina Liddell, and my best friend in the world is Sandy Fache."

His eyes narrowed on me. "That madwoman! I ought to have known that you had something to do with her. You're just as self-righteous as she was."

"*Is.* She's still alive, not that you've done anything to promote a long life." I took a long breath, and made the meanest eyes I could. "And I'm here to see to it that you pay."

"Ah, I knew at some point that we'd get around to money." His nostrils twitched as if he smelled something rancid. "Well, your little attempt at blackmail won't work with me. I have nothing to hide." He waved a hand to the side. "My life is an open book, and I most certainly do not have HIV. I would know if I did."

"Have you had yourself tested?"

"Yes," he said, taking me by surprise.

"You . . . you have?"

"I just said so, didn't I?" He drew himself up to his full height and glared down at me. "A year ago I was a bit unwell, and had occasion to undergo some medical testing, and I opted to include several completely unneeded tests, as it turned out. So you can see that your attempt to squeeze money out of me is going to fail abysmally."

"But . . ." I shook my head. He had been tested? Sandy hadn't mentioned anything about that. "But Sandy said—"

"She lied," he said loudly. Noticing a look from Fidencia, he dropped his volume to add, "Perhaps your friend didn't tell you the entire truth about our little liaison, but I assure you that she was not as selective as you obviously were led to believe."

"Selective?" It was my turn to narrow my eyes, and I did so. "In what sense? In regards to men? Don't be ridiculous—she told me she fell in love with you three years ago at the dig in Iraq. She wouldn't sleep around if she felt that way about you, more sorrow her."

"Not only would, but did. I heard from a reliable source that wasn't a digger, someone who was safe from her attentions. She was caught going at it like a rabbit on a stone altar that was in the middle of being excavated. Does that sound like a woman in love?" His voice was filled with mockery, and it just made me want to slap his face.

"She's not like that," I protested, putting my hands behind me to avoid temptation. "She wouldn't sleep around that way."

"My dear, naive Lori—there's a reason Sandy was asked back to the dig for two years in a row, and it wasn't due to her archaeological skills."

That did it. It pushed me right over the edge.

"You bastard!" I gave in to the urge and slapped him, pulling back at the last minute so it wasn't as hard as I wanted. "How dare you!"

"That will be quite enough!" he snarled, shoving me backward. "And don't waste your time coming across all high-and-mighty. Sandy, as my dear mother would have said, was no better than she should be. Ask the people who were there—they'll tell you what really happened at that dig. As for me, I have more important things to do than to put up with this sort of accusation."

I watched him go to the trench with a growing sense of irritation and unease. Could he possibly be telling the truth? But if he was, Sandy had outright lied to me, and I had an even harder time imagining that.

"No," I told his retreating figure, straightening my shoulders. "I'm not going to let you make me doubt a perfectly wonderful woman. She has no reason to lie to me, and you have every motive to throw me off your scent." Shaking my head at myself, I left the cellar and went upstairs to inquire if anyone knew what Gunner's cell phone number was, and when he was expected home.

I had several things I wanted to think over, and even more that I wanted to talk to him about . . . and an overwhelming urge to do the latter while lying naked on top of him. I felt extremely awkward wandering around the castle without permission while I looked for him, although I hoped a bit of latitude would be granted given that Gunner and I were ... That thought brought my feet as well as my brain to a halt.

Just what were we? A couple? Dating? Engaged? I laughed to myself at the last word, knowing full well that Gunner was pulling my leg about getting married—who in their right mind married someone after knowing her for a week? Such things did not happen in real life, and if they did, they ended up in a quickie divorce that was never again discussed.

"Are you lost?"

I twirled around at the voice, sighing in relief when Alice emerged from a room behind me. "In thought and in deed, yes. I was hoping to find someone who could give me Gunner's cell number. Roger told me he went off to have his cast removed, and I wanted to find out when he was going to be back. There's a ... situation ... I want to discuss with him."

Her expression didn't budge an inch, but a distinct look of mirth lit up her eyes.

"Oh god," I said, slapping a hand over my mouth before spreading my fingers to add, "Forgive me. I didn't mean to speak in innuendos. I really did just want to talk to him. Not that I didn't enjoy our time together, mind you, because the man is beyond talented that way, but you probably don't want to hear that sort of thing about your brother-in-law, huh? Anyway, I did want to talk to Gunner about something, something *else*, and ... I'm babbling now, aren't I?"

She laughed, and pulled me into a room. "If you are, you have the excuse of having spent an extremely trying night, even if it was spent with the delicious Gunner."

"Stop lusting after my brother, wife," Elliott said without looking up from where a laptop sat on a large desk. "Else I'll have to get the parrot out."

I stopped, feeling even more like I was an interloper. "Parrot?" emerged from my mouth before I could make a fast escape. "Sorry. I'm clearly interrupting—"

"No, you're not." Alice went around to the back of the desk, reaching between the baron's stomach and the desk. For a moment I thought she was groping him right there in front of me, but when she pulled her hand back, she was holding a small address book. "Sorry, my cell phone is on the fritz, or I'd look up his number on it. And the parrot is . . . er . . . a friend of ours. Kind of."

"Do not try asking her to explain—the answer will only confuse you," Elliott said in his clipped British tone. Even though Gunner was adopted, I expected him to speak in a similar fashion, but it struck me then that Gunner's voice, although sexy as hell with an accent, was much softer in cadence, and not so BBC upper-class.

Elliott looked up and eyed me. "Alice tells me you have a mutual friend in her foster sister, and that she tried to get you to stay in the castle. You're welcome to room here if you've had your fill of Cressy."

"Elliott, have you forgotten that everyone is going to be returning in six days?" Alice smacked him on the arm with the address book before leafing through it. "I wouldn't wish the full force of your family on anyone, especially someone who's had to put up with a bored Gunner. Ah, here it is. Let me write it down for you."

I took the number she scribbled on a corner of an envelope, thanking her, and making my apologies for interrupting. "I'm sorry to have been wandering around your castle—it's really amazing, I have to say—but I got a bit lost and there are no signs on this floor."

"This is private," Alice said, following me to the door. "The ground floor is where the *turistas* flock. No, no, that wasn't meant as an indictment—you're welcome to look around wherever you like, isn't she, Elliott?"

"Until the family returns, at which point she will be likely to have several unpleasant surprises should she wander unexpectedly into any of the boys' rooms." He donned an expression that could only be described as martyred and started tapping at the keyboard.

"The *boys* range in ages from eighteen to late thirties," Alice said, blowing her husband a kiss before closing the door on him, and gesturing to the left. I walked down the hall admiring the paintings. "Did Gunner tell you that Lady Ainslie—their mom—adopted a butt-ton of kids from all over the world? They have seven brothers and two sisters, and all of them are crazy as loons. But in a good way. Lately, Elliott and I have been working at getting them all settled."

"Settled how?" I asked, following her down a long flight of stairs, which led to the familiar small kitchen.

"I'm in need of some cinnamon toast and tea." Alice filled a toaster with bread, and got butter and some sugar and cinnamon out of a cupboard. "Well, gainful employment mostly, although with the older ones, I've decided it's my job to help them find the happiness that Elliott and I have."

I sat when she gestured, my eyes widening. "You're matchmaking?"

"That's such a stigmatized word." She flipped a switch on an electric kettle, and got out a teapot, rinsed it, and spooned in some loose tea. "I prefer 'happiness enabler.'"

"If you think you're going to matchmake Gunner and me—," I started to say.

"But that's the good thing!" she interrupted, spinning around to grin at me. "You guys did it all yourselves without my having to intervene! That's so awesome, even if it does mean that I won't get to count Gunner as one of my successes. Still, I'm happy to have him settled even if I didn't have a hand in it. Do you like milk in your tea? I can't understand how the Brits like it like that, but maybe you feel differently."

"No milk." I felt suddenly weak, as if all my energy had drained away. "Do you happen to know when Gunner will be back?"

She cocked her head a minute, then smiled. "I'd say in about three minutes. That sounds like his bike."

"Good lord, he has a motorcycle?"

"Of course. Didn't you guess he would?" She set a few cups on the table, followed by plates, teapot, sugar, cinnamon, and, as an afterthought, a small pot of marmalade. "He's totally the motorcycle sort of man. Did he tell you how he broke his ankle?"

"Doing something foolish," I said, wondering what on earth I'd gotten myself into.

Alice nodded. "It's just the sort of thing we expected him to do." With that, she turned to the door and smiled. "Hello, Gunner. Look at you with two feet in shoes."

Gunner peeled off a leather jacket as he entered the room, a helmet in one hand and a cane in the other. He smelled like the outdoors and sexy man, and the instant that scent hit me, I wanted to throw myself on him and kiss him until he couldn't breathe.

"I won't show you what's under my sock, though," Gunner said, giving me a grin as he sat down next to me. "The skin on my foot looks like the underbelly of a fish that has lurked in the depths of Loch Ness. Are we having tea? Oooh, cinnamon toast? Lorina, would you believe that the Ainslie family never had exposure to such delights as cinnamon toast before Alice arrived to save Elliott from becoming a curmudgeon?"

"I heard that, you pestilential blight." Elliott strolled into the room, sniffing appreciatively. "I hope you were planning on bringing me some toast and tea while I was slaving away trying to put food in our respective mouths, Alice. A man cannot survive on a mere sandwich for luncheon."

"You ate three sandwiches, and half of the pasta salad I was going to save for dinner, so don't try to guilt me." Alice ruffled his hair affectionately as he sat down. "As a matter of fact, I was planning on a nice little chat with Lorina to explain to her what a mad wonderland she'd stepped into, but I guess that will have to wait. More toast coming up. Help yourselves to tea."

Elliott reached across the table for the sugar and poured himself and Alice each a cup of tea. He paused, giving me an odd look. "Lorina."

I started guiltily, and stopped trying to ogle Gunner out of the corner of my eye. "Yes?"

"That's your name."

"Yes, it is. Is something the matter with it?"

He set down his toast and frowned, as if he was thinking hard. "What's your surname? Little?"

"Not quite—it's Liddell. Sounds almost the same, but spelled differently."

To my surprise, he started laughing, pulling Alice down onto his lap when she arrived with another plate filled with toast. "Wonderland is right."

"What on earth are you cackling about?" Alice asked, giggling when he obviously squeezed her on the behind.

"Lorina Liddell. Alice." Elliott looked from her to me to Gunner. We all stared back at him. "Have none of you ever read the classics?"

"Classic what?" Gunner asked.

"*Alice in Wonderland.* That Alice's sister was named Lorina Liddell."

"Oh," I said, the penny finally dropping. "Yeah, my mother was a big Lewis Carroll fan. That's why she named me Lorina. She never liked the name Alice. Oh, sorry. No offense intended."

"None taken," Alice said. She was about to say something else, but evidently changed her mind, because she slid off Elliott's lap and picked up a tray on which she collected one of the two teapots, a plate of toast, and a couple of cups. "My darling, I think I'd rather discuss this fascinating insight you have into classical literature upstairs. In your office. In private."

Elliott stood up slowly, frowning as she took the cinnamon toast from him. "Why? I'm quite comfortable here."

She gave him a look that had him examining first Gunner, then me, and finally nodding. "Ah, yes. I see your point. Privacy with cinnamon toast is much desired." He took the tray from her and, without a look back, left the room, Alice in tow.

"That was subtle," I said when they were gone. "Do they expect us to have sex right here on the kitchen table?"

Gunner, who was chewing a piece of toast, paused, considered the idea, and then shook his head. "Too messy. We'd get sugar everywhere. Plus, Cressy might walk in, and then I'd have to get her a second horse."

"Don't tell me she's already wrangled one horse out of you?" I asked with a little laugh.

"Not yet, but she's made me promise to get her one when she turns eighteen in six months."

"She's a fast worker," I said with approval.

"Truer words were never spoken. Now." He dusted off

his hands, wiped the crumbs and sugar from his lips, and smiled. "About that lovemaking you mentioned. Shall we go upstairs?"

I would like to say that I didn't hesitate to disabuse him of the notion that I had been hinting I'd like to get down and dirty with him, but the sad fact is that I actually thought about it for a few seconds before remembering why it was I wanted to see him.

"As a matter of fact, we don't have time," I said, ignoring the desire to jump him right then and there. "Paul found another mouse stone, but his translation seemed a bit iffy to me, and now Roger is off on some tangent about a pointing statue, and I might have confronted Paul about Sandy."

I had hoped to slip that last bit in there without him noticing, but damn him, that's what he chose to pick up on.

"You confronted him?" he asked in the middle of putting cinnamon sugar on another piece of toast. "I thought we were going to do that together? I hoped we could come up with a reasonable plan, a thoughtful plan, a plan that wouldn't be tantamount to slander, and then proceed from there."

I slumped in my chair. "I know. We were. And I meant to wait for you, but Fidencia was there accusing him of having crabs, and then one thing led to another and I was telling him about Sandy, and he absolutely denied he had HIV. Which, of course, we knew he would, but still, he's got balls looking me dead in the eye and lying like that. And then he said the most heinous things about Sandy, which had to be him trying to smear her name in the dirt, and after that, I just kind of lost control."

He set the toast down. "Do I want to know what happened?"

"I slapped him." I hung my head for a second, hoping

the appearance of sorrow would keep Gunner from being annoyed with me, which just annoyed me, because I
shouldn't care if my actions don't make a man happy.

But I did care.

*Dr. Anderson would tell you that it's more important
to approve of your own actions than to worry if others
approve,* my inner self pointed out.

Shut up, I told her. *Dr. Anderson doesn't know everything.*

Mmmhmm. You've got it bad, don't you?

"I really hate internal monologues," I said with a sigh.

"Conscience getting the better of you?" Gunner
asked a bit archly, which I resented for about ten seconds.

"I'd say yes, but then you'd have proof that I listen to
the voice in my head, and that just sounds too crazy for
words. Oh, Gunner." I put my elbows on the table and
my chin on my hands. "What am I going to do? Paul
swears he didn't give Sandy anything. He says she was
basically the equivalent to the camp ho, and that if she
picked up HIV anywhere, it was not via him."

"Hmm." Gunner tore the piece of toast in half, and
gave me some before popping the rest into his mouth
and chewing while he thought. "What we need is a blood
sample."

I shook my head. "He says he already had a battery of
tests, including HIV, and that he's negative."

Gunner eyed me. "Could it be possible that he's telling the truth?"

"Sandy isn't like that. She's not promiscuous. She's
barely had two boyfriends the entire time I've known
her, and even when she was seeing someone, she never
had him over at our apartment overnight."

"I don't know what to say, then. On one hand, we have

Paul swearing he's clean and that your friend was a tart, and on the other, you know your friend well, and say she's not likely to have picked up the disease from anyone else." He frowned at the teapot. "I just don't see that we're going to get very far unless we have proof of what he claims—that he doesn't have an STD."

"And I doubt if he's going to be willing to hand over his test results to prove it," I said sadly, feeling the full weight of the burden I'd set on my shoulders. "It's too bad Daria's husband isn't here."

"Why is that?"

"He's a lab tech. Evidently he does all sorts of health testing, and he'd surely be able to tell us if a sample of Paul's blood was infected or not."

"That would imply we had a sample to be tested."

I waved the fact away that I had yet to figure out how to get said sample. "So what are we going to do?"

"About Thompson?" He got to his feet, winced briefly, and carried our plates over to the sink. I gathered up the tea things and took them to the counter. "I'll talk to him later and see if it's possible to get a glimpse at his test results, not that I believe he carries them around with him. There's a chance he might show us the results in order to shut us up."

"You think he really is innocent?" I asked, a bit dumbfounded.

"I don't know." Gunner rinsed out the teapot. "But I don't like to judge people until I have all the facts."

"I hate it that you're more principled than I am," I said, shooting him a little glare. "I've always prided myself on being a nice person, and here you are making me look like a heel. All right, we'll ask him nicely for the test results."

"After I see this latest stone," Gunner said, pulling me

up against his body, and speaking against my lips. "Unless you'd rather go upstairs and indulge yourself in some hot, steamy lovemaking first?"

"You are incorrigible," I told him, gathering my things and sashaying out the door.

His laughter followed me, making me feel simultaneously happy and worried.

What was I getting myself into by indulging in a relationship with Gunner? He made me intensely happy, and yet at the same time, I had a desperate feeling that I was about to take a start down a path from which I wouldn't be able to return. The problem was that I couldn't tell if that was a good thing or not.

"Why isn't life simple?" I moaned to myself.

Chapter 18

"It's a ring."

"Where?" Lorina glanced around her.

"Not a physical ring—this." Gunner waggled the latest puzzle stone at her. "The answer to the puzzle is a ring. The kind with a seal on it. It's another famous riddle. This time, I came prepared."

Lorina watched with interest as he pulled out a small Latin primer and flipped to an appendix. "Let's see, it should be . . . ah, here it is. The English translation is, 'I cling to an extremity. You might say I'm part of it, so little do I weigh. My face makes good impressions every day.' And the answer is a ring with a seal on it, the kind used to seal letters and such with wax."

"'My face makes good impressions' . . . ha." Lorina looked smugly satisfied. "And it has nothing to do with a pointing statue. Roger is totally off track."

"He is if he's expecting this puzzle to tell us where a

treasure is." Gunner thought for a few minutes. "I have to admit that I'm not seeing where the clues are leading us. A ship, a greeting, a roof tile, and now a ring."

"Maybe the ring is the treasure?" Lorina suggested, examining the stone.

"Ring? What ring?" Roger bustled into the store-room. "You found a ring?"

Lorina explained about the stone.

"Oh." Roger was clearly disappointed, but recovered quickly. "Well, ring . . . statue . . . it doesn't matter what it is so long as it leads us to the treasure. How's your foot? We'd like to get a piece filmed later with you explaining to Lorina why the dig has shifted to the castle cellar."

"My foot is fine, although I'm supposed to use this cane when I do a lot of walking." Gunner indicated the implement leaning against the wall. "And I'd be happy to do the piece, so long as Lorina isn't busy molesting me."

Lorina's eyes widened for a moment before she narrowed them with a warning of later retribution. It just made him smile. She was so easy to tease, so delightfully open with her expressions.

He thought of telling her right then and there that he was becoming quite serious about keeping her in his life, but decided that what she needed most at that moment — other than him — was space. She obviously had some emotional issues to work through, and although he'd love nothing more than to help her master them, he'd be patient and let her deal with them in her own way.

He was feeling very noble until he realized that Lorina was chatting with Roger about some plan for dressing them all up as Romans to reenact the burning of the villa.

He leaned down and whispered in her ear, "If I told you that I'm aware you need time to process the emotional ramifications of our relationship, would you gawk at me for my singular ability to understand your inner-most self, kiss me because I am thinking only of you, or punch me in the arm because you're so overcome with gratitude that you can only express yourself by a slight physical attack?"

She spun around and gawked at him. And then punched him in the arm before turning back to Roger. "That sounds fascinating, Roger, but I'm not sure I'll have the time to do the pieces in front of the camera with Gunner as well as play dress-up Roman and still have time to take pictures—"

"Of course you will. We will make sure you have the time," Roger said, giving them both a toothy smile. "And perhaps Gunner would care to be—"

"Lorina is the lady of the manor, and I am captain of Lorina's guard," he said, wiggling his eyebrows at her in a way that he hoped signified that he'd be captaining her guard just as soon as they were alone together.

"Are you?" Roger frowned to himself for a few moments before bobbing his head in acquiescence. "That would work. There were bound to be some guards at the villa, after all. Very well, we'll do the piece for the camera first; then we'll start the reenactment of the villa burn-ing."

"Won't that take time away from the dig?" Lorina asked, sliding Gunner a look when he wrapped an arm around her and hauled her up to his side. "I would think that was the first priority."

"It is, of course, but the digging will be done by then. It'll be dark, you see. Torches! We must have plentiful torches. I'm sure the Romans had torches. I wonder if I could buy some locally. . . ." He turned on the radio and demanded, "Someone find me a torch shop."

Gunner watched as Roger bustled out of the room making a note that someone would have to get hold of the wardrobe department of the network. "There goes one very single-minded man."

"I know, right? I've tried to point out the obvious to him—well, you heard me just now—but he just gets an idea and goes full bore with it." She dug her elbow into his side. "And what's with this emotional ramification business? If you're trying to pressure me into something, I should warn you that I do not pressure well."

"On the contrary, I was simply pointing out that I'm well aware you are feeling trapped right now, and that I was giving you the time and space you need to work through that and come to the decision that marrying me is the answer to a great many problems," he said lightly, not wanting to add stress to the situation. "Also, I noticed that you didn't kiss me."

"Pfft. And not likely to when you make silly comments like that." He was about to object that he wasn't teasing her when she continued, setting the stone back in its tray. "Evidently Paul is in one of the other rooms looking at some foundation that one of the diggers uncovered. Shall we go tackle him?"

"If you like." Gunner strolled with her out of the room, feeling only a slight twinge of ache in his ankle. "Although you may wish to let me do the talking, since you've already confronted him about it, and he might be less happy to see you again so soon."

She made a face, but kept silent as they approached Paul, who was directing a pair of diggers on how to clean off the wall.

"What is it?" Thompson snapped when Gunner asked to have a word with him. "Can't you see I'm busy? Some of us have work to do, you know. We can't all swan around the castle like . . . like . . ."

"Like I lived here?" Gunner put a smile on his face even though he would have liked to kick Paul out of the cellar. "I believe you'd prefer the discussion to be a bit more private." He glanced meaningfully at the diggers. "I have a couple of questions to ask about a dig a few years ago."

Thompson glared at Lorina, and looked, for a moment at least, like he was going to refuse Gunner's suggestion. "Very well. You two carry on. I won't be a moment."

Thompson marched out to the room where the mouse stone was stored. Fidencia had evidently been ordered elsewhere, since they were now alone.

"I hope you are not going to slander me the way that one did," he said, nodding at Lorina. "And also, she's crazy if she thinks I'm going to give in to her blackmail."

"I don't blame you," Gunner said, taking Thompson by surprise. "If I'd been accused of something I didn't do, I'd say the same thing. The question is, can you prove what you say?"

"Prove it?" Thompson looked first appalled, then angry. "Why the hell do I have to prove anything?"

"Because it's the right thing to do. Because you are a decent human being. Because you are aware that the charges made against you by Lorina's friend Sandy are grave and you wish to assure her and any other women you've been with that you are not the cause of any illness."

Thompson's jaw worked a couple of times; then he finally spat out, "You have no right to the sort of proof you're asking for."

"No," Gunner acknowledged. "We don't. And we can't force you to give it to us—we can only ask you to do the decent thing because an innocent woman has suffered, and we would all like to keep others from going through the same thing."

"Very well." Thompson gave an annoyed sniff. "Because I have nothing to be afraid of, I will do as you ask, even though I consider having to prove my innocence an unnecessary inconvenience. As you say, I am a decent man, and if it will make Sandy feel better to know that our relationship did not end in her present situation, then I will e-mail my physician for a copy of the lab results. So long as the information contained therein goes no further than Sandy."

"Absolutely," Gunner agreed. "We don't wish to persecute the innocent, Thompson, or invade your privacy any more than we have to. We simply desire to locate the source of the infection, and ensure that person receives appropriate treatment."

"I just hope you have a suitable apology ready for me once you see the lab results," Thompson replied grandly, and stalked away.

Lorina sagged against Gunner when he was gone, releasing breath that she had evidently been holding. "That was the most horrible thing I've ever done. Dear god, I feel dirty. Do you feel dirty, Gunner?"

"Not dirty so much as guilty as hell." He pinched the bridge of his nose to forestall a headache he felt coming on. "I do admit that was one of the more unpleasant things I've ever done, and hope I never have to do it again. There is one thing worse, though."

"Ethnic genocide?" Lorina asked, releasing his hand and moving over to examine the stone and the other finds that sat on the makeshift table. "Baby-seal clubbing?"

"That he's as innocent as he says he is," Gunner said grimly.

Lorina shuddered. "Yeah, that's going to be seriously horrible. He could sue me."

"I doubt he'd do that, since he offered to let us see the lab results, but he could make things very uncomfortable for us." He caught her hand as she walked past him, about to head out the door. "Lorina, you're very certain—"

"Yes," she said without letting him finish. She hesitated a moment, then leaned in and kissed him gently before licking the tip of his nose. "I know Sandy. She's not promiscuous."

He took a deep breath. "All right, then. We'll just deal with the situation as it happens."

"You'll see. Sandy will be vindicated," she predicted, and, with an explanation that she needed to catch up with taking photos of the dig in the cellar, went off to gather her camera equipment.

Gunner had to fight back the urge to give her instructions on how to frame shots, but kept his advice to himself, and instead went to find his daughter.

He found Cressy as happy as a lark, and she quickly had him promising her she could spend the weekend assisting the stable owner with an overnight pony trek, which made her even happier.

"Thank you, thank you, thank you! You're the best dad ever!" Cressy yelled, doing a leap of happiness, and flinging herself on him to smother his cheeks in kisses. "Madame said we could do a little cross-country work, which is so awesome! This is the best summer I've ever had! Gran, did you hear?"

Salma emerged from her tent, a folding chair in her hand. "I did. I believe anyone within a five-hundred-yard radius heard your cries of joy. Good afternoon, Gunner. You look much better than this morning."

Gunner wasn't the sort of man who blushed at the drop of a hat, but he felt a little warmth on his cheeks that had nothing to do with Cressy's overenthusiastic signs of affection. He met Salma's eyes, wondering if he was going to see any reproach in them, but there was nothing but a little amusement that he could well bear.

"It's amazing what a meal and a shower can do to raise your spirits. How are things going out here?"

"Very well. Cressida had a nice lesson today, didn't you, dear? And we have decided to indulge ourselves in a little celebratory dinner in town tonight. You don't mind if we don't spend the evening with you and your family, do you?"

"We're celebrating the fact that you had illicit sex in the tunnel, and are getting married and getting me a horse next year," Cressy said in a rush, and then looked down at her walking shorts and *eek*ed. "Gotta change! Back in a flash, Gran."

"No, I don't mind you having dinner by yourselves, although I know Elliott and Alice are looking forward to spending time with both you and Cressy."

"I promised Cressida what she calls a girls' night out," Salma said. "And I hate to go back on that, but of course, if the baron and his wife would like us to attend dinner with them—"

"We'll do a family dinner tomorrow," Gunner reassured her, then grimaced. "Illicit sex in the tunnel?"

Salma just smiled. "You do that martyred look very well, Gunner."

"Unfortunately, it's a look that I'm going to be wearing a lot."

"Only if you keep allowing Cressida to find you in compromising positions." She lifted a hand when he started to protest, giving a gentle little laugh. "That wasn't a criticism, my dear, merely an observation. I do like Lorina, you know."

"Good. I do as well."

She hesitated a moment before continuing. "I hope you aren't allowing yourself to be swayed by empathy into actions you might later regret."

He puzzled through that for a moment before guessing she was talking about the marriage announcement. "Have you ever known me to be forced into something I didn't want to do?"

"No, but this is a situation where you're not really being forced, are you?" She sat on the folding chair, smoothing a hand over the skirt covering her knees. "You might not wish to acknowledge the fact, but you are a very empathetic man, and I can see that you feel strongly about Lorina."

He was genuinely surprised that Salma knew him so well, since he saw her so seldom. "Strongly empathic, you mean?"

She said nothing for a moment. "I suspect it started that way, but now other emotions have come into play, have they not?"

"I'd be a dead man if I didn't think Lorina was worth my attention," he said with a rush of gallantry.

"And that is very telling," Salma said, nodding. "Lorina is charming, quite charming, and I like her. But you clearly see much in her that perhaps others miss. No, I'm not criticizing her, so you needn't rush to her defense— I'm sure she's everything you know her to be. I'm simply saying that to those of us who don't have your sensitivities, she is a perfectly nice woman, no more and no less. What is more, she is, I suspect, quite vulnerable to your particular charms. I would hate to see that vulnerability exploited."

"If you're worried that I'm rushing into a relationship, I can assure you that Lorina stated several times that she has no intention of marrying me. Although I have to admit, the thought that she's so willing to spurn my offer has wounded my pride a bit."

"And perhaps your brother's recent marriage has made your own situation look a little less rosy?"

"My situation as in my inability to maintain a serious

relationship?" he asked, wondering if he should be offended that his feelings were so easily read.

She made a conciliatory gesture. "Let us say your choice to stay open to potential new romance rather than commit yourself to one person."

"I'm a free spirit," he said with dignity. "I always have been. Elliott's the one who had long-term girlfriends— I'd never found one that I wanted to be with beyond a few weeks."

She was silent for a moment, her gaze on Cressy's tent, from which came the sounds of both music and occasional crashes followed by muted cursing. "Until now?"

He opened his mouth to say that he would move heaven and earth to protect Lorina, but reality wasn't quite so cut-and-dried. "That is something we will have to wait and see. Unfortunately, the decision is not mine alone to make."

"And yet you announced your engagement in public without Lorina's consent."

He shifted uncomfortably, swallowing back the explanation that it had originally been made in jest, but now had taken on a much more enticing aspect. "Yes, well, I might have been a bit premature in that, but I'm sure that once a few problems are taken care of, Lorina will be more open to considering a future with me."

"And if she doesn't want a future with you?"

He straightened his shoulders. "I don't know. I'm hoping it doesn't come to that, because I'm not sure I could move on from her." Raising his voice, he added, "Cressy, do you need any spending money?"

Cressy stuck her head out of the tent, clutching the door tightly. Her hair, which had been contained in a ponytail, had somehow gone through a transformation, and now resembled several hedgehogs locked in mortal combat. "When *don't* I need spending money, Gunner?"

"I apologize," he said, pulling out his wallet and giving her a few bills. "That was a stupid question."

"The only stupid question is the one not asked," Cressy said, blowing him a kiss before disappearing back into the tent.

"I really do not know how she turned out as smart as she did," Gunner told Salma, "but I'll never stop being grateful to your daughter for her. Shall I see you two later tonight, or will your girls' night out be a lengthy one?"

"I don't think we will be back at a sociable hour. We plan on visiting the cinema after dinner." She gave him a knowing look tinged with amusement. "You are free to enjoy your evening without our limiting presence."

He bent down to kiss her cheek. "You're a witch, do you know that? In another age, they'd have burned you at the stake."

"In another age, I wouldn't have let them know the truth about me."

He laughed and, after a quick look at his watch, headed back to the castle. He had arranged to meet Lorina shortly before dinner, so they could meet Thompson together, and he had just enough time to shave and change his clothes before that.

It didn't escape him that he was almost giddy at the thought of spending the entire evening with Lorina. That excitement lasted until he had completed his ablutions, and then the thought struck him that perhaps Lorina had other plans for her evening.

"Impossible," he said aloud, refusing to give in to the doubts that Salma had started within him. "Lorina clearly can't keep her hands off of me, and I'm not going to encourage such subversive thoughts. The only question is whether she would like to go out to dinner or have me cook for her here."

The question was still uppermost in his mind when he thumped his way down the stairs to the small sitting room that the family used when they were home. To his surprise, Elliott was sitting with a book in his hand.

"Ah," his brother said upon sighting him. "There you are."

"I am indeed, although I'm about to leave. Did you need something?"

"Not need so much as wanted. I thought we could catch up."

Gunner paused in the act of gathering up the keys to his motorcycle. "That sounded very older brother. You wouldn't, by any chance, be wishing to question me about the fact that I announced I was going to marry a woman I've known for a week?"

Elliott looked surprised. "No, actually, I wasn't going to mention that. I assume you know your own mind."

"Thank you. Then you, like Salma, must be warning me about stomping all over Lorina's heart. If so, I can assure you that I have no intention of doing anything to hurt her."

"Again, that wasn't what I was going to say." Elliott cleared his throat. "It's another matter that's become quite obvious."

Gunner crossed his arms over his chest. "You know full well that I would never have been in the middle of carrying on with Lorina had I known that you had broken down the door to the bolt-hole and crept along the tunnel to us—"

"We weren't creeping!" Elliott said loudly. "The amount of noise being generated was enough to wake the dead, but evidently not enough to distract you two."

"I would point out that when I make love to a woman, she's oblivious to all else, but you're well aware of tales of my prowess, so I won't."

"Don't you try to look modest at me, Gun," Elliott said, pointing the book at him. "I know full well you haven't a shred of modesty, and yes, I'm equally well aware of both your reputation and the fact that when one is so pleasantly engaged, trivial things like an awareness of one's surroundings get lost. That was, in fact, not what I wanted to talk to you about, either."

"Well then, what the hell is?" Gunner asked, running out of patience. He hated being called on the carpet, especially when he knew he was guilty of misdeeds.

"It's come to my attention that you are blackmailing a member of the dig team."

Gunner stared at his brother for the count of twenty before speaking. "That bastard ran to you, didn't he?"

"If by 'that bastard' you mean a perfectly charming woman, then yes."

"A woman? What woman? Not Lorina!"

"No, although the fact that you've mentioned her makes me believe she knows what you've done." Elliott gave him a long look, one that made Gunner think of their father. He felt even more like a naughty schoolboy, which in turn just made him even more irritated.

"Of course she knows—she's the whole reason we're blackmailing that bastard Thompson."

"So you admit you *are* blackmailing him?"

"No, of course not, I was being facetious. We simply asked Thompson about a situation that is worrying Lorina, and he offered to give us the proof that he wasn't guilty of instigating the situation. There was no blackmail involved, although I have no doubt he thinks we pressured him into doing the right thing." Gunner took a deep breath and tried to think of the names of all the women diggers. He had met only a couple of them, although the one he knew best was Daria. "It couldn't have been Daria. . . ."

"That was, I believe, her name." Elliott set down the book. "Gun, you know I hate to do this just as much as you hate to have me rail at you, but really, we can't have you harassing anyone, let alone people who have given us a substantial amount of money to spend a month on the castle grounds. They may not be guests per se, but they are tantamount to guests, and I draw the line at extorting money from guests. At least, not money they haven't agreed to pay, although god help us if Alice continues to hold those Historic Ainslie Castle events. I may just go mad if she goes through with her plans to have a Victorian Month. Can you see me in a cravat for an entire month?"

Gunner couldn't help but laugh despite the dressing-down he was receiving. "No, although I'm willing to wager that Alice would come up with some costume for you that made you look even more the lord of the manor than you already are."

Elliott made a rude gesture at him. "Do you want to explain just why you and Lorina see fit to not-quite-blackmail one of the archaeologists?"

"It's not even remotely blackmail, and no, I don't wish to explain," Gunner said smoothly. "It's not my explanation to give. I will inform Lorina that you're concerned about the situation, and see if she'd like to explain the whole story."

"Uh-huh." Elliott gave him a sour look. "I'm sorry, Gunner, but that's not going to be good enough. I want an end to this right now. At the very least, you need to apologize to Thompson."

Gunner was silent for a few minutes while he struggled between loyalty to his brother and respect for Lorina. In the end, he couldn't resolve the two and simply said, "You've known me my entire life, El. You know I have done things that aren't quite as respectable as you might wish, but I am not evil. You're just going to have to take it on faith that if I make a few waves, I have a good reason for doing so. You can rest assured that if Lorina and I are in the wrong, then I will most definitely apologize."

"That's just the problem," Elliott said, ruffling a hand through his hair and making the curls stand out in spikes. "I said the exact same thing to Alice, and she took it further and said that Thompson probably deserved being accosted for doing something so bad that you'd have to talk to him about it, and she was all for kicking him off the property. But that aside, I really have to ask you to fix the situation. I don't care how you do it, but make it good."

"I said I would if it's warranted. And I should know that"—he consulted his watch—"in less than two hours."

"Thank you." Elliott was silent for a moment; then his eyes grew amused and he grinned. "I can't believe you've finally fallen for a woman. You *have* fallen for her, haven't you? Yes, I can see you have—you've got that same expression on your face that I started seeing in the mirror after I met Alice. Plus there was that marriage proposal."

"Yes, that was a bit of a surprise to me, too," Gunner said, relaxing into a chair to ease his foot. "It just kind of burst out without my being aware of it until after I'd spoken. Lorina thinks it's all a joke, of course."

"Of course." Elliott leaned back in his chair, propping his feet up on an open drawer. "I notice, brother mine, that you are trying deftly to avoid addressing the issue of having fallen for Lorina."

"Not avoided, simply not acknowledged. And stop

being so nosy—my romantic life is none of your business."

Elliott took the abuse as it was intended—with half-hearted sincerity. "And should I let Alice go ahead with plans for a wedding?"

"Eh . . ." Gunner didn't like being put on the spot, and wondered if he could distract his brother. He decided he had a morsel of news sufficiently intriguing, and gave it a shot. "Let's put plans for a wedding on hold until I've had a chance to talk more about it with Lorina. But I meant to ask you, did you hear that they've found another treasure stone today? In the cellar, actually."

Elliott sat up at the word "treasure." "No, I didn't hear that. I was going to ask you why you authorized a cellar dig, but tell me more about this stone. The TV producer was going on and on about the potential treasures to be found, but it didn't seem realistic."

"We don't know that there is a treasure, but it seems more possible than it did a week ago." He spent twenty minutes going over the history of the dig finds, with emphasis on the riddles and how they could be pieced together. "The greeting is clearly exactly what it says it is—the start of a series of communications."

"In this case clues," Elliott agreed. "And the ship and roof tile can only mean a decoration on an upper story."

"But the ring . . . that one has me. You're the scholar in the family—what do you think of the riddles? Do they seem to point to something specific?"

Elliott thought for a few minutes, idly turning back and forth in his swivel chair. "It could be . . . do you remember a program on TV some years back about a series of Roman decorations found near Hadrian's Wall? As I recall, they were round in shape, and bore a distinct resemblance to coins. What if the ring clue doesn't mean a ring itself, but a circular decoration?"

"Now, that's a good idea," Gunner said, mulling it over. "So you think the decorations were along the roof-line of the second villa, the one that's now under the castle?"

"Not necessarily the second villa."

"So you think the treasure is behind the decoration?" Gunner thought about that for a moment. "Makes sense to me, especially if there's precedence."

"I believe there is." Elliott got up and went to a computer, typing for a few minutes before he said, "Ah, I thought I remembered that correctly. It *was* a temple, not a villa."

"What was a temple? Where they found the ring decorations?"

"Yes." Both men stared at each other.

"The temple is where all those people were killed. The ones from the original villa, and probably the one under us as well."

"A temple in the grove," Elliott said, his eyes alight. "How very dramatic. I wonder if I could use it in a book."

"You're brilliant," Gunner told his brother, his mind racing. "It all fits: the clues leading away from the villas, the sacred safety of a temple—at least sacred in the mind of the Romans—being used as a hiding place for their precious items, hidden away behind seemingly innocent decorations. It's all there. And even if there are more stones and we don't find them, at least we have a definitive place to look."

"If the decoration was plaster, as they frequently were, then it's not likely to have survived," Elliott warned.

"True enough, but whatever treasure was hidden behind it or beneath it—assuming we have the solution to the puzzle in the first place—whatever was hidden may well have been protected in a box or chest. I'll discuss it with Lorina. I'm due to meet her shortly."

"Should we tell the TV producer?"

"Not just yet. Let me talk to Lorina, first. She's been as much a part of this as me, and I'm willing to bet she'll want a chance to locate the treasure before the TV people or Thompson are unleashed on it."

"That's not very professional," Elliott chastised. "They are, after all, paying for the right to dig on the grounds."

Gunner sighed. "I know. Sometimes I hate having a good upbringing—it makes it so much harder to be immoral. The film crew and the archaeologists all have a dinner in town tonight where they will be feted by the mayor and town council. Roger invited me to attend, but I made my excuses, since I'd much rather spend it with Cressy and Lorina. Once he's returned from that affair, I'll tell him about your ideas."

"That sounds much wiser than trying to dig it up yourself," Elliott said with obvious approval.

Gunner grinned. "That doesn't mean I'm not going to take a stab at a little exploratory digging while everyone is off at dinner, mind."

"Just so long as you don't irritate the production company, or give them cause to complain you're keeping all the glory to yourself," Elliott warned. Then, with a wry twist of his lips, he added, "Let me know if you find something promising; Alice would love to be there to see it dug up."

"Definitely."

"Not that we'd be able to keep any of the treasure if it was found, what with the law forcing us to give up anything of value," Elliott said somewhat wistfully, "but it might bring in more tourists, and we could include a tour down to the cellar to see the remains of the villa.

Alice is already brimming with marketing ideas for fans of the TV show."

Gunner grinned. "Good for her."

"And about the other thing—" Elliott gave him a look that was meant to be stern.

"Consider it taken care of." Gunner left before Elliott could chastise him further, his mind on Lorina.

Chapter 19

"About this wedding of yours, Lorina—"

"What the—" I stopped dead in my tracks, looking around wildly until I noticed Roger sitting in the shadow of his RV, tweaking his tie and brushing off a suit jacket. "Oh, hello."

"I had a thought, and I know you will like it. Rather than simply having the wedding at the end of the show, as we originally thought, what if we have a Roman wedding?"

I stared in disbelief. "A what?"

"A Roman wedding. You know, a reenactment of the sort of wedding that the lord and lady of the manor would have had."

"They weren't a lord and lady, were they?" I protested. "I thought Romans were just . . . citizens."

Roger waved that idea away. "Anyone can have a wedding. Just last season, *Britain's Got Mimes* had a wedding, and if the mimes did that, then we have to go one step better."

"Mimes have their own TV show?" I asked, dazzled at the thought.

"Yes. They were forbidden to speak when they were in costume, which was all the time, and let me tell you, if you think you can generate drama by a couple of mimes sissy fighting, you should think again."

"I beg your pardon?"

"Sissy fighting. You know," he said, paddling his hands in the air. "A slap-athon. It was the lamest thing you've ever seen."

"I can imagine," I lied, not being able to wrap my brain around the idea of a reality show that featured mime fights.

"So *we'll* do a Roman wedding. Clever, eh? It ties in with the program, allows us to set up some epic reenactments—the making of the bride's dress, getting the groom to the church, et cetera—and yet has something that no other reality TV show has. Viewers will love it, absolutely love it."

"I won't, you know. But it doesn't matter. There's not going to be a wedding, Roman or otherwise—"

I stopped talking when Roger's phone started blaring an obnoxious pop song.

"Hold that thought. It's the studio head," he said, lifting up a hand as he took the call. "Gloria, darling, how nice to hear from you. I was just going to call you up and tell you about the ever-so-exciting discoveries we've been making—" He wandered off chatting gaily into the phone.

Luckily, the rest of the dig and film crews were busy getting ready for a big dinner in town with local officials, so no one paid me any mind except to ask if I was going with them. I made my excuses, took a quick catnap, and was out a short time later taking pictures of the abandoned trenches in the golden afternoon sun.

Gunner sauntered around the corner of the barn behind me, a sultry smile clinging to his lips. He wasn't quite as graceful as I suspected he would be normally, since he still limped a little while walking, but that didn't mean I couldn't ogle him. "You clean up very nicely," I told him, having to restrain myself from removing the black shirt that clung to his chest in a way that came close to making me drool.

He glanced down at himself, clearly surprised by my comment. "Thank you, but I didn't actually dress up. I would have worn boots, but my ankle is just swollen enough to keep me in trainers."

"Those jeans have been ironed," I said, pointing at the faint creases on the fronts of the legs. "And that shirt is pretty nice. I consider both dressing up. And here I am in nothing but a sundress, and sandals that have seen better days, and my hair is sticking out all over because Cressy confiscated my hair dryer this afternoon, and I have no idea where she put it."

"You look divine," he said, taking my hand and bowing over it before he kissed my fingers. "I like your dress because it thrusts your breasts upward, where they clearly are waiting for my attention. I like your sandals because they draw my attention to your long, glorious legs. And I like your hair curly like that because it means you have a strong mind."

"Oh, it does not," I said, taking the arm he held out for me.

"No, but it sounded good. Ah, I see you're taking pictures."

"Yes, I thought it might be an interesting contrast to the other pictures. And speaking of interesting contrasts, Roger wants us to have a Roman wedding," I said with disgust as we slowly made our way along the line of RVs. "He thinks we'll beat the mimes that way."

"Mimes?"

I shook my head. "You don't want to know. Although, word of warning—never get in a fight with one. I guess it's a slap fest if you do. Are we going to dinner?"

"We are, but I thought we'd get the meeting with Thompson over with first, if that's agreeable with you."

"I'm sure he's at the big dinner in town."

"He wasn't about ten minutes ago when I saw him run to his caravan."

"Oh. Good." I made a face. "Or not good, depending on your frame of reference. I really wish it was over with."

"If you'd rather not be there—"

"No, no, I just meant that my stomach is tied in knots thinking about it. But you're right—let's get it over with. Only . . . what on earth are we going to do if Paul comes up with some proof that he's not the source of the disease?"

"We'll apologize for taking up his time," Gunner said, placing his hand over mine and giving it a supportive squeeze. "I should warn you from speaking around Daria, though. Evidently she went running to my brother with tales of us blackmailing Thompson."

"Blackmail? We didn't blackmail him."

"No, but evidently he presented the situation to Daria that way."

I frowned. "That's . . . surprising."

"Why so?"

"Because Daria doesn't like Paul. She said as much the first day I was here, and she's been even angrier ever since he removed her from the dig team in the cellar. I gather that they do things by seniority in the archaeology world, and as the second most experienced archae-

ologist, she should have been working in the cellar rather
than Dennis."

"Who's Dennis? The one with the hat?"

"Yeah. He's nice enough, although he seldom talks,
and Daria was really annoyed when Paul assigned him
to the trench instead of her. Why would she tattle on us
like that? It doesn't make sense."

"Human nature seldom does," Gunner said, and
stopped in front of the door of Paul's RV. My stomach
gave a lurch. "Courage, my love. We'll get through this
together."

Most of the tension eased from my tightly wound gut.
I leaned in to give him a little kiss, breathing in his heady
scent. "Thank you, Gunner. It's nice to know that you
are so supportive. It's not something I've seen a lot of in
my life."

"I gathered that to be the situation. Who was it who
mistreated you? Your father?"

His eyes were warm, and filled with understanding. I
wanted to cling to him and sob out the story of my life,
but I hadn't learned to be strong for nothing. I kissed one
corner of his mouth and pulled away. "Let's leave that
for another time, shall we?"

"I'm here whenever you want to talk," he said simply,
and, lifting his hand, knocked on the door. "And I do
mean whenever. Middle-of-the-night consultations are
my specialty."

"I'll remember that—"

The door opened. My stomach gave a warning jump
when Paul gave us both a haughty look before handing
Gunner a piece of paper. "I think you'll find everything
is in order. Not, I wish to point out again, that I need
your approval for my lifestyle, but as you can see by the
copy of the lab results, it would be quite impossible for

me to infect anyone, let alone Sandy Fache. Now, if you'll excuse me, I'm late for that important dinner."

He shut the door on us before we could respond.

"Well, that was both anticlimactic and oddly dramatic," I said, my stomach settling down to normalcy. I leaned into Gunner's side to read the paper. "What does it say? Is it from his doctor?"

"No. Better than that—it's a copy of the result from the lab itself."

"*Specimen number . . . date of birth . . . clinical information . . . physician ID . . . Ah, here it is. Test name: HIV. Test name: syphilis. In range: nonreactive. Test name: hepatitis B. In range: nonreactive. Test name: hepatitis C. In range: nonreactive. Analysis performed by: Hollingberry Laboratories. The performance of this assay has not been approved for pediatric populations. . . .* Blah, blah . . . the rest are just disclaimers. What the hell, Gunner? Nonreactive? Does that mean what I think it means?"

Gunner sighed, and folded the paper, tucking it away in his pocket. "It means, my sweet one, that we owe Thompson an apology. These results show he did not have any of the diseases listed, including HIV."

I shook my head before he stopped speaking. "No. I don't buy that. Sandy isn't the sort of person to sleep around. She said she fell in love with Paul, and that means she wouldn't sleep with anyone else. He's got to have done something to get a false report. Maybe he had someone else send in blood for him."

"That's not very likely. Should we get it over with now, do you think, or would he be more annoyed at being interrupted to appreciate an apology?"

I slumped against him. "This is my fault, not yours. I will be the one to apologize, but I think I'd better do it with a written apology as well. It looks more substantial than just sticking my head through the open door and yelling, 'Sorry we accused you unjustly.' I just can't believe that the report is right, though. Maybe he paid someone off?"

"I think you're just going to have to accept the fact that he isn't the source of your friend's woes." Gunner took my hand, leading me away from the RVs and out toward the fields. "Most labs have stringent requirements in place so that the samples taken are from the correct donor."

Something was itching at the back of my brain, some idea or fact or *something* that I couldn't quite put my finger on. "I just don't believe it," I repeated, only then noticing that Gunner had paused to collect a couple of shovels and my dig bag. "What are you doing? I thought we were going to have dinner."

He grinned, his teeth flashing in the sun, which was beginning to set. "We are, but I want us to check on something first."

"Out here?" I asked, glancing around. We were headed toward the field where the main number of trenches were, but bypassed those for the small hill just beyond the fence that was covered in trees. "You're not planning on digging where the bodies were, are you? Because, although Roman skeletons don't weird me out, the thought of spending the night digging in what is basically a massacre site is a bit unsettling."

"It was a temple before the people from the villa were killed there," Gunner said, giving me another smile.

"Right, that's a smile that knows something. That's a smile that says, 'I have a secret, and you don't know it,' which is only going to irritate me. Why are you smiling that smile, Gunner? What secret do you have, and why aren't you telling me?"

"I haven't told you because my mother taught me it

wasn't polite to talk over people, especially people you like. And I like you. A lot. Are you done analyzing my quite innocent smile?"

I made a face at him, and felt my psyche relax even more. I wanted to do a little dance of joy that I found a man with whom I could be myself without worry. "Innocent, my shiny pink ass. Spill."

"Shiny pink . . ." He stopped walking for a moment, his fingers white around the shovel handles. After a few seconds of deep breathing, but before I could ask him what was the matter, he shook his head. "No. I must focus on this right now. Later, my delicious little squab, later we shall address the issue of your attempting to distract me with your shiny pink ass, but until then, I want to do a little digging before Roger gets back from his dinner."

"Hullo. What are you two up to?"

We stopped midway across the field. Daria had evidently been sitting on the floor of one of the deeper parts of a trench, and popped up now, dusting herself off.

"Oh, hi. I thought everyone had gone off to have dinner. Gunner seems to think that we need to do a little digging." I glanced at the man in question, unsure if he wanted me to mention more.

"We do," Gunner agreed.

"For something in specific?" Daria started packing away her tools.

"Good question." I turned to Gunner. "OK, now you really do have to tell us what's going on. What brilliant deduction did the baron have? Why are you worried about Roger? Did you find a mouse stone that gave directions?"

"Better than that—I have a brother who loves word puzzles, and has a history degree." He stopped, clearly loath to say more in front of Daria.

"Ah," I said awkwardly, wanting to help Gunner, but at the same time disliking his desire to keep Daria out of it. "That sounds . . . promising."

Daria looked from me to Gunner, and evidently realized what was going on. She gathered up her bag of tools, and said simply, "I'll leave you to it, then. Happy treasure hunting."

"Thank you," Gunner said, waiting until she was out of earshot to say, "That was a bit awkward."

"Only because you wanted to keep your news secret from her. She's nice, Gunner, even if she did tattle to your brother on us."

"Which makes me hesitant to trust her overly far."

I took two of his shovels and marched alongside him. "That was personal drama. She's probably just one of those people who likes to gossip about others. Archaeology is different, though. I've seen how dedicated she is to it. She could probably help us."

Gunner glanced at his watch. "Knowing the mayor and how he likes the sound of his own voice, we have at least two hours before Roger could return, and we'd be obligated to fill him in. Given that, I have to admit that it's more fun to chase the treasure when it's just us."

"True," I agreed. "So what is it exactly that your brother said about the treasure?"

I listened with growing excitement (and admiration for the baron's deductive reasoning) as Gunner explained why he felt the treasure would be found in the grove. "But would this roof-decoration circle thingie survive?" I asked when he finished. "Wouldn't the attackers go after the temple? I may not know a whole lot about English history, but if I was pissed at invaders to my country, and trying to destroy them, I'd sure as shooting go after their religious places along with their houses."

"Yes, they would have most likely burned the temple

as well as the villas, and it may well be that the decoration was destroyed along with the rest of the structure. But I'm hoping that the treasure itself was protected and is just waiting for us to find it. Whoever hid it went to considerable trouble in a time of great stress to leave behind clues as to its whereabouts, so I assume he or she took precautions to ensure the survival of the treasure itself."

"I sure hope so," I said. We made a detour to the far end of the field in order to go through a gate, and then turned northward to the small stand of trees that marked the temple ruins. "It would be really annoying to have all these great clues and not have resolution to the mystery. Who do you think left the stones?"

"There you have me," Gunner said, setting down my dig bag next to a large fragment of stone. I realized with a start that it was likely a chunk of the temple wall that had survived enough to push its way out of the dirt. "We'll have to ask Elliott what he thinks. He's clever that way. Now, then, let's see if we can align the geophys results with the walls that were uncovered, so we can find the front of the building."

We consulted the black-and-white printout, which to me looked like nothing but a bunch of black blobs and lines and squiggly bits. Gunner eyed first the line of wall nearest to us, then the paper, rotating it several times before he nodded. "The door faces south, I think. Now, if you were a treasure, and your hiding spot over the mantel of the front door was destroyed, where would you fall?"

"Why the front door?" I asked, looking around for something that screamed "treasure hiding spot." "If you were hiding something, wouldn't you put it where no one would see it?"

"Ah, but you're forgetting that our individual didn't

have much time to hide his belongings. He would have had to use what was at hand, and since the decorative medallions were easy to remove and could be replaced just as easily, it's likely that's where the treasure was placed."

"It seems kind of improbable to me, but I'd be lying if I said I wasn't thrilled by the whole idea."

Gunner pulled some white fabric tape out of my bag and handed me a number of little wire stakes. "Let's mark the foundation that hasn't been excavated yet."

It took us about fifteen minutes to get the remainder of the temple physically notated, but by the time we were done, we had a pretty good outline of just how the building lay under the surface of centuries of dirt. The sun was starting its descent behind the trees when Gunner picked up a shovel.

"Ready?" he asked, striking a pose at the area we had deduced was the front entrance.

"Ready." I stuck my shovel into the earth. "Let's find something exciting to show Roger when he returns. Hopefully something we can rub Paul's nondiseased nose in."

Gunner's brow wrinkled. "That's strangely specific, love."

"I know." I put my foot on the shovel, and dug out a wad of dirt and grass. "It's going to take me a while to work out my anger at him. Although I still think that somehow Paul has faked that report. Sandy might be many things, but a ho is not one of them."

We discussed the idea of Paul trying to deceive people with a false report during the time it took us to dig down a few feet, the shadows from the setting sun behind the trees stretching across the bumpy ground, reaching with long fingers into the trench we had cut. I figured we had a half hour of light at best before we'd have to stop, and was about to mention that when Gunner suddenly stopped digging and said, "Hmm."

"Hmm, what?" I looked up from where I was on my knees, using a trowel to scrape back the dirt. "Did you find the medallion thing?"

"No, but I've found something metal. Come and tell me what it looks like to you."

I knee-walked over to where Gunner was bent over an object. It looked like a yellowy white wire bent in a curlicue. "Holy crap, Gunner. Is that a bracelet?"

"I believe so." He was using a small paintbrush now to brush away the clots of dirt from the intricate spirals of metal. "That or an armlet. Good lord. That's a coin next to it."

I squatted down next to him and scrabbled around in my bag until I found a toothbrush. I brushed around the curved edge of a lumpy black object. "How can you tell? It doesn't look like a coin to me."

"It's not one—it's several coins." He looked up, his eyes bright with excitement. "Do you know what I think we've found?"

"The treasure?"

"At least part of it. You work on the coins, and I'll try to get the rest of this bracelet cleaned off."

"This is seriously the best thing I've ever found," I said, brushing carefully around the blackened blob. And I'll be damned if Gunner wasn't right—along one edge it was possible to discern the rounded form of coins.

"Do you have your camera, love?"

"Yeah, it's in my bag." I gave it to Gunner, alternating between mentally squealing over the endearment and watching with much interest how he took photos of the objects before they were excavated. After a few minutes, he lifted the bracelet out and inserted it into a plastic bag.

"Do you see this?" He pointed with the paintbrush to a curved shape in the dirt. "I believe that's the outline of a round wooden box, probably used to hold the treasure. Damn, we're going to need some light here soon. And this dull piece of metal here is most likely a metal band that held the box together. I think you're right—this is the best thing I've ever found as well. Christ, here's another one."

"Another bracelet?" I tried to look around his head to see what he had found. "Or more coins?"

"Neither." He grinned at me. "How about some gold earrings?"

"You're kidding!"

He moved aside so I could see what he was bent over. Two blobs of gold metal lay bare, their heavy round bottoms narrowing up to looped wires.

"Good god, those are gorgeous. I'd wear those! Wait, let me get the pictures this time. It's good practice." I got several of the artifact lying in situ, adding, "Holy mother of chicken mole, Gunner! We found it! We found actual treasure!"

"We did indeed." He laughed aloud when I grabbed him with one arm and kissed him. "And we had best stop now, lest we leave Roger with nothing to film."

"That's fine. I feel guilty enough that we pulled the couple of things out already. But hooray! We found the treasure! Paul can just go suck a lemon, because we did it! We found it without him!"

"It certainly looks that way."

"Ooooh, did I hear you say you found the treasure?"

I jumped a few inches at the sound of the voice behind us. Daria stood with a thermos in hand, and two mugs. She held them up, saying, "I thought you guys would enjoy a quick cuppa."

"Oh, how nice. I'd love some tea. I never knew how thirsty you could get just digging around in dirt." I accepted one of the mugs with tea, smiling gratefully.

She filled the second mug and gave it to Gunner. "Is that gold?"

"It is. Earrings. Aren't they pretty?" I told her. "And look, Gunner found a gorgeous spiral bracelet, although I don't know what it's made from."

"Silver," Gunner said. "And there's another one below the earrings. See the edge of it?"

"Man alive, this is just like never-ending treasure!" I took more photos, adding, "Roger will crap himself when he finds out what we discovered."

"This is terribly exciting! I can only imagine what Paul will have to say when he sees the results. Shall we toast your find?" She poured a little tea in the cap of the thermos and held the cup aloft. "To the Ainslie treasure hoard, and those who found it!"

"Nicely put," I said, and took a big swig of lukewarm tea. It trickled down my suddenly parched throat, prompting me to drain the rest of the mug. Gunner sipped at his tea, thanking Daria as he set the mug aside, spilling a bit of it on the spoil pile. He shifted it to a safer distance, and contemplated the trench before us.

"You're welcome. Paul arranged for some tea, since he knew I stayed behind to do some work, but I thought you guys would like to share it. I didn't know we would be using it to toast a celebration, or I would have brought something a bit more dignified!"

"There's nothing wrong with a good cup of tea," Gunner said, bent over another piece of jewelry—a brooch, I thought, since there appeared to be a broken pin attached to it.

Daria knelt next to us, admiring the find. We didn't want to excavate any more treasure, sure that Roger would want to film the rest of the items being removed, but we all agreed that it wouldn't hurt to do a little digging in the area surrounding the find.

The sun burned red as it slid downward, forcing us to stop after about twenty minutes of brushing away dirt. We hadn't found anything else, but the metal of treasure still clutched by the earth glinted temptingly.

"It's like an endless pit of goodies," I said, stifling a yawn. "And there's more down there."

"That there is. I can make out at least two more bracelets, and more rings, not to mention that mass of coins that has corroded into a blob of metal," Gunner answered with a yawn of his own.

"This is so exciting." Daria stifled a yawn, too. "How many items altogether, would you say?"

"There's no way of telling. Do you see—" He paused to yawn again, giving his head a little shake as if to wake himself. I knew just how he felt—I was in the grips of a growing sense of sleepiness that I couldn't seem to shake. "Do you see this? It's the other side of the metal tape, which means that the wooden box was only about so . . . wide. But we don't know how deep. . . ." He yawned once more, which just triggered me into yawning, and the next thing I knew, Daria was saying something in a slow, hesitant voice that I didn't seem to be able to take in.

"Lorina?" I heard Gunner ask, his voice thick. "I think . . . lord . . . I think we've been . . ."

I blinked several times, trying to get my eyes to stay open, but they refused. I seemed to slide into a warm, black pool, but before I went under, I managed to finish Gunner's sentence with one single word. "Drugged," I said, and curled up next to the treasure, one hand draped protectively over it.

Chapter 20

"Gunner."

The voice came from a long way away. Possibly a different planet. What was Lorina doing on another planet?

"Gunner, wake up. Oh man, my head."

"I think I may vomit," another voice said. It was female, and vaguely familiar, but not familiar enough that he could put a name to it.

"Ugh. Don't say that, or I will, too," Lorina said, and he felt someone give his shoulder a little shake. "Gunner, I know you're alive, because you were making snorting noises just a few minutes ago. Good god, I feel awful. Wake up so you can pamper me and make me feel better. Gah. Dr. Anderson would have my hide if she ever heard me say that."

He cracked one eye open, and immediately wished he hadn't. The light shot into his brain with the velocity and effect of a laser cutting through butter. "Christ," he swore, and closed his eye.

"No, but I know how you feel." Lorina pried open one of his eyelids, and peered at him with concern. "Assuming, that is, that you feel like you've been run over by a herd of elephants, following which you were beaten by several anvils, and possibly licked some hallucinogenic frogs."

He opened his eyes again. "You've done frogs, too?"

Her eyes widened. "No. I was speaking metaphorically. Wait, you have?"

"Just once." He rubbed his forehead, and slowly sat up. He had been lying on the floor of what appeared to be a disused barn. "It wasn't an experience I am eager to repeat. Where are we? What happened? Who is Dr. Anderson? And who is about to vomit?"

"We're in a barn, I think. There appears to be hay in a loft over there. The door's locked, though, so we can't get out. We were drugged, and that was Daria who said she was feeling sick."

"Drugged?" He took stock of his body. Nothing seemed to hurt, although he was feeling less than fit. "Who the hell drugged us?"

"That is a very good question." Lorina's eyes were half-closed, as if she had a hard time staying awake. Gunner knew just how she felt. There was nothing more that he'd like at that moment than to go to sleep for about ten years. Possibly twenty. "We—Daria and I, that is—we think the tea was drugged, since that's the only thing that all three of us had."

"The treasure!" Gunner said, memory returning to him. He got to his feet with a lot less grace than was normal, and held out a hand for Lorina. "We've got to tell Roger and Thompson so that they can fetch the treasure and take it to the conservation room. They'll want to stabilize the metals before they are exposed to too much air."

"Too late," Lorina said wearily, and took the hand he offered, rising and brushing off dirt from the packed-earth floor. "Daria says she remembers hearing someone before she passed out. I'm willing to bet that they took the few things we excavated, and most likely the other stuff we were starting to uncover."

He rubbed his head again. "Are you saying that we were knocked out so that someone could steal the treasure?"

"It looks that way." Lorina looked sympathetically at him. "The big question is, who would do that? Who doesn't give a damn about sharing the find with the world?"

"Thompson," Gunner said, automatically picking the most annoying person on the dig at the same time he massaged the back of his neck.

"Who has such a lack of respect for archaeology that he'd blatantly keep items of such great value from the public?"

"Thompson," Gunner repeated, although less certainly. "Christ, I feel like I've been through the wars."

"Who would put himself above everyone on the production team?"

"Thompson?" It was a question now, but Gunner hated to give up on the idea, despite the fact that, his personal behavior aside, Thompson had shown only professionalism regarding the dig itself.

Lorina gave him a weary look. "Just because we don't like him doesn't mean we can peg him for the villain. Although I would love for him to have done it, because then we could call in the cops and have them work him over."

"A strangely enticing idea," Gunner agreed. "And I fear you are correct about his not being the person responsible, although it leaves us with a dearth of suspects. The doors are locked, you say?"

She waved a hand toward them. "Feel free to give them a try. Daria and I got nowhere. If it wasn't Paul, who did this to us? It had to be someone who wouldn't care that the archaeology company lost the prestige of finding the treasure, which means someone outside of their organization."

"That's the question I'd like answered most right now," Gunner said, trying the door. He eyed Daria when she returned from the other end of the barn. "Unfortunately, I don't have a suggestion. I'm hot. Are you hot?"

Lorina gave a weak smile, and took his arm. "Normally I'd tease you about having to ask, but I'm just too tired. I thought I was having a hot flash earlier, but Daria said she was feeling warm, too."

"It's not an enjoyable experience," Daria agreed, sitting down on an overturned bucket. There wasn't much else in the barn—until the film crew's arrival, it had been used to store antique farm equipment. Since the crew had no need of farm tools, now the barn was empty of all but them. "What are we going to do? We're trapped in here while Paul is no doubt secreting away the find."

"Surely you can't seriously think Paul would do that," Lorina protested, releasing Gunner when he tried the double doors of the barn. "I know he's not your favorite person, but you work with the man—is it likely he would do something so at odds with his job?"

"He might," Daria said darkly, narrowing her eyes. "If he had sufficient cause to think he could get away with it."

Lorina shook her head a little, her eyes drooping. She yawned as she said, "I don't see that, but maybe I'm too muddleheaded to figure it out. Don't get me wrong— there's no love lost between Paul and me—but that doesn't mean he's responsible for this. He's just too much of a professional to do something so heinous as steal archaeology."

"Don't let that professional persona fool you. He's only after what he can get. I should know," Daria said, leaping up to pace the floor.

Lorina drooped against the wall, and Gunner wanted badly to let his eyes just close for a bit. He rattled the door again, and tried to get his mind working at its usual speed.

"Why should you know?" Lorina asked, rubbing her eyes. "Because the board of your company gave him the head-honcho job instead of you?"

"That, and ... well ... it's not widely known, but we dated a short while before I met my husband, and I can tell you from experience that Paul Thompson is not a man who takes other people's successes well. I found a number of important artifacts at two of our digs, and it destroyed our relationship. Not that I'm unhappy about that now—I'm quite happy with my husband—but it did open my eyes to Paul's true character."

Gunner cocked his head, putting his ear to the door and listening.

"Wow," Lorina said, giving Daria a look of surprise mingled with admiration. "I had no idea he was so vindictive."

"Ha! That's one word for it." Daria gave a short laugh. "He's had it out for me ever since I dumped his ass. Why do you think he insisted I be assigned trenches that aren't likely to provide the treasure? Jealousy, pure and simple. And now this. I just bet you if we searched his caravan, we'd find the jewelry."

Gunner straightened up and moved a few steps away from the door, standing next to Lorina so he could put his arm around her. Immediately, she sagged against him.

A wave of protectiveness welled up inside him. He was angry with himself for allowing harm to come to Lorina, but at the same time, he realized that the situation was not one he could have foreseen. Still, he chided himself, he'd have to do better if he wanted to keep her where she belonged—right in the center of his world.

"But to drug us!" Lorina protested. "That's so extreme. Wait. . . ." She frowned, looking puzzled. "I really am not thinking straight. How could he know we were going to find the treasure? Oh, wait. . . . He might have noticed that Gunner had shovels when we went to see him earlier, and figured out we were going to do some digging. Still, that doesn't mean he'd know we were going to find anything valuable, and even if he did think that, where did he get the drugs to knock us all out? And when would he have time to do it? He said he was late for a dinner with the mayor."

Daria shrugged, and continued to pace. Gunner eyed her, wondering where she got the energy. Perhaps she hadn't been drugged as heavily as Lorina and he had been.

"Some of that might have been my fault," Daria admitted. "After I saw you two heading for the grove where the temple was, I went back to camp for a little break. That's when I met Paul, and he asked if I was the only one who was digging late. I mentioned you two. He said something about praising such dedication, and that the least he could do was make sure some refreshments were sent out to us. By the time I was ready to go back to my trench, he had the thermos of tea and a packet of biscuits for us."

Gunner frowned. "It seems like such an out-of-character thing for Thompson to do."

"I agree, but at the time, I didn't think anything about it," Daria answered.

"Even assuming he had some psychic intuition that we were going to find treasure, where did he get the drugs to doctor the tea?" Lorina asked with another yawn.

Gunner yawned in sympathy, and wondered if he had misheard voices at the door. He badly wanted to get Lorina tucked away safely so he could figure out who it was who had attacked them with drugs.

"Who knows? Oh!" Daria stopped and pointed at Lorina. "Didn't you say you had some knockout drugs?"

"Me?" Lorina frowned. "I . . . I don't remember saying anything like that."

"You must have, or else I wouldn't know about it," Daria observed, and rubbed her chin.

Gunner looked in surprise at Lorina, who he had to admit looked just as taken aback. "I told you about my drugs?" she finally said in a voice that squeaked.

"You did," Daria said calmly.

Worry was clearly visible in Lorina's eyes. "I don't remember that. I would never—I mean, it's not like me to tell people—Gunner is the only one I ever wanted to blurt the truth to, and even then, I didn't for a week."

Daria shrugged. "I don't know why you can't remember telling me. It was the second day you were here, I think."

"I just don't seem to remember—"

"But regardless," Daria said despite the fact that Lorina was talking, "it explains the time you caught Paul hanging around your tent. No doubt he was looking through your things and found your Mickey Finn ingredients."

Lorina rubbed her eyes again, her body drooping heavily against him, her words sounding thick and slow. "That makes sense, I guess. Oh, what do I know? My brain is so fuzzy I can't think straight. I just want to sleep. Gunner, what are we going to do?"

"We're going to wait about thirty seconds, and then have a doctor check us out. Following that, we'll talk to Thompson."

"What do you mean, wait thirty seconds—"

At that moment, the voices that Gunner had heard in the distance grew louder, followed by a demand to know if they were inside.

"Yes, we're here," Gunner yelled in response.

"Thank god Cressy tried to find you before she left for her evening out. Hang on—we'll have you out in a minute. Someone's jammed a wedge under the door," Elliott called.

Cressy's head popped into a window that was visible in the upper loft. "You guys aren't having sex in here, are you? Because if you are, I'm going to want a horse trailer to haul my new horse in. Oh. You're not."

"Get down off that ladder," Gunner told his daughter.

"How do you know I'm on a ladder?" Cressy asked, trying to look coy. It didn't work.

"I know because the last time I looked, you weren't twelve feet tall, and I happened to see a ladder lying around from where the film crew was hooking up lights. Now get down."

"I'm not hurting anyone," Cressy protested.

He donned his very best Annoyed Father Expression. "If you fall and break your ankle, you won't be able to go riding."

Cressy thought about that a second, made a face, and disappeared from the window.

"Did you know there was a window up there?" Lorina asked him, taking his hand.

His fingers tightened around hers while he wondered if she'd let him lock her away until he found the culprit who had drugged them, and immediately discounted that thought. Lorina wasn't the type of woman to allow others to fight her battles. Share them, yes, but fight them? He smiled at her, wondering if she knew just how delightful she was. "Yes."

"Then why didn't you say something?" She dropped his hand and gave him a thin-lipped look. "We could have gotten out of here!"

Damn, she was even adorable when she was annoyed with him.

"What are you laughing at?" she demanded to know.

"You," he said, pulling her to his chest, and kissing the edges of her mouth. "You're the only woman I know who looks sexy as hell even when she's half-asleep and irritable."

"If I'm irritable, it's because you're driving me insane." She kissed him back, then suddenly moved to the side, her face flushing as she glanced at Daria.

"Don't mind me," the latter said, picking a piece of hay off her clothing. "Just pretend I'm not here."

Gunner gave her a long look, was about to say something, but decided better.

The door gave a creak, followed by a nerve-rending squeak as the wedge was removed. Immediately thereafter, the darkness of the barn was flooded by the camping lights held by their rescuers.

Gunner straightened up to face his brother, who had a particularly long-suffering look on his face. "What have you done now?" Elliott asked. His glance moved on to where Lorina stood. "Ah. I see. At least this time you've managed to keep your clothing on."

"They have, but that's probably because of my presence," Daria said, coming forward quickly. "I really need the loo. If you'll excuse me—" She dashed off with her hand over her mouth.

Lorina took an unfortunately good look at Daria and made an odd *guh* sound, looking a bit green about the gills.

With one eye on Lorina, Gunner took his brother aside and quickly filled him in on the happenings of the evening.

"You were drugged?" Elliott asked in stark astonishment. "Are you sure?"

"Am I sure that we didn't just suddenly fall asleep in the middle of uncovering what looked to be an unprecedented cache of silver and gold jewelry and coins? Yes, I'm certain we were drugged."

"How did you get here?" Elliott looked around them in search of an obvious vehicle.

"I have no idea, but I suspect via one of the wheelbarrows used by the diggers. Everyone is off at dinner, and since this barn isn't visible to the tents, I suspect someone simply wheeled us down from the temple and dumped us here. It would only take a few minutes."

"True," Elliott agreed, frowning at where Lorina weaved her way over to the door.

Gunner immediately went to her, and supported her with an arm. "I'd like a doctor to see Lorina. She seems a bit woozy."

Elliott made no protests; he simply took charge of the people gathered around the door and sent them on various tasks. In no time, Gunner had tucked an only mildly protesting Lorina into his bed, and was waiting outside the room while the family doctor examined her inside.

For the first time in his life, fear clutched at him, and he was not enjoying the experience. Lorina had become more and more woozy, dropping off to sleep in the middle of sentences. What if the drug had seriously harmed her? He'd just found her, dammit—he didn't want to lose her now.

He leaned against the wall across from the door to his bedroom, his palms sweating as he gave in to his fears. She could be ill, gravely ill, and what could he do about it? Nothing! Dammit, why hadn't he stopped her from drinking that tea? If he got her through this, he would take far better care of her in the future.

No more playboy ways for him. Not just for Cressy's sake—it was himself he was thinking about now. He didn't want to live a life that did not include Lorina in it, and just the thought that she could even now be fighting for her life . . . "Dammit!" he exploded, and took a step forward to fling open the door and demand the doctor do whatever it took to save Lorina.

"Is the doctor done?" Cressy trotted down the hall, her face twisted with worry. "Are you guys all right?"

"I'm fine. It's Lorina I'm worried about. The doctor is in with her now." It took a heroic effort, but Gunner managed to not charge into the room, instead returning to leaning against the wall outside the door.

"She looked pretty sleepy at the barn. Is the doctor going to give her something to wake her up?" Cressy asked, pacing nervously up and down the hallway. "How come you aren't sleepy like she was? Who would drug you guys? I just don't get it!"

"Lorina will be fine," Gunner said, making an effort to chase all the dire thoughts from his head. He sagged tiredly against the wall, suddenly so overwhelmed that it was a struggle to remain upright. He wanted so badly to crawl into bed next to Lorina, to hold her and keep her safe from the world, but there were things he had to do, and he had to do them now, before too much time passed. "I spilled some of my tea, so I didn't drink as much tea as she did. And I'm not sure there's anything to get."

"You didn't say who drugged you," Cressy said suspiciously, stopping in front of him. "You know, don't you?"

He rubbed his jaw. He needed a shave and a hot shower, and about three straight days of sleep. But most of all, he needed Lorina hale and hearty. If they got through this, then he'd make sure that things were different. He'd make sure she understood that he had changed, and was a better man. The sort of man who deserved her. "I have an idea, yes. The problem is, I don't know the reason for it."

"I thought someone drugged you to take the treasure."

"Possibly. Possibly there was another motive."

"Well, for god's sake, Gunner!" Cressy all but jumped with excitement. "Uncle Elliott and that TV guy know the guy who took the jewelry you dug up. That's got to be the one who drugged you, right?"

Gunner straightened up at that. "What man who stole the jewelry?"

"The one who Uncle Elliott found with the jewelry," Cressy said impatiently. "That is, the jewelry was found in his trailer. You know, the head guy who Lorina was pretending she really liked."

He gave his daughter a piercing look. She met it with eyes that were bright with intelligence. Damn, he'd forgotten for a moment just how perceptive she really was. "They found the jewelry in Thompson's caravan?"

"That's what Uncle Elliott said a couple of minutes ago. He wants to call the police, but Roger is insisting that they wait until he can talk to the head of the studio. Uncle Elliott said he'll wait until you go down to talk to them, but after that, he'll get the police in. I just hope Lorina is all right. Can I be your best man? Only I'd be a best woman, obvs. Or do you want Uncle Elliott to be best man? Can you have two? I wouldn't mind sharing with him."

"I believe most women tend to go for bridesmaid," he answered, rubbing his head and willing the massive headache away. Why was the doctor taking so long? Should he call for a helicopter to airlift Lorina to the nearest hospital?

"I'm not most women," Cressy said, whomping him on the arm. "I want to be your best woman."

Distracted from his dark thoughts, he smiled and

pulled her into a hug, kissing her on her head. "You *are* my best woman."

"And Lorina," she said, giving him a fierce hug. "She's best, too."

"Yes, she is." He released her to search her face. "If we did get married—yes, you can be my best man. Or one of them, because I would like Elliott for that position as well—if Lorina and I did get married, would you be happy? You like her, yes?"

"Of course I'd be happy. She's cool, and she likes Gran, and she's deep, you know? I like deep."

"I like deep, too," he said, relieved that his marriage would pose no issues with Cressy. He wondered how he could ever consider Lorina without the thought of marrying her, and decided that wasn't important. What *was* important was getting Lorina on board with the idea.

The doctor emerged from the room at that point, a woman in her sixties who was semiretired, but who still oversaw the health care of the Ainslie family. "Your friend is fine," Dr. Magnus said before Gunner could ask. "I've taken blood and urine samples from her, and I'd like to get the same from you as well, but I suspect you are correct and that you've both ingested some form of benzodiazepines. I've given her a little stimulant to help combat the effects of the drug, so she's feeling much better. Now, let me take a look at you."

"I don't need an exam. I had less of the drugged tea than Lorina. Is there any reason I can't go in and see her?" Dammit, why was the doctor getting in his way when there was a woman to cherish?

"None," the doctor said, flicking a penlight across his eyes, and *tsk*ing to herself. "She may have moments of sleepiness, though. I urge you both to get some rest, actually. You'll feel better for it."

"Is there anything we should do for her?" he asked,

relief filling him at the knowledge that Lorina wouldn't be taken from him.

"Nothing at all other than to make sure she stays hydrated. And you both might wish to go light on food for a day or so until the drug leaves your bodies. You look a bit pale—I suspect your stomach is queasy, yes?"

"Just a bit—not too much," he admitted.

"Where is the third patient?"

"Elliott will be able to tell you that." He told Cressy to fetch her uncle, thanked the doctor, and, with no patience left, entered his room.

Lorina sat on the edge of the bed, her head in her hands. She looked up as he entered, and gave him a wan smile. "Got a clean bill of health. How about you?"

Dear god, she was beautiful. Her smile lit up not just the room but all the dark corners of his soul. How could he ever have imagined life without her?

"The same." He sat next to her and was pleased when she scooted over to snuggle up with him. He thought of telling her of his feelings right then and there, but he wanted to give her time to get used to the idea that he intended for her to be around for more than just a short period of time. "You know, the thought of being alone with you here in this room has been uppermost on my mind for the last few days, but I'm afraid that if I tried anything right now, I'd be doomed to disappoint."

She laughed, and kissed his jaw. "That goes for both of us. I'd really like nothing more than to strip you naked and rub myself all over you, but not right now. Not until I feel like I wouldn't fall asleep in the middle of it."

"Which is a good thing considering Elliott will be here in a few minutes."

"Why?"

"I asked him to come. Evidently he discovered that Thompson had the few pieces we uncovered."

Lorina gaped at him. "No!"

He nodded. "I'm afraid so. We were both quite wrong in our estimation of him."

"Not once, but twice," Lorina said with a wry twist of her lips. "Only the first time we were in the wrong, and now . . . Gunner, this just seems so convenient."

"Doesn't it?"

She slid a look at him from the corner of her eye. "You don't think he drugged us and stole the jewelry?"

"No, I do not."

"Neither do I." She made a quick gesture of defiance. "Oh, don't get me wrong, I don't like the man. No matter what that test says, I know he is guilty of infecting Sandy, and for that, he should rot in hell. But even considering all that, he doesn't strike me as a thief, not of archaeological artifacts, no matter what Daria says."

She stopped abruptly, then sucked in a large amount of air and turned to him, grasping his arm in a hard grip. "Gunner, that's it! That's what's been bothering me! Man alive, I can't believe I missed it!"

"Missed what?"

"The name on the report, on Paul's report. Do you still have it?"

"I think so." He went through his pockets and pulled out the folded sheet of paper. "I was planning on writing my part of our apology on the back of it."

"Look," she said, smoothing it out over his leg. "The name of the lab."

"Analysis performed by: Hollingberry Laboratories," he read. "What of it?"

"Hollingberry is Daria's surname. And she said when I first met her that her husband ran a lab that did medical tests. That's got to be more than a coincidence."

Gunner thought for a minute. "That would explain a lot."

"Does it? Like what? Speak to me in words of few syllables, since my brain is evidently made of molasses."

He squeezed her and wondered what he'd done in a past life to have landed Lorina in this one. It must have been something hellaciously wonderful. "We both agree that Daria's suggestion that Thompson drugged us in order to steal the treasure is very unlikely."

"Very."

"The question of how he knew that we were digging isn't really answered by Daria saying she'd seen us heading out to the temple. There was already a trench there, so why would more digging there send him into a panic that resulted in his drugging our tea?"

"Good point. Someone had to have been watching us to know we found the treasure," Lorina said slowly, enlightenment dawning in her eyes. "And he was going to the mayor's dinner. So how did he know? He couldn't. Which means . . ." Her eyes opened wide.

He nodded. "The rest of the crew was at the mayor's dinner. There was no one around but Daria and Thompson, and he was to leave shortly after we met with him. I can't help but wonder if there's a reason why Daria would want Thompson out of the picture."

"There is," Lorina said, sitting up straight and turning to him. "She wants his job. She's very bitter over the board of the Claud-Marie company picking him over her. If she set him up for drugging us and stealing the treasure, then she'd be a shoo-in for his job. But . . ." She gnawed for a second on her lower lip. "That doesn't explain the coincidence of the lab situation."

"That's been bothering me as well." He glanced at his watch. "Elliott should be here in a few minutes. Are you up to talking with him, or do you want to rest? Perhaps you should rest. You've been through a lot."

She pinched his arm. "Stop mother-henning me."

"I can't help myself. I feel responsible for the situation."

The look she gave him was one of genuine confusion. "Why?"

He didn't want to admit the truth, not sure how she'd take it, but if he wanted to have a future with her, he had to be honest about his feelings. "Because I should have watched over you better."

She pulled back, giving him an odd look. "Watched over me? Like . . . stalking?"

"No, of course not." He was silent a moment, unsure of how she'd take his intentions. "I . . . oh, to hell with it. I want to take care of you, Lorina. It would give me the greatest pleasure to ensure that your life was one of happiness and pleasure, and lots of romping in bed with me. There. I've said it. If you're going to yell at me for challenging you as a strong, independent woman, you'd best do it now before Elliott gets here."

She opened and closed her mouth a couple of times before wrapping her arms around herself and shaking her head. "You want to take care of me?"

"I do."

She had been staring at the floor, but slipped him a look out of the corner of her eye. "Because you think I need you?"

He hesitated, treading carefully. "Partly that. But also because I need you, too, and evidently part of that need is to make sure you're safe and happy."

"Safe," she said on a sigh, shaking her head again. She turned to him, putting her hand on his, slipping her fingers around his. "If you knew how important that word is to me, but I really don't want to bore you with my hang-ups. . . . Oh, you're right—to hell with it. I'll just tell you and let the chips fall where they may." She took a deep breath. "You were right when you guessed that I grew up in an abusive environment. And yes, it was my father who was the one who did the abusing—verbally, not physically—but my mother was too much of a doormat to ever stand up to him and stop the damage. I got away from them both when I was eighteen, and went to college, which is where I met Sandy. When I was in my late twenties, I fell into a relationship with a man who turned out to be just like Dad."

She rubbed her arms, and Gunner had to fight himself to keep from folding her against his chest, and placing himself between her and the rest of the world.

"That only lasted for a year, and after that, Sandy convinced me to get some counseling. That's who Dr. Anderson is—she was my counselor for five years. She taught me that I don't have to be a victim, and that not all men are like my dad and ex, and most importantly, that I am a strong person on my own, and don't need approval from anyone to be happy. And that was good, but every man I met since then has been . . . ugh. I can't describe it. It's like I'm in a person-sized hamster ball, and I can't stand having them in there with me. I don't like men touching me, and I certainly haven't been able to trust one to not go ballistic on me like Dad and the ex."

He put his hand on hers, touched by both the fact that she opened up to him and that she obviously felt differently about him.

"Until you." She gave him a slow look, one that carried many emotions in it, all of which warmed him to his toes. "You're different."

"I've been told that many times, but never before has it been a compliment," he said with a little tightening of his fingers against hers. He wanted to dance and sing with joy at her statement, but knew instinctively that he needed to let her finish her confession. "Just so you know—I think you're different as well. From any of the other women I know, that is."

She smiled in response, her fingers lingering on his for another few seconds before she withdrew her hand. "So now you know the worst about me. I launched a revenge plan against Paul—"

"Which you couldn't complete."

"And I allowed men to dominate me when I should have stood up for myself."

"You did stand up for yourself, love. I have a brother who suffered some pretty horrendous abuse before our parents adopted him, and I know how much blame he put on himself for being in a situation that was out of his control. You aren't responsible for the actions of others."

"You sound just like Dr. Anderson," Lorina said with a light laugh. "And I know that—I truly do. I guess I was just trying to bare my soul to you, all of the ugly bits of self-doubt and such."

Once again he had to struggle against the urge to take her into his arms. His wounded little Lorina, so bravely determined to share with him her innermost secrets. He blinked a moment at that thought and, without realizing it, asked, "Why?"

"Why?" Her brow furrowed. "Why did I bare my soul?"

"Yes, why? Why tell me this now?" Hope flared to life within him when she bit her lower lip and slid another sidelong look at him.

"Um. I guess . . . I just . . ." She stopped and turned to face him, slapping him on the knee. "Dammit, you're going to make me say it, aren't you?"

"I'm not going to make you do anything," he said softly, and hoped she understood he was making her an oath.

"That's not what I mean, although . . ." Her militant expression faded into something softer. "Although I do appreciate that. I bared my soul because what you said about us earlier—I like it. I like *you*. A lot. And I think maybe we might have something other than just wickedly hot sex going for us. So I wanted you to know just what you would be getting in me." She took a deep, quavering breath.

"I'm sorry," he said, pulling her into his arms. "I tried to stop, but I can't. You just send all my senses reeling, and I have to hold you. Tell me you don't mind."

"I don't mind," she said with a little giggle, leaning into him. "But you have to understand that I'm not surrendering myself to you. I won't be anyone's doormat. I won't be my mom."

He kissed her forehead, knowing full well if he kissed her anywhere else, they'd end up beneath the covers. "I wouldn't want you any way other than how you are. Now, I believe you need to distract me."

"Really?" She must have sensed how difficult a time he was having leashing his desire, for she scooted off his lap and moved off the bed to pick up a pillow that had fallen to the floor. "Why?"

"My brother and his wife will be up here any minute, and if you don't distract me, I'm bound to pounce on you and demonstrate in no uncertain terms just how much I admire your strength of purpose and delectable body. And mind. I like your mind, too."

"Nice catch," she said with another light laugh, and sat down in an armchair a few yards away. "All right, let's go over what we're going to say to Daria."

Before he could answer, there was a knock at the door, and Elliott popped his head around the door. "You decent?"

"Quite," Gunner replied. "Come in; we have a few things to say to you."

"Oh, I hope it's about the wedding, because I'd like to get that planned before Lady Ainslie comes home. Elliott and Gunner's mom, that is." Alice bustled in after Elliott, giving them both concerned looks. "The doctor says you're fine, which is good, although if you need anything, Lorina, let me know. Your sleepiness aside, I'm dying to talk wedding with you. Mom-in-law will be back in less than a week, and we need to have the plans firm or else she'll take over, and then you'll have every Ainslie relation in the British Isles descending upon you. The woman dearly loves a wedding, and Elliott and I only got away with a minor one because she didn't yet realize how much fun she could have planning one."

"Wedding talk will have to wait," Gunner told his sister-in-law with a sidelong look at Lorina. "We're still working things out in that regard, and I don't want Lorina rushed."

Lorina wrinkled her nose at him. "If only you'd thought about that before you announced to everyone that we were getting married. Go on, tell them about Daria."

"Daria?" Elliott asked, sitting on the second armchair and pulling Alice down onto his lap. "Ah, the woman who told us about the blackmail. What does she have to do with your wedding?"

"Nothing." Gunner quickly explained their theory on Daria's involvement with the drugging. "The part we don't understand is whether her husband running Thompson's STD tests is a coincidence or by design."

"That's one heck of a coincidence," Alice said, leaning back against Elliott. "Although maybe Mr. Thompson knew Daria, and that her husband was a lab guy, and he asked her hub to do the tests, so it wouldn't get around?"

Gunner stared at her for a second, then turned to Lorina, who moved over to stand next to him. She gripped his arm in excitement. "There's a connection, isn't there?" he asked her.

"Yes," she said, all signs of fatigue having disappeared. "Daria used to date Paul. Before she was married, of course, but I gather they were an item. And then they broke up, and things kind of went downhill for Daria."

"If the relationship ended badly, then that might give her even more motive for throwing suspicion on Thompson," Gunner said, getting to his feet. "I think we need to have a chat with her."

"I agree," Elliott said, patting Alice until she got off him. "I'd like this taken care of quickly, and with minimal police involvement. We don't need any negative publicity surrounding the dig if we want to draw tourists in to view the excavations. Where is Daria now? Does anyone know?"

It turned out that no one did know, and when they all trooped down to the tent area, Daria's tent was empty.

"Her things are still here, though," Lorina said as they glanced around. "So she hasn't done a runner."

"That we know of," Gunner amended, and emerged from the tent to find Roger striding past, a frown firmly affixed to his brow. "Roger, hold up a minute. Do you know where Daria is?"

"Hmm? No, I don't. What's this I hear about you finding treasure? Why would you dig without us? It's too late to film now, but Sue is no end of furious that you'd dig without first telling us. I understand that you feel proprietary about the finds, but really! I thought we were on the same page regarding digging. Your discovery would have made for excellent viewing, and now the best we can do is have a reenactment of you finding the treasure, and then an analysis of just what was buried, and when, and by whom."

"I think we need to have a discussion with both Mr. Thompson and Daria," Elliott said at the same time

Gunner started into an explanation of why he had started digging before Roger had returned from town.

"We weren't sure if there was going to be anything there at all, especially since part of the temple had already been dug up," Gunner finished. "Has someone been to the trench to see if any of the uncovered archaeology is still there?"

"There's nothing but a big hole in the trench," Roger said, giving him a sad look.

Gunner exchanged glances with Lorina. "It's as we thought. I'm truly sorry, Roger. I had no idea it would end this way. We should talk to Thompson and Daria as quickly as possible. Are they around?"

"Paul's in his trailer." Roger shot a distressed look at Elliott. "He says he won't come out until his name has been cleared. Daria's whereabouts are unknown. I asked some of the diggers to scout around for her."

"Then we shall go to him," Elliott said, and they all turned as a group and went to find Thompson.

Roger trailed after them, calling into his radio for a camera crew to meet him at the caravans. By the time they arrived, Thompson was standing in the open doorway, his arms crossed, and an obstinate expression settled firmly on his face.

"If you've come to arrest me for the theft of the archaeology found in my caravan, I demand legal representation." Thompson looked along the line of them one by one. "I am innocent, not that I expect anyone to believe me." He looked hard at Gunner and Lorina. "It's obvious that someone planted the archaeology here to make me look bad."

"If you don't mind, we'd like to come in and discuss that," Gunner said, and, without waiting for permission, pushed his way past the archaeologist, taking Lorina with him.

Thompson sputtered a bit, but gave way when the others followed. They arranged themselves on the available couch and chairs, with Gunner taking a stand behind the chair in which Lorina sat.

"I believe I'll nominate myself as speaker," Gunner said, glancing around at the others. They all nodded. Lorina leaned back and gave him a supportive smile. "First of all, we'd like to get the situation with your tests cleared up."

Thompson's face went black. "I do not believe I gave you permission to discuss that with others."

"I'm afraid I had to tell Elliott and Alice about it," Gunner said, feeling like a heel, but knowing he'd have to continue in order to get to the truth. "I am confident, however, that they won't speak of it to anyone."

"Absolutely," Alice said. Elliott murmured his compliance.

Roger looked confused. "What test is this?"

Paul sighed heavily. "It's nothing, just proof I provided to squash an ugly rumor about my health."

"What we'd like to know is, how did you go about picking the lab for the tests? Was it one your doctor selected, or did you find it?"

Paul looked surprised at the question. "The lab? What does that have to do with anything?"

"It might be the answer to a great many questions, particularly why the stolen archaeology was hidden in your caravan."

"As a matter of fact, my doctor left the choice up to me, since I had been out of the country for some time on a dig. Daria said her husband ran a lab that performed the tests I desired, and she could ensure speedy results if I used him." He snorted disgustedly. "The length of time it takes to get results back these days . . . it's positively scandalous."

"Daria suggested the lab?" Lorina looked at Gunner. "For what purpose? To falsify the results, do you think?"

"Not necessarily," Gunner answered. "If Daria had access to her husband's records, she might well have been the one to alter the results. We won't know which it is until we talk to her."

"What's this about falsifying the results?" Thompson asked. "I've told you numerous times I do not have a disease, any disease. Yes, I've been tired a lot lately, but I'm sure it's just overwork."

"I think you'd better get yourself tested again," Lorina told him. "And by a different lab. Also, don't have sex without a condom."

Paul snorted again. "I always do use a condom, not that it's any of your business."

"I know of one time you didn't," Lorina said darkly.

Paul frowned.

"Do you think Daria set him up to make people think he had HIV *and* stole the Roman stuff?" Alice asked, looking somewhat confused. "She really has it in for him, doesn't she?"

"I'm afraid it's more serious than that," Gunner said, his hands on Lorina's shoulders. Just knowing she had the same sort of warm feelings toward him as he felt for her gave him a sense of peace that was strangely fulfilling. The world felt right, as if it had been off-kilter all this time, and he only just now realized it. "Daria gave him false results simply so he wouldn't get the drugs he needed to keep the disease under control. She didn't want anyone to know he was infected."

"Did Daria break off the relationship with you, Paul, or were you the one to end things?" Lorina asked.

"I did," he said, his frown deepening. "But I hardly think Daria would plant the stolen archaeology on me over a long-forgotten failed relationship."

"Long forgotten by you, but not by her," Gunner said.

"You think Daria would do that simply because Thompson dumped her?" Alice asked.

"No," Lorina said slowly, glancing at Gunner. "But she might if she was infected, like Sandy was."

"Hell hath no fury," Alice agreed, nodding.

Paul paled. "You mean I really am sick and it's not just work wearing me down?"

"I'm not a doctor, so I can't say for sure, but it's looking very much like you have HIV," Lorina said solemnly. "I'm sorry, Paul. I wouldn't wish that on anyone, even though there are lots of drugs these days that keep people with HIV living healthy and happy. I should know— I went with Sandy to all her doctor appointments, and got the scoop on the antiretroviral drugs that are working wonders. You really should see your doctor pronto, though."

"Indeed, he should," Gunner agreed.

"Does that mean you think Daria is infected, too?" Alice asked, looking worried.

"Not necessarily," Lorina said. "She told me she dated Paul before she met her husband, so that had to be some time ago."

"About fifteen years, yes." Paul sank into a chair, his expression stunned. "I had no idea. . . . I thought it was just back-to-back digs, and then the long hours, and . . . Christ! HIV."

There was a moment of awkward silence before Gunner spoke again.

"If Daria is a particularly vindictive person, and it seems like she is, then I can see her fixing the report so that it made Paul think he wasn't sick when he was. She probably hoped that if the disease ran amok in him, it would do some serious damage, and it would be too late for treatment. Or at least sideline him so she could take his job. That she could so cold-bloodedly allow other women to become infected speaks a lot to her nature."

"Psychopath," Alice said, shaking her head in dismay. "Revenge-driven and intent on doing anything necessary to see Paul suffer."

Lorina shifted uneasily. "Yes, well, not everyone who seeks revenge is really bad. Anyway, I guess we won't know the truth until we can find Daria and ask her."

"Where does that leave me?" Paul asked. "Yes, I'll see my doctor immediately, tonight if possible, although I don't hold out much hope for that. But what about these charges against me? Am I going to be arrested? I did nothing wrong! I can't stay to talk to the police when I have to get to a doctor. I could be dying!"

"I don't think you're dying. You seem in pretty good health other than you said you've been tired a lot," Lorina pointed out.

That seemed to cheer up Paul. "That is true. And they have wonder drugs these days, don't they? But what about the police and the baron's intention to have me arrested?"

"We know you are innocent," Gunner said before Elliott could respond. "We know you didn't drug us or take the artifacts. Where are they, by the way?"

"Safely locked up in my trailer," Roger said. He'd been so quiet, Gunner had forgotten he was there with them. "And there they'll stay until I can get them in the hands of the conservator that the Claud-Marie people are sending out."

"Wise," Gunner said appreciatively, and pulled Lorina out of the chair. "I believe we've cleared up all the mysteries, other than hearing what Daria has to say, not that there's much doubt about it. But since Lorina's eyes are drooping, and I myself am about ready to drop down and fall asleep on the ground, I believe we're going to bed. To sleep, I should point out lest some of you think otherwise. Although the other will follow, not that you need to know that. Christ, now my mouth is running away with me."

"It's the drugs," Lorina said, giggling, and stood up. "Come on, Mr. No Verbal Barriers. Let's get some sleep so we can be fairly intelligent when people find the missing Daria."

"Sleep sounds good. Sleep with you, fair lady, sounds like heaven on earth," he said gallantly. "Sleep with you every night is beyond my wildest dreams of happiness. Marry me, Lorina. Marry me and love me as much as I love you, and end my hedonistic ways."

Lorina's eyes widened when he took her hand and got on one knee. He winced and, with a muttered apology about his ankle, sat on the couch and pulled her onto his lap, still holding her hand.

"Did you just propose to me? In front of everyone?" she asked, the scent of wildflowers making his head spin. It was a delightful sensation, one that he fully intended to enjoy for the remainder of his life.

"Yes, yes I did. I felt it was necessary to have an actual proposal if Alice is at some point going to all the trouble of planning our wedding."

"A Roman wedding," Roger said, looking up from where he was sending a text message. "We talked about that. A nice, authentic Roman wedding with slaves and a captain of the guard. Which reminds me, I really must call costuming to see how many Roman outfits they have."

"I don't want to press you, love. You don't have to answer me now, but I do feel it necessary to say in front of my family that I want you in my life. Every day. Starting now, and going forward for as many years as we have. Tell me that you'll think about marrying me. Tell me that the idea of spending your life with me isn't repugnant, and that you will save me from spending my life flitting from woman to woman in a desperate attempt to forget the love that I lost."

"Poetic," Lorina told him. "Very poetic, and I like the part where you want me to marry you just to save you from all those other women out there who covet you. Not that I blame them, of course, but they can just keep their hands to themselves, because I have decided that I will consider marrying you. *Consider*, mind you, because in-control women don't rush into things like marriage, and there are some issues still to be worked out, such as where we would live, but yes, I accept your proposal to consider marrying you and your fabulous chest that I want to touch more than anything."

Gunner laughed at the shocked look that came over her face. She had covered her mouth at what was obviously a slip, and now slid her fingers open to say, "Dammit, you are a bad influence on my mouth. Stop encouraging it to say things like that."

"But I like it," he said, nipping at her delectable lower lip. "I like it a lot. I like *you* a lot. I love you, Lorina, and that's not something I say lightly."

"It's not. I've never heard him say it about any woman who isn't a family member. This is a momentous occasion," Elliott said.

Gunner nibbled the top of Lorina's lip, and willed her to say the words he suddenly quite desperately wanted to hear. "Tell me you think fondly of me. Tell me you want me over all other men. Tell me you'll take pity on me and save me from hordes of unbridled women. But mostly tell me that someday you could love me."

Lorina leaned back in order to eye him, sighed, and said with a curl to the corners of her mouth, "Oh, very well. In the interest of saving you from being ogled and molested and forced to sexually gratify hundreds if not thousands of women, I will admit that you're not half-bad, and I might already be the tiniest bit in love with you."

"A tiny bit?" he asked, giving her his best puppy dog eyes. "That's good. That's a start. It's a good start. Do you think it might improve? I'm not pressuring you, or hurrying you, mind. It's just that the love part is important. Tantamount, you might say."

She glanced at the others, and then said slowly, "Joking aside, Gunner, I've never been one to blare my emotions to all and sundry."

"I know," he said, swallowing back a sense of despair that she would ever come to feel about him as he felt for her. "And that's fine. I won't ask you to do so now. I just wanted to make it clear to everyone that I was committing myself to you, if you'd have me."

Her lips twitched. "You're going to make me say it in front of everyone, aren't you? No, no, don't tell me you won't make me do anything—I know you won't. Dammit, it's still such a new feeling that I hate to put it into words, but since I can't resist those big blue eyes . . . fine. I love you more than just a tiny bit. And I suppose I even need you a little, although not as much as you need me to keep you in line so all those women stop bothering you. And, hallelujah, I can finally tell Dr. Anderson to stop worrying about me. There, are you happy?"

"Deliriously so," he said, kissing her the way he'd wanted to kiss her ever since he'd woken up from the stupor. He smiled when she whispered into his mouth that she loved him more than she ever thought possible.

"All right," he said, gently pushing her off his lap so he could get up. "The show is over. She's formally accepted the proposal to think about marrying me."

"So nice to scratch one of your siblings off my matchmaking list," Alice said as Gunner wrapped an arm around the woman who he knew truly needed him just as much as he needed her, smiling when Lorina leaned against him as if they were longtime lovers.

How right he had been to listen to Elliott talk about how happy marriage made one. And how smart he had been to pick Lorina as the woman to fill his life. Now if he could just figure out how he was going to keep his mother from making a huge event out of their eventual wedding . . .

To: Alice Ainslie <imabaroness@ainsliecastle.
co.uk>

From: Lorina Liddell <l.liddell@tddcc.edu>

Subject: I can't believe we're doing this!

I know we said we were going to Oregon just so
Gunner and Cressy could help me pack up a few
things, but the silly man wore me down, and
after I finally gave in, he and Cressy made an
executive decision while we were still in the air,
so instead of going to Portland, we ended up in
Anaheim.

Yes, we're getting married. In Disneyland.
Don't ask who is officiating—it's one of Gunner's
Internet religion buddies—which I guess means
you and I have officially started a tradition of
Ainslie wives getting married to their husbands
twice—once via a ceremony of dubious authen-
ticity, followed later by a legal one.

Please consider this our request to organize a
very small civil ceremony for us when we get
back.

Thanks for the update on Daria. I'm glad they
caught her before she could get out of the country with the remainder of the Roman treasure,
although it would be nicer if she admitted what

she'd done rather than denying drugging us, or keeping the truth about Paul's condition from him and any women he's been intimate with. It bothers me that Daria's been released on bail—does anyone else but me think she's going to bolt?

Regardless, it's a shame that her husband got dragged into the whole mess, but good to know that he and their kids don't have HIV, or that he was involved in Daria's scheme to punish Paul. Poor man. I can't imagine what he's feeling, knowing his wife altered documents that seriously endangered all those women (and, of course, Paul), not to mention drugging Gunner and me and stealing valuable artifacts. Shall we take bets as to whether he divorces her and then sues her for almost destroying his livelihood?

I have to say, I feel a lot sorrier for Paul than I expected. It couldn't have been easy to have contacted all those women he's slept with, although thank god he used condoms that worked with them. It doesn't help Sandy, but at least we know there's no one else out there suffering because Daria was trying to destroy him and take his job. Boy, did she have me fooled. What a heartless bitch.

Gunner asked me to thank you and Elliott for taking over the archaeology "expert and an idiot" spots (as I thought of them), although you are by no means an idiot. We both appreciate your doing so, and if the rave reviews are anything to go by, you and the baron are a big hit. We should be back from Disneyland in time to participate in the last few days of the dig, so if you could keep taking a few pictures while you're running around the cellar and the other trenches, I'd be grateful. Gunner seems to think I can really pull together a book, although I'm not so sure. Still, it'll be a fun project to work on together.

Gunner and Cressy send their love, and Cressy made me promise that I'll send you a picture of her as Gunner's best man. Oh, and she wants to remind Elliott that she will need stable space for a horse next year.

It's going to be a wild ride with the two of them, but you know I'm going to love every minute of it. There's just something about those Ainslie boys, huh?

Must dash. All our best,

Lorina (and Gunner and Cressy)